ON ALIEN SKIES

ON ALIEN SKIES

ICARUS CODE BOOK FOUR

RYSA WALKER

For information:

www.rysa.com

For those who understand that power untempered by justice and mercy is tyranny.

Fight on.

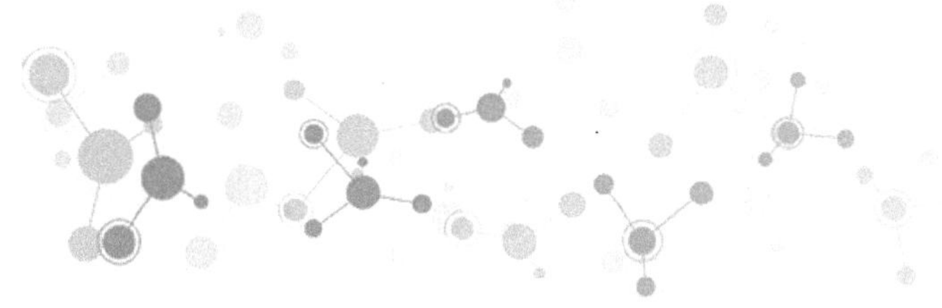

So dreamt thy sons on worlds destroyed
Whose dust allures our careless eyes,
As, lit at last on alien skies,
The meteor melts athwart the void.

So shall thy seed on worlds to be,
At altars built to suns afar,
Crave from the silence of the star
Solution of thy mystery.

~ George Sterling, "The Testimony of the Suns" (1903)

CONTENTS

PART I

PART II

PART III

EPILOGUE

PART I

FROM THE JOURNAL OF EBERIN DAS

(Translation by Alice Dobroski)
18.11.508

I DO NOT SLEEP WELL, here in the hideaway that will soon be my crypt. Last night, I awoke after only a few hours in the middle of the strangest dream. I rarely recalled my dreams in the past, and when I did, they were usually reenactments of daily activities. When I worked in the lab, I would often dream of whatever experiment I was working on. Occasionally, I dream of places on Ufretas, but they are static in my memory, like thumbing through a photo album.

Salaia, a woman with whom I had a brief romantic relationship when I lived in Peira, would often tell me of her dreams the next morning over breakfast, as she browsed through a little book that she claimed helped to decipher their meaning. Her dreamscape was a strange forest of shifting realities where natural laws did not seem to apply, where childhood memories blended with fictional characters and nursery stories. Sometimes, dream monsters chased her until she jolted awake. She was rarely able to sleep again that night for fear that they still lurked, teeth bared, waiting to pounce the instant her eyes closed. On a few occasions, the fear stayed with her for days.

I found Salaia's dreams interesting and understood that she was afraid, but I could never relate on a personal level. My dreams were dull, quotidian things, easily forgotten.

Last night was different. In my dream, I sat beneath the esmar tree behind the house where I lived during my last assignment. It was summer, I had a book and a tall glass of bergan tea, and I was enjoying the shade of the tree's wide willowy branches. As I turned to the next page, however, something fell from the tree and landed near my foot.

It was a ripe usimi, a fruit that does not grow on an esmar tree, or on any Martian tree, but only on Ufretas. I've loathed usimi since I was a child and bit into the pale-yellow flesh one day to find that it was filled with tiny worms.

I instinctively kicked the fruit away and looked up to find the esmar tree had vanished, replaced by a massive usimi bearing hundreds of ripe yellow fruits on its gnarled branches. Before I could scurry away, the tree sprouted wiry new limbs. They pulled me tight against the trunk as others pelted me with fruit bombs.

And then, in one of those fantastical twists that never happen in my dreams, I sank into the tree. I *became* the tree and I controlled the branches. It would have been a simple matter to stop the assault, but I didn't. In fact, I called more of them in, and it wasn't just usimi branches now, but branches of every sort, including the thin, vinelike limbs of the esmar in my backyard. They squeezed the tree—the tree that was somehow also me—tighter and tighter, stealing my breath until I jolted upright as Salaia had on those long-ago nights in Peira.

I now have a better understanding of how such a dream might haunt you long after you awaken. But I do not need Salaia's book to interpret my dream. I am part of the monster I seek to tame. It is part of me. And if I cannot tame it, I must try to kill it.

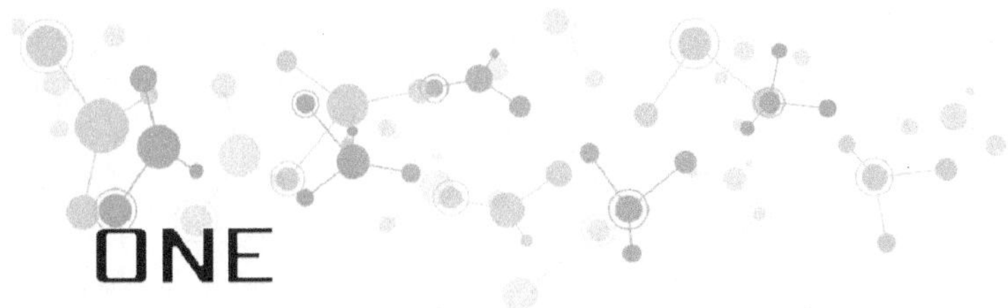

ONE

Tuesday, October 3
New York

"AND HERE ON the right we see that same eye with three lines extending from the bottom." The woman on the wallscreen tilted her unruly gray curls toward a rudimentary drawing of a human eye, one of several Egyptian hieroglyphs on the stone tablet depicted behind her. "Even young children would probably recognize that as a *crying* eye and associate it with sadness or grief, because tears seem to be another constant between human civilizations."

A subdued chuckle ran through the classroom as the closeup of the Rosetta stone gave way to an assortment of alien eyes from science fiction and horror films. A student near the front said, "You should add the ones from that swimming pool video."

A few of the others laughed out loud now.

"Oh my god, yeah. I saw that."

"It's fake, though. Gotta be fake."

The professor paused the lecture. "What video are you talking about?" Her tone was pleasant, but with just enough edge to make it clear that they needed to get back to the lecture.

"Sorry, Dr. Dobroski," the first guy said. "Didn't mean to interrupt. Surprised you haven't seen it, though. It was everywhere a few days back. It's drone footage of something that looks like a yeti in a swimming pool. Big green eyes that reflect back at the camera. I'll send it to you."

"Thanks." She pressed play again and the woman on the

screen, the late Dr. Holly Leffler proceeded to explain why things like differences in anatomy would complicate and probably even doom efforts to translate a sample of the alien language recently uncovered on Mars.

She hadn't really planned to use these prerecorded lectures when she was assigned to take over for Leffler. It felt wrong. Borderline ghoulish, like she was yanking the woman out of her grave and forcing her back into the classroom. She'd rationalized the decision by reminding herself that the twenty-two students currently in the classroom and the ninety-five others who were participating virtually had signed up for a course taught by Holly Leffler, not Alice Dobroski. She was just making sure they got what they paid for.

It was true, but it wasn't something she'd even thought about until after the fact. Her real reason for taking the video shortcut was that the alternative was canceling class or preparing a lecture. Canceling was a bad idea for someone still on probationary status, especially when her students had already missed two sessions—one due to Holly's murder and the other due to minor flooding on campus after the hurricane that had skipped along the New York coastline the previous week before heading back out to sea. But she'd had no time to put together lectures for this class or any other because she'd spent every waking moment since the semester began doing the very thing that Holly was on the screen declaring to be impossible.

Even though they'd worked together for several years, the only memory Alice's brain fetched when she thought of the woman were those last moments at Mount Sinai's emergency ward, with Holly thrashing in the bed and Claire begging the nurse to check for neurotoxins.

Would it have made a difference if she'd chimed in and seconded Claire's request? Maybe. But Alice had known Claire Echols for less than twenty minutes at that point and had no reason to believe that her mentor's symptoms were due to anything other than heatstroke, as the nurse claimed. It had, after all, been the most logical conclusion in the middle of a record heatwave.

"Even the assumption that they *had* eyes requires a leap of faith," Holly continued on the screen, "given that the only writing we have from their civilization was etched, rather than printed on a smooth surface. Some species of bats here on Earth can detect minute differences in texture through echolocation. Likewise, ancient Martians might have read these symbols by hearing or touching them, so we cannot know for certain that they had a symbol or word for sight. And this is but one of countless unknowns."

Alice fought back a wild urge to stop the video and dispense with a few of those *unknowns*. She could tell her students that the name on the chamber door was Eberin Das. That he'd definitely had eyes based on the descriptive words in his journal. That he was not, in fact, an ancient Martian but an ancient Ufretan. She could tell them that the words etched into the walls were a parable about the danger of lies, could even pull her computer out of her bag and walk them through the similarities between ancient and modern Ufretan. And while she couldn't say exactly how or when Eberin had died, she *could* tell them that he spent his last days attempting to save not just the people of Mars, but any later civilization that might stumble upon his burial chamber.

She could also tell the class that they'd almost certainly found Eberin's warning too late to save the Earth, but … maybe she should skip that part. Their first essay was due in two days, and existential angst about the near future might make it hard to focus on established methods for deciphering clues about the distant past.

Of course, she couldn't actually tell them or anyone else what she knew, and that was making her more than a little crazy. Keeping secrets was nothing new. Her entire identity was a carefully crafted fiction that she kept from her colleagues and the vast majority of her friends. But she'd always had at least one person she could talk to about *that* secret, since her mother had joined her when she left her old life behind.

But this? Her mom was happily remarried to a lovely man in Pittsburgh, working at a job she enjoyed and coparenting two teenage boys. If the world was ending, why ruin her mother's final days?

The bigger issue, though, was that she was pretty sure her mom would panic if she found out about the translation project. Either she'd decide Alice had finally cracked and have her checked in at a psychiatric hospital or she'd tell her to bail—destroy the files, pack up her things, and hit the road. Again. And her mom would empty her bank account and ditch her happy suburban existence to make it happen, just like she had last time.

But Mitch had been something they could outrun. An attack by an advanced alien civilization? Not so much.

The video had another fifteen minutes to go, and she was sorely tempted to duck out. Her brain needed caffeine and fresh air. But her thermos was in her messenger bag beneath the desk, and the door was on the other side of the wallscreen, so both of those objectives were out of reach. She couldn't even check for messages in the darkened room, because her armscreen would be a distraction. So, she closed her eyes and popped a stick of gum into her mouth, hoping that the peppermint would overpower the smell of a humid classroom packed with too many bodies at the end of another scorching early October day.

When the lecture concluded with Holly's confident but decidedly false declaration that the Icarus code was an unsolvable puzzle, Alice reminded the class of their essay assignment and dodged the few students who had questions, saying that they would have to send her a message because she needed to get to a meeting. Untrue, and not entirely credible at eight-thirty at night, but it was enough to get her outside.

She sank down onto one of the metal benches, still warm to the touch more than an hour after sundown and pushed a stray dark curl behind the vivid aqua frame of her oversized glasses. Then, she cracked open her thermos, took several bracing gulps of iced coffee, and tapped her armscreen.

Four messages. Still nothing from Claire. One was from Josh Hardt, who was stumbling through the duties that had landed on his shoulders as interim head of the department now that Holly was gone. The next two were brand new messages from students, almost certainly the ones that she'd evaded getting out of the classroom, and the fourth was yet another call from a truly annoying FBI agent named West.

This was message number eight from West in the past two weeks. At first, his questions had mostly been about Holly's death, but once he discovered that his primary target—Claire Echols—was no longer on the planet to answer his questions, he shifted to asking what Alice knew about Claire, what she knew about the Flock member whose body they'd found in the house at New Haven, and the nature of the work that Claire had hired her to do. Alice answered some of his questions and leaned heavily into the NDA she'd signed to avoid the others, pointing him toward Jamal Sellers, the attorney Claire had hired to represent her, when he got pushy.

After the third or fourth call, Alice had laughed and said West must think she had Claire locked inside a closet, given how often he was contacting her. It was obviously a joke, but the man had a grossly underdeveloped sense of humor. He'd simply said no, he didn't believe that, but he did think she knew a lot more than she was admitting.

West may not have been happy with her responses, but Alice was equally unhappy with him sniffing around. She was reasonably sure that her identity was solid—her mother had certainly paid enough to make sure of it—but there could always be a loose thread. Any small, incongruous detail might prompt a dogged, humorless man like West to tug at it out of curiosity and that could unravel her entire life.

Admittedly, her personal problems paled in the face of everything else that was happening, but she had no control at all over the looming alien apocalypse. She'd had one very short, cryptic phone call before Claire left the planet on what she'd claimed was a last-ditch effort to avert the attack. The good news, Claire had told her, was that she wouldn't need to rush the translation. And there was no longer a reason to worry about anyone coming after the documents, since Durav no longer needed to keep their mission secret. He was more concerned about getting a message to the Ufretan Alliance to let them know that Earth had achieved both milestones and they were now free to bomb the planet into oblivion with a clear conscience.

Alice still wasn't entirely sure why they were going to Mars, aside from the fact that it had something to do with Tobias Shepherd. Claire had promised to send a more detailed email from the ship—in Ufretan, since Beck was traveling with them and that would be a code Anton Kolya's censors couldn't hack. But two weeks later, the promised email still hadn't materialized. She'd even sent two vague messages to nudge Claire about it, but they were apparently in silent mode. That had Alice torn between being annoyed and worrying that something awful had happened.

She tucked the thermos into her bag, turned off her armscreen, and took the stairs down to Amsterdam Avenue. The temperature had dropped a good ten degrees since she entered the building around four, but the night air still held a hint of metallic haze from the rail hubs downriver. It was just shy of nine now. The streets still teemed with life—students waiting at bus stops, a couple drifting out of a corner café, a woman outside a juice cart laughing much too loudly at whatever she was watching on one of the old-style Vis-a-Visors.

Alice's current dinner plans were a bowl of Cheerios and a sliced-up banana when she got back to her apartment. But she hadn't eaten since midday, and the food carts proved too tempting to pass up. There was only one person waiting at the tamale stand where she had grabbed lunch at least twice a week for the past few semesters. She merged into the line and inhaled deeply, savoring the aromas of masa and chiles.

When she reached the front, the vendor—a guy named Emil who was probably still in his teens—glanced up and gave her his usual wolfish grin.

"Ah, *mi bella profesora!* Cheese and green chile, comin' right up. I was beginning to worry that you moved away without ever letting me take you dancing." The kid was at least ten years her junior, but he'd started up an easy flirtatious banter on her first visit a few years earlier.

"I'm still here," she said. "I've just been busy with a side project."

"*Qué mal!*" he said in mock horror. "He must be very handsome, this *side project* who keeps you too busy to visit me."

She was tempted to say that her side project had actually been dead for millions of years, but she just laughed and shook her head. "Don't I wish. No, I've just had a ton of extra work."

"So, they stick you with the night class this semester?" He nodded toward the university across the street, not even looking down as his hands deftly wrapped the tamale in waxed paper.

"Yeah. I don't mind, though. Better than teaching at eight a.m.."

"Oh, *si, si*." He handed her the warm fragrant bundle, along with a couple of napkins. "I like the city at night much better. Sure you don't want to wait around for another hour or so 'til I lock up? There's this club over on ACP…" He performed a deft little dance move.

She laughed and pressed her thumb against the pay pad, adding his usual generous tip. "I've got too much work, Emil. Can you give me a rain check?"

"Again, with the rain check! You break my heart, *profesora*." Then he laughed and greeted the next customer.

Alice walked down 120th toward Morningside Park and unwrapped the tamale for an experimental bite. It was hot, but manageable as long as she didn't wolf it. Inside the park, the path curved downward through a stand of tall trees that were probably older than the university itself. An ambient glow from the city lights filtered through the leaves. Two teens shared a vape on one of the trailside benches. A jogger pushed by in the opposite direction, pounding up the steps on the illuminated path. Distant whoops and hollers of a late-night basketball game drifted through the woods from the Athletic Field, but it was still much quieter than the street.

When she reached the bottom of the path, she turned left toward the fieldhouse, stopping at the first trashcan so that she could toss the tamale wrapper. She pulled her thermos from the front pocket of her satchel and took a long drink. That's when she heard it.

Or maybe *sensed it* was more accurate. She couldn't pinpoint exactly what it was that set her nerves on edge. Someone was definitely behind her—no surprise at all when you live in the city —but they'd halted when she did. It was probably nothing, but...

She chugged the dregs of her iced coffee, screwed the cap on, and turned to stick the thermos back in her bag, risking a quick glance behind her. No one was there. She'd probably just imagined it.

But the footsteps started up again as soon as she moved back to the trail.

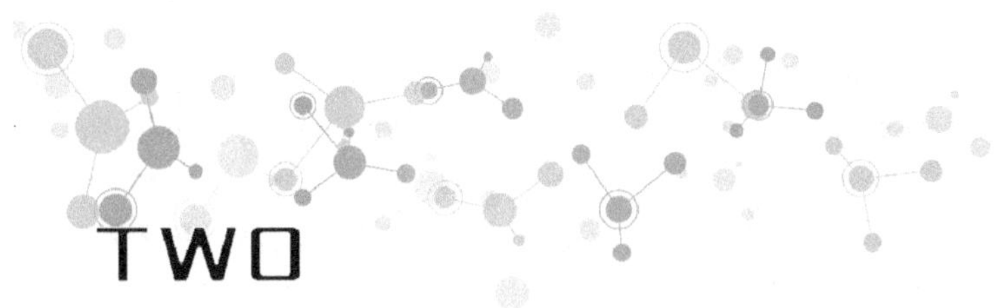

TWO

ALICE ADJUSTED the strap on her messenger bag, using the movement as a cover so that she could slide her weapon out of the holder just inside the front flap and slip it into the pocket of her skirt. She'd usually be carrying a pistol, but handguns weren't allowed on campus. Ironically, her pistol was completely legal, licensed and tagged. The wireless taser now in her pocket, on the other hand, was black market and packed twenty milliamps beyond the legal limit, so she really hoped she didn't have to use it. Given the events of the past few weeks, Agent West would be on her doorstep in a heartbeat if the NYPD informed him that she'd so much as jaywalked let alone brandished an amped-up taser.

Taking the 123rd Street exit, she crossed Morningside and blended into a cluster of pedestrians waiting at the light, still watching the path from the corner of her eye. As the signal flipped to walk, a tall figure slipped out from behind one of the concrete pillars that flanked the exit, moving quickly so that he could cross before the light changed. He was dressed in varying shades of gray and was unusually tall. Around six-five—too tall, too thin, and too pale to be her stalker ex. Almost certainly law enforcement, possibly someone Agent West had assigned to tail her.

The street narrowed on the other side of the avenue, boxed in by buildings that hadn't been maintained properly since well before the Secession Crisis. About halfway down the block, she paused at the door of a CVS as if debating whether to go in. Two buildings back, the man stopped, too, looking inside the darkened window of a vintage clothing shop. When she moved again, so did he. Matching her pace. Not attempting to close the gap.

Normally, she'd have turned left when she hit Douglass Boulevard. Her apartment was only a block beyond that point. But there was still an off chance that the guy wasn't a cop. He could be someone Mitch had hired. He'd done that once, the first time she tried to break up with him. With daddy's money and influence behind him, he could afford to hire actual humans, and not just the drone surveillance she'd caught him using on her a few times when they were still together. But she'd had no indication that Mitch knew what name she was using or even knew for certain that she was alive.

Still, whoever this guy was, did she really want to lead him straight to her apartment? No, she did not.

Instead, she kept going until she reached Powell, where she took a right, heading for a green awning at the other end of the block with the letters *DLS* printed on the side. According to the owner, Juno, who was ... well, not exactly a *friend*, but a fairly close acquaintance, the letters stood for Dirty Little Secret. The *secret* part was on point, given that the place was half hidden, wedged beneath a pawn shop and a quaint-looking place that sold vape herbs and designer teas. She'd never heard anyone else call it by the full name, though. To the rest of the neighborhood, it was just the DLS.

Alice fished around inside the front pocket of her bag until her fingers landed on a tiny metal box that had once held breath mints. She flipped the top up and peeled a microcamera about half the size of her pinky nail from the waxy strip of paper inside, making a mental note to reorder, since she only had one more in the tin. When she grabbed the black metal railing on the steps that led down to the club's entrance, she left the tiny camera behind.

Inside, ambient synth mixed with the faint buzz of conversation. Two screens above the bar—mercifully silent—were showing a soccer match and a news story about a mostly peaceful protest outside the old Javits Convention Center, which the city planned to begin using as a Rejuvesce distribution hub in just over a week.

Alice hadn't paid much attention to the furor over the new drug before meeting Claire. She'd received her lottery number like everyone else and was near the middle of the pack for her age group. While she suspected it would be years before supplies were plentiful enough for them to start distribution to anyone younger than fifty, she certainly wasn't going to pass up a few extra decades of life ... or more.

Claire had never explicitly admitted that the drug offered anything beyond what had been announced, but Alice now had enough pieces of the puzzle to read between the lines. The two milestones that the Guardians in the Eberin Das journal had been looking for were expansion beyond the solar system and biological immortality. That appeared to be the same for their modern counterparts. In the video Beck sent to Claire, he'd told her he was around eleven hundred years old, adding that this made him one of the younger members of the Watch. Given lifespans that were measured in millennia, it stood to reason that the few extra decades Rejuvesce officially promised might not be significant enough for the Alliance to consider the milestone met.

The bartender's eyebrows arched in a blend of recognition and curiosity when he spotted her. "Juno was just sayin we haven't seen much of you lately. He's not in tonight, though."

"Yeah, I've been working. I'll have to catch up with him later."

She ordered a sativa seltzer with a shot of curaçao, turning to keep an eye on the door while he prepared her drink. Three people came in, including a tall, long-haired man wearing a Yankees cap. He was well over six feet, tall enough that she thought for a moment he might be her pale gray shadow. But unless he'd changed clothes and slapped a wig on his head, it was a different guy.

She carried her drink over to a small booth near the back where she could see the door and still have a bit of privacy. After a few sips and some deep breaths to steady her nerves, she extended her armscreen and opened the app to see if the man was still outside. It took a moment to get her camera oriented correctly, since she'd accidentally placed it at a slight downward angle. But once she panned up, she had no trouble spotting him. He was across the street—almost *directly* across the street—leaning against the wall of an abandoned restaurant and staring intently at the door of the club. He wasn't even trying to be subtle about it.

Alice zoomed in and was hit by an immediate sense of unease. It wasn't that she recognized the guy, and between his height and his facial ink, she *would* have remembered him. The thing setting off her alarm bells was the man's expression—or rather, his *lack* of expression. His face was blank, almost like a mask.

She took a picture, then zoomed in even closer to focus on the facial tattoo and realized there were actually *two* of them. Both were on his forehead, just above the right eye. The larger of the two was a black crescent, with something that reminded her of a misshapen musical note inside. It wasn't familiar. She then shifted her attention to the smaller marking, and her breath caught in her throat. That one, she knew. It looked a bit like an upside-down U, with a wavy line similar to a tilde bisecting it at a forty-five-degree angle. She'd translated that symbol several dozen times in the past few weeks. It was the Ufretan number fourteen.

"You're right. He's watching you." The man's voice, which was unusually deep, came from directly behind her.

She quickly retracted her armscreen and moved her hand toward the weapon in her right pocket. It was the *other* tall guy, the one she'd seen enter when she was standing at the bar. He had longish, light brown hair, a pronounced jaw, and a nose that looked as if it might have been broken at some point.

"That's why I wanted to talk to you." He slipped into the seat opposite her and placed his beer on the table. "To warn you. That same guy was following me earlier in the day, but I managed to throw him off by circling around. Decided I'd return the favor and see if I could track him back to his boss. But then he ducked into that park about twenty minutes ago, like he was expecting someone. When he comes back out, I find that he's now following *you*."

She opened the camera app again. Tall, gray, and dead-eyed hadn't budged an inch. He reminded her of a living statue performer she'd seen in Times Square a few months back.

"Did he see you come in?" she asked.

"Possibly. I ducked out of the alley when he was crossing the street, but … I wouldn't put it past Durav to have guards with extra eyes on the backs of their heads."

Durav. That was a name that both Claire and Beck had mentioned.

The man watched her closely, and she thought he'd picked up on the look of recognition in her eyes. "Given the location of the park," he said, "I'm guessing you were coming from campus. Your bag suggests either a student or a professor. So, who are you and why is he following you?"

Alice wasn't about to give him any information. "I'm thinking *you* should go first, since you plopped down at my table uninvited."

"That's fair, I guess." He stared at her for a long moment, long enough to make her a bit uncomfortable. Then, he pulled a piece of paper out of his pocket. "Do you have a pen or pencil?"

Alice frowned in confusion. "Yeah. Hold on." She wasn't inclined to take her eyes off this guy, so she fished around blindly in the front pocket until her fingers finally closed around a pen.

"Thanks." Taking the pen in his left hand, he quickly sketched something on the paper, then slid it and the pen across the table to her.

She dropped the pen back into her bag and stared down at the three Ufretan letters he'd written. The first was one that she'd been pronouncing as *ow*, based on the guide left behind by Tobias Shepherd. The second was a hard *s*, and the third was their equivalent of a soft *n*. So, putting it all together, *Owsin*.

The name didn't ring any bells. She'd watched the video that Beck sent to Claire multiple times and couldn't recall either him or

Claire mentioning anyone with a name similar to that. One thing that Claire *had* mentioned, however, was that the Watchers were all unusually tall.

She looked up at the man and shrugged. "Am I supposed to recognize these symbols?"

"Depends. Since Durav seems to have you in his sights, I'm guessing you're the professor who took over after Dr. Leffler was murdered. If so, then they should at least look familiar."

Okay, then. He had a decent idea who she was after all, so it was reasonable for him to assume that she was familiar with the images of the text in the Icarus chamber. And even if she hadn't worked directly with Holly Lefler, any student of archeolinguistics would have been curious enough about the discovery that the symbols might look familiar. He should *not*, however, know that she had a pronunciation guide. Nor should he be aware that she knew anything about the Watch or the fact that there had been aliens on this planet for well over a century.

She decided to neither confirm nor deny her identity for the moment and just focused on the paper. "Now that you mention it, they do look a bit like the symbols that were found on Mars. But this sucks as an introduction. You can't seriously expect me to translate the word or have any idea how to pronounce it." She shrugged. "Guess I'll just have to call you Martian Man."

He grimaced. "Let's go with Housen."

After weeks of working on the translation day and night, the first thing that popped into her head was whether he'd added the aspirated *h* at the beginning of his name to make it closer to English or if that was the standard pronunciation of his name on whatever Ufretan world he called home. But she pushed down her internal overeager schoolgirl, the part of her that always wanted to be first to solve any riddle, and just repeated the name back with a curt nod.

Housen waited for a moment before prodding. "And *you* are?"

About five seconds from getting the hell out of here, she thought.

But he had information that she obviously needed, so maybe she should stick around for another minute or two.

"Alice Dobroski. And yes, I did work with Holly Leffler." That much he could probably get from the campus website or newspaper if he dug around a bit. "I don't know who that man is, though, or why he's following me. You, on the other hand, seem to have a pretty good idea. Perhaps you'd care to clue me in?"

Housen thought for a moment, tracing his finger around the red and black label of his beer and most likely, debating how much he could tell her without her either leaving or laughing in his face. When he looked up, his pale blue eyes fixed resolutely on her own. "The man across the street is watching you because his boss is hunting for something. He thinks there's a decent chance that you have it. And he's perfectly willing to kill you to get it back."

THREE

"AND YOU KNOW THIS ... *HOW?*" Alice asked.

Housen's mouth twisted. "How do I know he's willing to kill? Because he's done it before. Your Professor Leffler is just one of many."

"No. I don't doubt that he's willing to kill. His eyes…" She shuddered. "They're soulless. I'm sure he'd be more than happy to deliver death—preferably in the most painful way possible. What I meant was how do you know that's why he's following me?"

"Just to be clear, I was referring to his boss. The guy across the street *will* kill you, but only if he's ordered to do so. He won't get any pleasure out of it, but he also won't feel even a smidge of guilt or remorse. Durav's got several of these guys, and they're basically human versions of the drone that killed your colleague. As for how I know…" He shrugged. "Reasonable conclusion, since that's also why they're following me."

Alice motioned for him to go on. She could pepper him with questions, but he'd probably reveal a lot more if she just let him talk.

"Okay. I'm just … debating how much I can say without you thinking I'm crazy and walking out. Maybe even deciding this is some sort of a tag-team con I've got going with the *ipret*…" He paused and took a deep breath. "With the *individual* across the street."

He'd been about to say *ipret-tai,* and she definitely knew *that* word. If you took the two halves separately, they translated as *blood-body*, but judging from context and one cryptic note Beck had left, the combined word meant *servant*.

"The thought *did* cross my mind," she admitted. "The two of you showed up at pretty much the same time."

It was true, although if she was being honest, the man's expression when he talked about Durav being a killer had been so unguarded that it had gone a long way toward pushing at least that one element of suspicion out of her head. There were still a few dozen others bouncing around, though.

Housen gave her a point-taken look. "Can I ask you one question? Kind of an odd one, I guess. How many apartments are in the building where you live?"

He hadn't waited for her answer before asking his *one question*, but she'd always thought the whole *can-I-ask-you-a-question* bit was weird anyway. The only honest response was *it depends*. It didn't matter who the person asking was, there were always some questions you weren't going to answer or at least weren't going to answer truthfully. And there was no way to know whether any given question fell into that category until it was asked.

The question he'd asked her certainly wasn't one she'd expected, but she could answer it as long as she gave him a vague approximation that kept him from pinpointing her address. Not that she knew the exact number of apartments in her building, anyway. She did a quick mental tally. There were around twenty floors in the main building, twenty-four in the newer tower. Maybe twenty apartments on each floor, although they were larger on the upper levels where the view was better and the owners could command a higher rent. There might be only a dozen units on those floors.

"I'd say between four-fifty and five hundred. Maybe a bit more. Why?"

He nodded, looking somewhat relieved. "How good is the security there?"

That was a *second* question, and he hadn't bothered to respond to hers. But she answered. "Decent."

That was the case for the building as a whole. Her own private security system, however, which covered not just her apartment but her entire floor, was top-notch. Her mom called her place Fort Knox. It was a seriously dated reference—every ounce of gold had been moved farther to the North prior to the Secession Crisis, once the neighboring state of Tennessee began openly toying with the idea of leaving the union. It was still a pretty apt analogy, though. In addition to an entire fleet of locks and alarms, her camera app had views from receivers that she'd placed outside her apartment, outside the elevator, and facing every entrance to her floor. They were positioned at strategic locations on the exterior of the building, too, but those were of limited utility since they could be knocked out of commission by severe weather or by someone leaning against the wall where she'd stuck them. She'd lost a few dozen in the past several years, including one that had ended up on someone's coat, treating her to a knee-level view of the man's walk home, an enthusiastic greeting by his dog, and then the inside of an unknown closet. That pattern had repeated daily until the coat was retired for the winter.

Housen had only asked about the building, though, not her personal setup, and she didn't see any reason to go into detail. Instead, she repeated her earlier question that he still hadn't answered. "*Why?*"

"A larger building makes it less likely that Durav just reduces the place to rubble and has his guys dig through the remains. He wouldn't worry about the loss of life, but I don't think he's got enough people to comb through the debris of four or five hundred apartments. And it would be harder to get his people in position to do that here in the city than it was in the suburbs."

He said these last words almost as if talking to himself. *Suburbs*? Was he talking about the drones that firebombed Claire's house? Last she'd heard, Claire had believed the Flock was behind that attack and that they were trying to destroy the files. The same files that she'd explicitly told Alice were a moot point now, since both milestones were met and the doomsday clock was ticking.

"You're saying this Durav person thinks I may have something of his that's important enough to destroy an entire apartment building?"

"Yes. He has other candidates, but we both seem to be on his list. Although, like I said, given the size of your building, I think they're far more likely to snatch you off the street and interrogate you."

"What is it they think I have? Do you know?"

"A signaling device."

"Well, they're wrong," she said, relieved to find that they were after something that wasn't actually in her possession. "I don't have anything like that."

"I know. But it doesn't matter whether you have it, Alice. Durav thinks that you *could* have it, so you're in danger. He's not just going to ask you a few questions and then let you go about your business."

And … here it comes, she thought. *Here's the part where you say I need to trust you. That you can keep me safe from the big bad wolf. Well, news flash, alien guy. I've been keeping myself safe for nearly a decade and a key component of that is not trusting strangers who pop up at my local bar.*

As Alice had told Claire when they were at the restaurant in New Haven, she wasn't the type to trust anyone without a considerable amount of background research. Even then, if her instincts said no, she kept her distance. But if this guy was a member of the Watch—if he was an *alien*—then she wasn't going to uncover anything meaningful with a background search. All she'd unearth is a fake identity as carefully crafted as her own. She certainly wouldn't find anything to help her understand his motives.

So, she was back to her metric of last resort—her instincts. And even though the snarl when he spoke Durav's name had seemed genuine, there was no way she was placing her safety in a stranger's hands. Which meant it was time to go.

She tipped back the last of her drink. "Do you want another round?"

"No. I'm fine." He lifted up his half-full bottle.

"Well, *I* do. It's not every day I have to deal with the fact that there's a maniac out there who wants to kill me." This was absolutely *not* true unless Mitchell Morris had dropped dead of a coronary, and that seemed unlikely. She had an alert on her phone with his name and identification number so that she could pop a bottle of champagne on the happy occasion of his death.

She pushed the menu button on the table and ordered a second seltzer. Then she grabbed her bag and told the alien another lie. "I need to make a quick trip to the restroom. When I get back, maybe you can tell me how you *know* I don't have this thing that Durav is looking for. Because it seems like the only way you could know for certain is if *you* have it."

The restrooms were down a series of narrow hallways. She stopped in front of the community wallscreen, which displayed local ads for dog walkers, childcare, and music lessons, and checked the view from the camera outside the club. The creep was still there, still staring at the front door. *Good.*

Alice pulled up a map and found the address closest to where the alley behind the building intersected with 122nd Street and ordered a car to meet her there. The app said three minutes, which based on past experience probably meant five. Two people were outside the restroom door, so she fell into line and debated her options while she waited.

She could get a hotel room for the night. Her salary didn't leave much room for splurges like that, but she did have some extra money coming in at the end of the month from the translation project. Another possibility was to call one of the numbers that Claire had given her, just in case she encountered any security threats. But based on Claire's comments about her brother's reluctance to pursue the translation project, she wasn't sure he'd be willing to help. The second number was the chief of Jonas Labs Security. Claire clearly trusted him, and yes, he was *private* security, but it still felt too close to police for her comfort.

When the timer on the app was down to one minute, she

headed toward the rear exit, still undecided. A fetid stench hit her nose as soon as she entered the alley. The dumpsters at the far end had been baking in the sun all day, and the smell seemed to be trapped in the narrow space between ten or more stories of brick on either side. She held her breath for the few seconds it took to reach the end of the alley, where she was relieved to see her ride waiting.

She fell inside and closed the door quickly. "Bryant Park," she said, picking a destination at random. As the car merged into traffic, she extended her screen and opened the camera app.

The *ipret-tai* continued staring at the door, barely moving. She watched him through the app for the next twenty minutes. Four or five people left the club during that time, but not Housen. She didn't think it likely that he'd still be waiting at the table, so he must have found the rear exit, as well.

Her car had already left FDR Drive and was navigating through the crowds around Beekman Place when a movement on her armscreen caught her attention. The *ipret-tai* tapped behind his ear and listened to something for a moment. Then he mouthed a few words and began walking back in the direction of Morningside Park.

"Change of plans," she told the car. "Take me to 2300 Frederick Douglass."

The fact that she'd blurted out the first destination that popped into her head when she first got into the car showed how rattled she'd been. Had she been thinking rationally, she'd have told the car to simply drive around the neighborhood. If she'd stayed within a mile or so of her apartment, she could have darted back without worrying that the *ipret-tai* might be there waiting for her. True, he was walking in the other direction, but she was nearly half an hour away. Plenty of time for him to circle back around to 124th.

She switched to current views from the sixteen cameras she had scattered inside and around the perimeter of her apartment building. The system was already set up to send an alert if it detected anyone whose facial features matched those of her ex. It wasn't perfect by any means, but it had screened tens of thousands of people in the past few years, and there had been only two false alarms. Time to add a second image—the one she'd saved earlier of the *ipret-tai's* face.

The lighting in the photo wasn't great, but the tattoos were very distinctive. She focused on those and enhanced them so that the crescent with the squiggly shape inside and the bisected upside-down *U* were clear. Then she initiated a search of the archive. It only went back thirty days, but the sole connection she'd had to all of this before that was working in the same office with Holly Leffler, who had still been very much alive and firmly convinced that the symbols found on Mars couldn't be translated.

By the time the car was back on FDR, she had the results. No one matching that description had been skulking around her building. For the first time since she realized she was being followed, she relaxed and leaned her head against the back of the seat.

At about ten minutes after eleven, the car arrived at her building. She had it circle the block a few times while she ran a facial recognition search on the footage from the past half hour. It came back clear, so she grabbed her bag and got out at the building's side entrance.

When she pressed her palm against the entry panel, however, nothing happened. The panel didn't even light up and the door, which would have slid open under normal circumstances, remained stubbornly closed. Maybe her palm was sweaty? She wiped it on her skirt and tried again. Still nothing.

She turned to see if the car was still there, but it was already halfway down the block. Cursing softly, she pulled the wireless taser from her pocket and began down the sidewalk toward the front entrance, which faced Douglass Boulevard.

About twenty yards from the intersection, a figure darted out from behind two parked cars on the other side of 124th. He was dressed in black and crouched over, but she could tell that he was tall even before he straightened to his full height. When the streetlight hit his face, however, she saw that it wasn't the same man that she'd seen outside the club. He had the same zombified expression, and the crescent tattoo above his eye, but his hair was different. His build was heavier. Which didn't make sense because the notes she'd read in the files about the *ipret-tai* had explicitly said that they were *cloned*.

She didn't have time to ponder that fact, however. The man was now charging toward her at a full run with what looked like a gun in his hand.

Alice raised her taser, flipped the dial to max, and fired. Her projectile connected with the right side of the man's chest and emitted a bright blue flash as she held down the trigger. The *ipret-tai* staggered backward for several steps but didn't fall.

Her mouth went dry. That was a clean hit. It should have been enough to fully incapacitate him, even as large as he was. But the guy just yanked the barb out, flung it aside, and kept coming.

The taser had two chambers, so she fired again. Another blue flash, followed by three clumsy backward steps. He must not have completely recovered from the first jolt, because the second one forced him down to one knee, even though her aim was slightly off this time and she'd only caught his upper arm.

It didn't matter. He was halfway to his feet by the time Alice turned to run. She made it exactly five steps before the gun sounded, and she felt the searing pain of a bullet entering her shoulder.

TRANSCRIPT FROM THE ATLANTIC POST

SEPTEMBER 29, 2084

BRYCE AVERY: Good morning, everyone. I'm Bryce Avery and this is Science Newsmakers where we bring you interviews with the people behind the latest and greatest scientific innovations. As always, for those of you joining us live, feel free to send in your questions during the interview and we'll ask our guest to respond to as many as possible at the end.

Joining us today is Dr. Kai Jonas, CEO of Jonas Labs. She needs little introduction, of course, given her groundbreaking work on the anticancer medication, Arvectin, and the promising new life extension drug, Rejuvesce. Welcome, Dr. Jonas.

KAI JONAS: Thank you for having me.

AVERY: I must admit that I was a bit surprised when you accepted our invitation since you haven't given an interview to the *Post* in nearly four years.

JONAS: Why should you be surprised? My daughter was employed with your organization during that period. Anything your paper reported about me was automatically suspect for many readers. Now that she has resigned, however, I'm happy to add the *Atlantic Post* to my rotation for an occasional chat about the exciting work we're doing at Jonas Labs.

AVERY: That's a good point, Dr. Jonas. We obviously wish

Claire the very best in her future endeavors. Before we get started, though, I wanted to offer my condolences on the recent terrorist attacks against your organization. How is everyone holding up?

JONAS: Thank you so much for asking. We're all doing the best we can under these trying circumstances. Jonas Labs lost several employees at the three locations that were hit, and would have lost far more if not for a heroic effort by our security staff to clear the buildings as soon as the warning came in. And, obviously, it's heartbreaking on a personal level to see our primary research facility reduced to rubble. I don't know if you're aware, but both the buildings and our lovely biodome were designed by my late husband, Martin Echols. We're not going to be cowed by acts of terrorism, though. We will repair and restore the buildings *and* the biodome. The attacks on our overseas facilities are even more troubling in many ways, since those two labs are our largest producers of Rejuvesce, and this will inevitably slow our ability to distribute the drug. Not dramatically, mind you. We now have twenty-seven manufacturing centers, and I intend to bring two new centers online a few months earlier than anticipated to lessen the impact. I expect only a minimal decline in production. But it's still disappointing to those on the waiting list.

AVERY: While we're on the topic of Rejuvesce, I'm sure you're aware that there has been considerable speculation surrounding your comments at the Ares Consortium dinner on the night of the attacks. If I'm not mistaken, your exact words were, "I will soon be asking our investors the same question that I am about to pose to you—how long might you be willing to wait for a return on investment if you knew your lifespan was potentially *unlimited*?" Could you explain to us exactly what you meant by that?

JONAS: Have you never heard of a hypothetical, Mr. Avery? It's a marvelous teaching tool. What would you do if your lifespan was unlimited? Okay, now consider what you would do if you had a century longer. Fifty years? Thirty? My intention was to explore this with you and the rest of the audience, before coming back to the idea that we truly do not *know* what tomorrow will bring or which breath will be our last. Ten years ago, no one would have imagined we'd be looking at several extra decades of life. Ten years from *now,* we may well view that as a paltry achievement, due either to new research from Jonas Labs or from one of our competitors. Unfortunately, I was—as you are well aware—interrupted by the Flock's announcement of their attacks, which left journalists such as yourself to make some rather wild assumptions.

AVERY: But you *were* planning to announce a breakthrough at the dinner, correct? Concerning updated figures on life expectancy for those taking Rejuvesce?

JONAS: I wasn't planning to do anything of the sort. Do you really think Anton Kolya would have invited me as a speaker in order to have me upstage his own announcement? If so, you clearly don't know the man. Again, it was a hypothetical. My point was that we cannot know the future. Things move quickly in the world of science. Why not take a few chances with your investments? You never know what will pay off or when it will do so.

AVERY: That's true, I suppose. So ... shifting to a slightly different topic, I'm guessing you've seen the recent drone footage depicting a rather odd-looking creature outside one of the homes in your neighborhood. Is this another new project?

JONAS: I beg your pardon?

AVERY: I ... was just asking if the ... um ... creature in the video was part of a new project. Perhaps another collaboration with Anton Kolya?

JONAS: Could you please refresh my memory as to the name of this interview series?

AVERY: Um ... certainly. It's called *Science Newsmakers.*

JONAS: Thank you. That explains why I came here under the impression that we would be talking about *science news,* not about conspiracy theories. I also believe I'm beginning to suss out why my daughter decided to take her talents elsewhere.

AVERY: I obviously didn't mean to offend, Ms. … I mean *Dr.* Jonas. I just—

JONAS: The footage that you're referring to was taken by members of the Gates of Destiny, who claim to oppose Rejuvesce on religious grounds. They've caused nearly as much damage to my organization as the Flock, parking themselves outside our research campus and outside my home for the past year, and wreaking such havoc that I had no choice but to buy out my neighbors and surround the place with guards. After the Flock destroyed our lab, I moved a few employees into those homes and now these appalling people are invading our privacy and circulating clearly fabricated videos suggesting that I'm housing some sort of cryptid. Or maybe *breeding* such creatures.

AVERY: I understand. Let's just move on to the next question.

JONAS: Oh, no. We're *done* here, Mr. Avery. Enjoy the rest of your day.

FOUR

Wednesday, October 4
Ares Station

CLAIRE'S SHOULDERS pressed into the seat harness as the laser array at Ares Station hit the solar sails, and the ship began to decelerate. Paul Caruso, who had served as their pilot during the nearly three-week voyage from Tranquility Base, entered something into his armscreen. An authentication code, apparently, because the ship chirped three times and then altered course slightly to the left, almost as if it were being dragged.

A few seconds after that, a familiar female voice came over the ship's comm system. "Welcome to Ares Station. *Velox One*, you are cleared to dock at 5-B. Estimated arrival in seventeen minutes and forty-three seconds."

Beck, who was in the seat on Claire's right, turned toward her. "Isn't that…"

Paul answered him before she could. "It's automated. But yes, they used Stasia's voice as the model. We definitely need to change that at some point, but to get her completely out of the system would involve finding a new model for the avatar and I haven't had time to deal with it. And she and Kolya may have patched things up after three weeks in tight quarters. The *Velox Two* is about the same size as this ship so it would be kind of hard to avoid each other." His face brightened. "Who knows? Maybe he even rehired her."

Wyatt, who sat on Claire's left, bristled at that. "You'd actually trust her enough to work with her again? The woman is responsible for blowing up *six* buildings, and that's not even counting what she did at Icarus."

Beck didn't say anything, but Claire felt his shoulders stiffen. The chairs weren't exactly spacious to begin with, and it now felt like she was wedged between two stone pillars.

Wyatt almost certainly hadn't meant to jab at Beck, but this was a sore point. Technically, Stasia Ljubic hadn't blown *anything* up. Yes, she had helped facilitate the bombing when Claire was at Icarus Camp. As for the more recent attacks by the Flock, though, Corbin Drexel had been the one in charge of planning. While Stasia had known what was about to happen, the same could be said for Beck. He'd only found out a few hours before the attacks, though, and he did try to stop the one that took out most of the Jonas Labs main campus. Still, he clearly felt guilty about the aid he'd provided. Even with advance warning so that they could clear everyone out of the buildings at those research facilities, people had died.

Claire wasn't sure that Wyatt's assessment was fair even in Stasia's case. Three weeks earlier, when she and Beck were searching for Ro and Jemma in the tunnels beneath the Triad's compound, she would probably have agreed wholeheartedly. But she'd had a lot of time to think since then. As much as she wanted to believe that she would have handled things differently at Icarus Camp, Durav had been pulling Stasia's strings. What if someone had been threatening Joe or Wyatt? Or Ro? Or Jemma? Claire would have tried to minimize harm as much as possible, which is exactly what Stasia did. But would she have been able to refuse?

Even in the case of the attacks by the Flock, knowing that the entire world was in danger of being wiped out in a matter of months, what might she have been willing to do to wake people up? To buy time for a miracle? She wasn't sure.

Claire thought she might be at the point where she could forgive Stasia, but she was nowhere near being able to trust her. Which is why she was glad that the woman hadn't traveled on the ship with them. It would have been awkward constantly bumping into her—*literally* bumping into her in all likelihood, given the tight quarters and the lack of gravity on the *V1*.

"Who said anything about trusting her?" Paul spoke without looking up from his screen. "All I'm saying is that it would give me the perfect excuse to quit."

Paul made threats like that several times a day, but Claire was beginning to think he might actually mean it. The original plan had been for him to accompany Claire, Wyatt, and Beck to Tranquility Base, help prepare their ship for departure and then return to Earth on the next shuttle. He'd been promised three days off, after which he was scheduled to spend a week in Minsk and another in Nairobi to discuss plans for rebuilding two of the Kolya International facilities that had been destroyed by the Flock. His husband Ayman had planned to come along. Not the most cheerful vacation, perhaps, but they had learned to grab time together whenever they could fit it into their schedules.

When they reached the lunar base, however, they found that Kolya had already departed on the *V-2*, along with Stasia and Macek, who had arrived with the previous group of tourists. Kolya had left behind a message informing Paul that someone else had been assigned to handle the trip to the bombing sites and that he was now tasked with piloting the *V1* to Mars. Given the late hour back on Earth, Paul had to tell Ayman their vacation was canceled via text.

Kolya hadn't been happy about having passengers on this trip in the first place, but with Tobias Shepherd insisting that Claire was the only person he trusted to negotiate the hostage standoff between his people at Ehden and the scientists at the KTI lab at Doba, she had enough leverage to insist on bringing Wyatt and Beck. While Kolya clearly suspected—with good reason— that one or both of them had played a role in convincing Shepherd on that point, his primary goal was to resolve the hostage situation as quickly as possible. Once it was over, his people could certify that stage six of the terraforming project was complete and end the planetwide lockdown that had been going on for nearly six months.

Taking the two raptors instead of a single larger ship had in fact shaved nearly two days off their travel time, but it wasn't enough. It was now four days past the point when Kolya had tentatively promised that Mars would reopen. And even if everything went well, it would likely still be several days before he could give the all-clear.

Either the *V-2* was a bit faster than its sister ship or else Kolya had pushed the ship harder than Paul was willing to, because they'd arrived at Ares Station about ten hours ahead of them. Kolya had messaged Claire a few hours earlier requesting a meeting in his office at Ares Station as soon as possible to discuss strategy for the negotiations with Shepherd. In her reply, she'd asked to bring Beck along, but Kolya said she could just fill him in later, adding something about too many nannies leaving the baby unattended, which she guessed was the Russian equivalent of too many cooks spoiling the broth.

The ship made another slight course correction, giving them a clear view of Ares Station, which had roughly the same orbit as Phobos, the small, unstable moon that had been demolished by the Ares Consortium as part of the initial stages of terraforming. Seven months earlier, when Claire had first viewed the spaceport from her cabin on the Ares Prime, it had been a large gray ellipse against the tawny backdrop of Mars, which lay about six thousand kilometers beyond. While there were still a few patches of reddish-brown sand in the mix, most of the terrain was now green. Not the neon green that had covered the surface as KTI's modified version of *Azospira oryzae* gobbled up the perchlorates in the Martian soil, or even the spring green of fields and lawns you might see from the air on Earth. The palette here leaned toward darker shades ranging from deep pine to a greenish black that reminded Claire of the roasted seaweed snacks Ro liked to munch on.

In fact, the land resembled the inside of the test dome she and

Kolya had visited at Canillo, filled with flora that the AE—accelerated evolution—biobots had determined were most likely to thrive this far from the sun. Mars was now filled with the type of plants that Davina Monroe and her team believed would have developed naturally on a planet this distance from the sun. If they were right, the planet had looked a bit like this millions of years earlier when Eberin Das was trying to save it from the Alliance.

And here they were again, facing the same battle.

Mars itself had obviously gone through the most dramatic change, but Ares Station was different, too. About half of the docks had been occupied then. Now, everything at the main station was full and two smaller satellite stations, each with four docks, had been constructed on either side of the main facility.

Wyatt apparently noticed the same thing. "Guess we're parking in the overflow lot."

"You're right that it's getting crowded," Paul said. "Kolya's not happy about the competition, but I think it's good that the mining colonies are building a separate station for worker transports and so forth. It should be operational in a few months and then Ares Station will just be for tourists and maybe we can get rid of the satellite docks. But no, we're docking at the main station, next to the *V-2*." He tapped to awaken the console controls and zoomed in to magnify a square near the bottom of the station's outer ring. Then he zoomed in again, to show a single, impossibly small space in a row with about a dozen other ships.

Claire's throat tightened and she squeezed her eyes shut. There were hand controls on the console, but she hadn't seen Paul touch them even once. Everything was automated, and she knew on a logical level that the space was plenty big enough for the raptor. Still, there was no way she was going to sit here and watch as the *V1* was sucked into that tiny dot on the viewport.

"Is it safe to go back to my bunk now that we've decelerated? I … forgot to pack something."

Paul gave her an incredulous look. In zero-g, you never

*un*packed unless you wanted things to go flying around the ship. "As long as you're back in your seat in…" He glanced at his armscreen. "Fifteen minutes and eleven seconds."

She unlocked the magnets that kept her boots attached to the metal floor and wriggled out of the harness. "How about I just strap into my bunk?"

"Fine. Just stay there until I give the all-clear."

Wyatt grinned. He knew exactly why she was leaving. "You're *sure* you don't want to watch?"

"I'd rather shove hot nails into my eyes. Or watch Avery's interview with my mom."

The interview had been published several days earlier, but she still hadn't watched it. Leave it to Kai to rub salt into what was a surprisingly painful decision to quit her job at the *Post*, now that she'd had a few weeks to mull it over, with nothing else to occupy her time aside from reading and rereading Shepherd's memoir, along with a few articles and books she'd downloaded on negotiation strategies. It wasn't that she'd expected Kai to grant her interviews or exclusives when she was working there. In fact, she would have avoided the ethical conflict by passing anything of that nature to a colleague. She definitely wouldn't have given it to Avery, but any of the others would have been fine.

What had chafed was the fact that Kai had decided that her daughter's job meant that she had to completely avoid any sort of cooperation with the *Post*, and she'd gotten grief about that from her editor and co-workers. And then, as soon as she was out the door, Kai decided to grant an exclusive to Avery, someone Claire had grumbled about on multiple occasions during their mandatory family dinners at Christmas and Joe's birthday. Which either meant that her mother hadn't paid attention to anything she said on those occasions or else she'd listened carefully and knew exactly where to insert the knife to inflict maximum damage.

"If those are the only two options, I'd recommend the interview." Wyatt laughed at her expression then nodded toward the screen. "I'll give you a shout when it's all over. Assuming, of course, that we don't crash into the side of the station."

Claire dug an elbow into his ribs, then pushed off toward the bunkroom on the other side of the corridor.

To say that accommodations on the *V1* were spartan was a major understatement. While the room was taller than the cabin she'd occupied during her previous trip onboard the *Ares Prime,* it was about the same dimensions otherwise and she'd been the only person residing in that space. This room was currently housing four. Apparently, the ship was rated for two additional passengers, since there were six padded compartments in all, stacked along one wall in two columns of three. Each had a narrow mattress, a storage bin, and a privacy net. There was just enough headroom for you to sit up in bed, although it was a pretty close call for Beck. Two small, enclosed cubicles on the opposite side of the room held a toilet, a mini-sink, and a hydrosonic shower that was even less useful than the one she'd tried at Tranquility Base.

Pushing off and up, Claire coasted toward her bunk, then crawled inside and secured the restraining net. She and Wyatt had taken the top two bunks on the left hoping to get at least a modicum of privacy. They'd tried sharing, but the mattresses were too tiny for them to sleep together ... or to do anything else together for that matter, unless they were very careful, very quiet, and very quick. On the plus side, Beck and Paul either didn't snore or else the rumble from the various machinery on the ship was loud enough that it covered the noise.

Privacy issues aside, the trip hadn't been too bad once they adjusted to microgravity. Paul had been fine, of course. This was his sixth trip to Mars onboard a zero-G ship, or a *floater,* as he called them. She and Wyatt had both been a little queasy at first, even with the anti-nausea ear cuffs. Wyatt had gone through vestibular training before covering a labor dispute at one of the lunar mining operations not long after he started work at the *Post,* so he was pretty much back to normal the next day.

To her surprise, it was Beck who'd spent well over a week barely leaving his bunk. About an hour after they'd left Tranquility Base, Paul had told them they were at cruising speed, and it was safe to go get some sleep. He hadn't needed to tell them twice. They were all exhausted—unsurprising, given that none of them had slept the previous night. Beck hadn't even made it into the hall, though. He'd lowered himself back into the seat closest to the door, his eyes closed and his face even paler than usual.

At first, she'd thought that exhaustion had finally caught up with him. The man had lost a lot of blood less than seventy-two hours before they boarded the ship. He should have spent several days in bed recovering, but there had been no time. The alien super-drug she'd injected into his side before they went to New York had kept him moving and apparently pain free while they searched for Ro and Jemma, but maybe it had finally worn off?

She had asked if he was okay, but even as the words left her mouth, she'd known what was wrong with him. He looked exactly like she'd felt on her first trip, when she'd just stepped into the lobby at Tranquility Base. The problem was weightlessness this time, not spin, but Paul said it could have a similar effect.

It didn't make sense, though. Even if Beck hadn't had a chance to do the vestibular training, the man was an *alien*. It wasn't his first time off planet.

"You traveled to Earth from the Ufretan system," she'd said. "How can this be affecting you?"

Beck had shaken his head, wincing and looking like he was going to hurl at even that tiny extra motion. "This body was in stasis for that trip. Also, Ufretan ships maintain gravity without spinning like a damn centrifuge. And before you ask," he added, in response to her expression, "I don't know how their system works. I'm not an engineer. I'll be happy to put you in touch with one if I ever make it back to Parda, but I don't think that's going to be an option."

It was a fair point. Given that the Ufretan Alliance was on the precipice of eliminating Earth, there was little chance that they'd be sharing technological secrets. Her mind had from force of habit simply jumped straight to what an incredible scoop that information would be for the *Atlantic Post* ... before remembering that she'd sent in her resignation that morning.

Beck had been completely miserable for the first week. Even with the anti-nausea ear cuff, he'd been unable to eat without throwing up later—an act that was even more unpleasant and awkward in microgravity. Every time Claire heard him retching or saw him clomping around in the magna-boots he used most of the time to keep himself upright she felt guilty for insisting that he come along. Motion sickness aside, he'd made it clear that he did *not* want to be here.

She hadn't lied. She really *did* believe that Beck had a better chance at convincing Tobias Shepherd to help them than she did alone. But she also hadn't been entirely honest with him. The truth was that she didn't want full responsibility. She didn't even feel qualified to handle the hostage crisis, and there were only a few dozen lives on the line at Nepenthes, between the Flock members being held at the lab in Doba and the scientists being held by the Flock in Ehden. If what they suspected was true, however, the fate of the entire Earth rested on the alien gadget currently in Shepherd's possession. And they had absolutely no idea how the man would react when he discovered that her main reason for making this trip wasn't to settle his standoff with Davina Monroe and the other scientists, but rather to secure the beacon before Durav got his hands on it and signaled the Alliance.

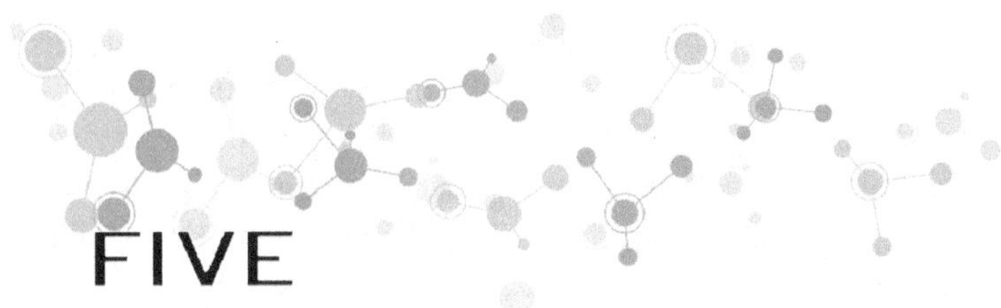

FIVE

THE *VELOX ONE* did not crash into the side of the station. In fact, Claire didn't even realize they'd docked until Wyatt pulled back the net around her bunk and told her they were ready to disembark.

"Do you think we have time to grab a bite to eat before your meeting with King Kolya?" he asked. "I don't know about you, but I'm way past ready for food that doesn't come out of a pouch, and from what you've said, we'll have a lot more choices here than we will at Nepenthes."

"Definitely. But you guys might need to go without me. We'll need to get through security first and I'm guessing Kolya—"

Paul's voice drifted up from the bunks below. "We don't go through the security line. Traveling on one of the *king's* private ships has its privileges." There was a note of reproof beneath his words as he repeated Wyatt's nickname for his boss, even though she'd heard Paul call the man an entire litany of names that were far worse.

Despite three weeks in close quarters, Paul still hadn't really warmed toward Wyatt. He was a friendly guy, for the most part, which left her wondering exactly how much of a pain in the ass Wyatt had been while trying to get information for his story about the deaths at the Millex mining camp.

"Go ahead and eat," Paul said, as he yanked his bag from the storage compartment inside his sleeping nook. "I've been ordered to report to His Royal Highness immediately, and I'll tell him to expect you at ten."

They all grabbed their bags and made the very short trip down the hall toward the exit. Paul pressed his hand against a security pad and the door to the docking cubicle slid open. Once they were inside with their bags secured in the bin, Claire slipped into one of the indented spaces along the wall, grabbed the handles on either side of her, and waited for the others to get into position.

Her stomach tugged sideways as they accelerated to match the spin of the station. Gravity slowly settled in. It was a familiar sensation, but not entirely welcome. The leg she'd injured at Icarus Camp—and further aggravated by vaulting over the gate at Beck's cabin—throbbed as her weight settled onto it. The pain wasn't as bad as she'd feared, however, so her daily rounds of stretching and using the exercise machine over the past few weeks had paid off. Not that it had been hard to carve out time given the limited options for diversion onboard the *V1*.

She looked across at Beck, wondering whether the motion sickness was going to hit him again, as Paul had warned them it sometimes did when the body readjusted to normal gravity. Beck smiled back and gave her two thumbs up. It was one of the few genuine smiles she'd gotten from him since they left Earth. Hopefully he'd still be fine once they started walking.

The docking cube, which was now rotating at the same pace as Ares Station, dropped into its slot with an audible click, and then the door whooshed open. A guard stood on the other side. He glanced at Paul briefly, nodded, and then waved the four of them through the gate.

Once they were on the other side, Paul pointed to a hallway on the left. "That will take you to the main concourse. I transferred your handprints to the system with level 2 access before we left the ship, so you can get where you need to go and won't need to worry about purchasing Martian credits. Anything you order goes on KTI's tab so live it up—well, as much as you can in an hour, since that's when you're due at Kolya's place, Claire. Find one of the guards when you're done and they can tell you how to get there."

She said okay, then followed Wyatt and Beck into what was almost certainly an average-sized hallway. But after three weeks on a raptor class ship, where her shoulders were mere inches from either side of any corridor, it felt like she was walking across an open field.

That feeling evaporated as soon as they stepped inside. It wasn't that the concourse was small. It was, in fact, enormous. But it was also packed. Wyatt mouthed the word *wow*. Or maybe he said it aloud. She couldn't hear much of anything over the noise. Judging from Beck's expression, he was equally overwhelmed, although she wasn't sure if they were reacting to the crowd or to the view.

Ares Station was at a different point in its orbit of Mars now than it had been the last time she was there, so the curved wall of windows at the front of the concourse no longer looked out over the massive, barren trench that she'd easily recognized as Valles Marineris. Now, the entire landscape was flat, much like the vast stretches of desert she'd flown across with Kolya on the way from Daedalus City to Nepenthes. Only now, the land was covered in a carpet of deep green, broken here and there by lakes that reflected the gray-brown light from the fledgling atmosphere. The station was on the same clock as Daedalus, where it was now well after nine p.m., so it was disconcerting to look down on a section of the planet where it was clearly the middle of the day.

The rotunda had been crowded on her first visit, but it was absolutely packed tonight. There were at least twice as many people. And the mood seemed off. Before, there had been a mix of tourists and workers, even a couple of school groups, and you could feel excitement and anticipation in the air. Now, it was almost entirely workers, aside from the security guards. The guards didn't have identifying information on their uniforms, but they were dressed in the same body armor as the dead guard she'd found in the tunnels at Conclave. There had been security the last time she was here, but she didn't think there had been as many of them. And they definitely hadn't been as conspicuously armed.

Once her brain adjusted to the barrage of sights and sounds, her nose kicked in. She smelled food. And she was hungry enough that the competing and far less pleasant aroma of too many people who'd only had access to hydrosonic showers for weeks on end wasn't a dealbreaker.

She turned and scanned the food kiosks along the back perimeter of the concourse, searching for one where the line wasn't totally insane. Her primary requirement was that the place had to offer salad. She'd been starving for leafy greens since they used up the last of the fresh veggies around the end of week one. The second requirement was something fried and salty, because whoever chose the provisions on the *V1* had apparently never heard of chips. Or spices, for that matter. They'd mostly stocked about a dozen varieties of healthy, bland, vacuum-sealed entrees. It was a satisfying enough selection for the first week, but after multiple repetitions of that same limited menu, they were all craving something different.

Beck wandered off toward a Nepali place. Claire opted for a kiosk that had a fairly wide variety. Thirty tedious minutes later, she began inching her way back through the crowd toward the table Wyatt was holding for them, carrying a tray ladened with a large salad, a calzone, an order of something called Italian eggrolls, the burger and fries Wyatt wanted, and two bottles of diet soda. There were no carbonated drinks at all on the *V1*. Paul said the bubbles caused digestive problems in microgravity. And the ship had run out of decent non-carbonated drinks midway through week two. The only ones left after that were the weird ones that Paul said Kolya liked. They smelled and tasted like licorice and were an odd green color—a lot like the *Azospira oryzae* now that she thought about it.

Claire was about halfway to the table when two guys in their late teens or early twenties very purposefully stepped in front of her. They looked like brothers. A girl standing next to the one on the right leaned forward, peering closely at Claire's face.

"That's *definitely* the reporter. Can't remember her name, but I watched that bullshit reveal she recorded at least a dozen times. If she was in on *that* stunt, I'm guessing she's in on this one, too."

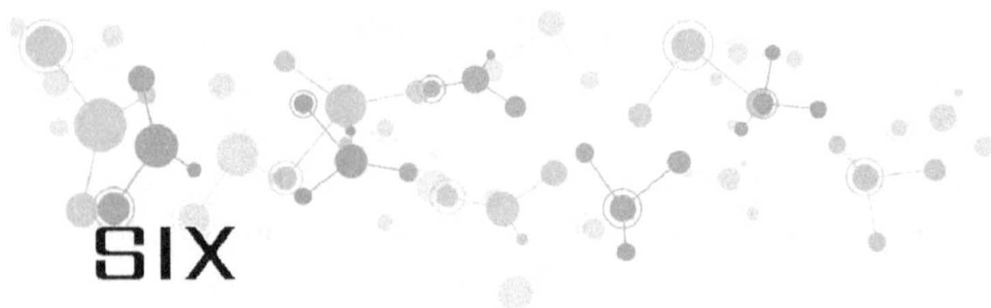

SIX

THE GIRL REACHED OUT, plucked a couple of fries from Claire's tray, and popped them into her mouth.

"Ooh, good idea," the one on the left said, as he and the other guy helped themselves to the fries. "I hear Kolya has finally arrived. We've been in dock for nearly a week waiting on the all-clear."

"I don't have anything to do with that," Claire told the man, hoping that the lie didn't show on her face. Technically, she was even more at fault than Kolya, who would probably have been able to resolve the standoff at Nepenthes remotely if Wyatt and Housen hadn't intervened.

"Well, maybe you can pass along a message when you see him, then, since you're such good friends and all," the second guy said. "Tell him this isn't what we signed up for. Pretty sure it's not what our bosses signed up for either. Kolya thinks he's the damned king of Mars, but he don't have the right to dictate when and where we go."

"Sure. I'll tell him if I see him."

"You do that."

The first guy was reaching for the burger when a security guard grabbed his arm and yanked it back. "Ow! Let me go!"

Claire backed away before she got pulled into the dispute and hurried toward the table, where Wyatt was tapping away on his phone. This was the first chance he'd had to message his source about the incident at Millex since leaving Earth. Connectivity had been almost non-existent on the ship, something she hadn't really anticipated. She'd gotten a short message from Joe and a slightly longer one from Ro a few days after they left, but nothing since then, and she had no idea whether the message she sent to Alice Dobroski had made it through.

Wyatt inhaled deeply as she slid the tray onto the table. "Oh my god. That smells incredible. Wait ... what are you doing?"

She scooped up the remaining fries with a napkin. "I ran into a few ... fans ... of Kolya's on the way over. They decided to help themselves to your fries. One of them didn't look like he worries too much about personal hygiene, so I'm thinking you might want to skip these. They would have gotten your burger, too, if one of the station's guards hadn't intervened."

"What did they want? I mean, aside from my dinner..."

"For me to let Kolya know that they are *not* happy with the delay."

He made a rueful face. "Can't really blame them on that point. They're stuck sleeping on the ships for an extra week after what? Four or five weeks in transit. Probably longer, even, given how slow some of those older ships are. Time at Ares Station is time they're not getting paid. And I'm pretty sure their employers aren't providing meals, either, judging from the length of these lines. I feel kind of bad about it, but I'm guessing they wouldn't be nearly as upset if they understood the alternative."

"Did you get through?" she asked, nodding toward his phone.

"Yeah. I'm just waiting for them to get back with a specific time so we can work out travel."

Macek was now fully behind Wyatt's quest to find out what had happened at Millex and had even managed to get Kolya onboard. Unfortunately, that cooperative attitude didn't extend to the main reason they were here. Kolya's entire team—including Paul—still seemed skeptical about the true origins of Sandjeel and the Watchers. Whatever cooperation Wyatt was getting would vanish in an instant if they learned about the subterfuge that he'd engaged in to ensure that they were included on this trip.

Beck joined them a few minutes later. He seemed a bit on edge, looking back over his shoulder before sitting down.

"Glad to see you've gotten your appetite back," Claire said, nodding toward his tray, which held two heaping plates. One looked like a curry of some sort and the other was piled high with fried onions.

"Huh? Oh. The bhajis are for the table. But yeah, it's nice to have options. It was hard to be too enthusiastic about anything on the ship after I'd upchucked most of it at least once."

"Thank you so much for sharing that lovely memory," Wyatt said with a grimace. It didn't seem to be putting him off his burger, though.

"Apologies." Beck popped one of the bhajis into his mouth. "Even though I'm pretty sure it was *already* a shared memory given the utter lack of privacy on the *V1*."

"On that note," Claire said, "I'm glad you're back. I don't have long before the meeting with Kolya and I wanted to make sure all three of us are on the same page now that we have some privacy."

Wyatt glanced around the packed concourse and laughed.

She rolled her eyes. "You know what I mean."

They'd decided before leaving Earth that the best course was to keep Kolya—and by extension, Paul and Macek—in the dark about Shepherd having the beacon. Given the decision to take two ships, that had simply meant excluding Paul, but anything you said on a ship that small was at risk of being overheard, so they'd just avoided talking about any of it even among themselves. She had taken the opportunity to have several long conversations with Paul on the more general topics of the Watch and the Alliance, though, and he was still firmly agnostic about the whole thing. Was he simply toeing the company line? Maybe. Either way, though, she wasn't comfortable telling him everything. And that went double for Macek. Triple for Kolya.

"Personally, I still think we should hold off," she told them. "I mean, I'll feel Kolya out during our meeting, but he's known for having a vindictive streak. If we tell him about the beacon, it's going to confirm his suspicion that Wyatt was involved in Shepherd's calling off the virtual negotiations. We could find ourselves locked out completely."

Beck raised an eyebrow. "You really think he'd do that at the risk of the entire Earth? I don't know the man, obviously. But Stasia and Drex said it wasn't just about power with Kolya. They said he was an idealist at heart."

Wyatt snorted. "So was Hitler. Not all idealists are noble or humanitarian. Idealism is no guarantee that Kolya will be willing to abandon his personal goals or loosen his grip on power."

Beck gave him a point-taken look. "Still ... he already *tried* reasoning with Shepherd on his own, right? His failure is the whole reason you're here."

"True," Claire said. "But he might have better luck in that regard if he could convince Shepherd that he'd been played. That we had ulterior motives. The man is paranoid. And even if Kolya didn't go that far..." She glanced at Wyatt. "It's entirely possible that they could have a sudden change of heart about you investigating the Millex story."

"You know I don't like having to back off from a story, *any* story. But you can't let that be a consideration."

"I know. And I wouldn't. It's just a ... side point."

They all focused on their food for a while, although Beck seemed distracted. He kept glancing back at the curved mezzanine level that wrapped around the rear half of the concourse. She was about to ask him who or what he was looking for, but then someone triggered the information kiosk and snippets of Virtual Stasia's spiel about KTI's terraforming efforts broke through the roar of conversation around them.

Claire could only catch occasional glimpses of Stasia's avatar through the crowd, which was gradually shifting in that direction. No one seemed to be paying much attention to what was being said but were instead focused on a group of hecklers near the front. She felt a small pang as she remembered Kimura doing the same thing just before they left for Daedalus City. He'd worn a self-satisfied smirk as he peppered the AI with questions about the logic of KTI's work on Mars when the money could be better spent on Earth. Kimura had been a hypocrite and an asshole, but he wasn't entirely wrong on that point.

Either one of the other people didn't like the heckling or something else riled them up because a few seconds later, a body went flying toward the stage. The younger, chirpier version of Stasia rippled and then cut out entirely as the man's shoulder smacked into the display.

Four security guards rushed over to break things up. One of the men shoved back at a guard, and for a moment it looked like weapons would be drawn, but they eventually let both men off with a warning. Two of the guards tried to clear people away from the booth, but there wasn't anywhere for them to go. Another crouched down next to the display, maybe to get it going again or see how much damage it had taken. A fourth guard, who seemed to be in charge, tapped something behind her ear, listened for a moment, and then began scanning nearby tables. She stopped when she spotted Claire, said something else to whoever was listening, then headed toward their table.

"Sorry to interrupt, Ms. Echols," the guard said when she reached them. "Chief Macek is waiting for you. Given that you seem to have attracted the attention of some of our other guests and"—she tilted her head toward the info kiosk—"the general chaos here, he'll be escorting you to your meeting."

Claire glanced down at her mostly finished dinner. Reluctant to jump at Macek's command, she debated asking for another five minutes. But it didn't seem fair to make the guard wait so that she could spite the woman's boss by stuffing the last few bites of calzone into her mouth.

"Chief Macek also suggested that you gentlemen might want to head back to your ship for the next hour or so once you're done eating," the guard added. "We're going to need both shuttles to get at least some of these folks back to the overflow docks, but after that we should be able to transport you to the surface."

Claire told Wyatt and Beck she'd see them back at the ship, then followed the woman through the crowd to where Macek stood waiting. The guard headed back into the concourse. Macek didn't say anything but simply nodded toward an elevator on the left side of the entrance doors. When they reached it, he pressed his palm against a panel of black glass. Once the door opened, he waved her inside.

"The guard just told us there are only two shuttles." Claire said when the elevator closed and the racket was gone. "Is that right? I traveled on shuttle number eight last time, so I would have thought that there were considerably more than two."

Macek pressed his hand against another black glass panel and the elevator headed up. A *private* elevator, apparently, since there didn't seem to be any way to select a floor.

"There are two shuttles here at the moment if you don't count Kolya's personal shuttle," he said. "Or the raptors, I guess. Those aren't really *designed* for surface landing, and they're too big to set down at Nepenthes or any of the smaller stations. Normally, though, we have ten shuttles. Six of them are the large models that can only land at Daedalus. The others are in drydock right now because we took advantage of the lockdown to do some routine repairs and upgrades. If things had gone according to schedule, all ten shuttles would be back here and running by now. Although if things were on schedule, it would be less of a problem in the first place, since half of the ships currently docked at Ares Station would have dropped off their cargo and passengers and would be on their way back to Earth by now."

"Why didn't they hold some of these ships at Tranquility? I mean, they knew the lockdown was going to be extended after the attack at Nepenthes happened, right?"

He raised an eyebrow. "Of course, they knew. And they *did* stop all departures … well, all of them except for our two raptors. But the ships currently docked here were already in transit when the Flock attacked. And since turning back mid-journey isn't exactly a simple matter with the laser propulsion system, we're stuck with them for the time being." He gave her a mocking grin. "But at least we won't have to worry about the overcrowding for much longer. Now that you've arrived with your *many* decades of hostage negotiation experience, I'm sure you'll have the situation at Nepenthes solved in no time at all."

GREETINGS FROM CAMP UFRETE

Dearest Anak –

I HOPE you're now fully adjusted to life on the ship. Travel of any sort is miserable outside of stasis, at least in my experience. But it is doubly so when you are physically ill.

We are all doing well here in Massachusetts, aside from the indignity of repeated poking and prodding from the people at Jonas Labs. The physical testing seems to have finally come to an end, but now they've taken to poking and prodding our minds, trying to find holes in our story. Trying to analyze how our minds work, I guess? I spent several days recording my personal biography and a general history of Novera and the Alliance—abridged, of course. Sandjeel did the same. Today I was hooked up to some sort of brain scan and asked a series of questions based on those histories. I'm pretty sure they're trying to determine whether we're lying.

The strangest thing is that Sandjeel seems oddly happy here. Even though he's losing weight—and hair—without the replicated supplements, he seems happier than in all the time I've known him, to be honest. I wouldn't have imagined it. While the house he's living in is large by Earth standards, it's much less space to roam about than he had in the tunnels. He must feel hemmed in, even more so now that the disaster with the drone curtailed even stepping out for a nighttime swim.

I think the child helps. She is a regular visitor, and she keeps him amused. I assumed Sandjeel was a novelty that she would grow tired of—or vice versa—but I often find her on his lap playing games or watching this cartoon show about cats on her tablet.

And yes, Joe is doing his best to make sure that we have what we need. I gave him the specifications for a *padjit* board, and he had someone print out a decent facsimile, although I really do wish the wooden version I made could have been salvaged from the fire. I spent so many hours carving the game pieces and it makes me sad to imagine them reduced to ashes.

Sandjeel has begun teaching Joe the game. He shows promise. Although, to be honest, I think Joe is less interested in *padjit* than he is in listening to Sandjeel's stories of his life on Novera.

In my last message, I told you about Nali as a youngling. I planned to write more—which I suspect you could surmise from my abrupt change of topic—but I couldn't bring myself to go beyond her first posting after university. That's not because I wish to hide anything from you, but because it hurts. I don't simply mean the fact that I will never see her again, although that is painful. It's not even my worry she could face repercussions from my decision not to return. Mostly it's because things were not good between us when I left and now they never will be. Barring a miracle, I won't have long to live with my regrets. She will, however. And that leaves me torn between hoping that she will miss me and hoping she has so thoroughly moved on with her life that she will never think of me at all.

The rift between us was one reason I joined the Watch. I thought that time and some distance would help, that perhaps her anger at me—and yes, my anger at her—would dissipate if we were forced to plan our conversations rather than simply yelling at each other. But the conversations have been almost entirely one way. I record long messages on my *rezlat* and wait for a response that rarely comes. A few cycles back she did send me a brief note and a short video from her commitment ceremony. It's a match her father wanted. I know the person well, and he will almost certainly make Nali as miserable as her father made me. But she is stubborn and will have to learn the hard way, just as I did.

Stasia has not contacted me. Once you arrive on Mars, please be sure that she's okay. I know I'm probably worrying excessively. She seemed quite certain that she would be physically safe the last time we spoke, but her extended silence troubles me. I've also had no word from our *absent friend*. They found another body out west, however, so I fear the worst.

Your cat misses you and wishes you were here. So do I. But I still believe that Claire was right that you can help convince Shepherd. You can be very persuasive when you want to be. When you return home, we will find that beach you mentioned and lie on the sand watching the sky. As I told you before, I don't believe in miracles, but if you happen to work one, then we will watch for seabirds instead of the *naidar* bubble. And if not, we will all enter our final rest far more at peace knowing that we tried.

Be safe, *amali*.

Arbet

SEVEN

BECK STOOD near the back of what he really hoped was the line to the Nepali food stall. He'd been craving something, anything, with flavor since he finally emerged from space sickness. His mind kept returning to the Durbar Grille, a little hole in the wall where he'd eaten during his years at Trinity College. Their vindaloo was so spicy your eyes watered just reading the word on the menu, and while he was under no illusion that a space station food stall would come even close, he was willing to roll the dice.

The lines stretched so far into the concourse that it was hard to tell which one went where. When he asked the man in front of him, he got a grunt that might have meant *yes*, accompanied by a scowl that discouraged him from pressing for clarification. Almost everyone in line was male, with the vast majority under thirty. That was about the average age for colonists and maybe five years over the average for guestworkers. The odds of anyone being gracious enough to let him switch lines if he'd miscalculated seemed exceedingly slim. Everyone was in a poisonous mood—the word *hangry* popped into his head, although he couldn't remember where or when he'd heard it.

As he inched forward, he reread the message from Arbet that had come in a few hours earlier. It was the second message he'd received, but she'd written others. Some of the references to things she claimed to have told him previously made him certain on that point. For example, she'd never mentioned her daughter by name before this most recent message. The only time that she'd mentioned her at all was the oblique reference in her note at

Conclave telling him that Sandjeel wasn't the only one who had to worry about offspring back on Novera. He'd tried to talk to her during the few minutes they had together before he left Earth, but there were too many people around for him to feel comfortable bringing up something so private. Instead, he'd waited and simply let her know in the first message he sent to her during the trip that he understood the sacrifice she was making, at least in the theoretical sense. He wasn't sure that anyone who had never had a child could fully understand.

The date stamp on her latest message was three days old. While there was definitely a lag this far from Earth, it would be measured in minutes, not days, for text-based communication with no images. Which meant that KTI's censors had spent some time trying to decipher it before deciding whether to pass it on. Beck would have loved to be in the room while they tried to make sense of Ufretan. He had a hard enough time translating it himself, given that Arbet was reduced to typing in Earther symbols and spelling the words phonetically.

The fact that KTI was letting the messages through at all had him suspicious that they *had* in fact been able to decipher them. Joe had shared the Eberin Das journal with Kai in his ongoing effort to convince her that Jonas Labs needed to abandon the stretch goals for Rejuvesce. He might have shared Shepherd's diary and the translation of *Tales from the Aveezi Forest*, as well. And since Kai and Kolya seemed to be in collaboration mode now, she'd probably shared anything she had with his people, which could mean that an entire team of archeolinguists were pouring over their messages. For that matter, given that Arbet and the entire Watch were now technically "owned" by Jonas Labs and living on company property, Kai could easily have some of her own people screening their communications.

Arbet's comment about their *absent friend* was ominous, though. She'd avoided mentioning Housen by name in her messages, and while Beck wasn't entirely sure of her reasoning, he'd followed suit in his replies. In her first message, which he'd received about a week after they left the lunar base, she'd mentioned news from out West. It had taken a bit of hunting, especially with the slow connection, but he'd eventually pulled up a story about a triple homicide at the gift shop for the roadside tourist attraction that the Triad owned near Kingman, Arizona. The bodies had been found the day they left. Two of them were the Earther employees that the Triad had hired to run the place. The third was an *ipret-tai* assigned to keep an eye on the remnants of the ship they'd arrived in, along with the spare beacon housed inside.

His search for the second article she'd mentioned in this latest message hadn't taken nearly as long, since they were closer to Ares Station and the ship was able to tap into its communications system. The same paper, the *Mojave County Standard,* had an article from three days earlier noting that local police were trying to identify a fourth body they'd found in a shallow grave about halfway between the gift shop and the entrance to the mining tunnel.

Beck was well aware that whatever fate had befallen Housen would have happened even if he'd stayed behind. The same was true for the chaos surrounding Sandjeel. But at least he'd have a better idea of exactly what was going on. Instead, he'd only gotten a vague explanation of how the drone had captured video of Sandjeel gingerly lowering himself into a swimming pool about a week back. He'd hunted the video down after reading her message, of course. The video had gone viral, so he'd had no trouble pulling it up. Waiting for the entire thing to come through on his phone, however, had brought back unpleasant memories of the early internet days, sitting in front of his Mac and listening to the ping and whine of the dial-up modem and then waiting … waiting … waiting for a game to download.

The drone's video quality was crap, so Kai's people had been somewhat successful in passing it off as fake. It had been dark in the backyard, aside from a pale turquoise glow from the pool lights and the half-moon above. Still, the area was bright enough to pick out three people creeping through the patio door and slipping into the pool. If it had just been Sandjeel, it might not have been as bad, but with others in the frame for comparison it was a bit startling. He was only about a foot taller than Joe … but nearly three times the height of Jemma.

Once they were in the pool, the camera had zoomed in on Sandjeel's face and for a span of about three seconds, his oversized eyes were cat-green reflections. You could even pick out the faint shape of the canula running from his nostrils into the shadows near the patio door which had resulted in all sorts of speculation from the "experts" who chimed in with comments. Were those fangs? Whiskers? Everyone had an opinion.

The audio quality was even worse, since the drone had been hovering near the industrial-sized walk-in freezer Jonas Labs had attached to the rear of the house in order to keep at least a few of the rooms at a reasonably comfortable temperature for Sandjeel. One high-pitched giggle had broken through the hum of the motor, but that was all you could hear from the roughly forty-five seconds of footage the drone managed to record before Joe spotted it and scurried out of the pool to grab a zapper. He was either too late, or it was one of the models that the drone zappers didn't affect, because it took off toward the trees. By noon the next day, the snippet of video was everywhere.

Someone nudged Beck from behind. "Move up or get outta the way, man."

He mumbled an apology and moved forward the two steps—*small* steps—necessary to close the gap. At least he could now see that it was indeed the right line.

Around ten minutes later, tray in hand, he scanned the crowd trying to find the table that Wyatt was holding for them. Or *trying* to hold. Given the surly demeanor of pretty much everyone they'd encountered so far, he could easily imagine people coming to blows or worse over someone saving a couple of seats. But Wyatt was exactly where they'd left him, phone screen expanded and still typing away, so Beck began moving in that direction.

When he was maybe halfway to the table, a woman came to an abrupt halt in front of him. He lifted his tray and turned sideways to avoid crashing into her.

If not for that small shift in perspective, he'd never have noticed the man on the mezzanine level.

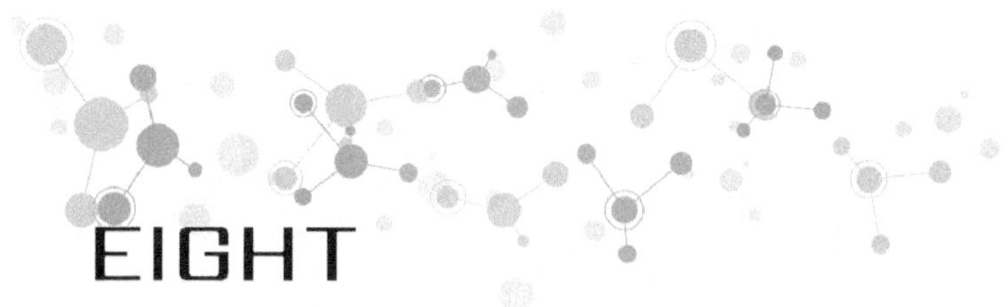

EIGHT

THE MAN LOOKED like the Earther guard Beck had seen tagging along with Maela at Conclave. According to Wyatt, his name was Jason Boudreaux. He'd been a low-level officer in the Lone Star Militia and was the same guy Claire had seen trying to break into the archeolinguists' lab at Columbia.

From here, there was no way Beck could be certain the man was Boudreaux. It might just be the angle, because he'd also been staring upward the last time he saw the guy. It was at Triad headquarters, and he'd been heading toward the front door, pissed that Reese had spilled beer on him and wondering what the hell was going on. When he heard voices from above, he looked up and spotted Boudreaux talking to a couple of the *ipret-tai* on the second-floor landing. The man had been wearing jeans and a shirt with rolled-up sleeves, same as now. His shirt, which was light blue today, might have been a different color then. Either way, it was a fairly standard uniform. At least half of the men in the concourse were dressed similarly, although most of them wore work boots—the kind with the wide toe that probably meant they were reinforced for safety. The guy on the mezzanine also wore boots, but they were of the cowboy variety. Not remarkable in any way, but they looked a lot like the ones he'd seen Boudreaux wearing at Conclave.

The guy wasn't talking to anyone now, just looking out at the Martian terrain through the expanse of windows at the front. Beck watched him for a moment or two, hoping the man would turn toward him so that he could get a better look at his face. Then a small cluster of people on the mezzanine crossed his line of sight. By the time they were gone, so was Boudreaux.

Or more likely, he thought, someone who bore a faint resemblance to Boudreaux from a hundred paces.

Beck scanned the concourse again, now looking not just for the mercenary, but for Durav. The man was a head taller than almost everyone in this crowd. If he was around, he'd have a hard time hiding.

He felt stupid even considering the idea. Even if Durav or some of his people were following them, there was no way they could have gotten here ahead of the *Velox Two*. Tranquility Base was the only commercial facility with a high-speed laser array and Kolya's people handled security there. While Kolya still seemed skeptical of the larger story he'd been given about the Watch, bodies had been found in the tunnels under Triad headquarters before they even left Earth. One of them matched Drex's dental records, and Kolya had apparently taken his ex-wife's death pretty hard. He might not be sure whether Durav was the guilty party, but Beck knew for certain that Kolya's people were looking for him. He'd seen an image on one of the screens at Tranquility Station claiming that both Boudreaux and an unknown man were wanted for questioning in regard to the terrorist attacks at Icarus and Millex. They included a picture of Boudreaux from the days when the guy was with the Lone Star Militia, along with an AI composite photo of Durav. That one must have been based on a description they'd gotten from Stasia, because it was a fairly good match.

So, no. The man on the mezzanine couldn't have been Boudreaux. It just wasn't possible.

Having mostly convinced himself, he began walking back toward the table, where Claire was now sitting with Wyatt. He joined them, and for the next ten minutes or so, they ate mostly in silence, scarfing down food like they hadn't eaten in days. The bhaji were a touch on the greasy side, but the vindaloo was good. Not Durbar Grill good, although to be fair, he hadn't eaten there in over five decades, so the food might be better in his memory than it ever was in reality.

The biggest difference between what was on this plate and what he was used to on Earth was the meat. This stuff must have been grown in a Martian lab, because the texture was off. It was softer, with a different mouthfeel from most lab-grown meat on Earth, which made him think the manufacturer hadn't fully adjusted their equipment to account for the lower gravity.

Even the distraction of decent food and stray thoughts about the differences in off-world techniques for growing vat meat couldn't keep his mind off the guy on the mezzanine. Every minute or two, he scanned the room again. The only time he was able to keep his mind fully in the present was when Claire brought up the question of whether to tell Kolya that they knew Shepherd had the beacon. While he leaned toward full disclosure, he didn't push the point. He'd never met Kolya. Claire had actually spent a good deal of time with him, and she and Wyatt both raised valid points.

Chaos erupted at the information kiosk a few minutes later. He half expected it would be Boudreaux, but it wasn't. Security broke up the scuffle and then one of the guards stopped by their table to escort Claire to her meeting with Kolya and to suggest that he and Wyatt wait on the ship until a shuttle was available to take them to the surface.

Before the two women were even out of sight, Beck felt Wyatt's eyes on him. *Again*. He'd caught the man watching him surreptitiously on multiple occasions during the trip. At first, he thought it was some sort of macho bullshit, that maybe Wyatt was holding a grudge over Claire's long-ago crush. But then he noticed Paul Caruso watching him, too, and realized they were playing Spot the Alien, hunting for any telltale signs that he wasn't a native Earther. He'd even seen Claire, who had known him for years, watching him on a few occasions. The whole trip, he'd felt like he was pinned under a microscope. It was one reason he'd spent most of the time inside his bunk, even after the space sickness dissipated.

In Paul's case, he could chalk it up to skepticism. Judging from the snatches of conversations Beck had overheard between him and Claire, the man still hadn't decided whether he believed their story. But in Wyatt's case? He clearly *did* believe. Maybe it was just one of the quirks of being a reporter.

He couldn't really blame them for being curious. It should actually be freeing—he didn't have to worry about dropping too many anachronisms into his conversations now. But their scrutiny made him self-conscious. For the first time in years, he felt *alien.* He kept second-guessing not just the things he said, but even his physical movements and gestures. The awkwardness of floating through the ship was partly to blame, but so was the knowledge that this body was now his endgame. Whatever time he had left would be in *this* body, *this* form. No matter what happened, he'd never see Parda again. His real body would either be revived without any memory of this assignment, or his family would be given some excuse for why they couldn't revive him. Malfunctioning equipment, perhaps. Or some fabricated story about his conduct on the trip that never mentioned the real reasons behind his treason. He didn't regret siding with Earth. If he could go back and change it, he wouldn't. But the full weight of the decision had finally settled in during the trip.

Or maybe it had settled in before they left Earth. He'd told Claire he didn't want to make the trip because it seemed unfair to saddle Joe and Arbet with the responsibility of dealing with Sandjeel and the very real possibility that some version of the truth would get out. That wasn't a lie, but there were personal reasons, too. He wanted to be around people who understood how he was feeling right now. Most of all, he wanted to be there for Arbet. She was clearly hurting. And Sandjeel? Sure, he'd known what he was signing up for at the beginning of the mission, and he was complicit in condemning the planet to destruction for the grievous sin of curiosity. Beck knew he shouldn't feel sympathy for him, but he still kind of did. Sandjeel couldn't even slip out for a dip in the pool without it going viral. And it wasn't like the man had ever *wanted* Earth to be destroyed. He just didn't think there was any way to stop it.

Neither did Beck, if he was being fully honest with himself. Earth didn't stand a chance against the Alliance. He didn't want to believe that, and he'd do his damnedest to at least delay the day of reckoning. But that didn't keep the thought from coming back time after time—*you can't stop this.* Because no matter how much he hated it, it was the cold, awful, and inevitable truth.

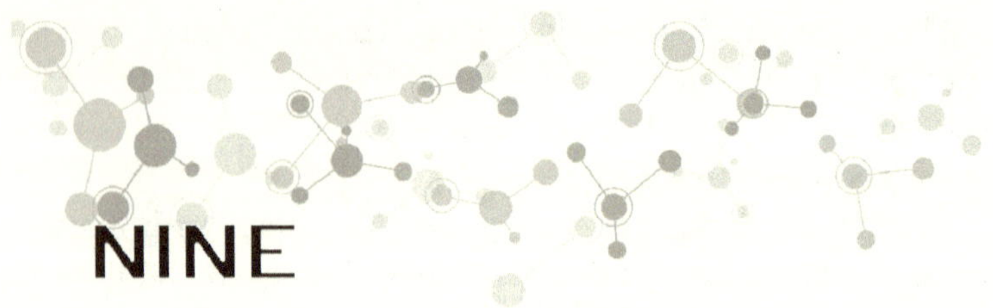

NINE

BECK LOOKED UP, not bothering to hide his annoyance. "What? What are you looking at? You think maybe I'll sprout an eyestalk on the top of my head?"

"No." Wyatt seemed mildly disgusted at the suggestion. "God, no. I was just wondering what has you so jumpy. Didn't want to say anything while Claire was here since she was already on edge over her run-in with the jerk who swiped my fries."

"Someone swiped your fries?"

"Oh, right. You missed that part of the conversation. Some idiot recognized her from the Icarus chamber video and wanted her to tell Kolya to hurry up and give the all-clear." He grinned and grabbed the last bhaji from the plate. "And you're deflecting. So ... why don't you tell me what's up?"

Beck pushed the last bit of vindaloo around with his fork, debating whether to tell Wyatt what he maybe perhaps possibly might have seen. No. He was going to sound paranoid.

"It's nothing. Really. Well, nothing except I wouldn't have eaten nearly as much if I'd known they were sending me back into zero-g so soon."

Wyatt gave him a look of sympathy but shook his head. "Nope. Not buying it. You've been glancing over your shoulder every thirty seconds since you sat down, well before you found out we were heading back into the Nauseator. Hope you're not looking for Stasia, because if people recognized Claire, they'd recognize her, too, especially with her virtual doppelgänger over there at the info booth. She'd be crazy to show up here." He gave a sideways nod toward the windows and the planet below.

"Kolya is arguably the most powerful person on Mars. But as much as we joke about it, he's *not* a king and his protection might not keep Stasia safe. Not when she literally has a bounty on her head in several colonies. So, if you need to talk to her, you should get Paul or Macek to set something up before we head down to the surface."

Beck actually *did* need to talk to Stasia, mostly so that he could reassure Arbet that she was fine. Stasia was not only a fellow member of the Watch, but Arbet now viewed her as her *client*, and wasn't happy that Kolya had whisked her halfway across the solar system where she couldn't see with her own eyes that the woman was safe. And her instincts in that regard were probably solid, given how long she had worked as a legal advocate on Novera.

"But," Wyatt said, "Stasia's *not* who you're looking for, right?"

Beck sighed. Wyatt would just keep pressing if he didn't get an answer. And maybe it would help to have someone point out that he was letting his imagination run wild.

"No. I mean, I do need to talk to her. But I thought I saw one of Durav's mercenaries earlier. Boudreaux."

"Really?"

"Yeah, but I was probably imagining it. I've only seen the guy a few times, and it was partly the cowboy boots…"

"Hold on." Wyatt expanded his phone screen, swiped, then pushed the phone across the table. "In case you need to refresh your memory. The photo isn't all that recent, but Claire says he hasn't changed much."

Beck turned the phone around and looked at the image for a few seconds. It was the same picture he'd seen briefly on a security screen at Tranquility Base, and it definitely looked like the guy on the mezzanine.

"It *could* be him, based on the picture. But there's no way they could have beaten us here, right? I mean, even if they somehow got past security at Tranquility, Caruso says the Velox is top of the line, the fastest model in the raptor class."

Wyatt laughed. "Fastest *legal* version, maybe. But there are plenty of raptor narcoships that can outrun anything Kolya owns."

"You think so?"

"I know so. Same basic setup as the *V1*, but they only have life support on the bridge, for the pilot and maybe a copilot if they're willing to be extra cozy for a few weeks. They hollow out the rest of the space for cargo. Dangerous as hell, but the money is good, so they still get takers. China also has a few Class C ships that are nearly as fast and can carry more people. Pretty sure the UAR does, as well. But it would take longer and a lot more cash to arrange that kind of transportation."

"Either way, they'd still have to go through Tranquility Base, though. Right?"

"Not necessarily. Some still do, because it's easier and cheaper. The trade isn't illegal on the Moon or Mars, so there's no risk as long as they take off from some place on Earth with lenient laws or lax enforcement. If you've got enough money, there are several … *cooperative* governments that are perfectly willing to lease out their military facilities. Hell, that was Plan B if Kolya didn't come through with transportation. I really didn't think he would, so Housen and I were looking at a couple of other options. None of which should have gotten him killed," he added quickly. "He could still turn up, you know."

"Maybe. Arbet seems convinced that he's dead, though, now that they found another body at the mining attraction. How sure are you that he'd already disposed of the other beacon?"

"All I know is what the man told me. But I can't think of any reason he'd have lied or any reason he'd have gone back to Arizona for that matter, so I doubt that's his body they discovered. Durav's people could have caught up with him somewhere else, though. I've sent multiple messages to the only contact info I have for him, and I haven't heard back. Although given the connection issues on the V1, some of those messages may not have gotten through."

Beck glanced back up at the mezzanine. "So … if Durav was checking out these other transportation options, which cooperative government would have been at the top of the list?"

"Idaho," Wyatt said, without hesitation. "It's the closest. They have almost as many illegal launches as legit going out of what used to be Mountain Home Air Force Base, although unless they've gotten some serious upgrades, I don't think they could launch a Class C. But if the guy you saw is actually Boudreaux, that's home turf for him, so it was almost certainly his departure point."

"Thought you said Boudreaux was with Lone Star?"

Wyatt shrugged. "Refugees from the Texas militia and Southern Sons probably outnumber natives in Idaho at this point. Boudreaux's got plenty of connections there. And plenty on Mars, which is why Kolya and Macek are willing to let me poke around for evidence that ties the militias to that containment breach at Millex."

"That still seems like a pretty big coincidence to me. I mean, Durav hires someone from the same group that—"

"I'm not saying it's the *same* group, although Lone Star did become sort of a catchall militia after reunification. Most of the hangers-on merged back into society, but the diehards didn't have a lot of choices when Texas reentered the union. The Dakotas are super strict about who they let in, so it was pretty much Idaho or Mars." He gestured toward the planet. "And I'm sure you can see why Mars would be a magnet for that type. The place is lawless, or at least that was the case twenty years ago. Now, though, you have Kolya trying to organize and civilize it."

"Is that such a bad thing?"

"Not in my book," Wyatt said. "Having seen firsthand far too many places where civilization has broken down, I'm a big fan of the concept. But there are plenty who disagree. Kolya had to twist a lot of arms and pay out some hefty bribes to get everyone to sign on to the lockdown, and that's partly because some of them really don't want the place to be terraformed. The way they see it,

Kolya has covered the surface with plant life now, which is good, because it will eventually mean they can get around without biosuits. Animal life, on the other hand, is not a requirement for the planet to be livable. There's a pretty vocal group in favor of ending the terraforming process now, in part because they're starting to wonder how long it will be before they're once again dealing with laws dictating where and how they can extract their opals or whatever because they might endanger some fragile life-form. The one good thing about the planet not having breathable air or a functioning environment was that they couldn't really screw it up worse than it already was. Anyway, you're *probably* right that it wasn't Boudreaux that you saw. I'd say at most, it's like a ten percent chance. But we should let Macek know. Give him a heads up, just in case."

Beck looked around again. Still no sign of Boudreaux or Durav, but he did catch the eye of the guard who'd led Claire over to the elevators. She gave him a stern look and gestured toward the exit, which was a few meters to her right. Then, she tapped her earpiece and began talking to someone. Her expression unnerved him. Something was up.

"Yeah," he said to Wyatt. "Macek needs to know. Although, it might be quicker to simply tell *her* on our way out." He nodded toward the guard as he slung his bag over his shoulder.

By the time they reached the exit, though, the guard was no longer there. They made their way back down the corridor they'd come through earlier, thinking they could tell the guy who was posted outside the docking cube instead, but he wasn't at his station, either.

Beck pressed his palm to the panel and opened the cube. They stepped inside, secured their bags, and grabbed the safety handles.

"Take us to the *Velox One*," he said. "Bay Five."

He braced himself for the onslaught of nausea as the cube decelerated and they reentered microgravity. His stomach did make one ominous little dip, but he took a few deep breaths and kept his eyes squeezed shut. By the time he opened them again, everything seemed to be stabilizing. Just fifteen more seconds to their destination according to the timer.

He relaxed. *Everything was going to be fine.*

The thought didn't even have time to fully form in his head before something large and heavy whacked into the outside of the cube.

FROM AWAITING THE SENTINELS

BY TOBIAS SHEPHERD

Appendix: The Sentinel's Manifesto (Lesson One)

THE SENTINELS HOLD the hourglass of time in their hands. Each time a species vanishes or a glacier melts, a few more grains of sand trickle through the narrow opening that determines our fate. Each time a child is born into a world where the air and the water are tainted, the sands fall faster. The actions of the planet's people determine whether the Sentinels tip the hourglass or hold it steady as the final grains slip away.

Do not, however, mistake the Sentinels' judgment for cruelty. It is not we who condemn the Earth, but its inhabitants. Every act you take to heal this planet tilts the glass in your favor. And if we decide that the Earth must die, it is only so that it may one day return—green, verdant, and alive.

May you walk in the light of the Sentinels.

Res esdoden ojiri ensilar ufretas.

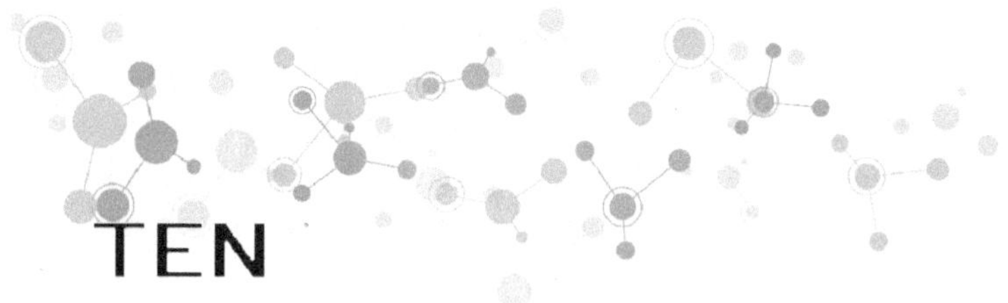

TEN

A STRONG SENSE of déjà vu hit Claire as soon as she stepped out of the elevator and into Kolya's quarters. She'd never been inside this particular apartment. But she'd been in two others that were identical in almost every way.

She'd noticed the strong similarities between Kolya's penthouses at the Red Dahlia and at Hotel Mir in New York when she dropped in to see if he had information to help her find Beck. This place was yet another matching pea in the pod. All three apartments had the same circular configuration, with transparent outer walls and ceilings. Or to be more precise in the case of this apartment and the Red Dahlia, with walls and ceilings covered in screens showing scenes from outside that made the walls *appear* transparent, since showing the actual gravity-maintaining spin would have resulted in nothing but a blur. The apartments all had the exact same artwork on the interior panels separating the private areas from an outer ring designed for entertaining. The same long wooden bar with wine and whiskey glasses dangling from overhead racks above bottles of liquor, with Kolya's favorite *krambambula* in pride of place. The same plush gray sofas strategically angled to maximize the panoramic view. As far as she could tell, the exterior view was the only thing that varied between the three apartments.

Back at Hotel Mir, she'd speculated that these similarities indicated a lack of imagination on the part of the designer, but she was now leaning strongly toward it being a very intentional choice on the part of the client, maybe even a matter of psychological necessity. Kolya had once told her that his various business ventures meant he rarely stayed in one place for more than a week or two at a time. Was this his way of maintaining the sense of being at home? He probably kept identical clothes in every closet, all arranged in the same order, so that even though the physical locations were millions of kilometers apart everything was familiar.

Macek must have read her expression, because to her surprise, he laughed. "It's a bit disconcerting, isn't it? His quarters at Tranquility Base are the same, too. I told him once that he should put up a sign to remind him what planet he's on. Only his places in Minsk and the cabin at Ehden are different, but he inherited both of those, so…" He gave an expressive shrug, as if to say *what can you do,* then nodded toward one of the sofas. "Wait here. I have things to deal with downstairs, but Kolya will join you shortly."

She expected a long wait, since Kolya wasn't exactly known for being respectful of other people's time. But she'd barely settled onto one of the sofas when she heard a door open behind her.

It was instantly clear that Kolya was in a foul mood. He didn't bother with the usual niceties but simply pointed toward the outer wall, where one section of wallscreen now displayed a video. "Care to tell me who that is?"

"Why, hello to you, too, Kolya. I *do* hope you had a pleasant trip."

When he didn't respond to her sarcastic greeting, she turned her focus toward the screen, which displayed the road outside the Triad's compound in the Bronx. The entire scene was bathed in a hazy reddish glow, with occasional flashes of light from above that she assumed came from the helicopter. On the right side of the screen, Macek was talking to the firefighters who had arrived on the scene in response to the explosives Durav's people had set, which caused fire to engulf not only the tunnels below, but also several of the homes owned by the Triad.

Since Kolya clearly wasn't asking her to identify Macek, she looked at the other side of the screen where Wyatt was talking to someone in a white car. She had the sense of time folding in on itself, remembering the deep sense of relief she'd felt as she stared out the window from the study at Lavender House and saw Wyatt below, standing in the road at the base of the hill. She'd even been relieved to see Macek. Kolya's chief of security wasn't exactly at the top of her most-trusted list, but she hadn't had the luxury of being picky, and he'd come through. Without his help, they'd have been forced to cart a nearly eight-foot-tall alien who was recovering from heatstroke down the hill and through the neighborhood to a helipad nearly a mile away, where they'd hoped to be picked up by one of the Jonas Labs Aerolyfts. Even in the middle of the night, they'd almost certainly have run into someone. And unless that someone was blind or extraordinarily high, they would have remembered seeing Sandjeel.

"If you're asking about the guy in the blue T-shirt, that's Wyatt."

"I *know* that. Who is the man he was talking to?" Kolya paused the video. The car had already turned around by that point, and all she could see were two red taillights heading out of the neighborhood.

"I ... have no idea. Probably someone asking him about the fire. At least, that's what I assumed when I saw him that night. I was looking through a phone camera, and from a different angle. Plus, I was kind of distracted by Stasia freaking out because she was worried that Macek was going to kill her."

"Well, Stasia always was a smart girl. You're telling me you didn't ask Garcia who he was talking to?"

"No, Kolya. I didn't *ask*. We're both adults. I don't report every conversation I have to him, and I don't expect him to report every conversation to me. To be honest, I'd completely forgotten that a car was even there. I was a little preoccupied with getting everyone to safety before another explosion went off down in those tunnels and killed us all."

Kolya sighed and told the screen to roll the video back thirty seconds. When the car was once again in place next to Wyatt, he told the computer to find the frame with the clearest image of the man inside the white car, then enlarge and enhance.

After a few seconds, a man's face filled the screen. It was vaguely familiar, with a square jaw and a slightly crooked nose. Light brown hair. Kind of shaggy. Claire frowned at the screen trying to remember where she'd seen the guy.

"You know him." Kolya stated this as a fact rather than a question, seeming far more certain on the point than she was.

A moment later, her stomach sank. She did indeed recognize the man. He was Wyatt's source, Housen. The one who had contacted Shepherd and convinced him to cancel his planned negotiations with Kolya and hold out until Claire arrived at Ehden.

"I wouldn't really say I *know* him," she said. "All I know is that he's one of the Watchers. I saw him only once, when I was looking at the video footage from the cameras that Wyatt posted around the Triad's headquarters. I only remember because he arrived at Conclave at the same time as Reese. That's the guy Beck carried out of Jonas Labs just before—"

"Yes, yes. The one who died." He nodded toward the screen again. "So? Tell me his name."

She considered lying. Not because it would serve any real purpose, but because his imperative tone of voice was pissing her off. Old King Kolya—decidedly not a merry old soul at the moment—was pushing her around like one of his fiddlers three. But if she didn't comply, he'd just drag Wyatt in and ask the same thing. She might as well tell him what little she knew, even though there was a very real risk that this would open up new avenues of questioning that she really didn't want to travel at the moment.

"His Ufretan name is Housen. That might not be the name he's been going by on Earth, though. I only saw him that one time, and again, not in person. I've never spoken to him at all. Aside from that, the only thing I know is that he's missing. None of the Watch have heard from him since the fires at their headquarters. I suspect Stasia could tell you far more than I can. You just spent the last three weeks together on the ship. Why didn't you ask her?"

He ignored the question and tapped something into his phone. The video flickered out, replaced by a still image with a full body shot of the same man, standing on a narrow dirt road in front of a cornfield, talking to two other people. All three were dressed in the standard uniform of the Earth Watch Alliance, AKA the Flock —faded jeans and a T-shirt bearing the group's logo of an eye with a globe superimposed over the iris. Claire didn't know who the woman was, but she immediately recognized the other man as Tobias Shepherd.

"I suspect Garcia could *also* tell me far more than you can," Kolya said. "Because I'm certainly not buying that he just *happened* to be the person this Housen guy stopped to ask about the fire. Not when just a few hours later, Shepherd reneges on his previous agreement and suddenly decides you're the only person in the universe he trusts. So, why don't you tell me why you're *really* here, Claire? What is so damned important that you're willing to risk the lives of the people that Shepherd is holding? One of those people is Davy's second-in-command who has to sign off on the inspections before we can lift the lockdown. Another is Idi Ademola, who is not just an employee but also a friend. And Davy herself? She's at risk, too, and as annoying as the woman may be at times, I consider her family."

"They're both okay, though. Right? Nothing else has happened to them?"

Kolya stared at her for so long that she grew very nervous that something else *had* happened during their trip. Claire had only met Davy and Idi once, and she wouldn't presume to call them her friends. But she genuinely liked both of them. She certainly didn't want their deaths—or anyone's death—on her conscience.

"No. They're both fine. Well, as fine as anyone can be under those circumstances. But whatever game you and Garcia—and

I'm guessing Beckett, as well—are playing has resulted in an untenable extension of this lockdown."

"Can't you waive the second-in-command signing off on lifting the lockdown? I mean, you run KTI, right?"

"Obviously. But I'm not going to violate my contract with the Ares Consortium. Official protocol for stage six requires that human teams confirm the sensor readings before lifting the lockdown. The other colonial leaders would love an excuse to challenge our lease on the Arsia Mons hyperlift. Or halt the remaining stages of terraforming entirely. So, we're kind of stuck. And I don't know if you've noticed, but there are some very angry people on this station at the moment. Every extra day they're here is costing a bloody fortune and—"

"God. I should have known." Claire barked out a short laugh. "It's about the money."

"Well, it's obviously a consideration," he admitted. "Why wouldn't it be? Personally, I can handle the loss, although if you remember I already took a sizeable financial hit in order to get the mining companies to settle with the workers so that we could even start the lockdown. For most of the ships docked at this station, though? Absolutely, yes, it is *one hundred percent* about the money. I guess it's easy for people to scoff when they have plenty of it."

ELEVEN

CLAIRE RESISTED the urge to roll her eyes. It took an incredible amount of nerve for Kolya, who was almost certainly the wealthiest man on Earth, to lecture *her* about being an insensitive rich girl.

"I'm not *scoffing* at anyone. But there's a lot more than money on the line at the moment. Like I said, you spent three entire weeks in transit with Stasia, so I'm guessing you and Macek have both grilled her thoroughly. You've also gotten back information from the DNA samples you and my mother took from the Watchers and Sandjeel. You *know* they're not … human." She considered amending that to say they were not Earthers. Beck would certainly object that they were *all* human—and with some justification based on the section of the journal that Alice translated. But she didn't want to give Kolya an excuse to start an off-topic argument.

He shrugged. "I know their DNA has some unusual markers. It's a shame I didn't get the opportunity to interrogate this Sandjeel character before leaving. Maybe if I had, I'd have a bit more confidence that he's what he claims to be. Your mother promised to let some of our experts in to run tests, but your brother seems disinclined to share the data."

Claire felt a chill at the words *run some tests,* remembering the fears Sandjeel had expressed as they fled the tunnels beneath the Triad's compound. On the trip from Earth, she'd watched the movie he mentioned. It was very easy to imagine Kolya's people —or some of her mother's—swooping in on Sandjeel like the government agents had done with E.T. And she doubted it was a matter of Joe being stingy with data. He was far more of an open-source scientist than their mother, so if he was withholding access to Sandjeel, it was because he was worried about the nature of these tests KTI was proposing.

"Either way, it doesn't prove anything," Kolya said. "They could have been altered—even *created*—on Earth. You've seen the kind of work that Davy and her team have done at Nepenthes."

She gave him a grudging nod, since she couldn't really argue the point. It wasn't just the lemur dog she'd seen in person, or the menagerie of creatures specially adapted for the Martian environment that Kolya had introduced in his video at the Ares Consortium dinner. Authoritarian leaders and the uber rich had been making copies of themselves for decades. It didn't always work well, and most of them did it for spare parts, but North Korea was now on its third copy of Kim Jong Un. Plenty of people in the good old USA used the technology, too. It was illegal, so they had to hide it, but it was odd how many of the rich and powerful suddenly developed extraordinarily strong genes, resulting in offspring that were virtual carbon copies of themselves. She'd even had the accusation thrown at her a few times, given her strong resemblance to Kai, and might have asked Joe to test it if not for the fact that her father's eyes stared back at her from the mirror each morning.

"Then I'm sure you'll agree that Davy could quite easily engineer a creature like this Sandjeel," Kolya continued. "And while I would argue that she's undoubtedly the best synthetic biologist on—well, I was going to say on Earth, but she hasn't been back there for several decades, so let's just say the best in this solar system. That doesn't mean, however, that there aren't others who are *almost* as gifted. They can't exactly run an advertisement in the *Atlantic Post* offering their services, due to the harsh penalties for such work under international law. But they *do* exist, Claire. I don't see how you can deny that the story we've been told is far less likely than the possibility that Shepherd found a black-market scientist who agreed to whip him up a few *aliens*." He made air quotes around the word *aliens* and added an unpleasant little smirk. "And it's an even simpler matter to tweak DNA to the extent that we see in Stasia and these other so-called Watchers. I'm just mystified that you and your brother fell for this ruse so easily. Your mother is, too."

"And I'm mystified that you can't see the massive holes in your theory. If Stasia was working for Shepherd, why would she have tried to kill him on the *Ares Prime*?"

"I believe the operative word there is *try*. Rather convenient that she failed, don't you think?"

It wasn't an *entirely* unreasonable argument. Claire had at one point even wondered whether Kolya himself had done something similar, staging the attack to frighten Shepherd in the hope that it would help convince him that he was in enough danger that he'd agree to remain on Mars and bring in his followers to colonize Ehden. She'd dismissed the idea then, in part because of how risky it was. The woman who was volunteering as the ship's doctor during the trip said that Shepherd very nearly died—*would* have died, in fact, if Claire hadn't spotted the drone as quickly as she had.

"Oh, come on, Kolya. You were *there*. Do you think the doctor was in on this grand scheme, too? But fine … there's plenty of other evidence. They've been on Earth since the 1950s. A little basic detective work proved to me that Beck was working for VersaBio years before he should even have been born. And I've already told you about the journal. It was in the sample I brought back from Mars—a sample I collected from a chamber that you know damn well was buried many meters below the surface. You saw it wedged into the rock inside that mining tube. Are you actually going to claim that Shepherd somehow arranged that, too?"

"It's not … impossible. And you could be in on it."

"Seriously? Why would I help the Flock?"

"Maybe out of spite," he said with a careless flick of his hand. "You've made it clear that there's no love lost between you and your mother."

"Not going to argue that point. But here's a news flash for you. Yes, Kai owns the company. And yes, she headed up the team that developed Arvectin. But Rejuvesce? She may be making a ton of money off of it and taking the public kudos, but that's *Joe's* research. Leaving aside the fact that it's an incredible advance for humanity, that work means everything to him. I love my brother. If there was another choice, I wouldn't dream of doing anything to take this accomplishment away from him. And you're forgetting about the sample that Kimura collected from the surface several years earlier. The NASA samples, even before that. The journal was encoded in *all* of them. It was seriously degraded in those earlier samples, given its exposure on the surface, but it's *there*. Are you going to tell me that all of those people were working for Shepherd? All of them were part of some grand scheme? By your logic, Kimura was a suicide bomber hired by the Flock. How does that make sense?"

Kolya leaned his head against the back of the sofa and rubbed his eyes with the heels of his hands. "We can go round and round on all of this, but I've had three weeks to think about it and none of it adds up. I think Shepherd has been playing a long con. And I'm not the only one. Kai agrees. Maybe you *weren't* in on the scheme. But the only other possibility I can come up with is that you've been duped, and I'm fairly certain you'll take even more offense at *that* suggestion. Personally, though? I don't believe a bunch of terrorists should dictate the future of humanity."

"Oh, why not be honest? This is all about your ego. You think *you're* the only one who should have a say in determining the future of humanity."

His eyes narrowed slightly, but then he laughed. "I'm the one with the resources to determine it, so … yes. Maybe I'm not the *only* one who should have a say, but I definitely get to sit at the head of the table."

Claire stared at him, momentarily stunned into silence. She'd hoped that poking at him about his ego would make him see how ridiculous he sounded. Instead, he'd doubled down. But maybe she shouldn't have been surprised. He'd made a similar comment about Mars, where he clearly viewed himself as a benevolent king bringing order to chaos, or at the very least, as first among equals. The various colonies had elected leaders, but they were just figureheads. It had been the mine owners and Kolya, not the government leaders, who had met at the Red Dahlia to negotiate terms for the lockdown. The real power on Mars was money, and Kolya controlled far, far more of it than the other corporate leaders combined.

"Even if a majority of the people there don't want the same thing you do?" she asked.

"Ah. So we're talking about Mars now. If it wasn't in the original Ares Consortium agreement, I'd delay the vote on the constitution for another year or two, but ... we can't. In time, we *will* have open, fully democratic elections on Mars. But at this stage? Public opinion needs to be molded, and candidates need to be chosen with care."

"So, you'd rig the election?"

"I absolutely did not say that. But if lobbying behind the scenes and skillful advertising are considered rigging an election, there's not a free and fair election anywhere on Earth, either. I have the resources to make sure my views are heard above others and I fully intend to use them."

She opened her mouth, ready to toss out the fact that Drex and Stasia, two people who apparently knew him well, believed that he was better than that. But as Wyatt had pointed out at dinner, being an idealist didn't make Kolya a good guy. It definitely didn't mean that he'd make the right choices. Either way, mentioning his recently murdered ex-wife seemed like a bad idea when the man was already in a pissy mood. Maybe she should cool things down a bit.

"Okay," she said. "Fair enough, I guess. But why not wait? There's no reason to rush. You haven't even finished terraforming Mars. There's plenty of room for expansion still. Wouldn't it be better to take your time? Do it right?"

And ... that was clearly the wrong thing to say.

His eyes flashed. "We'll do it *right*. Do you think this is some idea that just popped into my head? Davy had a team working on the exoplanet project before we even began stage five on Mars. We've had at least a dozen candidate worlds lined up for nearly a decade. That section of her lab didn't take much damage, so we could launch within weeks. Like I said at the Ares Conference, I could easily fund this on my own. Not much expense now that the R&D is done. But fortunately, I'll have help. Quite a bit, actually. Despite the disastrous end to the dinner that night, I've managed to convince several high-profile investors to come on board."

Even though he didn't say it, something about his expression left Claire with absolutely no doubt that one of those investors was her mother. In the one message she'd gotten from Joe, he'd said Kai was coming around, that he was convincing her. But maybe she was just telling him what he wanted to hear. It wouldn't be the first time she'd lied to him.

"And here's the thing," Kolya continued. "Even if I believed everything you've told me, that just makes it even more imperative that we move on to the exoplanets. If there really is some superior alien race coming to wipe out Earth ... then we need to make certain that we have other options. Mars can only hold so many people."

"You really think the Alliance is going to ignore Mars? They wiped it out once. If they're going to all this trouble to remove Earthers as potential competitors, I think they'll want to make a clean sweep of it. So, who exactly would you be terraforming those worlds for? And did you even read the journal? You talk about saving intelligent life, but the Alliance *is* intelligent life. They almost certainly seeded Earth—or Mars—the same way you're planning to seed those exoplanets with your biobots."

"Claire." He said her name with a touch of long-suffering amusement, as if he'd been negotiating with an unreasonable child. "As I said before, there's no point in arguing. I didn't ask you here to debate all of this and you're not going to change my mind. We have more pressing concerns at the moment. Whatever the reason—and I'm convinced that *Garcia* is the reason—Shepherd is determined that you will be part of these negotiations. So we need to hash out which elements you will handle and which you will leave to me."

"From what I recall, Shepherd didn't say anything about *you* joining me. I'll be going in with Beck."

"And from what *I* recall, Shepherd didn't mention Beck joining you, either. What makes you think he'll be okay with someone he doesn't even know tagging along?"

She was tempted to point out that according to his grand conspiracy theory, Shepherd already knew Beck. That would have to be the case if the man had hired, or even genetically engineered, the Watchers. But she didn't want to get into all of that again.

"I doubt Shepherd expects me to go in entirely on my own. And he seems dead set against negotiating with anyone connected to you or to KTI."

"Why not take Garcia, then? Back on Earth, he seemed determined to be your big, brave protector. Is he really going to let you walk into the lion's den without him?"

Kolya was obviously goading her. Maybe she hadn't kept her expression as neutral as she'd hoped during that teleconference. Wyatt had announced that he was coming along because she'd nearly been killed on that first trip while traveling under Kolya's protection, and he probably *was* a bit nervous at the idea of her going in alone. But it was also a convenient ruse that allowed him to follow the story about the attack at Millex, something he was increasingly convinced was connected to Durav and the Alliance.

"Wyatt will be fine," she said, "because he knows that what you're unwilling to accept is actually true. Whether or not *you* believe the Watchers and the Alliance are real, Shepherd has been waiting for decades for some sign from his Sentinels. If Beck can convince him that he is in fact one of those Sentinels, that will go a long way toward helping me talk the man off the ledge. We have a better chance of ending this quickly and without further loss of life if Beck goes with me."

Kolya was quiet for a moment, and she was surprised that he actually seemed to be considering what she'd just said. But then he shook his head.

"I don't trust Beckett. Not entirely sure that I trust *you* at this point. Maybe Shepherd will allow Macek or—"

Whatever else he was going to say was drowned out by a loud, percussive thump that shook the entire room, followed by the sound of breaking glass.

TWELVE

CLAIRE WATCHED THIN, spiderweb cracks travel across the wallscreens. What had previously appeared to be a seamless clear dome looking out into space was now a series of blank gray panels. Tiny pieces of the screen tumbled to the floor, along with one jagged chunk the size of her head.

"What was that?"

Kolya shook his head. "Maybe something hit the station? It's never happened before, though. We've got a detection system. I … I need to find out if it's safe here. Just hold on." He tapped behind his ear. "Call Macek."

As Claire turned to survey the rest of the room, the smell of alcohol hit her nose. She had assumed that the wallscreens were the source of the shattering noise she'd heard, but the hanging rack above the bar had come loose, smashing not only the glasses it held but most of the bottles beneath it as well.

"Damn it," Kolya muttered impatiently. He waited another couple of seconds, then tried to reach Paul. When that failed too, he said, "Come on, then. We'll take the emergency exit."

He started to get up, but a second *whump* rocked the station. Not as strong as the first, but strong enough to knock him back onto the sofa.

It was also the last straw for the lights. Claire fumbled for her phone, but emergency lamps kicked in first. She tugged it out of her pocket anyway. Whatever caused those explosions, they had definitely come from below and that's where Wyatt and Beck were.

Kolya had her arm now and was yanking her up from the sofa.

She grabbed her bag and followed, even though it felt like they were going in the wrong direction.

"Call Wyatt."

He tugged her toward the interior of the apartment. "You can call him once we're out of here."

Her phone—unlike Kolya—understood that she hadn't been asking for permission. It picked up her command and began ringing as they crunched their way across the strewn glass. Kolya pressed his palm against a black square near one of the emergency lights. A section of the wall slid away to reveal a closet with a wide dark hole in the floor.

"Just wait," Kolya said, as if he actually thought she was going to jump into it. After a couple of seconds, something clicked into place and dim lights flickered on to reveal a tunnel.

"Go! I'll meet you at the bottom." Kolya had his phone out again, too, presumably still trying to reach Macek, but he didn't seem to be having any more luck than she was having reaching Wyatt.

She winced and mentally shoved away the very unpleasant image of being crushed inside the tunnel if another explosion hit. But they clearly did need to get out, and the elevators probably weren't an option. There was only one conceivable way to follow Kolya's command, so she sat on the floor, lowered her feet into the opening, and placed her bag on her lap.

"Just leave that!"

She ignored him. After the recent burning of her house, the bag contained every item of clothing she owned, and she had no intention of leaving it behind.

The phone should have kicked over to Wyatt's voicemail by now, but it was still ringing. She ended the call and pushed off. The tunnel curved downward. It looked a bit like a corkscrew slide, and that's exactly what it felt like for the first few seconds. Then it straightened out and dipped sharply. She was moving fast. Too fast, she thought, but then her stomach flipped slightly, and she discovered that her butt was now several inches above the smooth surface of the tunnel. By the time the chute spat her out into a narrow room at the bottom, she was completely weightless.

Kolya's call had gone through, apparently, because she could hear him talking behind her. She pushed off against the wall next to the tunnel to free up space for him to enter and floated over to the airlock. Looking to the right through the narrow window in the door she could see a row of shuttle docks, but as best she could tell in the glow from the emergency lights, they were all empty. To the left, however, a single shuttle was parked in the third slot down. That must be their ride.

She started to call Wyatt again, but Kolya's feet were now in view. A second later, he was in the room, still talking to the person on the other end of his call.

"No. I need you on the surface. Wheatley can handle it." He was looking through the window into the shuttle bay now, and judging from his expression, something wasn't right. "And tell her to fire the idiot in charge of my shuttle. What's the point in having an emergency exit if the damned shuttle is two bays over?"

Claire couldn't hear what was being said on the other end, but whatever it was, Kolya didn't like it.

He yanked open a small closet on the other side of the tunnel opening. "Never mind," he snapped. "We have suits, assuming I can find one small enough for Claire. We'll meet you there." As he spoke, he began pushing items from the cabinet in her direction.

Boots. Helmet. Biosuit.

A tiny worm of panic gnawed at her stomach as she remembered frantically pressing together torn fabric around the edges of Laura Brodnik's helmet in an ultimately failed attempt to save the woman's life. These suits weren't like the ones they'd worn on Mars, though, or even the cheaper puffsuits that had been issued to the miners at Icarus. These had a more rigid outer casing.

"Does Macek know what happened?" she asked as she plucked the items from the air. "How bad is it?"

"He's not sure yet. We think it was one of the freighter ships, since both explosions happened on the docking level one section over. Most of the damage and casualties are there and in operations, but we've got scattered reports of injuries on the main level, too."

"The main level is where I left Wyatt and Beck." Claire pulled her phone from her pocket again.

"You're not going to be able to reach them. I was talking to Macek on a closed channel. Regular communications are down until we get the primary power system back online. But Wheatley —she's head of security for the station—says she told them to head back to the *V1*. They're probably already on the ship." He held up a hand, anticipating her next question. "That's in Area Five. All the way across the station, so I'm sure they're fine. The explosions were closer to *this* side, and there's a report of hull damage, which is why I need you to hurry up with that suit so that we can get to the ship."

"I *am* hurrying." It was true. The sooner she got into the suit, the sooner she could reach Wyatt. But it was also true that Kolya was making much better progress than she was. Of course, he'd probably had more experience getting into these damn things in zero-g. You'd think the lack of gravity would make it easier, but it really didn't. "Why don't they just stock biosuits?"

"Those are rated for Mars, where there's at least some atmosphere. These are for the ship maintenance crews that have to be tethered to the station while they do repairs. You wouldn't last long out there in a standard biosuit. The length is somewhat adjustable—just press the buttons on the outside until it feels right."

She followed his instructions, adjusting the leg, arm and torso sections. It was still a bit large even after the adjustments, but the boots fit okay. She had just gotten into the helmet and was pulling on the gloves when it occurred to her that Kolya had said Wyatt and Beck were on the other side of the station. "So … wait. Are we taking the shuttle around to Area Five to pick up the others?"

"Not quite." He grabbed her shoulders and spun her around so that he could check the seal on her helmet. "We're taking the shuttle to the surface. Macek is on this side of the station, so he'll be joining us. He should be here shortly. The others will take the *V1* and we'll see them later."

"No." She yanked away so that she could face him. "I'm not leaving the station without knowing if they're okay."

His exasperated sigh buzzed into her speaker. "Macek was calling Caruso next. He can fill us in on everyone's status when he gets here. We still don't know what caused the bloody explosions or whether there are more to come, so can we please just board the ship and get the hell out of here?"

As much as she would have liked to argue the point, she knew he was right. And she really didn't have any other options if the *V1* was, as he had said, on the other side of the station. There was *probably* another route to get to this shuttle bay, given that Macek was on his way to the ship. But the only route she personally knew involved crawling back up that escape tunnel and taking the elevator down to the concourse—an elevator that might not even be functional if the station was on auxiliary power.

She gave Kolya a terse nod and yanked the strap to tighten her glove.

"Check your stats," Kolya said.

She tipped her helmet toward her right shoulder. A display popped up in the top right corner of the face shield.

"All green."

He gave her a thumbs up, then pulled a metal cable out of the wall and clipped it to the belt at the waist of her suit. He then attached a much shorter elastic cable and handed her the carabiner at the opposite end. "Clip this to your bag so that it doesn't go floating away. Once you're inside the shuttle, send the tether back and I'll join you."

"Okay." She pulled her bag, which was floating nearby, over one shoulder and attached the clip while Kolya opened the airlock. He motioned for her to step into the doorway. She did, realizing for the first time that while she'd become somewhat accustomed to life in zero-g, she'd always had a wall or some other surface within easy reach. Now she was staring out at a massive shuttle bay, and beyond that, open space.

She cursed under her breath.

Kolya's laugh over the helmet speaker made it clear that he'd caught her reaction. "You'll be fine."

The shuttle was about fifteen meters away. It had a tube like the one that they'd used earlier when exiting the *V1*, but it was on the *other* side of the ship, attached to another doorway into the station. On this side, the shuttle was one solid sheet of metal. She was about to ask Kolya how they were supposed to get inside, but then the panel slid away, creating an opening about a meter wide near the center of the craft.

Kolya pointed her toward the steadily widening gap and gave her a push. It was, admittedly, a rather gentle push, but she was now moving at a speed outside of her comfort zone. She couldn't help imagining missing the door, bouncing off the side of the shuttle, and drifting helplessly toward that ominous opening at the far end of the bay.

Get a grip, Claire. That's why you have the freakin tether.

While Kolya's aim hadn't been perfect, it got her close enough to the shuttle door that she was able to angle her body slightly and hook one arm through the opening. That motion triggered the interior light, revealing a much smaller vehicle than she'd imagined, with only four seats. She'd been expecting something like the shuttle in which she'd traveled to the surface on her first trip, which seated about twenty. She should probably have realized it was smaller based on the outside, but she never paid attention to the exterior of the first shuttle she boarded because she'd entered through one of the tunnels. And when they landed, she'd been far too fascinated with the Martian landscape and the amusement park atmosphere inside the dome at Daedalus City to pay attention to a transport that wasn't all that different from the Aerolyfts she routinely rented on Earth.

After pulling herself inside the shuttle, she shoved her bag under one of the seats. Then she unhooked the longer tether from her belt and tossed it out the opening.

"All yours," she said. "How are you going to close the airlock from here?"

Kolya didn't respond. He clearly heard at least the first part of what she'd said, however, because he yanked once and the tether zipped back toward the door where he was waiting. After clipping it to his suit, he pushed off toward the shuttle, seeming much more confident about the short trip than she'd felt a few moments earlier.

Apparently, she hadn't *looked* very confident either, because Kolya's voice was decidedly cocky as he entered the shuttle. "See? Nothing to it. You just have to—"

The explosion that vibrated through the shuttle was louder than the previous two. Closer. It tossed both of them into the wall. Kolya was facing her, and his body partially blocked her view of the station, but she saw the airlock door, still open, when it snapped back from the force of the blast. The door was gone, along with several chunks of the wall next to it. It was just a ragged hole now, the space in front of it littered with debris. A sheet of metal drifted past, a lazy guillotine tumbling slowly in the faint glow of the emergency lights.

She caught a brief glimpse of the tether whipping behind it like the tail of a kite.

And then all she could see was Kolya's stunned expression as the cord yanked him across the shuttle toward the open door.

THIRTEEN

CLAIRE FELT a tug at her waist. Her eyes locked on Kolya's boot, which had snagged on the handle of her bag. Then the second tether, still clipped to the belt of her suit, snapped tight like a leash, dragging her behind it.

Kolya's gloved fingers closed around the edge of the shuttle. The other hand braced against the lip of the hatch, his arm straining to counter the momentum that was trying to tear him away.

"Unfasten the cable!" she yelled, as her own fingers fumbled with the clip on her belt.

"I'm trying!" Kolya cursed, hard and low, his voice laced with panic and fury.

A second later, the handle snapped, leaving the tether attached to her suit as the bag careened past Kolya into the shuttle bay. Claire was free, but now the only thing keeping Kolya in the shuttle was his tenuous grip on the edge of the hatch. He'd abandoned his attempt to disconnect the tether and was now holding on with both hands, but he was losing ground.

For a moment, she considered simply letting him go. If he drifted away into space, it would increase their chances of stopping the Alliance. Without Kolya, the plan to terraform exoplanets would almost certainly end. They'd only have *one* selfish, self-centered trillionaire with a gargantuan ego to convince. And she and Joe could figure out a way to handle Kai.

Kolya's eyes met hers through his visor, wide and wild. It was almost as if he knew what she was thinking.

She couldn't have done it anyway. Bracing her left shoulder

against the wall and her boots against the rim on the other side of the shuttle door she stretched forward and finally caught the tether. It vibrated from the tension, and she doubted her gloves would hold out for long, but she had to try. She locked her grip and pulled.

For a second, she actually thought they had a chance. There was no gravity here. And the piece of metal attached to the other end of the tether wasn't even as large as her bag, which she could still see, floating out toward open space.

But then Kolya's grip failed and his gloved hands slid across the slick surface of the shuttle. Claire managed to hold onto the tether, but pain struck through her bad leg, and she could feel her muscles giving way.

"Just let go, Claire. I've got at least four hours of air. Macek should be here soon, and he can come after me."

What he was saying made sense, but she couldn't make her hands release the tether. Which was borderline insane, when she'd been thinking not fifteen seconds earlier about how much easier things would be if she just let go. There was no way she could save him, and he'd just given her permission. If she didn't let go soon, they'd both be sucked out.

"Dammit, Claire, just—"

"Got you." Macek's deep voice came through her helmet speaker, blocking out what Kolya was saying, as his arm wrapped around her waist. He was standing upright, his boots magna-locked to the shuttle floor. His other hand reached across and joined hers on the tether.

Kolya said something in Russian.

Macek snorted. "You can thank me when your ass is in the shuttle. And don't unlock that clip until we have hold of you."

A few seconds later, Kolya was inside. Macek took a beat to catch his breath, then sealed the hatch and unlocked his boots. Claire steadied herself against one of the seat frames, heart still pounding.

After a long moment, Kolya pushed off against the wall toward the console. "Strap in. We need to get moving."

"We should do a full systems check first," Macek said.

Kolya was already tapping something into the console. "We don't have time. Not unless you can tell me Wheatley has already detained the people who caused those explosions and has them under lock and key?"

"Of course not," Macek said. "But there's debris flying all around out there. One of the side panels is dented. We may have taken additional damage."

The AI, a female contralto voice, was now calling out the checklist for takeoff. *Outer doors secure. Pressure stable.*

Kolya pulled off his helmet. "We could take far more damage if we wait around. Strap in *now*."

Claire opened her mouth to object. But power was already surging through the shuttle's systems, and she was pretty sure the arrogant ass would take off whether she was strapped in or not. Since she had no desire to careen around the cabin like a billiard ball, she slipped into the harness and turned toward Macek. "Kolya said you were checking in with Paul. Did Wyatt and Beck make it back to the *V1*?"

"Yes," Macek said. Only there was the faintest hesitation before the word and his eyes drifted ever so slightly toward Kolya.

"You're *lying*. Did something happen to them? Were they in the areas that were hit?"

"No, no. I'm sure they're both okay. All three explosions were on *this* side of the station. No one would be stupid enough to damage the other side."

"Why is that?"

"It houses the main laser array," Kolya said. "Whoever did this is almost certainly pissed off because they should already be headed home. Damaging the system that gets them back to Earth would be counterproductive."

"Then what is it that you're not telling me, Macek? Did Paul say Wyatt and Beck were on the ship or not?"

"When I spoke to Caruso a few minutes ago, he hadn't made it to the ship yet. He insisted on going back to get Stasia."

Kolya turned and pinned him with a stare. "I didn't authorize that. Taking her to Daedalus before we're there to organize the trial is a bad idea."

"I get that. And I didn't authorize it either. But he said he wasn't willing to leave her on the station with someone trying to blow it up. And ... he's right."

Kolya apparently didn't agree with that assessment. He huffed loudly, then turned back to the console and began tapping something into the screen.

"What are you doing?" Macek asked.

"Messaging the storage bay at Daedalus. I'll tell them to go ahead and send the full fleet of shuttles back to the station, just in case we need to evacuate everyone."

The maneuvering jets were now nudging the craft toward open space. As they neared the outside of the bay, however, something smacked into the side of the shuttle. There was a loud scraping noise. The shuttle rocked slightly from the impact but quickly steadied. Claire watched through the viewport as a chunk of metal from the earlier explosion went flying off at an angle. She wondered briefly where her bag was, imagined Ro's snarky response when she told her that the infamous blue dress was floating somewhere in space, and then pulled her mind back to the conversation.

Macek was saying something about the other shuttles technically being restricted from returning to Ares Station until after lockdown officially ended. She knew that he had a lot of people on the station to worry about, but he still hadn't answered her main question, so she cut him off in mid-sentence.

"So will Paul be bringing Wyatt and Beck to Nepenthes in one of *those* shuttles?"

"No," he said. "He'll be taking the *V2*."

He was still dodging, so she pressed on. "But *Wyatt and Beck* are waiting for him on the *V1*."

"It's ... *possible* that they are on the *V1*," he said, again casting a wary eye at Kolya. "But if so, they are not *waiting*. The *V1* left Ares Station about ten minutes ago."

FROM THE RED PLANET

MONDAY, 541/69

Kolya Responds To Vogt Announcement

AS REPORTED LAST WEEK, Käthe Vogt, current chair of Daedalian Council, announced in a letter to *The Red Planet* last week that while she intends to finish out her current term, she will not submit her name as a candidate in the upcoming election, scheduled for Tuesday, 654/69. ("Vogt Announces She Will Not Run," 543/69)

Councilmember Vogt is the third member of the fifteen-person board—and the highest ranking—to announce that they will not seek reelection. Previous statements by Ms. Vogt over the past year have suggested a growing dissatisfaction with the direction in which the colony is moving, but she stated that her decision was a recent one, and one that she arrived at only after months of deliberation.

"When I first ran for this position twelve years ago, it was because I wanted to make a difference," Ms. Vogt said. "Because I wanted to represent the people who have chosen to make Mars—and specifically, Daedalus—their home. But the current council has devolved into little more than a rubber stamp for whatever corporate leadership decides. And with the constitutional question on the ballot in the upcoming election, corporate is pushing hard for us to support a unitary system. At one point, I was ambivalent on the issue, but I am increasingly convinced that this plan will not work for Mars, given its current stage of political advancement and the uneven economic development between the colonies. One has only to look at the tense situation here in Daedalus during lockdown to understand the sort of conflicts a close union would invite. I believe Mars will be far better served by continuing with a looser confederation that avoids placing too much control in the hands of any one individual or political body. I also believe that we need a constitution that will move us away from corporate control and allow for a government that is fully supported by taxpayer contributions once terraforming is complete. Unfortunately, I've been told that these positions aren't in keeping with my leadership role on the Council."

The Red Planet immediately reached out for a response from Anton Kolya, who is currently in transit back to Mars. We received the following message this morning, which we are printing in its entirety:

"I have no idea what Councilwoman Vogt is talking about. Käthe is free to hold whatever opinions she likes concerning the proposed constitution. I have never said anything to the contrary. But the polling is clear. Daedalians support a unitary constitution by double digit margins, and support is growing rapidly in the other colonies as well. I believe we now have a majority of all Martian colonists, and I am certain that the measure will win.

I never suggested that Käthe's opinions are not in keeping with her role on the Council. I simply advised her that it was risky to take such a firm stance against a unitary constitution—which the people clearly favor—when her name will be on the same ballot as the measure. As for her suggestion that the people shoulder the full cost of running Daedalus, that's many decades away from being feasible and the amendment process to the proposed constitution will allow flexibility for that sort of change if and when the time comes. I would double down on my advice to her on that point, as well, because throughout human history, you'll find few populations that would support a candidate who suggests that the government multiply their tax burden tenfold.

Let me add that Daedalus owes Käthe a debt of gratitude for her long service and we certainly wish her the best in her future endeavors."

A poll of 400 Daedalian citizens conducted by *The Red Planet* on 432/69 showed 44.7% favoring a unitary system, 34.1% favoring a federal system, and 21.2% undecided. Rounded up, this does indeed indicate double-digit support for a unitary system over a federal system within Daedalus among potential voters who have made a decision on the issue. A planet-wide poll has not yet been conducted, but we have applied for a funding grant from KTI and hope to complete the poll once the lockdown is lifted and citizens returned to their home colonies.

The deadline for candidates wishing to run for a seat on the Colonial Council is Wednesday, 627/69.

FOURTEEN

THE DOCKING CUBE ZIPPED FORWARD SO FAST that Beck nearly lost his grip on the safety handles. After a short burst of speed, the cube braked sharply, jerking him back in the other direction. A compartment with a tiny blue silhouette of an emergency mask lit up for about a second, then went dark again. Was that a good sign or bad?

"What *was* that?" he asked Wyatt, who had looped an arm through one of the handles and was now fumbling with his phone.

"An explosion of some sort. I need to check in with Claire. And Macek. Because now I'm thinking the odds I gave you a few minutes ago are way too low. I'm not sure *why* Boudreaux or Durav would be targeting the station, but Boudreaux's a big fan of making things go boom."

A red light flashed inside the cube, and then the automated Stasia-voice came over the comm system. "Please state your destination."

"We already did," Beck said. "Bay 5. Space B, *Velox One*."

"I'm sorry, but that isn't an option. *Velox One* is currently locked down for departure. Please state an alternate destination."

"What the..." Beck exchanged a confused look with Wyatt. "Okay, then. Can you take us to *Velox Two*?" It was worth a try. He had no clue what the access level Paul had granted them included, but if it would get them onboard the *V1*, maybe it would also get them onto its sister ship.

"*Velox Two* is docked at 5A. Please hold onto the handles with *both* hands so that we can depart." That instruction was for Wyatt, who was typing something into his phone. He stopped and did as he was told. The cube then moved forward for maybe five seconds, and the voice chimed in again as it decelerated. "Now arriving at 5A. Please wait while I engage the passenger tunnel and ensure proper life support."

After a series of hums and clicks, the door opened, and Beck followed Wyatt through the tunnel into the ship. The layout felt very familiar after three weeks onboard its twin. They stashed their bags in the bunkroom, then turned left into the tiny bridge area. Beck remembered what Wyatt had said about the narcoships and tried to imagine spending three weeks in a space as small as this bridge by himself, let alone with a second person. Moral quandaries aside, he wasn't sure that he'd be able to tolerate those living conditions, no matter how well it paid.

As they entered, the viewport showed the *V1* slowly moving away from the dock.

Something didn't add up. Why would the security officer have told them to go back to the *V1* if it was scheduled to depart?

"*V2,* who is onboard the *Velox One*?" he asked.

The *V2's* voice was identical to the voice on the *V1,* with a smoky baritone that always made Beck think it was going to burst into a Lou Rawls song. When the AI didn't answer immediately, Beck was pretty sure it was going to say that it couldn't tell him. But apparently their access level included some degree of information, as well.

"Janelle Tuller and an unidentified guest are onboard the *Velox One*."

Wyatt stared at Beck. "That's … Drex, right? I thought you said she was dead."

"She *was* dead. *Is* dead. Claire and I both saw her, and she is most definitely dead."

"Then who…" He gestured toward the ship, which was now approaching the outer hull of the station. "You think it's Stasia? I mean, I'm sure Macek took away her employee access but … she could have Drex's information, right?"

"She could, but..." Beck shook his head, remembering the bloody circles at the ends of Drex's fingers when he and Claire found her body inside the Triad's chambers. "No. I'm guessing it's Durav. Or one of his people. He tortured Drex before he killed her. Which means he probably has her phone and any codes that he'd need to access her credentials. We need to follow that ship."

Another thump jostled the station as he spoke. It was farther away this time, more of a gentle shake than a shove.

"What? No. We're not leaving without Claire."

"I don't like the idea either, but she's with Kolya. He needs her to negotiate with Shepherd, so he'll get her to the surface safely. And if Durav is on that ship..." He gave a helpless shrug. "Even if it's Boudreaux, we can't let them reach Shepherd first. *V2*, can you follow the *Velox One*?"

"I'm sorry, Mr. Beckett, but that is not possible, as there is no pilot currently on board."

"Okay. Can you contact Paul Caruso, then? Or Macek? Either one. Just tell them it's an emergency."

"The only communications channel open is reserved for security personnel. Ares Station has multiple emergencies at the moment, including at least a dozen casualties."

Wyatt rubbed his temples. "Can you at least tell us whether any of the passengers who came in on the *V1* ... or on this ship ... are among those casualties?"

"I'm sorry, but I don't have that information. Should I let you know when communications are open again?"

"Sure." Wyatt shook his head and stared down at his useless phone. "So, we just wait?"

"Looks like." Beck pushed gently against the wall, drifting forward until he was almost pressed against the viewport. As he watched, the *V1* cleared the edge of the station, arced to the left, and then zipped out of sight.

"What kind of idiot lets his ex—who is a *known* terrorist, I might add—keep the go-codes to his spaceship?" Wyatt asked.

"I doubt that he did. Drex had high-level access for years.

Stasia for even longer. One of their first tasks would have been to make certain that they or another member of the Watch could get back into Kolya's systems."

"Is that what you did at Jonas Labs?"

"It is," he said, trying not to sound defensive. "There, and everywhere else I worked. It was the job. And since it's Alliance tech we installed, it's not likely to show up in most Earther security scans."

"Yeah. Guess you can't fault Macek's people for not catching a rootkit hiding out in their system if it was from an advanced alien civilization."

They waited. Wyatt tried his phone every couple of minutes. Either he didn't trust that the AI would actually let them know when communications were back up or he just needed to be doing something. You couldn't exactly pace in zero-g.

After five minutes or so, Beck paged the AI again. It probably wouldn't give him any answers, but like Wyatt, he couldn't just float around doing nothing. "I know communications are locked down right now, but can you tell me whether anyone else asked who was onboard the *Velox One*?"

"Based on my survey of messages logged into the system over the past hour, you are the only one who has made that inquiry, Mr. Beckett. I don't have access to the secure channel, however."

"Too bad there's no fire alarm we can pull," Wyatt said. "Or, for that matter, something to start a fire with. Bet they'd—" He broke off as a clattering noise filled the docking tunnel. A few seconds later, Paul entered the ship, followed by Stasia.

Beck was glad to find that Stasia looked relatively healthy. The dark circles under her eyes suggested that she wasn't sleeping well, and the vivid blue dye in her hair had faded to something closer to a robin's egg, but otherwise, she seemed fine. Not that he'd really thought she was being physically mistreated during the trip, but Arbet's worry was a bit contagious.

"What are you doing here?" she asked. "Paul said you took off in the *V1*."

Wyatt turned to Paul. "Why did you think it was us?"

"Because you were the only ones who had permission to enter! I just couldn't figure out how you managed to steal it without a pilot. But if you're here, who the hell—"

"We think it's Durav," Beck said.

Wyatt nodded. "Stasia was also a suspect, at least in my book, but since she's here…"

Paul huffed. "Why exactly do you think it's Durav?"

"Because when we tried to board the *V1*, the station's computer system told us that it was occupied by Janelle Tuller. And Durav could easily have gotten Drex's phone and access codes when he … um … before she died." Beck exchanged a look with Stasia, who went even paler than usual at the reminder that her friend had been tortured. "And … I think I saw Jason Boudreaux in the concourse. That's—"

"The militia guy, yeah." Paul drifted over to the ship's console and pressed his hand against the panel. "Well, if that's the case, the joke's on them, because we know exactly where they're going. Daedalus is the only station on Mars that can accommodate a raptor class ship. None of the hyperlifts at the other stations are wide enough and they don't have a strong enough boost to break out of the atmosphere. An actual spaceport has to be constructed close to a spot with enough elevation that we can build a hyperlift up the side of the mountain. Daedalus uses Arsia Mons, and Elysia will eventually use Elysium Mons. Constructing those systems is very expensive, so the Ares Consortium decided that it made more sense in the early stages to route all off-planet arrivals and destinations through Daedalus and construct additional spaceports as demand and resources permit."

Beck shook his head. "They're not stupid, Paul. No way they'll land at Daedalus."

Paul pulled himself down into the captain's chair and slipped his arms through the harness. "Even if the person piloting it is a genius he won't have a choice. The AI won't land at a station that isn't certified to handle a raptor, not without level one override.

They'll *have* to land at Daedalus. I'll message ahead once we're in range and have a welcoming committee waiting for them."

Wyatt threw his hands out in frustration. "It's *not their ship*! Why would they be worried about getting the thing off the ground again? They'll just leave it there and book passage back to Earth, probably with the same people who got them as far as Ares Station, so…" He stopped and stared at Paul. "Wait a minute. *This* ship is a raptor. Are you saying *we'll* have to land at Daedalus, too? Because we're supposed to be going to Nepenthes."

"Yeah. Not much we can do about it. We'll join them as soon as we can. Right now, though, you guys need to strap in. *V2*, prepare for departure."

Paul kept his eyes fixed on the console as he spoke. While Beck obviously wasn't a pilot, he couldn't see anything on the screen that required the man's undivided attention. Paul had even noted on the trip from Tranquility Base that the AI did the lion's share of the work. His tone of voice was off, too. He was lying about something, and he wasn't particularly good at it.

Judging from the set of Wyatt's mouth as they strapped into the passenger seats, he also sensed that something was up. And Stasia's expression confirmed it. She'd known Paul for years, so she was probably pretty good at reading the guy.

"We were never actually going to Nepenthes," Beck said. "This was always the plan, wasn't it?"

"Not … *exactly* the plan. We were supposed to take the *V1* and then head to Nepenthes as soon as the lockdown is lifted. Macek was supposed to be with us, in case you … objected to the new travel arrangements. And *she*"—Paul shot a look at Stasia—"was supposed to remain on the station. It would probably have been poetic justice to leave her there despite today's events, given her penchant for blowing shit up in recent months, but I didn't want that on my conscience. To your key point, however, yes. Kolya *did* intend to separate you. He informed me about an hour ago that he'd decided it would be unwise to let Claire go in by herself. So, he'll be joining her."

"Probably couldn't stand someone else getting the credit," Stasia said.

Paul shrugged. "You'll get no argument from me. His ego didn't magically shrink during your absence."

"Claire wasn't planning on going in alone," Beck said. "I was supposed to go in with her. That's the only reason I'm here."

"You'll have to take it up with Kolya," Paul said. "*V2*, navigate to Daedalus Station."

The ship began moving toward the exit, gradually picking up speed.

"I already set up a meeting with one of my contacts," Wyatt said. "A guard at Nepenthes Station. He was working at Millex earlier this year, when the…" He glanced at Stasia.

"I had *nothing to do* with those bombings." Her tone suggested this wasn't the first time she'd said those words.

Paul waved his hand in a *so-what* gesture. "Then you reschedule the interview. We should be within range of the Daedalus communications array in ten minutes or so. Tell your source we'll be at Nepenthes less than six hours after the lock-down ends. It's not like he's going anywhere, right?"

"That still doesn't fix the main problem," Beck said. "Kolya going in with Claire wasn't the deal. I don't think Shepherd is going to respond well to that change of plans."

Wyatt nodded in agreement, something that Paul caught because this time, he *did* make eye contact as he spoke.

"Funny how you both seem so damn certain you know what Shepherd wants even though you claim you've never met the man and that you had nothing to do with his about-face on the previous negotiations. That's the reason Kolya doesn't trust you. Well … not the only reason, but it's fairly high on the list."

FIFTEEN

SHORTLY AFTER THE *Velox One* reached cruising speed, Stasia tapped Beck's arm twice and nodded toward the hallway. Then she unfastened her harness and pushed off in that direction.

Paul gave her a sideways look. "It's less than an hour to Daedalus City. Just stay in your seat."

"No. I'm hungry. I was about to order dinner when the first explosion happened."

"Again, it's less than an hour to Daedalus," Paul said. "Why not wait until you can get *real* food? I thought you hated floater rations."

Beck had a flashback to some old movie with two siblings arguing in the back of a station wagon.

"Everyone hates floater rations," she said. "But needs must when the devil drives."

Paul frowned in confusion as she disappeared around the bulkhead, apparently unfamiliar with the saying. Given her sarcastic tone, he may have thought it was a crack about his piloting skills.

Wyatt had extended his screen and was furiously typing away. They weren't in communications range yet, so he must have been queuing up messages to send as soon as he could. Beck didn't disturb him but just slipped out of his harness and followed Stasia, ignoring the look that Paul gave him as he passed by.

When he reached the tiny galley, he found Stasia rummaging around. After a brief search, she emerged with crackers and cheese, a nutrition bar, and a packet of yogurt.

"Guess you weren't lying," he said as she took a savage bite from the bar. "I thought you just wanted to talk."

"I do want to talk. But I also haven't eaten since last night. We docked around three a.m. I never sleep well on floater ships, and after three weeks of listening to Macek snore, it was so nice to be sleeping in my own bed in my own room— well, what *used* to be my own room—at the station. So, I overslept and never quite managed breakfast. Unfortunately, it's very slim pickings in here since they didn't have a chance to restock." She lowered her voice and slipped into Ufretan. "I *would* have lied, though, if I didn't have a convenient excuse. It feels like I've been in solitary confinement for the entire trip, even though I was never actually alone … just stuck in a tiny little sardine tin with two large and exceptionally surly men."

"They gave you the silent treatment?"

"Between interrogations? Yes. To be honest, Macek seemed to be coming around a bit toward the end. Not that I think he really believes anything I told him, but he seemed less angry. Anton though … I think he blames me for Drex being dead. And maybe for Drex ever being with him in the first place, which is ridiculous because the Triad assigned her as his Watcher first. She's the one who pulled *me* in. I was probably just a handy punching bag for him. *Verbal* punching bag," she added quickly, in response to his expression. "Although if looks could kill they would have jettisoned my corpse before we made it to Tranquility Base. The main issue is that I really didn't need that much time with my own thoughts right now. Between Drex's death and all the others, and what Durav told me about my mother staying behind when Seset left the Alliance … well, I haven't been sleeping too well."

"You don't know anything for certain, though. Durav would rather lie than tell the truth. Your mom could be safe in Seset."

"Maybe. I've suspected for a long time that her sympathies had shifted toward the Hodjeri. It's an occupational risk for intelligence officers. You have to learn so much about the other side—their languages, their customs, their beliefs. To be effective, you have to learn to think like they do. It's hard to maintain emotional distance. But the more I think about it, the more I suspect he's right that she requested asylum from the Alliance. They have a hostage, after all."

Beck gave her a puzzled look.

"My body. It's being stored on Ufretas Prime. If she defected with the rest of Seset, they would have just pulled the plug."

"Yeah. I hadn't thought of that." He had actually thought that it might be a relief to Drex and Stasia that their homeworld switched sides in the seemingly unending war between the Alliance and the Hodjeri Union. With their families on the other side, they wouldn't have to worry about retribution against them if their actions supporting Earth were discovered, something that was a very real risk for his own family and the families of Arbet and Sandjeel. But in Stasia's case, the threat of retribution cut in both directions.

"Either way, I'm not sure that anyone is actually safe in Seset, at this point. It's been nearly three years since the last communication cycle, and from what Arbet told Drex, they were still fighting *ipret-tai* soldiers for control of several cities. If my mother is there and the battle is still raging, I doubt she's sipping *evir* by the fireside. She's probably on the front lines."

"Three years is a long time. She could be leading a classroom by now, teaching Sesetans to speak Hodjeri."

"Then she'll have her work cut out for her. If not for her tutoring, I'd never have made it past the beginner levels."

"I *didn't* make it past the beginner level. The Hodjeri alphabet is close enough to Ufretan that I think I would have been okay, but the tones killed me. And I wasn't alone. Nearly half the class dropped or flunked out. They joked that there's a damn good reason the Hodjeris allow member planets to keep their own languages, because otherwise, no one would join."

"True. Thanks for the mental image of her in a classroom, though," she said with a sad smile. "I'll try to keep that at the front of my mind. Maybe it will improve my sleep."

"Arbet has been worried about you. She tried to reach you but never got a response."

"Anton took my phone. Said he couldn't trust me not to contact the Flock or whatever terrorist group I was working with this week. How *are* things back at Camp Ufrete?"

He gave her a brief rundown on the news he'd gotten from Arbet. He'd completely forgotten that she didn't know Reese was dead, otherwise he would have broken that news a bit more gently instead of casually tossing it into the conversation.

She stared down at her fingers for a moment as she rolled the empty wrapper from the bar into a tight coil. "You think Housen is dead, too?"

"I don't know. Wyatt tried to contact him. Several times, apparently. So did Arbet, although I suspect the number she has for him isn't as recent. If he's alive he's not responding. She seems convinced that the new body they found near the mining attraction is his, but we can't think of any reason he'd have been in Arizona."

Stasia gave him an incredulous look. "Because that's where the backup *brelat* was, obviously. A better question is why Durav would come to Mars. Surely there are places he could hide out on Earth with the damned thing until the Alliance is in signal range. Mars seems like the last place he'd want to be."

"Oh," he said. "I guess I need to catch you up on a few things. First, Housen disposed of the backup beacon the week *before* Conclave. Or at least that's what he told Wyatt."

"How exactly does Wyatt fit into all of this? And … why are the two of you even here? I know Claire was roped in to handle the hostage negotiations at Ehden—which, to be honest, also makes very little sense to me. But the two of you being here seems…" She trailed off in response to his exasperated look.

"Could you let me answer your first set of questions before you start firing more at me?"

Stasia nodded and listened patiently while Beck brought her up to speed on how Shepherd acquired the beacon and the role that Wyatt and Housen played in convincing Shepherd to insist on Claire as mediator.

"And *I'm* here," he added, "because Claire thinks I stand a better chance of convincing Shepherd to hand it over. Personally, I don't believe he'll listen to me any more than he will to her, but she's going to have a much harder time talking to him with Kolya breathing down her neck."

"Assuming that they reach Ehden before Durav does, if that's really him on the *V1*. I'm still trying to picture him traveling in a floater ship. He's never been one to forgo creature comforts, and nothing with a gravitational system could have made it here ahead of us. But yeah, if Durav gets to Shepherd first, we've got problems. Fire won't hurt the beacon, I wouldn't put it past him to burn down the entire dome, along with everyone in it, and then just comb through the rubble for something that survived. Or gas the people. That's an obvious risk given that the domes are closed systems." She glanced in the direction of the bridge. "You've told Caruso all of this?"

"No. Claire tried. Which means we all heard." He gestured vaguely at the tight quarters. "There's no privacy on these ships. She even gave him the Eberin Das translation to read. But Paul kept shutting her down. He's still skeptical about ... well, about everything."

"Same for Anton and Macek. They seem determined not to believe. Anton is convinced that this is all a massive hoax perpetrated by Shepherd and we're all either his witting or unwitting pawns."

"Which is why Claire decided we needed to keep quiet about our main purpose for this trip. We were just planning to get into the same room as Shepherd—without Kolya or Macek around—and then play it by ear. Try to convince him to hand the beacon over. I don't see how that's going to happen now, though, unless we highjack the ship."

She shook her head. "Not an option."

"It apparently worked for Durav."

"Well, it won't work for us. Drex was in the system as a pilot. I never got certified. The simulator they used in the licensing class gave me a nasty headache. I can't operate anything larger than one of the surface planes. Caruso is the only person currently onboard that the navigation system will listen to. And ... he wasn't wrong about Daedalus being the only station equipped for passenger ships. Like he said, they're constructing another one at Elysia, but it's not due to open until the end of stage seven. He is wrong, however, in thinking they won't be able to override the AI to land somewhere else."

"Yeah. I kind of assumed that whatever backdoor Drex left for herself in the system would default to the highest level. I mean, I never set up anything less than that, and I'm sure you didn't either."

"Exactly. Like Wyatt said, they won't be worried about getting the ship back off the ground, so it's just a question of where they decided to set down. The landing strip at Nepenthes is nowhere near big enough ... which I consider very good news at the moment."

"What about Lyot? Wyatt seems to think that Boudreaux might have some connections to Westmoreland."

"Their port is plenty large enough, but keep in mind that we're still under lockdown. And while Lyot has a reputation for being lawless, they try to keep most of it under the table. People there have communications with other colonies and the outside world. Some of them may have seen the mug shots KTI posted of Boudreaux and Durav. I doubt Westmoreland would let them land there. But ... he has maybe as many as a dozen mines in the incorporated areas, just as Kolya does. They're all closed due to the lockdown. Most don't have large landing areas, but if the surface around the camp is relatively flat, it could be doable. And if someone gave them access, they could take a long-range buggy or even a surface skimmer. Some of the larger camps have those. Although, to be honest ... Wes Jr. is a wild card. He may thumb his nose at public opinion and roll out the red carpet for them."

"Great. Boudreaux could set the V1 down at Lyot or any one of a dozen mining camps they own. The negotiations will be over before we reach Ehden, and Kolya's presence will almost certainly keep Claire from accomplishing our main goal with Shepherd. Which means we're screwed."

He'd intended the comment simply as a restatement of their situation. But Stasia took a moment to consider, as she caught a floating square of cheese between two bite-sized crackers, then popped the tiny sandwich into her mouth.

"Maybe," she said. "At a minimum, we're *delayed*, and that probably amounts to the same thing. But being forced to land at Daedalus doesn't automatically mean we'll arrive after the negotiations are done. Based on my past experience with Shepherd, he'll want to determine the time, the place, and every other detail possible about these negotiations, and judging from Anton's complaints to Macek last night, he's refusing to make any of those arrangements until he knows that Claire is on the planet. I doubt things will get rolling before tomorrow morning. Under normal circumstances—by which I mean if I still had the keys to the kingdom and if said kingdom wasn't on lockdown—I would simply requisition a plane and a pilot as soon as we touched down and we'd most likely be at Ehden before they finished hashing out the details. But neither of those things are true."

"You're seriously going to tell me you didn't leave yourself a way to get into KTI's systems?"

"Oh, no. I can get *into* the system. Drex handed her access over to me when I joined KTI. And if that was Durav or one of his hired minions who just took off with the ship, it proves our backdoors are still there. But there are actual *people* handling the launchpad at Daedalus and in case you've forgotten, I'm persona non grata on the entire planet. I ... might be able to get in to override the lockdown protocol, but I don't have pilot credentials. If we want to get to Nepenthes quickly, we—or rather, I—will need to do something far more difficult than stealing a ship."

"What's that?"

Stasia gave him a weak smile and dropped her voice to just above a whisper. "Convince Caruso to help us. Preferably *before* we land. And this would be so much easier if Ayman was here, because any decision he makes affects both of them."

"You think Kolya will actually fire him?"

"Ha. Fire him? Definitely. He'll be lucky if Anton doesn't kill him. Or invoke some clause in his NDA and take back everything he's earned over the past few years."

"If money's the issue…" Beck began.

"No. It's not." She lowered her voice even more. "I mean, it's surely something that concerns him, but it's not the *main* thing. You should have seen him when he first started at KTI. This was his dream job. He knew more about the terraforming process when he came in than most people who'd been working here from the beginning and he … well, he idolized Anton when he first arrived, almost as much as the Flock looks up to Shepherd. Come to think of it, he was a lot like the Flock members in other ways, only he saw science as a means of saving the planet, rather than assuming that it was speeding along our demise. Paul believed Anton was this visionary who was not only transforming Mars into something livable but offering that same technology—for free—to clean up Earth's environment in the process. And he does, but then Paul gradually realized that KTI gets this gargantuan tax write off as a result. It actually costs the man *less* if he donates the technology than if he tries to extract payments. That's just one thing among many. Over time, I think everything just … chipped away at Paul's idealism."

"Never meet your heroes, hm?"

"I guess. It was tough watching the guy get slowly ground down by Anton's incessant demands … kind of like he was kicking a puppy. I actually thought Paul would quit, but he just grew a shell of sarcasm."

They were both quiet for a moment. Beck suspected Stasia was thinking the same thing that he was. Paul wasn't the only one whose idealism had taken a beating. The same was true for all of the surviving members of the Watch, aside from Sandjeel and Durav. It was tough thinking that you're working for the white hats, only to discover that you'd unwittingly signed up with the bad guys.

"Could that be a way to reach him?" he asked. "I mean, if Paul feels like he's been working for the Dark Side, maybe you can convince him that he'd fit in better with the Rebels."

"Maybe." Stasia smiled. "He *is* a little short for a stormtrooper."

"True. But you probably shouldn't lead with that."

SIXTEEN

BECK WATCHED as Wyatt dug around in the drawer that served as the ship's bar. As he searched, he kept glancing nervously toward the bridge, where the argument between Stasia and Paul had been going on for a good ten minutes.

"Pretty sure this is the last bourbon," he said when he emerged triumphant with a drink pouch. "But I saw a few of the margaritas if you want one."

Beck shook his head. Drinking really didn't seem like a good idea to him at the moment. He tried to keep his expression neutral, but apparently, he failed.

"Hey, don't judge me," Wyatt said with a wry twist of his mouth. "Their yelling gives me major flashbacks to when my parents split up."

Beck thought the vibe between Stasia and Paul was more like brother and sister, but he agreed that the argument currently raging on the other side of the bulkhead had the intensity of a family fight. And maybe it was, in a sense. Paul clearly felt betrayed. He and Stasia had worked closely for four or five years, much of the time off planet, dealing with a boss who was obviously demanding. That kind of environment was a crucible that tended to forge tight bonds. And the tighter the bond, the more it hurt when it was broken.

It was mostly Paul doing the yelling now, with Stasia only occasionally getting a word in. At this rate, they'd be at Daedalus before she even got around to *mentioning* what they needed him to do, let alone talking him into it.

"How old were you when your folks divorced?" he asked Wyatt.

"Fourteen. And yes, in case you're wondering, I coped by raiding the liquor cabinet back then, too. Then, I got packed off to live with my grandmother for a year while my parents got their act together. Well … not *together*, because they ended up apart, but you know what I mean." He sucked out the rest of the liquor, then shot Beck a curious look. "Or do you? How does a species that basically lives forever handle marriage? Does anyone on your planet actually do the whole 'til death do us part thing?"

"Not exactly. You contract for a set period, take a break, and then decide if you want to renew."

"That sounds very amicable and civilized. Maybe *too* amicable and civilized."

Beck thought back to the miserable first cycle after his split with Brinn, when he'd alternated between bouts of staring morosely at the walls of the apartment they'd shared for several centuries and bouts of wanting to track down and eviscerate her new partner. He hadn't seriously considered violence, of course, but there had been a whole lot of anger mixed in with the hurt.

"I guess it *can* be civilized when all of the partners want out. In practice, it's not all that different than anywhere else—it all depends on the situation and the people involved. Arbet spent much of her life as a legal advocate, which included negotiating separations. She told me about some cases on Novera that would rival any of the nastiest divorces I've heard about on Earth." The argument in the bridge had tapered off as he was speaking. After a moment, he said, "Do you think they're both still alive in there?"

"Only one way to find out." Wyatt shoved the empty liquor pouch into the trash receptacle and started to push off from the wall in the direction of the bridge.

"Wait. Let's give them a few minutes more."

Sure enough, the conversation started again after a moment, at a lower volume now, although there were still occasional and somewhat more subdued outbursts from Paul. These grew farther and farther apart, until about ten minutes later, when Stasia came back into the galley.

"He's … thinking," she said softly.

"Does he not get that we're under a bit of a time constraint?" Wyatt asked, matching her low tone, even though his expression suggested he was struggling to rein it in.

"He understands. But we have another ten minutes or so before we reach Daedalus. And he has a lot to consider."

"So … he believes you?" Beck asked.

"I *think* so. I'm not sure it had much to do with what I told him, though. He's been reading the Eberin Das journal for the past few days and weighing everything that Claire said. The thing I believe might seal the deal, though, is that he's only gotten one message from Ayman since we left Tranquility, and judging from what Ayman said, most of the messages Paul sent home never arrived."

"Yeah," Beck said. "We've had the same problem. Claire, too."

"I'm not surprised," Stasia said. "But in the past, our communications never went through Kolya's censors. That was one of the privileges of being in Kolya's tiny circle of trust. But—"

"But now," Paul said from the doorway, "they're combing through everything I say. On the one hand, that means this fun little act of subordination we're planning won't cost me my job, because I'll be quitting. On the other hand, it has me wondering what *other* privileges Kolya may have curtailed. We could get down there and find I can't even requisition a tram to take us into Daedalus City."

They all fell silent for a moment, and then Stasia said, "If you go into the system on your phone, I can reserve it under Kolya's authorization."

Paul laughed. "Afraid not. After getting burned by you, Kolya never moved me all the way into that *tiny circle of trust,* as you put it. And you don't have access at all. I was there when Macek locked you out."

"Out of the *front* door perhaps. But I got in to plant the message at the Ares Consortium dinner, didn't I?"

Paul peeled off his armscreen and handed it to her. "Fine. Knock yourself out. But keep in mind that you're on the wanted list in all five colonies." He tilted his head to the side and scanned her, from her faded blue hair to her generic sweats. "This get-up might fool the crew at Daedalus. I mean, no one there has ever seen you in anything other than *haute couture*. But it's not going to get you past facial recognition."

"I'm well aware of my legal status." Stasia navigated through a series of screens, then typed in a command that pulled up an interface written in Ufretan. A few minutes later, she said, "Okay. I have his … messages." A tiny frown flickered across her face and then vanished.

"What's wrong?" Beck asked.

"Nothing. I found what I needed."

"Request one of the Kotis," Paul said. "I'd really rather not fly an Engelbrodt until I know more about why Westmoreland's crashed."

She typed for about a minute, seeming to weigh each word as she entered it. Then, she hit send.

"Okay. *Kolya* just placed a request for us to be provided with a plane. A Koti," she confirmed before Paul could get the question out.

"And you're sure the confirmation won't go to *his* device?" Wyatt asked.

"Completely sure."

As she spoke, the armscreen lit up with a confirmation. The good news was that a four-seater Koti would be readied for departure. Paul was listed as the designated pilot, and he was transporting personal guests of KTI to Nepenthes to assist with the hostage negotiations. The bad news was that the planes had been stored for lockdown, and the support personnel were all furloughed. They estimated a delay of at least six hours, which would allow them enough time to pull someone in to take care of the necessary maintenance and safety checks.

"You should probably just stay here on the raptor," Paul said. "We'll sneak you over to the departure dome once we get a green light to go. The janitorial crews will be on furlough, too, so I doubt they'll pull in anyone to clean this ship until…" He trailed off as another message came in requesting level one authorization to override the lockdown protocol. He reached for the armscreen to enter his credentials, but Stasia shook her head.

"It needs to be Kolya's."

"You *do* know that's an entirely different code, right?"

"Of course, I know," she said, with a touch of irritation. "I sent the lockdown protocol out to every single resident on the planet. I helped write the damn thing. It's just … I combed through a couple of Kolya's other recent messages. You were right to worry. He revoked your override access just before they departed from Ares Station. I guess he thought you might help me escape once we land … although where the hell would I go?"

Paul gave a bitter chuckle. "Would have been nice to hear it from Kolya himself, but hey ... why am I surprised?"

Nothing happened for several seconds after Stasia entered the code into Paul's phone and Beck had the sense that she wasn't nearly as confident as she was pretending to be. But then the interface flashed green and returned to displaying the navigation console for the *V2*. The timer indicated that they would be landing in a little under five minutes, so they returned to their seats and strapped in.

The landscape on the viewscreen had changed dramatically while Beck was in the galley, as the shuttle skipped across time zones. Earlier, it had shown a bucolic late afternoon panorama of rolling plains, where the predominant palette was a mix of dark greens and browns. Now, the sky was black, highlighting the glowing neon hues from Daedalus City in the foreground. At this distance, the dome looked as if it would fit neatly on the tip of his finger. It reminded him of an exceptionally garish snow globe an officemate at VersaBio had brought back as a souvenir after her trip to Vegas.

They were nearing the landing pad now, and he was surprised to find Stasia gripping the armrest between them. Weird. She would have made trips like this dozens of times during her years at KTI. Maybe she actually *was* nervous about Paul's piloting skills.

He could now make out a series of smaller domes scattered around Daedalus City, including one adjoining the landing area that must be for departures, judging from the line of aircraft hangars at the far end. The dome that caught his eye, though, was much smaller. It was unlit, but there was just enough ambient light from the neighboring domes that he could make out a dark rectangular box near the center.

Beck felt an odd combination of emotions as he stared at the chamber that had been the final resting place of Eberin Das. He'd never been religious but imagined this might be similar to what people felt on a pilgrimage. It wasn't that he thought of Eberin as a god or anything of that nature, but he did feel a sense of awe as he considered the tremendous effort it had taken for the man to pass his warning down to a civilization millions of kilometers and millions of years from his own doomed world.

The oddest thing, though, was the twinge of hope in the mix. That was an emotion he recognized, even though he hadn't felt it in nearly a month. Everything he'd done since learning the true mission of the Watch had been the fruit of his conviction that he had to at least *try*. That it would be immoral, fundamentally wrong, and yes, *inhuman* to do nothing when faced with the information he now had. But he'd never truly believed they had the slightest chance of stopping the Alliance.

Now, though, looking out at the chamber, he couldn't help thinking about the incredibly unlikely chain of events that had placed Eberin's journal in his hands, when he was one of the few people on Earth who had even a remote chance of deciphering it.

The odds against that were astronomical. So why should he assume they would fail now?

That wasn't logical, of course. The fact that they'd overcome astronomical odds to get this far didn't mean they'd continue to have the same level of luck. He'd never believed there was a higher power guiding the course of history, and he now knew that the Alliance had been destroying emerging worlds for millions of years. Earth wasn't special. There was no reason to assume that its inhabitants were more worthy of being saved from destruction than the people of ancient Mars or any of the other planets the Alliance had summarily dispatched into oblivion.

Those were the facts—cold, bleak, and dark as Eberin's chamber. The facts hadn't changed, and he couldn't ignore them. But they were now joined by a tiny, inexplicable flicker of hope. And he couldn't ignore that, either.

FROM AWAITING THE SENTINELS

BY TOBIAS SHEPHERD

Appendix: The Sentinel's Manifesto (Lesson Four)

THOSE WHO JOIN TOGETHER as the Earth Watch must seek to restore the lost balance of nature, and to do this, you must change the hearts and minds of the people. Above all, you must teach them to reject the Janus-faced twins of Progress and Destruction, and embrace a fuller, more verdant life in harmony with nature. For only by this can the Earth be saved.

Walk in the light of the Sentinels.

Res esdoden ojiri ensilar ufretas.

SEVENTEEN

CLAIRE WAITED for Kolya's rant to wind down before even trying to interrupt. "Wyatt and Beck didn't steal your ship. There has to be another explanation."

Kolya shrugged. "Occam's razor. They were on the *V1*. The *V1* is now gone. Ergo..."

She had felt kind of bad for harboring even a passing thought about letting the tether yank Kolya into space. But the pretentious jerk actually said *ergo*. Now she was kind of wishing she'd pushed him out the door herself.

To her surprise, Macek agreed that they hadn't stolen the ship. "Caruso says he gave them level two access. But even if he *had* given them level one, neither of them is in our system as a pilot."

"Do you think maybe Stasia..." Claire began but stopped because Macek was shaking his head.

"She's not a pilot, either. She said the training interface gave her headaches and she quit halfway through. That was one reason Kolya agreed to hire Caruso. I also *revoked* Stasia's access before we even arrived. She couldn't buy a coffee on that station without one of us approving it, let alone take a ship out of dock. And, as I said, she's with Caruso."

"Can you call him and—"

He glanced pointedly at the phone in his hand. "What do you think I've been trying to do, Claire? I *should* be able to route calls through the shuttle's comm system. It's not working, though. I know you're worried. I'll keep trying. If nothing else, we'll be at Nepenthes in less than an hour. We may be able to piggyback off the relay at Elysia even sooner."

"My money is still on Garcia being the thief," Kolya said. "Someone messaged him with a lead, and he decided he couldn't wait until the lockdown was lifted. Plenty of raptor pilots are stuck at Ares Station right now. He probably paid one of them to help him grab the ship. I know your security team has been spread a bit thin lately, Macek, but this kind of lapse is really unacceptable."

"Screw the raptor!" Macek's tone was sharper than she'd ever heard him use with Kolya. "I'm more worried about the damage to Ares Station. Garcia and Beckett might be *on* the *V1*. I'll admit that's a possibility. But if you're sticking with Occam's razor, the most likely scenario is that the damned thing was hijacked by whoever set the bombs. And Garcia could not have done that. Not unless you think he got explosives past our people at Tranquility Base and transported them on the *V1*, and I can promise you that did not happen."

"Can you, though? Rather bold of you to promise *anything* given the security failure on the station today."

Macek said something in Russian. It sounded like *blue duck* to Claire's untrained ear. Whatever it meant, Kolya didn't like it one bit and for a moment it looked like they wanted to trade blows. The wave of anger passed as quickly as it had started, however. They just stared at each other, and the tension seemed to drain out of both of them at the same time.

Claire, on the other hand, was still fully wound up. Macek's point that the raptor was likely stolen by the bombers was probably obvious in retrospect, but it hadn't even occurred to her. There was nowhere to hide on that ship. And neither Beck nor Wyatt was armed.

"Why can't you track the *V1*?" she asked. "It's *your* ship. Just follow it!"

"We don't need to," Kolya said. "Whoever swiped the ship will soon find that their options are extremely limited."

Macek nodded. "He's right. Like I said before, we know where it's going. There's only one port on Mars that can handle passenger vehicles larger than shuttles like this one, and that's Daedalus. Even if they managed to override that, the raptor's AI won't allow it to land anywhere without a crew, and they're all closed due to the lockdown."

"What about supply ships? Aren't those still coming in? Surely they don't land only at Daedalus? And narcoships. Wyatt was saying earlier that a lot of those are raptor class."

"Supply ships are automated," Kolya said. "No pilot. No passengers. And narcoships don't *land*. They just swoop close enough to the surface to release their drone carriers, which take the shipment the rest of the way. There are currently no laws against the drug trade, but they have to pay taxes if they come through official channels and narcotics dealers generally prefer to avoid that. It's a tricky maneuver, even for experienced pilots. I've actually tried—not to drop off a drug shipment, but just to see if I could manage it. If you swoop too low, gravity gets you and you may not have time to parachute out."

"There's a ship skeleton just outside of Hellas Station whose pilot misjudged," Macek added. "A few more at Lyot, which handles most of that trade. So, yeah, they are heading to Daedalus. Anything else requires a level one override and there are only three people in our system with that clearance—me, Kolya, and Caruso."

"Two," Kolya said.

"Okay." Macek gave him a confused frown, as if wondering whether he or Caruso was the one who no longer had the clearance. "Two, then. But the point remains. The *V1* can't just land in the middle of nowhere and disappear."

"Well, they *could* force a crash landing," Kolya said. "And Davy *could* be wrong about the surface being safe now. I kind of like that possibility. A bit of *Azospira oryzae* in their lungs might teach them to respect private property."

"Stop trying to scare her. Davy is never wrong, and again, the only place the raptor can land is Daedalus. That's where you were sending them anyway, so what difference … does it make?"

Judging from the way Macek trailed off at the end, Claire was sure he'd let something slip. Her suspicion was confirmed when Kolya shot him a venomous look.

She didn't say anything, just leaned her head back against the seat and listened to the faint warble of the engines as she stared at the deep green carpet of the planet's surface, which was now displayed on the viewports. Kolya kept glancing in her direction, like he expected her to call him out on his very obvious treachery, but what was the point? He'd clearly been planning this all along.

Well, not the explosions at Ares Station or someone taking off with one of his raptors. But he'd definitely planned on separating her from Wyatt and Beck. That way, once they were at Ehden, he could tell Shepherd that of course he couldn't let her go in all by herself, without any sort of security. With no other options, he'd insist on accompanying her himself. Or, if Shepherd balked too hard at that, he'd send in Macek. Either way, Kolya would get what he wanted. As usual.

And while everything they'd just said about the *V1* having to land at Daedalus made sense in the normal operation of things, their current circumstances were anything but ordinary. Whoever stole the raptor either had high level access or had managed to forge the necessary credentials. Otherwise, how had they gotten clearance to leave Ares Station?

After several minutes, the silence was broken by a hoarse rumble inside her helmet, as Kolya cleared his throat. "We have about half an hour to Nepenthes. I'd like to be able to hit the ground running when we arrive. Where did we leave our conversation when the bombs started going off?"

"You'd just said that you didn't trust me. And I was about to respond that the feeling was entirely mutual."

"I believe I said that I wasn't *sure* if I could trust you, but perhaps we can set our reciprocal feelings of suspicion aside for the time being and focus on the greater good."

By which you mean your *own good,* she thought, but simply gave him a terse nod.

Kolya entered something into his phone and then aimed it at the viewport. "This was taken earlier today at Doba and..." He stopped and frowned when he realized that all three sections of the viewport were still showing the planet ahead, along with rows of control lights and other readouts that were superimposed over the scenery at the top and bottom. The screen flickered, then the section on the right, which was apparently the one to which Kolya had sent a signal, went dark. Two lights at the top of the screens switched colors, one going from green to amber, and another blinking back and forth between amber and red. Kolya gave the two remaining displays an angry glare, apparently hoping to cow them into submission. The only change, however, was that the flickering indicator made up its mind and was now flashing red.

The shuttle's AI chimed in with the entirely unnecessary announcement that screen three was no longer functional. Macek told it to run a full system diagnostic. After a short pause, the voice came back.

"Multiple systems inoperative or functioning below normal parameters."

EIGHTEEN

AS THE SHIP began ticking off the problem areas, Macek mumbled something in Russian. Based on Kolya's expression, it was a variant of *I told you so*. While the AI itself was speaking English, she didn't recognize most of what it was spouting out concerning damage to the shuttle, either, aside from a few ominous phrases like *external communications array* and *guided landing*.

"That last part doesn't sound good," she said.

Macek grabbed his helmet and tossed Claire's to her. "Just as a precaution," he said. "But no, it's not good. We shouldn't have been cleared to leave the dock if any of these systems were down."

"But they *weren't* down when we left," Kolya said, as he latched his own helmet into place. "Or at least, external communications weren't down. I exchanged messages with Daedalus as soon as you told me about the *V1*, which was before we got the green light to depart. And Nepenthes received and cleared our flight plan. But you're overreacting. I can navigate and land without feedback from the crew at Nepenthes if I have to. God knows, I've done it plenty of times in the past."

Claire glanced at Macek, who didn't seem nearly as confident on either issue. Maybe he was also remembering the ominous scraping sound of that flying metal panel smacking into the hull as they left the station. On Kolya's second point, she was tempted to ask exactly how many years it had been since he navigated and landed manually … but did she really want to know the answer?

"See if you can pinpoint the problem," Kolya said. "Or at least get those damned lights to stop flashing."

Macek, who had been out of his harness before Kolya even began speaking, clearly didn't need the instructions. He flapped a dismissive hand in Kolya's direction and opened a wall panel.

Kolya turned to Claire. "I suppose we'll have to do this another way."

He expanded the screen on his phone and tilted it toward her, revealing a satellite image of two tiny domes, roughly the same diameter, with a wide stretch of dark green foliage between them. As he zoomed in, the details gradually came into focus. Off to the right, a cluster of bamboo trees formed a dark line against the gray-tinged sky. For the most part, the domes looked fine, but they were marred here and there by irregularly shaped lighter patches that were merely translucent instead of transparent.

"What are those spots on the exterior?" she asked.

"Repairs. That was the sole concession Shepherd has made since this standoff began."

"Didn't you say he agreed to release the kids?"

"Well … yes. Aside from that. A few days after we left Tranquility, he agreed to let us send in repair drones to patch up the damaged panels at both Doba and Ehden. Otherwise, everyone would still be in biosuits. That would have been doubly miserable for his people, since the vast majority of the suits at Ehden are the bulky ones everyone calls Stay-Pufts."

He zoomed inside one of the domes to show a deep green glade. Several partially collapsed buildings were clustered near the center.

"This was taken earlier today at Doba. It's nearly dark there now, so you won't be able to get a clear view in person until tomorrow. That larger building in the center is the main lab."

"Looks like it took a lot of damage."

"The exterior did, yes. But there wasn't as much damage to the actual lab as it might appear at first glance. The more complex work happens underground. Most of Davy's lab—including the areas that handle her more *important* projects—were largely unaffected."

His expression was unbelievably *smug* as he delivered the last sentence. She knew she should let it pass, but…

"Yes, you mentioned that earlier. And I got it the first time. The Flock's attempt to slow you down failed and there's nothing to stop you from launching your little bundles of DNA at exoplanets. Who cares if you doom humanity in the process? Nothing else matters as long as you get what you want when you want it."

For a moment, it didn't look as if he was going to take the bait, but then he erupted. "It's not about what I bloody *want*, Claire! Why can't you see that? If all of this is actually true and we simply give in to their demands, we're *already* doomed. What right does this Alliance have to keep an entire planet from fulfilling its destiny? How is that fair? Humanity is *curious*. We are, by nature, explorers. Conquerors. If we can't expand, if we let your aliens confine us to a cage, are we truly human?"

"I'd hardly call restricting us to our own solar system being confined to a cage. You're right on one count, though. It's not fair. But that can be said for a lot of things in life."

"True. Including being held hostage for weeks by a bunch of religious fanatics."

"Or by a bunch of scientists," she countered. "It's an equal number of hostages on both sides, right?" She decided not to mention that it had been *his* bright idea to let Shepherd take over Ehden, even though pretty much everyone else had told him it was a mistake.

"Almost equal," Kolya admitted. "There was some confusion over the exact number at first. Shepherd's people had sixteen, but they released the four children. We have thirteen Flock members. Our guards caught them running through a field near the tunnel between Doba and Ehden right after the bombs went off."

"All young women?" It was a reasonable guess. Shepherd's followers were mostly female and Kolya's main reason for allowing Shepherd to set up camp on Mars had been to help correct the gender imbalance on the planet, which was roughly three-quarters male.

"All but two. Davy was willing to release the suspects into Shepherd's custody if Shepherd came to Doba for questioning. He seemed amenable at first. But some of his more ardent followers balked at that, saying they were concerned for his safety. Shortly after that, they took nine of Davy's people captive, along with a few spouses and children. They've been holding them there ever since. Well, except the kids. They're back with Davy's people now."

"Why were they in Ehden?"

"No clue."

"Do you know where Shepherd is staying?"

"He has rooms in that new construction across from the dining hall."

"Is that where I'll be meeting him?"

"No. I'm going to suggest we meet at my cottage. We'll have more privacy there."

Claire nodded vaguely, even as her mind whirred trying to come up with alternatives. Because that wasn't going to work at all. Kolya's cottage was at least a kilometer from the center of town. There was no guarantee that Shepherd would have the beacon on him, so they needed to meet on his turf. Preferably in his quarters, but at least within easy walking distance.

"No," she said after a moment. "He's not going to go for that. We should aim for neutral ground. Or … if you want him to think that you're acting in good faith, allow him some security. Offer to meet at the diner. Or, better yet, at his place. I mean, you're not seriously worried that Shepherd is a threat, are you?"

Kolya gave her an incredulous look. "Of course, he's a threat. He has nearly a hundred people there who will do anything he says."

"Yes, but the Flock has espoused nonviolence for decades. I have a hard time believing they've suddenly morphed into a band of highly trained terrorists. They're probably as scared as the hostages."

"Nonviolent people don't blow up buildings," Kolya said. "And they have weapons. Otherwise, we'd have sent in a security team to simply extract our people."

Macek snorted loudly. He didn't seem to be paying attention to their conversation, and his head was obscured by the open electrical panel. If not for Kolya's annoyed expression, Claire would have assumed the noise was in response to whatever was going on with the comms system.

"Shepherd claims he had nothing to do with the bombings. And there's some evidence to back him up on that point," she added, deciding that it was probably best not to remind him that *Drex* had taken responsibility, backed by both Stasia and Beck. "So, I think we have to at least consider the possibility. It's not going to be much of a negotiation if we go in automatically assuming the man is lying."

Kolya didn't say anything, but his jaw was tightly clenched as he flipped angrily through a series of images on his screen. A few seconds later, he found what he was looking for and shoved it toward her.

"This was one of the hostages. A security guard. They beat the holy hell out of him. Davy said the trauma to his body was probably enough to kill the poor kid on its own. But your *nonviolent* Flock shot him in the head just to make sure."

NINETEEN

CLAIRE STARED down at Kolya's phone. The young man in the picture was wearing a newer model biosuit similar to the one she'd worn on her previous trip to Mars, aside from the KTI logo on the front. A helmet lay on the ground next to his body, the visor broken and blood-spattered. His neck and one of his legs were bent at unnatural angles.

When she looked up, Kolya was watching her, his mouth twisted into a sneer. "Does that look *nonviolent* to you, Claire? Still so certain you want to go into Ehden on your own?"

Her mouth went dry. She'd already been nervous about the plan, but what the hell had she gotten herself into?

"I never said I wanted to go in on my own. My plan was to go in with *Beck*. You're the one who decided to send him to the other side of the planet." She nodded down at the image. "When did this happen?"

Kolya took the phone from her, retracted the screen, and shoved it into his pocket. "A few days after we left Tranquility Base. Shepherd sent Davy a message saying they'd left the body in the field near the tunnel. Told her he didn't want to hurt the other hostages, but he needed to make sure she knew that he would do whatever he had to do in order to protect his people."

"How did KTI respond?"

He shot her a disdainful look. "Do you actually think we killed one of his people and … what? Just tossed her out into the field, tit for tat?"

She shook her head, even though she hadn't entirely ruled it out. "I was just wondering if they agreed to the repairs on the dome before or after the man was killed."

"I don't know. It needed to be done quickly, otherwise the crops would be damaged. So, before, I think. Figuring out a precise timeline hasn't been a high priority."

"Well, it should be. It would be helpful to know the extent to which they're still communicating, if they were able to reach any sort of agreement after that. And..." She hesitated, pretty sure that he wasn't going to like what she said next. "And I think there's more to the story. Because if that's the sequence of events, it doesn't add up."

"How so?" There was an edge to his voice.

"It's just ... backward. In the immediate aftermath of the bombing, probably less than a day after your security team takes his people—" She'd been about to say *hostage,* but she knew he wouldn't like that terminology and caught herself just in time. "Takes his people into custody. They were making a bit of progress, right? Shepherd releases the children, and they agree to let the repair team in to patch up the dome. All that happened before tempers even had a chance to cool off. And then a day or so later, you get an act of such extreme violence against one of the hostages with no provocation? It doesn't make..." Realization dawned as she was speaking, partly because a flicker of guilt crossed Kolya's face. "The repair team. You tried to use them as cover for a rescue mission, didn't you?"

"Yes," Kolya said. "And it very nearly worked. All they had to do was get to the main gate, subdue or take out the guards there, and let in the team we had waiting just out of sight. But they were caught, stripped of their weapons, and kicked out of Ehden."

The sound Macek made this time was faint, almost inaudible. Claire might even have passed it off as feedback from the helmet speakers if not for Kolya's reaction.

"Oh, do go on, Macek. You're clearly itching to say it. I'm sure you think if you'd been on the ground it would have all gone differently."

Macek closed the electrical panel. "If I had been making the decision, it wouldn't have *gone* at all. As I told you at the time. We had no indication our people were being mistreated. And even though I am as suspicious as you are about Shepherd's sudden determination to negotiate only with Claire, we had an agreement with him. The security team breached that agreement."

"And you think that gave Shepherd the right to kill that man?"

"Don't be ridiculous. Of course I don't think that. What I do think is that their stupid mistake is going to make it harder to get him to trust us again."

"No kidding," Claire said. "Anything else you'd like to tell me before we get there?"

Kolya gave her a withering look, then glanced back down at his phone. About ten seconds later, her own phone buzzed. "There. You now have my correspondence with Davy since the bombing."

"All of it?"

"Yes, Claire. Do you really think I was able to read through and weed out sensitive info in less than a minute?"

It was a fair point, so she simply gave him a palms-up gesture to indicate that he'd won the round.

Kolya then turned to Macek. "Status?"

It seemed to take a moment for Macek to realize that he was asking about the shuttle. Claire thought the answer was kind of obvious, anyway, given that two of the indicator lights were still bright red.

"Nothing I can do," Macek said. "It will have to wait until we're at Nepenthes."

"Are you sure?" Kolya asked.

"*Yes*, I'm sure. The whole diagnostic system is screwed."

Kolya cursed, unstrapped his harness, then gave his head a quick jerk to the side to activate his helmet's control panel. A second later, one of the three tiny lights at the top of Claire's own panel blinked out. *Kolya has left the chat.*

They watched as Kolya stomped across the tiny cabin and

yanked open the very same panel Macek had been examining for the past fifteen minutes.

After a moment, Macek huffed and turned his attention to Claire. "I don't know what he's trying to prove. He's a better pilot than I am, but he knows far less about how to fix them. Breaking them, on the other hand…" He gave a bitter chuckle. "So now he will pout for a few minutes. I have known him since we were nine years old, and this is always his pattern when the universe fails to give him proper deference."

"Are you worried about the shuttle?"

He lifted one shoulder in an almost imperceptible shrug. "As best I can tell, it's just a communications issue. Nepenthes knows we are coming. We should be fine. The AI will still make most of the calculations. It just won't have real-time feedback from the landing pad." After another quick glance at Kolya, he lowered his voice to the point that it was barely a whisper inside her helmet. "While he stands there pretending he knows what he's looking at, maybe you can answer a few of *my* questions?"

"Sure…" Claire said, not entirely clear as to where this was heading.

"Stasia and I spoke a few times during the trip. Not many, because Kolya wanted to give her the…" He shook his head, trying to come up with the word.

"Cold shoulder?"

"Yes. To ice her out. But we had a few occasions to talk while he slept, and … what I don't understand is this. If everything you and Stasia have said about this Alliance is true, then why did you not contact the authorities? The governments that contribute to the Ares Consortium would be a good first step. They could activate their space forces. Get them ready to fight, ready to knock those *nadir* drones or whatever you called them out of the sky as soon as they appear."

"Because we can't win. Not with so little time to prepare."

He shook his head. "You can't know that for certain."

"No. *I* don't know for certain. But Stasia and Beck? The other

Watchers? They all have a far better grasp of the capabilities of the Alliance's weapons than I do. Stasia's mother is in the Alliance military. Sandjeel also had a long military career. He says we don't stand a chance."

"Even if that's true, it hardly seems fair to keep everyone else on the planet in the dark. You seem to have more than your fair share of curiosity. If the world was ending in six months, wouldn't you want to know?"

Having had several weeks to ponder that question, she didn't need to think before answering. "On a personal level? Yes. But on a societal level? I could easily see that going horribly, horribly wrong. If people believe there's no future, you'll need to hope their humanity overrides their animal nature. And hope that any religious beliefs about an afterlife restrain them from taking full advantage of opportunities in this one. Because no future means no time for punishment. Living for the moment could have an extremely dark side in this case. So, yeah. If the decision were solely in my hands, I'd choose to leave people in blissful ignorance."

"If it's as hopeless as you claim, why did the Flock or these renegade Watchers even bother blowing my buildings up?" This question came from Kolya, who was now strapping himself back into the captain's chair, apparently done with his sulk. She was fairly certain he hadn't fixed the larger issue, but the lights were no longer red … or amber, or green, for that matter. The offending row of lights was simply gone.

"I never said it was hopeless," she countered. "My point was that we can't possibly fight them with six months or a year at most to prepare. But if we can stop Durav, if we can delay him sending that signal for five years, ten, even longer—then maybe. Right now, though? We'd just be terrifying people for no reason."

And she knew it wasn't just individual people who might overreact. Governments would, too. They'd probably start by sweeping in and grabbing not just Sandjeel but also Arbet and the *ipret-tai.* Beck and Stasia, as well, once they returned to Earth. Kolya might even support that decision. Kai, too.

"Again," she said, trying to keep her tone calm and reasonable, "we just need a delay. I'm helping you with the standoff at Ehden, when I should be back on Earth trying to help locate and stop Durav from sending the signal."

"How do you know Durav hasn't already sent it?" He chuckled. "I mean, wouldn't that be priority one for a supervillain intent on destruction?"

"I told you before. They haven't entered the communications window with the Alliance yet. They're not in range. I just don't see why you can't at least hold off a few months on your exoplanet project. If Durav actually sends the signal, then there's no harm. You can go ahead and scatter your AE biobots to every planet in the—"

"Oh, we *will* find Durav. I may not be convinced by the rest of your tale, but I *am* convinced that he killed someone I … someone I once cared about. And there's no way I'm letting him get away with that."

She took a deep centering breath, mustering all of her willpower in order to keep her expression neutral. As usual, Kolya was determined to make it all about him. Durav had dared to harm someone who was important to him and now he wanted revenge. There was a time when she'd thought there was a compassionate core underneath the man's ego. He *was* capable of small acts of kindness and consideration. She remembered him going out of his way to ensure that she was able to keep her promise to bring Jemma peanut butter cookies on her last trip to Mars. Now she wondered if those kindnesses were only for the people in his immediate orbit, the chosen few. She'd fallen into that category when he was trying to get into bed with her and was probably still on the periphery as Kai's daughter. Everyone else, though? He acted as if they were a nameless, faceless audience in thrall to his magnificence.

Whatever his reasons, though, he currently had his battalions of paid minions actively hunting for Durav. And it wouldn't help their cause to question his motivations, so she ignored him and focused on the view of the planet.

It was twilight now, but they were close enough to the surface that what had previously appeared as a deep green carpet was revealed to be a mottled tapestry with irregular threads of brown and the reddish beige that had been the planet's predominant color on her last visit. She could even make out one manmade feature—the four inverted cone habitats at Elysia that she'd seen on her previous trip to Nepenthes.

From this far up, the Elysian pods were just four dots of light arranged in a square. But the configuration stirred a wrenching wave of homesickness. She had landed at Jonas Labs on multiple occasions, and the four buildings had looked a bit like this as her AirLyft approached the helipad. Of course, there would only be two buildings at Jonas Labs now—even the most ambitious estimates wouldn't have the others replaced before early spring. These thoughts brought a touch of guilt, as well. Joe was embroiled in that chaos and also having to deal with the refugees from the Watch all on his own. If what Kolya had told her earlier was true, he wasn't having much luck convincing Kai, either. Even though the situation with Beck was complicated, he was the one person Joe might have opened up to if he was feeling pressured.

And what had she done? She'd whisked Joe's entire support network off the planet … for no good reason, in the end, since Kolya had clearly intended to be the one joining her in the Ehden negotiations from the beginning. He'd merely let Wyatt and Beck tag along so that she'd agree to help.

"So. No more warning lights," Macek said dryly. "Turning them off is such a novel way to fix the problem."

"They were *distracting* me. Do you want me distracted while I'm landing the shuttle? Or maybe *you* want to land it yourself?"

"Oh, no, no, Kolya. You are the better pilot. No question. Carry on."

A few seconds later, Macek reached for his phone. "Ah, we're in range of Elysia's communications system. Good." He glanced at Claire, frowned slightly, and then tapped something in.

Her phone began buzzing inside the exterior pocket of her suit. Macek gave her a little grin and held a single finger up to his visor in a shushing gesture, but Kolya wasn't paying attention, anyway.

A surge of relief flooded through her when Wyatt's name appeared on the screen. Multiple messages, with the last one sent about five minutes earlier. Before she could open any of them, though, the entire shuttle began to shake so violently that she nearly dropped the phone. She pressed her head back against the seat and stared at Kolya's faint reflection in the viewport.

"Nothing to worry about." His voice was completely calm as he pushed the controls upward and the rattle began to calm. "Although the atmosphere *is* a little thicker than when I last did this manually."

The shuttle began shaking again before he even finished the sentence. This time, the AI chimed in. "Unable to connect to guided navigation. Adjusting descent path to recommended parameters."

Kolya tapped the screen on the console with his other hand, then pushed up again on the controls. As before, the shaking settled down somewhat, but it was still very rough. She put her phone back inside the pocket. If she tried reading her messages now, her stomach was going to revolt.

How long had it taken them to reach Nepenthes Station once they passed Elysia on the last trip? A little less than half an hour, she thought. But the shuttle was moving much faster than the plane Kolya had been flying then. He'd barely touched the controls during that flight, and she wondered again exactly how long it had been since he manually landed any aircraft, let alone a shuttle coming in from Ares Station.

Macek muttered something in Russian. Claire picked up the word *vector,* but the rest was unintelligible.

Kolya responded in English, his knuckles white against the controls. "You want the helm?"

Despite Macek's earlier statement that Kolya was the better pilot, Claire really wanted him to say *yes*.

"That's what I thought," Kolya said when Macek didn't respond. "Now shut up so I can focus."

The craft lurched downward at an angle that felt much too steep given how far they still were from Nepenthes.

Claire's stomach churned. She squeezed her eyes shut and clutched the armrests, focusing on keeping down her dinner and trying not to think about the ground rushing toward them.

PART II

FROM THE JOURNAL OF EBERIN DAS

Translation by Alice Dobroski
18.12.508

TOMORROW, I will place this journal into Navi's hands. If its warning reaches you, future explorer, she deserves far more credit than I.

As I read through one last time, however, I have one more regret to add to my total. Why did I devote so many of these entries to my own story, my own anguish and guilt?

I suppose you could argue that is the nature of a diary. One cannot, after all, chronicle the inner thoughts of anyone other than oneself. I do wish, however, that I had spent less time on introspection, and more time telling you of the world around me, the people, their cultures. My people will soon erase the entirety of Martian civilization, and the only record likely to survive is mine. Nothing will remain of their art, their music, the simple beauties of their day-to-day lives.

Instead, you have the tortured musings of a renegade alien. I believed I could save them, that I could convince the mighty beast to have mercy on the weak. But all I managed to do was convince the beast to devour several thousand of them ahead of schedule.

ONE

New York
Wednesday, October 4

THE BOTTOM of Alice's foot was cold. Just *one* of her feet, though. She thought it was her left foot, but her brain was too fuzzy for her to be certain at the moment. It felt like someone was pointing a jet of frigid air directly at her toes. She needed to move, to pull her foot back under the blankets and sleep for a few more hours, but her body wouldn't cooperate. It felt like she was fused to the bed.

And ... an alarm was going off. The sound was muffled, though. Had she knocked her armscreen to the floor when she placed it on the charger? But that didn't make sense, either. She always woke to music, not an alarm.

She tried to open her eyes, but after a few seconds gave it up as a lost cause and drifted back under to the alarm's faint *waa-waa-waa*.

Later—she had no idea how *much* later—another sound dragged her back to the surface. Closer and louder this time, and she had the vague sense that she'd heard it before. The blaring noise continued in the distance, but the new sound was a series of high-pitched beeps, more like a fire alarm, followed by a woman's voice. She couldn't quite make out the words, but the man's response was crystal clear. *Override,* followed by an alphanumeric string.

When Alice slipped back into the fog again, Mitch was there with her, silhouetted against the light from her bedroom. One hand gripped the frame of the closet door and the other—the one with the gun, the gun he'd just fired into her leg—hung limply at his side. *You never listen, Ceci. Never. And look what you made me do now!*

No. No. *No.* Someone had shot her, but it had *not* been Mitch. The voice she'd heard saying *override* wasn't his. It was a ... dead voice. Flat. Monotone. And she wasn't *that* girl anymore. Cecilia Cooper, the nineteen-year-old girl who had crawled to the back of her closet in a futile attempt to get away? She was long gone. Alice Dobroski fought back. Her taser might not have stopped the guy, but at least she hadn't frozen, cowering in the back of the closet, waiting to be shot.

And ... had she actually even been shot this time? Her shoulder was stiff, but it was nothing like the searing pain of the gunshot wound. It hadn't just been a flashback, though. She *had* heard a weapon fire right before she felt the pain in her shoulder. But given the fuzzy state of her head right now, maybe it had been a tranquilizer dart?

She tried to open her eyes again. This time, she managed a narrow crack and peered through her lashes. It was dark, with intermittent flashes of white and blue light against the walls of a tiny room.

No. Against the inside of a *car*. She was lying on a car seat, not on a bed as she'd originally thought.

And the man across from her wasn't Mitch. It was the *ipret-tai*. His eyes remained fixed on the window, his impassive face going in and out of shadow as the car passed beneath the overhanging lights along the highway.

Alice felt a rising sense of panic, but she fought it down and tried to regulate her breathing. There was nothing to be gained from letting him know she was awake. Her head still felt disconnected from her body, and she needed time to formulate some sort of plan.

She needed to *remember*. What had happened during those seconds after she felt the pain in her shoulder? Had the *ipret-tai* displayed any weaknesses or vulnerabilities she could exploit if she got a chance? She knew that she'd kept running but she'd only made it a few steps down the sidewalk before tumbling into a guerrilla garden one of her neighbors had planted inside the tree pits in the center of the sidewalk. Her clearest memory was lying on her side, thinking that it was a miracle her glasses hadn't been thrown off. A chili pepper so close to her nose she could smell it. Hearing footsteps pounding toward her. Thinking *that taser should have brought you down, should have killed you, you inhuman freak.*

With tremendous effort, she had managed to tip onto her back and aimed her taser up at the dark figure standing over her. It was pure bluff, though. She'd already fired both projectiles. And even if the weapon hadn't been empty, she couldn't have hit him. Not with her vision blurring and fragmenting like a frickin kaleidoscope.

Then, all of those fragments had merged into a wall of solid black.

How long ago had that been? She couldn't see the dash, and her phone wasn't on her arm. Not that she'd have risked turning it on. A quick glance down at the floorboard revealed her messenger bag, propped against the door. From the corner of her eye, she glimpsed her feet and found that her left shoe was indeed missing.

She closed her eyes again. A few seconds later, the beeping noise she'd heard when she first regained consciousness filled the cabin. Reflected light from the dash flashed in time with the noise and a woman's voice said, "Taking exit 27E to comply with law enforcement directive. Taking exit 27E to—"

"Override. 6743D22J."

While Alice had never actually owned a car, she was fairly certain that overriding police commands didn't come as a standard option for automotive AI. But the car complied. "Continuing to 167 Riviera Drive. Arrival in approximately 29 minutes."

As the AI was speaking, the *ipret-tai* tapped behind his ear, listened for a moment, then said, "*Bahnt, bahnt. Gerdez.*"

Her brain knew the first word instantly. A second later, the other word clicked into place. *Yes, yes. Twice.*

The *ipret-tai* spoke without inflection, flat and inanimate. In fact, he sounded a lot like the computer program that she'd set up to read the Eberin Das journal back to her. The accent was a bit different, though. Shepherd's pronunciation guide had the word for *yes* as closer to *baht* than *bahnt*, but it wasn't much more than the difference between a Brooklyn and a Jersey accent.

After a pause, the *ipret-tai* looked out the window. *"Ahn, Durav. Kai onig vint. Oza."*

No, Durav. I see ... There was a word she didn't catch in there, but the next word was *one*. Maybe *only one*? But only one what? Whatever it was, it was *oza,* which meant *blue*. One blue light? Was the flash she'd seen a police drone?

He listened and then spoke again. *"Vrash, Durav. Othren agar vrendt?"*

Sorry, Durav. For the first time, Alice thought she heard a tiny hint of emotion. Whether it was fear or regret or something else entirely, she didn't know, but the man's tone was different. Then it was back to business with the second sentence. The first word signified a question, like *do I* or *should I*. And the last word was a feminine pronoun, so he was almost certainly talking about her. The middle word wasn't *kill,* thank god. She knew that one. On the other hand, there could easily be as many synonyms for killing someone in Ufretan as there were in English, so it was probably a bit early to celebrate.

"Bahnt. Ahn Ufrete zhorg a vren'ga-tai o vren'thal."

She understood the first part. *Yes. No Ufretan thing...* She also picked up the phrase for *her body* and the word *or*. The last word she didn't know, but it had the feminine prefix. And she could make an educated guess, because he kicked at her messenger bag as he spoke.

Putting it all together, that probably meant he'd searched not only her bag, but also her person, a thought that made her skin crawl. At least she had no memory of the experience, so being unconscious had a silver lining. Or to use the Ufretan phrase, *the abeeda had a sweeter peel.*

"Bahnt. Vrash, vrash. Alduug New York *erd kait gerd-tai housen foont."*

Yes. Sorry, sorry. Something *New York* something *look second-body Housen traitor.*

Housen could be another word she didn't know, but it was probably the guy from the bar. If so, it was confirmation that he wasn't working with them, because she was positive about her translation of the word *foont*. Eberin Das mused about his status as a *traitor* in almost every journal entry.

The *ipret-tai* tapped behind his ear again, then switched to English. "Pulsar. Move to the shoulder of the road and stop."

"Finding first safe location to move to—"

"Override. 6743D22J. Do it now."

The car veered to the right and screeched to a stop. Alice fought the impulse to brace herself and very nearly tumbled to the floorboard.

"Delete all system data."

"I'm sorry," the AI said, "but—"

"Override. 6743D22J. Full delete."

The door opened and the car's cabin filled with light from the overhead lamp. Alice steeled herself for the *ipret-tai*'s hand to close around one of her limbs. Or around her throat. Instead, she heard the door slam, and the car was once again dark, except for the ambient light from the highway and the intermittent flashes of blue.

Her guess that those blue flashes were from a police drone was confirmed a few seconds later when the wailing noise was replaced with a verbal warning. "Stop and place your hands above your head. If you do not stop, this unit is authorized to use non-lethal force. Police will arrive momentarily. All interactions are being recorded. Stop and place your hands behind your head. If you do not stop—"

The light and the warning cut out abruptly. Apparently, the *ipret-tai* had a very illegal drone blocker.

Alice remained perfectly still, expecting the *ipret-tai* to return. When several minutes passed with no sign of him, she began feeling around on the floorboard for her bag. Once she found it, she searched the inner pockets, hoping her phone was inside.

No luck. She didn't see it under the seat, either.

The drone's warning that the police were on their way was no doubt true. And while *will arrive momentarily* could mean anything from a few minutes to a few hours with the NYPD, they were probably moving a lot faster now that he'd disabled their traffic drone. The question was whether she wanted to be here when the police arrived. There was nothing to link her to the owner of the car, and no drone to spot her leaving. Of course, with only one shoe, walking was going to be a challenge. And with no phone, walking was likely her only option.

She propped herself up on one elbow and did a more thorough search, but the shoe and phone were definitely gone. Which meant they had all of her data. They probably couldn't access it, but then again, she'd have said they couldn't override the car's AI to ignore police commands. She had backups on an encrypted server, so nothing would be lost. But the sooner she could log in and wipe that phone, the better.

"Pulsar?" Her words were slurred, but apparently clear enough that the AI recognized its name, because the console lit up.

"I'm sorry. This vehicle is no longer functional. A repair unit has been paged. Expected arrival in forty-six minutes and seven seconds."

So, the AI *could* dial out, even with the system data purged. That was good news.

"Thanks, but I can't wait that long. Can you call me a car?"

"I'm sorry. This vehicle is no longer functional. A repair unit has been paged. Expected arrival in forty-five minutes and fifty-eight seconds."

Resigning herself to a barefoot walk to the next exit, Alice slipped off her remaining shoe and stashed it inside her bag. But even those small movements were exhausting. She fell back into the seat and took a few deep breaths.

By the time she mustered enough energy for another attempt to get out of the car, lights flashed behind her, and she heard the crunch of tires on gravel. It was far too soon to be the repair unit. It might be the police, but if so, they weren't using their bubble light or siren. A good Samaritan? Maybe. But how often did people actually stop to check out a stranded vehicle on the highway, especially in the wee hours of the morning?

Did it matter, though? She didn't even know if her legs would support her at the moment. And even if they did, she couldn't outrun a car. She couldn't even outrun someone on foot, if they had the advantage of shoes. With her options severely limited, she pulled her knees up against her stomach, hoping she could at least get in a semi-decent kick if it turned out to be another of Durav's men.

With her eyes closed to tiny slits, Alice braced herself as footsteps approached the car.

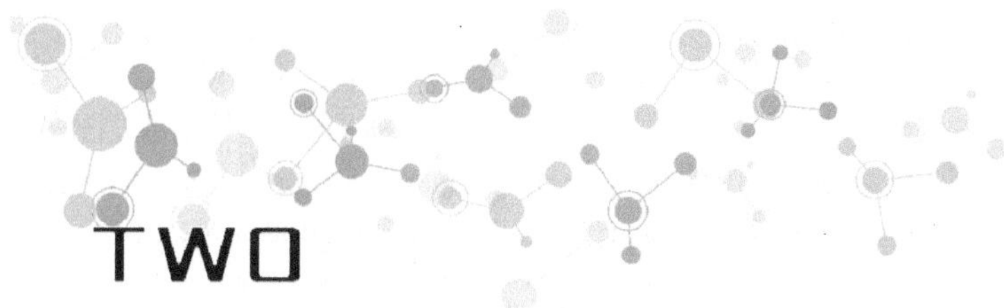

TWO

A SHADOW FELL across the rear windshield. Its owner hesitated for several seconds, then moved around to open the door.

"Alice?"

Deep voice. Definitely male. And ... she recognized it. It was the guy from the bar. Housen. She didn't move, hoping to give herself time to decide whether this was good news or bad. How the hell had he found her?

There was a touch of amusement in his voice when he spoke again. "I can tell that you're breathing, so if you're playing possum trying to decide whether you can trust me, the police are going to arrive any minute. Kind of surprised they didn't beat me here. I'd rather not deal with them. I get the feeling you'd rather avoid that, too?"

She remained perfectly still, debating her next move. But if Housen's motives were bad, he would have just grabbed her, right? He was more than a foot taller and could have overpowered her on a good day, let alone right now when her muscles felt like limp spaghetti.

"And Do'djat could come back," he said. "Where did he even go? I'm pretty sure I know somewhere you'll be safe, okay? I'd like to have checked in with Garcia or Arbet first, but my messages are either not getting through to them or they're not responding. Or ... can't respond. That's also a distinct possibility."

Do'djat was the number thirteen in Ufretan. Alice hadn't gotten a clear look at the ipret-tai who drugged her, but she now had a good idea what was tattooed on his forehead. One of the other names Housen had mentioned—Arbet—wasn't familiar at all. And Garcia was a very common surname, but he *could* mean Wyatt Garcia, who was currently on his way to Mars with Claire.

There was also the fact that the *ipret-tai* had called Housen a *foont*. That didn't necessarily make him a good guy, but it did mean he wasn't working with them and wouldn't turn her over to them. Probably.

Anyway, what choice did she have? She was going to have to trust *someone*.

"Fine." She opened her eyes and pushed herself up to a sitting position.

He exhaled visibly. "You're not hurt, are you?"

She shook her head. "My shoulder is a little stiff from what I assume was a tranquilizer gun and I twisted my ankle a bit, but I'm okay."

After one last, completely futile search inside the storage compartment behind her seat she gave up. "I need your phone."

"Now? We need to get out of here."

"*Now*." Something about her tone must have convinced him that arguing would be pointless, because he just sighed, unlocked his phone, and handed it to her.

She navigated to her server's website, entered a complex twenty-four-digit code, and stared into the screen that popped up long enough for it to confirm her identity. Then she sent another code to her phone that remotely wiped every trace of personal data along with all of the apps.

"Thanks." She returned his phone, grabbed her bag from the floorboard, and slipped her shoe back on. "I may need help getting to your car."

That prediction turned out to be accurate. Her knees buckled as soon as she tried to stand. Placing part of her weight on the foot with the shoe and the rest on Housen, she began moving toward a white Argo two-seater, the most common low-end rental model, which was parked straddling the shoulder and the breakdown lane.

Housen glanced warily around them, paying special attention to the woods on the other side of the narrow clearing.

"He's gone," she said as she slid into the car. "He took off after disabling the drone, apparently on Durav's orders. Probably realized the NYPD would send something a whole lot bigger and potentially more lethal than a fly-by drone once its signal went dead. He's heading back into the city."

Housen gave her a baffled look as he told the Argo to resume course. "How did you figure *that* out?"

She mentally kicked herself for the slip. "I ... heard part of his phone conversation. Just the one side. There were some words in another language, and I didn't understand all of it, but..."

He frowned, clearly preparing to ask another question, but she dove back in before he had a chance.

"How did you find me here? I mean, don't get me wrong. I'm *glad* you showed up. But you couldn't have followed the car from my apartment, otherwise you'd have been here ten or fifteen minutes ago. And unless you lied at the bar, you didn't know where my apartment was in the first place. Which makes me think you either had a tracker on that guy's car or..." She couldn't think of any point at which he'd touched her or been close to her bag and she had not only an app on her phone but also a standalone signal blocker in her bag. Still, it was the most obvious possibility. "Or you placed a tracker on *me*."

"Yeah." Housen gave her a sheepish look. "The pen you handed me in the bar."

She narrowed her eyes and dug around in the front pocket of her messenger bag, pulling out four different pens before she found the right one. It looked exactly like the others, aside from a minuscule silver dot on the cap that she was pretty sure hadn't been there before.

"What is this?"

"Um..." He frowned in confusion. "A tracker? Like you just said."

"No. What *brand*? What *model*? There seems to be a hole in my security, and I need to know how to patch it."

"It's ... sort of a custom build. Tracker and listening device combined. I don't have specs."

She lowered the window. He reached for her hand, but she flicked it out before he could stop her.

"I don't have another one of those. And it might have come in handy again at some point."

"Then you can go back later and hunt for it. Should be easy enough to track down since you managed to locate me."

"Fine. If it makes you feel better, I couldn't get anything at all from the listening device so maybe the hole in your security system isn't as massive as you thought."

She didn't respond. In one sense, it did make her feel better. On the other hand, an audio recording would have helped patch the gaping hole in her *memory* from the hour that she was unconscious.

"I'm sorry for tagging you," Housen said after a few minutes of silence. "But I could tell you were going to take the first opportunity to run before I even sat down. Your eyes kept going to the exits and you held one hand under the table the entire time. I assumed it was a gun, but..." He dug a taser barb out of his pocket and handed it to her. "I found this on the street. Guessing it didn't do much to stop him?"

"It did *not*. And that thing was ... supercharged. It shouldn't have just stopped him. It should have killed him."

"Not likely. Durav likes his security force extra sturdy."

"I don't suppose you by any chance found a shoe, as well? Or the taser that shot that dart?"

"Afraid not."

"I'm still a bit unclear on how you knew that guy abducted me. I drove around for quite a while before heading home."

"I know. You seemed to be a regular at the bar, so I assumed your place was nearby. I waited at the table for a bit, then realized you were gone. When the tracker showed your car headed out of the neighborhood, I thought you might have gotten smart and decided to stay elsewhere. I was pretty sure Durav would have someone waiting outside your apartment, though, and like I said before, I need to pin down their location. And I actually *didn't* know where you lived when I reached the bar. What I told you was true. I saw Durav's guy following you, and I wanted to warn you. But after you left..." He shrugged. "Let's just say I have experience getting into databases. It's kind of my business. Or *was* my business, I guess. Anyway, once it became obvious that you'd ditched me, I did a little digging around in public utility records and a few other sources until I found your address. Your *actual* address, I would note, not the one you give out when asked."

Alice pressed her lips into a tight line and stared out the window. It would have taken more than *a little digging* to dredge up that kind of information. She'd shared the apartment with her mother for about a year and a half, and even though Alice covered all of the bills now, her mom's name was still on the lease. They also left all utilities under her mom's name—and that was her mom's *new* last name, after the marriage. And as he noted, she routinely gave out the address of an apartment she'd sublet during her first few months in the city rather than her current address.

And what did he mean by saying that sort of sleuthing was his business? From what she'd gathered, members of the Watch were supposed to work on the two milestones, either in longevity research or connected to the terraforming projects. Why would they have needed someone working as a private investigator?

"I reached your place just as Do'djat was tossing you into the Pulsar," Housen continued. "Took me nearly ten minutes to page this car, so I called the police while I waited. And yes. I used fake names for both of us. I just told them that I saw someone snatching my girlfriend, so I triggered the emergency tracker"—he made air quotes around the last two words—"that she always carries. I thought they could force the AI to take one of the exits, but apparently Durav purchased some upgrades."

"Yeah. Douche Hat had an override code."

He chuckled. "It's pronounced *doo-djot*."

"I like my version better."

Housen went silent for a moment, then said, "I *get* why you left, okay? You don't have any reason to trust me. But will you at least believe me now when I tell you these people are dangerous?"

"I already believed that part."

"Then why did you go back to your apartment? You knew they were following you."

She shot him an annoyed look. "Because it's where I *live*. Because I don't have anywhere else to go."

That wasn't entirely true. But she wasn't going to endanger her mom, and it really hadn't seemed like a big enough deal to call Claire's brother. She didn't even know the guy. And, based on what Claire had said, he wasn't all that enthused about the translation project, so she wasn't sure this would be a priority for him.

"Plus, I didn't know that they—or you—had my home address. When I watched through the camera in front of the club, I saw the guy head off in the opposite direction. I've also got half a dozen microcams outside my apartment building and I ran his photo through my system. There was *no* sign of him. And yes, I know you said Durav has multiple henchmen, but they're supposed to be clones, so why..."

He raised an eyebrow. "Being cloned doesn't necessarily mean cloned from the same source."

"Yeah. I kind of figured that out on my own."

"Okay. But how did you know that *ipret-tais* are cloned? For that matter, how did you know the word *ipret-tai*?"

"That's what you called him. Back at the bar, remember?"

"I let the *word* slip. Actually, I don't even think I got the whole word out. But you recognized it. You knew what it meant. And I'm dead certain I didn't say anything about them being cloned."

THREE

ALICE DIDN'T ANSWER AT FIRST, TRYING and failing to come up with something that would explain that bit of knowledge.

"And come to think of it," Housen continued, "there's no way in hell Do'djat would have been speaking English. Not to his boss. Durav would consider that an insult of the highest order and Do'djat knows that *ipret-tai* who insult Durav don't live very long. So, why don't you just tell me who's been teaching you Ufretan?"

Maybe he was right. Maybe it was time to lay her cards—or at least some of them—on the table.

"A few weeks back, I started working with a journalist from the *Atlantic Post*. Claire Echols, the one who covered the opening of the Icarus chamber."

"Yeah. I kind of figured that out on my own." He gave her a tight smile, tossing back the same bit of snark she'd used a few minutes earlier. "In addition to your address, I uncovered a recent interview you gave the police while I was waiting in the bar. You were at the house in New Haven with Claire Echols when she found Devin Shepherd's body. But I seriously doubt that Ms. Echols speaks Ufretan."

"No, but she gave me some information she got from her friend Beck. You probably know him as Anak. He's the one who told Claire the *ipret-tai* were cloned." She actually had no idea what Beck had told Claire about the *ipret-tai*. But she wasn't sure whether Claire would want Housen to know about the Eberin Das journal or the documents from Shepherd, so she was sticking to the bare essentials, tossing in the occasional half-truth as needed. "Anyway, I've been using these notes that he gave to her along with some high-end gray-market translation software, trying to decipher the message on the walls of the Icarus chamber. I've been at it pretty much non-stop, hoping that I'll have something to report when she gets back from Mars."

Nothing in that explained how she'd be able to understand spoken Ufretan, so she wasn't too surprised that his expression was skeptical as she spoke. But his eyebrows shot up when she said the word *Mars*.

He let out a long breath, leaned his head back against the seat, and laughed softly. "I'll be damned. It actually worked. He managed to convince the son of a bitch to take them."

She frowned, confused at the sudden shift in his mood. "I ... guess? She said they were traveling with Anton Kolya, if that's who you mean."

"It is. That was the plan that Garcia and I set into motion, but I've been trying and failing to get confirmation that it worked for the past two weeks. I had ... a close call with a couple of Durav's hired hands. Mercenaries, not *ipret-tai*. Anyway, I caught a bullet in the arm when they tracked me down to my hotel. They got the phone with my contacts. Last I saw of Garcia was a few hours before that, when he was about to head into a burning building. I was a little worried that none of them made it out."

"Do you mean the fire at Claire's house in Maryland? Because she wasn't even there when—"

"No. Big fire in the Bronx."

"Oh. At the Triad's Headquarters?"

"Yeah. Exactly how much do you know about that?"

"About the fire? I vaguely remember a news story about a big fire, but I didn't know exactly where. I've been kind of preoccupied. Claire and I only had a few minutes to talk before she left. I'd messaged the night before, but she was in the middle of something. I think it was an emergency with her roommate's daughter. She was supposed to contact me with some information about our project during the trip to Mars, but I've sent her several messages over the past few weeks and so far … no response."

"Okay. But what I meant was how much do you know about the *Triad*? About the Watch."

"I know you're one of them. I know you guys had a big meeting in the Bronx a few days before Claire left. I also know about the two milestones and … I know what the Alliance plans to do now that Earth has achieved them. And I know Claire, Wyatt, and Beck are on their way to Mars in some sort of hail Mary attempt to stop it. Which you were apparently working with Wyatt on, based on what you said a few minutes back."

"Yes. Beck wasn't part of the original plan, but I'm glad to hear he made it out of the fire. Did Claire say anything about the others?"

"No. Like I said, it wasn't a long conversation."

"Okay. I just … there were reports of a lot of burned bodies in those tunnels beneath the compound and I'm wondering how many members of the Watch survived. I haven't been able to get up with any of them and … frankly, I was worried Durav had killed them all."

"How many were there?"

"Counting the *ipret-tai?* They're not all aligned with Durav," he added, in response to her expression. "Counting the *ipret-tai* that he hadn't already killed, there were around forty, including Sandjeel. He's the head of the Triad, and … well, by tradition, the head keeps his native form."

"Has that always been true?" The question was out before she even thought about it, because she didn't recall reading anything like that in the Eberin Das journal. But if Housen thought it was a weird question, he didn't let on.

"I think so? Anyway, if his bones were found in that tunnel, let's just say there are going to be some interesting tales circulating among the NYC first responders."

They both fell silent for a moment, and then she asked, "Where exactly are we going?"

"Not sure. But not back to NYC. Your place isn't safe right now."

"No," she agreed. "I'm not even sure I could get in. My handprint didn't open the door, and that's never happened before, so I'm thinking they've tampered with the building's security system. And Do'djat was definitely going back to the city." She frowned, trying to think of the Ufretan word for fourteen. "I'm guessing the one who was hanging around outside the club is named Ren'djat, judging from the tattoo above his eye?" When Housen nodded, she continued, "Durav ordered him to go back and help Ren'djat look for you. He called you a *foont*, by the way."

"Coming from them, that's a badge of honor. And they're a bit slow on the uptake. I've been a *foont* to the Alliance for about eight decades now."

Housen's words weren't as eloquent as the ones that Alice had translated from Eberin Das's journal, but the sentiment was the same. And the guy clearly meant it. His jaw was clenched so tight that she was afraid he'd break a tooth.

"So, if we're not going back to New York, where *are* we going?"

He shook his head. "Right now, we're just headed toward I-95. I haven't decided whether to go north or south. My funds are a bit limited at the moment, but I have friends in either direction who could put us up for the week, maybe longer. They're ... um ... working farms, so the accommodations won't be much. But they'll have beds, food, and enough weapons to keep us safe if Durav's people track us down again."

"Weapons? What kind of farm..." She shook her head when she made the connection. "The Flock? Seriously?"

He chuckled. "They're not *all* crazy. And they're on our side in this battle."

Alice sighed. Her time with Mitchell Morris had left her with a deep and abiding distrust of organized religion. Not small groups, so much, but the megachurches. And while the Flock might not be a religion in the traditional sense, they checked all of the boxes that set her teeth on edge—charismatic leader, thousands of fanatical followers, and a tenuous relationship with reality. But apparently, she didn't have many options right now, so…

"Fine," she said. "But I'm not staying anywhere for a week."

"Like I said, it could be longer."

"Not for me. I'll lose my frickin job if I miss classes for that long. We're a tiny department and we're already down one professor after Leffler's death. If I'm not there, Josh is going to have to handle everything on his own."

"Doesn't that make it *less* likely he'll fire you?"

"Nope. It will take a few days for him to line things up, but there are plenty of recent Ph.D.'s adjuncting at three or four different schools in order to make ends meet. Any of them will be more than happy to take my place."

She wondered for a moment if that would be true if they knew that the job carried the risk of death by nanodrone or abduction by alien zombies. For that matter … was Josh at risk now? He'd had nothing to do with the Icarus images, but he was chair of the department, and he had two small children. She felt like she should warn him but couldn't think of anything she could say that wouldn't leave him thinking she'd gone completely insane. At a bare minimum, though, she had to let him know someone would need to cover her classes—and the classes she was covering for Holly—for the next few days.

She borrowed Housen's phone again, logged into her university email, and made up a lie about a health crisis with her mom, something that she hated doing because it felt like she was opening a karmic door to bad luck. But Josh knew that she had precisely one close family member, so there was nothing else he'd even begin to believe.

After hitting send, she skimmed through the student emails that had come in after class to see if there was anything urgent. Her eyes landed on the one with the viral video. *Bigfoot in Boston Burbs?* According to the text, the video had been captured by a drone in a ritzy enclave called Everly Estates, about a half hour north of Boston. The house—in fact, the entire neighborhood—was owned by Jonas Labs. Curious, she clicked on the link and watched for a moment with the sound muted.

“We're coming up on I95,” Housen said, as the video neared the end. "If we go south, we're heading to the Flock compound in Virginia. North will be the one in Vermont. Do you have a preference or…?”

“We should definitely go north. Although…” She handed him back his phone and pointed at the screen, where she had paused the video. “If this is who I think it is, we may not need to bother your friends in the Flock.”

TALES FROM THE AVEEZI FOREST

THE THANKLESS CHILDREN OF MOTHER UFRET

Translation by Nathaniel Everett

AS EVEN THE smallest child knows, the Aveezi Forest is a place that you should never, ever go. Dark and wild, the forest teems with creatures that snap and snarl. They will happily gobble up any youngling so foolish as to enter.

But even in the Aveezi Forest, light and dark must find a balance. Deep, deep inside the forest—where, I must again caution, you should never, ever go—there is a wide glade called Alestria, where gloom and danger may not tread. Here, the trees hang lush with ripe babda and usimi fruits, the waters flow sweet and cool, and the wind hums a soothing song. Here, the suns shine brightly in the daytime, the sky shimmers emerald and violet as they set, and the creatures live (mostly) in harmony.

It is here in lovely Alestria, on an early spring evening, that we find Motz and Tibbo—the very best of best friends—lying on their backs and staring up at the night sky. Their teacher, Ossa, is next to their lantern, his long neck craned over a map of the stars.

"Who wants to go first?" he asked.

Tibbo scanned the sky, hunting for Greila. It was his very favorite of all the constellations, because it reminded him of a starsprite's wings. But that part of the sky was covered by dark clouds, so he had to keep looking.

"I see Narsa!" Tibbo said, pointing his tiny finger toward a cluster of stars. "See? It's the one with a curlicue at the end, like a tail. And right next to it is D'jar—"

"Don't be greedy!" Ossa said. "It's Motz's turn."

"Sorry."

"I see..." Motz raised a furry blue arm and squinted up at the sky for a long time. "I see D'jar...at. It's shaped like a ... like an usimi tree."

"It's pronounced *D'jareeshi,*" Ossa corrected. "And I suppose it does look a little bit like an usimi tree, now that you mention it."

Tibbo frowned. D'jareeshi was the one he'd started to say. It was the constellation just to the right of Narsa and it looked nothing at all like the wide drooping branches of the usimi tree. It looked more like the pail they used to gather wesselberries. The constellation that *did* look like an usimi tree—sort of—was Trexal, which sat on the *other* side of Narsa. It was very clear that Trexal was the one Motz had meant, and equally clear that she didn't study the star map that Ossa gave them the day before. If he'd been here alone with her, he would have pointed this out. But that would also have meant correcting Ossa, which would be very rude. So, he held his tongue.

It was Tibbo's turn again. After a quick search, he located Sisara, the tiniest, faintest figure in the spring sky. He told them it reminded him of a square popkin, with a single drop of jam hanging from one corner.

"I'm hungry," Motz said. "Can we have our snack now?"

"Not yet," Ossa told her. "You haven't had your second turn."

Motz thought for a few seconds, then said "I see ... Ufret!" and pointed to the biggest, brightest star in the sky.

"Very good, Motz!"

Tibbo tried hard to bite his tongue. But it was no use. "That's not a constellation! It's just *one* star. And you've known it for years. You could probably have found it when you were in nursery."

Ossa made a gentle tutting sound. "Oh, Tibbo ... why do you dismiss Ufret so quickly? She is the mother of all worlds. And she is *part* of a constellation. Does she not deserve recognition?"

"Well, sure, but..."

"Tell us the story, Ossa!" Motz clapped her hands gleefully. "I *love* the story. Tibbo does, too, don't you?"

Tibbo would really have preferred to keep looking for constellations. He'd studied the map so carefully, hoping Ossa would be happy. There were many, many things he couldn't do as well as Motz simply because he was tiny, but this was one task where size didn't matter.

And they'd heard the story of Mother Ufret *so many times*. Even the youngest children in the village knew that story by heart.

Tibbo smiled and nodded anyway. Maybe if he was good and he kept from doing anything else that annoyed him, Ossa would bring them back to look for stars another night. Maybe then the clouds wouldn't be blotting out his favorite constellation.

Ossa sighed and squinted down at the two of them. "No, Motz. You are too old for that story."

Motz's blue shoulders drooped, and Tibbo did his best to look disappointed, too. He didn't like to see his friend unhappy.

"But," Ossa said, "the story doesn't end there, you know. And you're younglings now. Perhaps you're old enough to learn what happened *next*."

Aware that he now had their full attention, Ossa continued. "As you know, Mother Ufret had many, many children. She had a thousand fingers and a thousand toes, and there were more children than she could count on all her thousands of hands and feet. Her children were bright and eager, but as they became younglings, they were too bright and too willful to contain to one area of the sky."

Motz nodded eagerly. This was the part of the story they

already knew by heart. "So, she sent them out to light the worlds. To show night travelers the way."

"Correct! But don't forget that many of her children are like our two suns—they help the crops to grow on the worlds that spin around them. And those crops give us life, so we too are the progeny of Mother Ufret. All she asks is that her offspring show her the proper respect." With this, Ossa cast a reproachful look in Tibbo's direction, making him feel even smaller than usual. "As you know, Mother Ufret has only *one* rule."

Motz nodded again. "We must save a portion of our harvest for her, so that she may continue to shine."

"Indeed. And now we have reached the *next* part of the story, the one that I believe you are now old enough to understand. Some of Ufret's star children—like our own two suns—showed respect. They stayed close, casting their light on the nearby worlds that gave their mother her due. Others, however, strayed too far. They left our galaxy and wandered into dark and twisted corners of the universe. Soon, they became dark and twisted themselves, like the creatures in and beyond the Aveezi Forest."

Tibbo shuddered, glancing toward the dark rim of trees at the edge of the fields.

"They forgot the mother to whom they owed their very existence," Ossa said. "Worse still, they cast their light on strange worlds that reserved no tribute for Mother Ufret. This made her sad. It also worried her, because she knew that the day would come when there was not enough light to feed all of these worlds. When that happened, she feared that her errant children would then turn on the others, and the fields of her loyal offspring would wither and die. So, she called her faithful children to her side. She commanded them to go forth and slay the worlds of their wicked siblings. And so, they did."

Tibbo frowned as he stared upward. Even with the big cloud covering more than half of the sky there were still far more stars than he could count.

"But why?" he asked. "We have *so* many stars. And you've

said that there are even more that we cannot see, and many worlds spinning around each of them. And each world has many lands, and each land has many villages like our own, and many fields of *sperza* and *usimi*. Isn't there enough to share?"

Motz nodded. "I know. It's so sad—"

"You're missing the point!" Ossa snapped.

"That's what I was going to tell him," Motz said. "It's *so sad* that he doesn't get the point."

"I agree," Ossa said. "Why don't you explain it to him?"

There was a very long pause as Motz thought. You could practically hear the gears grinding inside her big blue head.

"I got the point!" Tibbo said, sparing her the effort. "But you always tell us to compromise and share. I think what they did was cruel."

Ossa and Motz's eyes widened in shock that he would question the wisdom of Mother Ufret. And almost instantly, a cold rain began to fall. Tibbo looked up to see that clouds now blocked nearly all of the sky.

The lantern went out with a hiss. Ossa tucked the star map under his cloak and told Motz to grab the picnic basket. Normally, she would have crouched down and waited for Tibbo to scramble up onto her shoulder, but she took off after Ossa, leaving him to make his way back to the cabin in the dark and on his own. The cold rain was now tiny pellets of ice, which would not bother Motz with her thick blue coat or Ossa with his hooded cloak. But Tibbo's orange fur was much thinner. Every shard of ice felt like a needle against his skin.

When at last he arrived at Ossa's cottage, wet and shivering, the door was closed. He knocked, and for a frightful moment Tibbo was certain that they would not let him in. But then the door opened.

"Come in, Tibbo." Ossa's eyes were filled with disappointment. He waited for Tibbo to dry off and then pointed him toward the fire, where Motz was finishing off the last popkin in their basket. Normally, Tibbo would have been annoyed that she had saved nothing for him, but he wasn't all that hungry now. And maybe he didn't deserve a snack.

Ossa stood near the window, looking out at the storm. "Mother Ufret seems very angry tonight. I do hope the sleet won't damage the spring usimi harvest. They're so fragile this early in the season."

"I'm sorry, Ossa."

"No, no, Tibbo. It is not your fault. I mean, yes, I suspect that you *did* call down the storm with your disrespectful comments."

Tibbo nodded, even though he couldn't help remembering how the large cloud had blotted out part of the sky when they first arrived, long before he spoke out. But maybe Mother Ufret had *known* that he was going to say something awful.

"The real fault," Ossa continued, "is my own. My pride in my skill as a teacher led to my failure. I thought that I had prepared you well enough and taught you enough that you could understand the full story, but it's clear that I should have waited a few more cycles until you were ready. The one you owe an apology to —I suppose both of us do, really—is poor Motz. She played no role at all in bringing down the storm, and yet she also had to run through the freezing rain."

"I'm sorry, Motz." But when Tibbo turned toward her, Motz was curled up on her side, already sound asleep.

"That's okay," Ossa said. "You can apologize tomorrow, before you and I take an extra shift in the usimi orchard as penance. For now, can you tell me what you learned this evening? What are the two most important rules of our society? The first is..."

"Always pay our respects to Mother Ufret," Tibbo said, hanging his head in shame.

"And the second?"

"Never ever go into the Aveezi Forest."

FOUR

Wednesday, October 4
Near Hyblaeus Catena

THE SHUTTLE'S frame shrieked and groaned as it slammed sideways into the surface of the planet, bouncing once, twice. Claire's teeth clacked together, slicing into the edge of her tongue, filling her mouth with the coppery tang of blood. A brief flash of light from the viewport flooded the cabin, and then it was dark.

When the craft finally came to a stop, everything was eerily silent. Her head and legs felt unusually heavy, and at first, she wasn't sure why. She tentatively moved her limbs and realized that she was suspended midair. The shuttle had apparently landed on its side, leaving her dangling by her harness from what was now the ceiling. At some point her head had been yanked sharply enough that the control panel of her helmet was already activated. She scanned the readings, relieved to see that all of the lights were a steady green.

But what about the others? It was well after sunset now, and only the barest hint of light came in through the viewport. She squinted into the darkened shuttle and tried to make out their location.

"Macek? Kolya?"

No response.

She tried and failed to remember the wake word Kolya had used for the shuttle's AI. If he'd even used one. Come to think of it, he'd just started tapping something into the console.

"Computer?"

No response. And the cabin was completely dark.

She did her best to tamp down a rising wave of panic. *Deep breaths. You have your phone. It was working a moment ago when the messages came in. You can call for help.*

Call who, though? She seriously doubted that the local emergency number was 911. And did she still have a signal? It hadn't been long since they passed Elysia, but the shuttle was moving fast, and she had no idea how far the range extended.

She was about to reach for her phone to check when one of the shadows shifted on what was now the floor, almost directly beneath her. That had to be Macek.

"Macek? Can you hear me?"

Still no response. He hadn't activated his communications yet. Or maybe his comm system was broken. That would be a major complication. But at least he was alive.

She was less certain about Kolya, though. Her eyes had now adjusted a bit, and she could see that the front half of the shuttle was mangled out of shape. A long thin ceiling panel that was loose on one end partially blocked her view. She could see part of the captain's seat, though. It had originally been close to the front, positioned in the middle of the craft. Now it was seriously off-center, closer to Macek's side of the shuttle and wedged beneath a section of the console.

Macek was attempting to stand now, and the shuttle rocked slightly as he tried to find his footing. Once he was up and his shadowed form was distinct from the chair and other debris, she could see that he was clutching one arm to his side.

"Kolya?" he called out. "Claire? Are you injured?"

Her relief at hearing Macek's voice was tempered by a flashback to the last time she'd been on this planet, trapped inside a twisted hunk of metal at Icarus. His voice was the one that she'd heard through her helmet then, as well, as she fought to keep Laura Brodnik alive. That eerie sense of déjà vu was amplified by the fact that Kolya remained still and silent.

"I'm okay," Claire told him. "My readings are green. How about you?"

"I'm good, aside from shoulder. I think maybe is dislocated. Stay put while I check on Kolya." Macek's accent was more pronounced than usual, probably from pain, shock, or both.

As for staying put, Claire didn't really have a choice. She was only about three meters off the ground, but if she unhooked the harness from her current position, she'd land right on top of Kolya.

She reached into the external pocket, relieved to find that she'd remembered to seal it. Otherwise, her phone would almost certainly have fallen out. "Is there some sort of Martian emergency number I can call?"

"Out this far?" Macek gave a harsh laugh. "You would be yelling into void. Elysia is closest, but they will already have seen the ship's emergency signal. They will send help. I need to check on Kolya. Can't pull up the AI to turn on the lights. Can you point your phone's light toward the front?"

Claire pulled out the phone and turned the light to max. She followed Macek with the beam as he inched forward. He was clearly in a great deal of pain. When he reached Kolya, there was a long silence, then he muttered something in Russian.

"Is he okay?" Claire asked.

"He's alive. Not so sure he's okay, though. I think ... maybe we should not move him until the medic is here. Lucky he's in hardshell suit. Otherwise, it would be worse."

"How long do you think they'll be?"

"Not sure. Depends on how far we are from Elysia. How quick they respond. Maybe ... an hour. Maybe more. Afraid you're stuck up there for a while."

"I'm fine." It was true. Her neck wasn't *entirely* happy with the position, but the lower Martian gravity kept it from being too uncomfortable. "Are you *sure* the emergency flare went up even though our external comms were down?"

"I am sure. When we first hit the surface. Didn't you see the bright …" Macek made an odd squeaking sound when he pulled in a breath. "Bright flash of light. There are monitors at Elysia. They'll pick it up. They'll send … help." He slipped down to a seated position as he spoke, now fully in the shadows.

"Macek? Are you okay?"

"Yes. Just my shoulder. I need to relax. Five, maybe ten minutes. Long enough so I can try to put it back into socket. *Do not watch me.*"

"But … you just said that a medic is coming. Shouldn't you wait…" She didn't bother finishing the question. Macek's comms light inside her visor had already gone dark.

Since he clearly wanted privacy, she focused on her phone. She could check the messages that Wyatt sent and, if by some miracle she still had a connection, respond so that he'd at least know she was alive. For now. And maybe they could alert someone at Elysia or Nepenthes. Because while she *had* seen the bright flash of light when they landed, she wasn't nearly as sure as Macek that anyone else had seen it. Of course, she knew far less than he did about Martian emergency procedures.

Her phone didn't have a connection, but she spent the next few minutes going through the messages that had come in from Wyatt before the crash. He and Beck had not, of course, stolen the *V1*. The only surprise was that the main suspect appeared to be Durav. Wyatt and Beck were onboard the *V2* with Paul and Stasia, headed not for Nepenthes, but for Daedalus City, exactly as Kolya had planned.

She felt a momentary pang of guilt for being pissed at the man when he was quite possibly dying a few meters below her, but she pushed it away. There was no getting around the fact that Kolya was an ass. And his unsufferable ego was partly to blame for their current predicament. She would not wish him dead. But an injury serious enough to sideline him? To keep him from accompanying her to Nepenthes? Given how much was at risk, she could wish for that with a crystal-clear conscience.

Macek's comms light flashed back on. "Do not *record* me, either."

"What…? Oh." She glanced back down at her phone. The thought hadn't even occurred to her, although it probably *would* be excellent blackmail material should she ever need it. "I'm not *recording* you. This is me giving you the privacy that you requested. If I'm reading my messages, I won't be paying attention to you. But I still think you should wait for the … medics."

His comms light was out before she could finish. Fine. He was a grown man and if he was determined to torture himself, there wasn't much she could do to stop him.

That's when it dawned on her that Macek was lying. Not maliciously. More likely, he was just laying on a bit of false bravado for her benefit. He actually *wasn't* certain that Elysia would pick up their emergency flare. And if they really were out here on their own, he wanted to have two functional arms as soon as possible.

She knew exactly when Macek tried to put his arm back into the socket. He was a large man with a deep, booming voice, but the shriek he emitted reminded her of the time her dad had stepped on the tail of her grandmother's ancient cocker spaniel.

It only lasted a second, though, and then everything was quiet again.

Completely quiet. There was no movement at all from the corner of the shuttle.

Claire kept her eyes fixed on her phone. It was sheer pretense, though. She couldn't concentrate and the words seemed to float in front of her. All of her focus was on the huddled form below that she could barely distinguish from the shadows.

She waited a full minute, then called out Macek's name. No response.

He must have fainted. Popping his own shoulder back into place was a bad idea, but it couldn't have killed him, right?

Unless he had a heart attack. Or a stroke. He was Kolya's age, late forties or early fifties, and looked like he was in good health, so it wasn't likely. But it also wasn't impossible.

No. Macek would wake up in a few minutes and be highly embarrassed about the fact that he'd passed out. He was okay.

Only … he was in one of the fabric suits. What if it had been torn, either in the crash or from rubbing against the debris while he contorted himself trying to pop his shoulder back into the socket?

Her mind kept ricocheting back and forth between these possibilities. And there wasn't a damned thing she could do as long as she was dangling in midair like a fly that some spider had wrapped up and saved for its midnight snack.

Maybe this is where all the bug monsters are hiding, Claire.

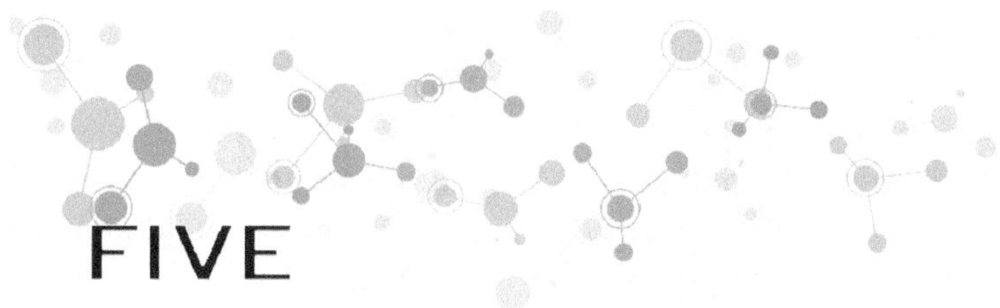

FIVE

"MACEK?" Claire raised her voice on the second syllable, making it almost a scream, hoping the higher pitch would carry her words through the thinner atmosphere. But there was still no response.

She turned on her phone light and pointed it at him. If he was conscious, that should get a response.

Still nothing, but the middle seat between them cast a shadow. The only thing she could see clearly was one of his legs and his other arm. Neither of them were moving.

Even though her options for helping him were fairly limited, she needed to get down there. The shuttle must have an emergency medical kit somewhere on board, but she had no idea where it would be or if she could even get to it in the rubble. Still, she could do chest compressions, right? And if he wasn't getting oxygen, they could share hers. It would be wicked cold without the helmet, but the surface was well above the Armstrong limit now, so at least her body fluids wouldn't boil away. She might not be able to do anything for Kolya, but if Macek was injured, she had to at least try to help. He could be a pain in the ass, but she'd developed a certain respect for the man, even as her respect for Kolya had nosedived.

The real question was whether she could get down without further injury to Kolya. Or herself, for that matter, since she really couldn't afford to aggravate her leg injury again. The harness holding her in place was made of thick straps of fabric and two buckles—one at her chest and the other at her waist. She wrapped one of the shoulder straps around her left wrist a few times, then unfastened the lower buckle, freeing her legs. Once she unsnapped the shoulder restraint and extended her body, it would be a fairly easy drop to the surface. The only hitch was that Kolya would be almost directly beneath her feet. If she could swing about half a meter to the right, though, she could grab the harness on the empty seat between her and Macek. The straps were too wide and stiff for her to get a good grip, especially with the gloves, and the fabric had absolutely no give. With the clunkiness of the hardshell suit, she figured there was at least a twenty percent chance that she'd misjudge the distance. Or she'd slip, in which case she'd likely land smack on top of Kolya. But her odds of success—and their odds of survival—weren't going to get better by putting it off.

She gripped the strap as best she could, then unfastened the second buckle to free herself from the shoulder harness. As soon as she was perpendicular to the ground, she began to swing gently back and forth. Once she'd built up enough momentum, she sent up a prayer that she hadn't miscalculated and then let go.

Her aim was off, and she missed the harness on the middle seat. In the end it didn't matter, though. Her right boot came down a few centimeters from the dangling ceiling panel. Landing only on her right foot was an intentional choice aimed at sparing her weaker leg, but it put her slightly off balance. She shifted her weight as soon as the other foot was down and narrowly avoided falling onto the console Kolya was pinned beneath. As much as she wanted to congratulate herself for that last minute save, she knew there was no way she would have pulled it off under Earth's gravity.

She ducked under the ceiling panel, which she could now see was actually loose at both ends, with the other edge propped up on a partition near the back of the shuttle. Once she was on the other side, she had a clear view of Macek. The awkward slant of his right shoulder suggested that his attempt to pop it back into place had failed, but his chest rose and fell in a steady rhythm. He was alive, he was breathing, and as best she could tell, there was no damage to his biosuit. Those were the only things she could check without removing his helmet so they would have to do for now.

Moving cautiously across the uneven surface, she worked her way a few meters over to Kolya. Much of his torso was hidden under the console, but the hardshell suit would probably have made it difficult to tell whether he was breathing normally anyway. She crouched down and aimed her phone light directly into the visor of his helmet. A moment later, his nostrils flared. It even looked like he squinted slightly at the unexpected glare, but she couldn't be certain.

She now understood what Macek had meant by it being a good thing that he was wearing the hardshell suit. The console probably wasn't *too* heavy, especially given the lower gravity. She might even be able to move it on her own. But as long as Kolya was breathing, it was probably safer to wait.

Claire felt a movement behind her a second before Macek's comms indicator lit up inside her visor.

"You said … you would stay … put."

"Yeah, well, that was before you passed out on me."

Claire thought that he'd deny it, but he just grunted. She went back over to his corner and carefully sat down across from him on the arm of one of the toppled seats.

"Kolya is still breathing?"

"Yeah. Thought I detected some eye movement, too."

"Good. I thought my shoulder was just dislocated, like one time a few years back. Now I'm thinking maybe something is broken."

"That's not good news."

"No kidding, Dr. Echols."

She chuckled at the sarcasm in his voice. "Exactly *how* not good depends on whether you were telling the truth earlier. How likely is it that Elysia picked up our emergency signal?"

Macek was quiet for several seconds. "I *was* telling the truth, but it is possible I was too … optimistic. As I was trying to relax enough to fix my shoulder it occurred to me that we are still in lockdown. So, there is no regular traffic. Will anyone be monitoring the logs?" He started to shrug, then sucked in a sharp breath at the movement.

Claire looked away, giving him a modicum of privacy to work through the pain. When he was breathing normally again, she pushed a bit further. "But … they have an automated system, right?"

"Sure. But everyone is inside the pods. The station is outside. Normally, people would be there to monitor but during lockdown? They're probably not manned. Nepenthes wouldn't even be manned except they are expecting us. Same for Daedalus. Maybe Elysia has an alarm that goes off, that notifies someone inside the pods. I don't know. I am no longer a regular visitor there."

Something about his tone suggested there was an interesting story behind that, but she didn't want to get distracted. "If they *did* get a notification, how long would it be before they arrive?"

"Depends on exactly where we are. I could check on my phone, but you would need to find it first." He waved his hand to indicate the rubble, making as small a movement as possible.

"Could you use mine?"

"Do you have a signal?"

"No."

"Then not unless your phone is already set to Martian GPS."

He had to know that it wasn't, so she didn't even bother to respond. Instead, she began combing through the debris on the floor. It took several minutes, but she eventually located the phone near the front of the shuttle, wedged beneath a crumpled panel from the console that was partially on top of Kolya. She stopped to check on him—still breathing—and then took the phone back to Macek.

"Okay." He held the phone in his right hand as he scrolled through with his left. "We are roughly four hundred fifty kilometers from Elysia."

"How far are we from Nepenthes Station?" she asked. "Like you said, they're expecting us, so maybe—"

"Closer to fourteen hundred klicks. Probably outside their range, although Kolya would know better on that. I also don't know how close we were to the flight plan, given that he was fighting for control during those last few minutes."

"And there's nothing between here and Elysia?"

"Nothing occupied. We are only a few klicks from the Hyblaeus Catena mining camp, but the crew is housed at Lyot for lockdown. No one..." He stopped, raising his eyebrows slightly.

"What?"

"No one is *there* now," Macek continued, "but communications equipment will be. If help does not come, I could walk to Hyblaeus and send a signal. But we should probably wait. It would be safer to..." He glanced at Kolya and then surveyed the rest of the shuttle.

"*What?*" she asked once again, since it was clear that something new was worrying him.

He sighed. "It would be *safer* to wait until morning. We're currently on the ship's life support. Even without the engines running, we should have ten, maybe even twelve hours. *If* the CO_2 scrubber is still working. Also, if the hull is not seriously damaged."

"That's two separate *ifs*," she said. "And considering the condition of the inside of this shuttle, I'd say the odds of the outside being undamaged are not good."

"Agreed. I will go check the scrubber now." He started to stand, clenching his jaw against the pain.

"No. I'll check. You can talk me through it. *After* I find the med kit. You need something for pain. And we should try to immobilize that shoulder."

Macek clearly wanted to argue. But he was hurting too much to make it convincing. He slumped back against the wall—the wall that used to be the floor—and took a few deep breaths.

"Okay. You win. Kit should be behind a hatch near the door. Port side. Easy to spot. A red cross on the front."

She frowned, trying to orient herself. In their current situation, with the shuttle tipped on itself, *port* and *starboard* meant *down* and *up*. The good news was that she wouldn't have to climb up to the ceiling to locate the medical kit. The bad news, though, was that she was pretty sure the only way out of the shuttle was through the starboard door, which was at least five meters above her head. There was no way Macek could make that climb. Which meant that if help didn't come on its own, *she* would be the one hiking out to the mining camp.

SIX

CLAIRE'S SEARCH for the med kit took a bit longer than Macek had suggested, but she eventually located it under something that looked like a large translucent platter. It had apparently fallen off one of the ceiling lights, which ratcheted her worry about the hull integrity up a few more notches.

Macek popped a couple of pain pills and washed them down with one of the water pouches she found in the hatch with the med kit. Luckily, the pills were small enough to fit through the same hole as the straw, so there was no need to remove his helmet. Immobilizing his shoulder was a process punctuated by many words that were almost certainly profane, some of them clearly aimed at her. They were all in Russian, though, so it was hard to take offense.

"Okay," she said, when they had his arm in something resembling a sling. "Where is this scrubber located?"

"Other end of shuttle. Around bulkhead."

The shuttle was small enough that she could see the bulkhead easily. It didn't seem to have taken any damage, aside from being slightly dented inward where the edge of the ceiling panel had landed. As she neared the back of the shuttle, she had a better view. When the ship was in its usual upright position, the wall spanned the middle two-thirds, with an opening of about a meter so that you could walk around it from either side. She was very glad for this design decision with the ship tipped over, because it meant she could go *under* the wall instead of being forced to climb up that loose ceiling panel and drop down to the other side. As she crawled under the opening, however, the dent in the bulkhead flashed through her mind along with several unsettling questions. How heavy was the panel currently resting on top of the wall? How much extra weight could it hold? This was followed by a lovely mental image of the bulkhead crumpling and coming down like the blade of a guillotine to slice her in half.

When she reached the other side—still in one piece—she found that there were two doors. The handle to the first one, which had no sign, was about chest high. The handle to the second door was a good meter above her head with a sign reading *Employees Only.*

"Which door is it?" she asked, even though she was pretty sure she knew.

"The one with the sign," Macek said.

There was absolutely nothing to climb on, so she went back underneath the bulkhead that might turn into a guillotine and dragged a chunk of debris back with her. Then she climbed on top, bracing herself against the wall. She had to stand on tiptoe, but on the second try, her fingers latched onto the handle. The door swung back toward her with more force than she'd anticipated, and she jerked backward to avoid it hitting her. She pinwheeled her arms in a futile effort to keep her balance but wound up on her ass, smacking her helmet against the bulkhead.

"What was that?" Macek said.

"Nothing. I'm fine. What next?"

"There'll be a panel on the device just inside the door. Bunch of readings. One will be labeled something like *power utilization*. It may be abbreviated. Just tell me what it says."

She'd barely been able to open that door. There was no way she could see inside.

"Hold on. I'm going to have to find something else to climb on."

"The other door is a storage compartment. Some boxes are inside with supplies that we're taking to the lab."

"That would have been nice to know earlier," she grumbled, as she opened the lower door and spotted four large crates. They were all tipped onto their side, which might be a problem for the contents given that the arrow marked *UP* now pointed to the left.

She hauled three of the crates out, turned them so that the arrow pointed in the proper direction, and used them to create a crude set of steps. Then she climbed up to peer inside the open doorway. Now that she was closer, she could hear a faint rumble from what she assumed was the backup generator Macek had mentioned. It was located on what should have been one wall of the closet but was now the bottom. There was no visible panel on that side, just a flat metal housing, so she leaned into the opening and looked up.

"KT-03A CO_2 Scrubber Control?"

"That's it," Macek said. "Give me the CO_2 reading."

She squinted up at the dimly lit display. "CO_2 is at point four eight."

"Okay. Should be at point four but could be normal fluctuation. What about the flow rate?"

"I only see *oxygen* and *humidity*."

"What are those at?"

"Oxygen is twenty point eight. Humidity at eighteen percent."

Macek didn't comment on those numbers, but he didn't need to. Both had a flashing yellow light next to them.

"Scroll down," he said. "The flow rate should be on the next screen."

"Hold on. I can't reach the display. I'll have to crawl inside."

Claire hoisted herself up and into the closet, then lay down with her back against the metal casing. It was slightly warm to the touch, even through the gloves, but the hardshell suit was thick enough that it wasn't uncomfortable.

She scrolled down past readings for temperature and pressure. "Got it. The flow rate is eighteen point four liters per minute. Which is one point six meters above nominal according to the readout."

He went quiet for a moment, and she heard only his breathing. "Pressure differential? That should be the reading just below."

"Point eight kPa. Oh … wait. It just changed to point nine."

"Can you check the first screen again?"

"Sure." She scrolled back up to the first screen. "CO_2 is point four nine, now. Oxygen is twenty point seven. Humidity holding at eighteen."

Macek mumbled something in Russian, then said, "You should get back here."

She left the boxes where they were, slid back under the bulkhead, and returned to the front of the shuttle.

"Any chance it could just be a problem with the scrubber?"

"No. We have a leak. It may not be severe, but … I don't think we can risk waiting until morning."

"Won't Nepenthes send someone out to search? I mean, we should have been there … what? Thirty minutes ago?"

"About that, yeah. But … it's lockdown. KTI is in charge of Nepenthes Station. Only three KTI people are authorized to send out a ship during lockdown. Two are on this shuttle. One is at Daedalus. It will take time to get in touch with her. When they inform Dr. Monroe she will say to hell with the chain of command and authorize a search on her own and no one at the station will have the nerve to tell her no. But we're about ninety kilometers north of the path Kolya submitted in the flight plan. Finding us will take time and…"

"And we don't have a lot of that."

"We do *not*. I'm also beginning to worry about how long Kolya has been unconscious. If no one arrives in the next few minutes, I think we need to assume the emergency signal went unnoticed."

"Am I correct in assuming that the only door is up there?" She tilted her head in the general direction of the hatch through which she and Kolya had entered at Ares Station.

"That's the only useable door, yes. Assuming we could open the other one, you'd see only dirt and rock on the other side. I don't think we have time to tunnel out. I've been examining our options while you were off exploring, and the only way I can see to reach the working door is to crawl up that ceiling panel. Which may not hold, and even if it does, it doesn't line up directly with the hatch." He held up a hand. "Yes, yes, before you even start, I *know*. There's no way I can make it. Not with my shoulder like this. And even if I wasn't injured, I'm nearly twice your weight and we don't know if the panel would hold me. So … how do you feel about taking an evening stroll?"

SEVEN

FIFTEEN MINUTES LATER, Claire stepped off of the panel, perched cautiously atop the bulkhead, and aimed her phone light at the shuttle wall about half a meter above her head. It took a bit of searching but she finally made out the seam of the hatch.

"How far is it?" Macek's voice was tight and slightly out of breath. He was currently on his back inside the engine room, with only his feet sticking out, ready to hit the manual control to open the hatch on her signal. Getting into that position with just one good arm had been a slow endeavor. A painful one, too, even after the medication. He'd turned off his comms until he was in place, but she'd been close enough to pick up his muffled moans. On the positive front, he hadn't fainted again.

"It's ... doable," she told him, hoping it wasn't a lie.

"Just imagine you are back in ballet class. Stand on your toes and make a small leap into the air."

She laughed nervously. "Hate to shatter your stereotype of little rich girls, but I never took ballet. Or gymnastics. And I don't think my piano skills are going to be much help."

It really *wasn't* that big of a jump, though. Only a matter of inches above her fingers if she could stand on tiptoe, which unfortunately wasn't an option in the stiff boots. The problem—and it was a major one—was that the edge of the hatch wasn't directly above her. That meant she'd need to jump at an angle to grab the rim. If she missed, she'd *probably* land back on the ceiling panel and would *probably* be okay to try again. There was no guarantee, however—even if she landed in the right spot, the panel had creaked ominously several times on the way up, and she thought there was a good chance that it would break under impact. Either way, any error would increase the time that the hatch would be open, venting breathable air from the shuttle. Unless…

"Can you open the door only *part* way? That way I can jump straight up. Assuming the door is sturdy enough. We need to be sure the seal will still be okay when you close it."

He snorted. "That door held while entering the atmosphere. I think it can hold you. Only problem is you will have to tell me exactly when to stop. I can see nothing inside this coffin."

She shuddered at his word choice, although he wasn't wrong. The engine room was a glorified closet. It might not have been too bad when the ship was upright, and you could just walk out, but when you had to lay down inside it to reach the panels it was claustrophobia-inducing even for her and Macek was much larger.

"Okay," he said. "I'm ready. Just say *go*."

"Yeah. Give me a sec." She took several deep breaths, keeping her eyes on the spot where she needed the ledge of the door to be. "Okay. Go."

As soon as the hatch began to move, an alarm pierced the air. It was the first alarm she'd heard since the shuttle crashed and it nearly threw her off balance. But she kept her eyes on the hatch. When the edge of the door came into view, she yelled, *"Stop!"*

After a quick check to make sure the gap was wide enough to accommodate the suit, she raised her arms above her head. Then she bent her knees and jumped.

It went better than she'd anticipated. She cleared the top of the shuttle easily and quickly lowered her arms, catching herself on both sides. The only thing she'd failed to account for was the slick surface of the door, which she should have remembered given how hard Kolya had battled to hold on a few hours earlier. Her gloved fingers slipped across the smooth metal on her left. There was no edge on that side, nothing at all to grab onto. But just as they lost purchase, her right hand latched onto the metal ledge directly above the seal. She held tight and twisted around quickly to grab the hull with her other hand. It was the same slick surface as the door, but before her fingers began the inevitable slide, she hoisted her upper body through the gap and slid down the hull toward the ground.

"Close it!" She shouted the command a second before she hit the surface, landing on her side in a pile of dirt that the shuttle had scraped up when it crashed.

"Got it," Macek said. "Are you okay?"

"Yes."

"Double check your settings before you go."

"Doing that now." It was true, although she had no idea what difference it would make. If something was malfunctioning, she would be hiking off to Hyblaeus Catena regardless. She'd never be able to climb back up the side of the shuttle and even if she could, there wasn't much they could do to fix any problems. "Everything looks good. Oxygen at one hundred percent."

"Not for long. You've got four, maybe five hours."

"How much did you lose while the hatch was open?"

"Enough that you should start walking."

Claire started walking. A few steps in, she turned slightly to the right, aligning herself with the orange arrow that hovered near the bottom of her visor, courtesy of the rudimentary map app that Macek had transferred over from his phone. She flicked on her helmet lamps, squinting momentarily as her eyes adjusted to the glare from the dust particles dancing in the twin beams of light. Ahead, past the path of destruction that the shuttle had carved, the ground was even darker than the sky, which still held a faint hint of light directly ahead. That seemed a little odd given how long ago they'd crashed, but she hadn't spent enough time outside in the early evenings on her last trip to know how quickly the Martian sky went from twilight to pitch dark.

"Okay," she said. "I'm walking. You're sure this arrow knows which way I'm supposed to go?"

"I'm sure it knows better than *you* do."

She couldn't argue that point.

The ground was fairly level as she started out, covered with the dark green grass she'd seen from the shuttle. A few spindly plants with wide leaves rose up from the terrain, similar to ones she'd noticed in the dome at Canillo. Either they were small by design, or they were still growing. None of them rose above her knees.

"We should be able to maintain connection," Macek said. "I believe the helmets have a range of about five klicks. Just … be careful and go slowly. Remember the ground will be uneven. In some places, the turf may be loose like it was before the terraforming. And yes, I know I have already said all of this, but…"

He probably *had* said all of it earlier, while he loaded the maps and she filled the outer compartments of her suit with one of the remaining water pouches, her phone, and the pocketknife that he insisted she carry. She hadn't argued even though it seemed ridiculous. There was no animal life out here and little in the way of plants, so she had no idea what she was going to do with a knife.

She hadn't been able to fully focus on much that he was saying, though. Her mind had been preoccupied with the fact that she was about to head off on her own on a lunatic hike across the Martian tundra.

"I'm fine with you repeating yourself," she told him. "Just keep talking. It's nice to have the company."

There was a faint crackle and then his voice came in again. "Um, yeah. But … I do need to sign off for a few minutes. I have to look in on Kolya. And you don't want me cursing in your ear while I try to crawl out of this sarcophagus and back under the bulkhead."

"Oh, sure. No problem." That was a lie, and he probably knew it. He was right, though. Hearing him curse as he worked his way back to the front of the shuttle wouldn't have bothered her. But the sound of him screaming if he moved his shoulder the wrong way? She wasn't sure her nerves could take that when she was all by herself with just a pocketknife and the faint beams from her helmet against the cold, bleak Martian night.

"I'll be back as soon as I reach the front of the shuttle. Try not to break your neck while I'm gone."

Macek said the words lightly, but there was definitely a risk. The map wasn't topographical. He'd been able to pull up information about the overall change in altitude between the shuttle and the camp. The increase was only a few hundred meters, overall—slightly uphill for about the first half kilometer, followed by a brief downhill stretch, then a smaller rise and a final descent leading down to the camp. That didn't, however, tell them anything at all about the nooks and crannies along the way that might be disguised by the new groundcover that had sprouted during stage six. She had debated searching through the rubble inside the shuttle to see if she could find something to serve as a walking stick but quickly abandoned the idea. While it would have been nice, she'd have had to haul it up the ceiling panel and toss it through the hatch. And maybe it was for the best. Poking the ground in front of her before each step would have seriously slowed her down.

"And *yes,*" Macek added, "I *do* know there is nothing I can do about it if something happens. But like I said earlier about those Alliance aliens, I'm the type who wants to know something is wrong, even if I can't do a damned thing to change it."

Then his comms light was gone.

The surge of panic that followed was stronger than Claire had anticipated. Which was stupid. The shuttle was barely fifty meters behind her. She was no more alone now than she'd been a few seconds ago. Nothing had changed.

Self-admonishment didn't do much to tamp down her nerves, though. All she could do was take deep breaths and move on, letting the tiny orange arrow lead the way while she kept her eyes on the ground in front of her.

What surprised her the most about the terrain so far was that the grass, or what she'd taken for grass, was more like a thin layer of greenish-black moss. It didn't seem to have a root structure, coming up easily any time her boot skidded even slightly across the surface, which happened every ten steps or so because it was a bit slick. When she stopped to figure out the best path around an outcropping of rock, she noticed the grass was also eerily fast-growing, beginning to fill in the gap left by her heelprint as she watched.

Growing like kudzu, she thought, flashing back to something that her great-aunt from Georgia would say every time she visited back when Claire and Joe were kids. Or maybe Dr. Ademola's fast-growing bamboo was a better example. The grass felt slightly spongy, too, reminding her of the rubber turf at one of the playgrounds where she sometimes took … Jemma.

Claire tried to pull back before the conclusion of that thought. Any memory of Jemma under her current circumstances was destined to bring back their shared joke about bug monsters and her imagination didn't need extra fuel at the moment. If she kept feeding it, she'd be seeing giant spider legs coming over the ridge up ahead.

For the next ten minutes, she walked, glancing far too often at the clock in the far-left corner of her visor. What was taking Macek so long? Had he passed out again?

A few steps later, she planted her foot wrong going down a slight hill. Her boot slipped and she skidded a few meters before losing her balance and landing on her side. As she was picking herself up, Macek's voice sounded in her ear.

"Still alive?"

"More or less. Remind me to tell Davy that her Franken-grass is much too slippery. It's also kind of creepy how fast it grows."

"The grass is not designed for walking. It's designed for maximum oxygenation. That stuff is the reason that this planet won't need domes five years from now. Maybe even sooner. Slipperiness wasn't really a consideration given that you're the first person—actually, the first *creature*—to ever walk on that stretch of land."

"Well, the first Earther, at any rate," Claire said. "For all we know, this may have been a major Martian metropolis before the Alliance destroyed the planet."

Macek snorted, but he didn't contradict her. She decided to change the subject, anyway. Talking about the millions of inhabitants who were suddenly wiped out on this planet felt a bit too creepy out here on her own, especially when it could so easily happen again in the near future.

"Is Kolya still unconscious?"

"Yes, but I think he is starting to come around. I've had to wake him plenty of times when he is still tired, and I saw the same annoyed twitch just now when I shined the light into his visor as when I turn on the lights or open the windows to jolt him awake."

"Waking Kolya sounds like dangerous duty. How long have you worked with him?"

He seemed to be considering whether to answer, although it didn't feel like a particularly personal or difficult question to Claire. She'd mostly asked it just to keep a conversation going.

"I suppose it depends on how you define *work*," he said, eventually. "My father was a groundskeeper for Kolya's uncle—not that well paid, but a steady job, and I often came along to help. Kolya's uncle would make him help, too, from the time he was seven or eight, so you could say I've been working with him for more than forty years now. We went to the same local school. Then, Kolya went away to prep school. After the first year, he convinced his uncle to pay my tuition as well. Same for college. Later, for law school. All with the understanding that I would pay back every penny, with interest, pass or fail. Which, by the way, is the exact same agreement he made with Kolya."

"And you stayed on after the debt was paid?"

"I did," he said, sounding a little defensive. "We *both* did. Kolya took over a couple of satellite resorts his uncle launched and then neglected to the point that they were floundering. We paid him off in five years. And a little less than five years *after* we paid him off, I helped Kolya take over the entire company to keep the stupid son of a whore from bankrupting it. If we hadn't, the Ares Consortium would have found a way to boot KTI from the terraforming project before they finished stage four. So, yeah, Kolya and me, we go way back. I've covered for him more times than I can count. But just so you know? I had nothing to do with Westmoreland's crash."

EIGHT

THE SUDDEN SHIFT in the conversation caught Claire by surprise. She'd certainly never told Macek about her suspicions that he might have played a role in Westmoreland's death. Had she even told Kolya that she suspected Macek? She didn't *remember* telling him. But she'd been pretty drugged up during their conversation at the hospital after the attack at Icarus camp, so she supposed it was possible.

"Macek, I didn't actually think that—"

"Yes, you did. Kolya told me you saw our … disagreement on the patio at the Red Dahlia during the negotiations with the mine owners."

"I *did* see you. And yeah, I'll admit that it seemed a little suspicious at the time. But that was before I knew that pretty much the entire planet hated the man. And … I eventually decided you probably weren't the type."

There was another long pause, long enough that Claire had the distinct feeling that he was weighing his words carefully. "What you saw was Wes trying to bribe me into sabotaging stage six. I lost my temper at first, but I cooled off. At that point, he tripled his offer. He apparently thought my hesitation was because he hadn't sweetened the pot enough. So, I let him think he'd convinced me, then I turned it over to Kolya."

"How did he react?"

He huffed out a laugh. "How do you think? He was pissed. But if anything happened to Wes's craft, it was not with my knowledge. I'll admit I've done things I'm not proud of, but … not that."

"I believe you." It was true, although she couldn't help wondering why he'd brought up the issue now. Surely her opinion didn't matter enough that it had been weighing on his mind all this time.

And then she realized that her opinion probably *didn't* matter that much to him. He might not care what she thought at all. But she was the only one around at the moment and he thought there was a decent chance that he might not make it through the night. Suddenly, that little pause before he told her about the bribe felt ominous. And that last bit, saying he'd done things he wasn't proud of? Was he about to launch into some sort of final confession?

While she was trying to think of something, *anything,* to change the topic, she realized she was almost at the crest of the first ridge now. There were no spider legs creeping over the top, thank god, but … was the sky getting brighter?

"Hold on a sec. I need to check something." She flicked off her helmet lamps and turned around in a slow circle. Behind her, everything remained inky black, aside from a scattering of early evening stars. When she pointed back in the direction suggested by her friendly orange arrow, however, there was a definite glow. And it wasn't a diffuse glow, spread across the horizon. It was clustered directly in front of her.

She hurried to the top, nearly slipping over the side. Downhill, just over the second slight incline, a dome of pale-yellow light covered a crater. A fairly *small* crater compared to most that she'd seen on her first trip to Mars. Several brighter dots of light were scattered around the inside. And it looked like something was moving along the far edge.

"You still there?" Macek asked.

"Yeah. Is there a—"

"Kolya's awake. He's not coherent, but I think I've convinced him that he needs to remain still."

"That's good news. But can you tell me if there's a zoom

feature on these helmets? Because otherwise I need to get out my phone."

"Should be in the menu on the right. Why?"

"I'm at the top of that first hill you mentioned, a little under a kilometer in. I've got a decent view from up here. Hold on, okay?"

Once she had the menu open, she blinked to select the zoom level, then watched as the crater below came into focus. Something was indeed moving. A massive drill, just like the one she'd spotted boring into the wall of Clark Crater during her night walk at Icarus Camp. Beyond that, visible through the tridygel walls of the dome, were several outbuildings and two planes, one small and one large.

"Yes!"

"What is it?" Macek asked.

"We're in luck. I thought maybe someone had just left the lights on for the past six months, but nope. Hyblaeus Camp has a massive drill running. Looks like somebody decided not to wait for KTI to officially end the lockdown."

She expected a laugh or a sigh of relief from Macek. Instead, he let loose with a few of the same Russian obscenities she'd heard while helping him get his arm into the sling.

"What? How could this possibly be *bad* news? If there are people down there, they'll have a medic, right? And I can see that they have transportation. At the very least, they'll be able to call Elysia. Or better yet, Nepenthes."

"All of that is true ... but Hyblaeus is managed by Lyot. The colony is basically in Westmoreland's pocket. And the younger one is maybe even worse than his father. Which I'm guessing you recall from when I caught you spying at the Ares Consortium conference."

"Yeah. But you can't actually think they won't help." A long stretch of silence. "Seriously? You think they'd refuse to make an emergency call?"

"They might. What you're looking at is a major violation of the agreement between the colonies, and they probably aren't going to be happy about having a witness. If you can get someone alone and let them know there's a substantial reward involved, maybe they'll help. If they contact Wes, Jr., though? I think he'd tell them to let us rot. But Claire ... you should really just come back. You could find yourself in a bad situation down there. Lyot is a lot ... rougher than Daedalus. Rougher than any of the colonies. Disputes are settled with fists or worse. And unless his son has changed the standard policy, they don't hire women for the mining camps. They also don't tend to hire *gentlemen*."

He left that hanging, but he really didn't need to say anything else. She got the picture loud and clear. But what choice did she have? There was nowhere else in walking distance and going back was pointless. It would essentially mean giving up and hoping that a search party from Nepenthes found them in time. She couldn't even get back into the shuttle.

"Maybe once I get close enough I can piggyback on their signal and call Wyatt. If not, let's hope I'm lucky enough to find a good Samaritan. Or at least someone who can be bought. And..." She dropped her voice to a lower pitch. "Given the hardshell suit, maybe I can pass as a man."

"You are very short," he said dubiously.

"Not much shorter than Caruso."

"He is very short, too. But the voice is okay. You might fool them. On the other hand, they will be far less likely to shoot you on sight if they know you're a woman. Not from any sense of chivalry, but ... women are a scarce commodity on this planet."

"Hey, watch who you call a commodity. I just wish you'd given me a freakin gun instead of a pocketknife." She shook her head in amazement when the words left her mouth, thinking how very hard she'd fought Joe on that issue only a few weeks back.

"You weren't supposed to encounter any *people*. And a gun wouldn't have been much use for cutting through the tridygel panel so that you could get inside. Did you think you were going to just walk in through the airlock tunnel?"

"To be honest, I didn't think about anything past getting to the camp."

"Okay. But … whatever you do, do not mention Kolya. Or me. Or Nepenthes, because that's KTI territory and it will be a dead giveaway. Just tell them we were traveling from … Noachis to Elysia and we crashed. You need to contact Marisol Alvarado at Elysia. When you reach Marisol, tell her you are calling for Jaromir Ambrosevich, pilot of the shuttle DS9."

"Jaromir … I saw that on your name card at the Ares Consortium dinner."

"Yes. Can you repeat it all back to me?"

"We crashed coming from Noachis. Contact Marisol Alvarado. I'm calling for Jaromir Ambrosevich, pilot of the shuttle DF9."

"*Dee-Ess-Nine*."

"Okay. *DS9*. And she'll know that's you?"

"She'll know. I doubt she knows another Jaromir, but just in case, Ambrosevich is my patronymic. Or middle name, as you would say. And the shuttle name is from a … shared interest."

Again, Claire suspected there was an intriguing story to be had. Macek had apparently visited Elysia frequently at one time but did not do so currently. Someone there—apparently someone with a certain degree of authority—knew him as Jaromir, which was so rarely used that Caruso had joked that it was a *silent* first name. Not only that, she knew his middle name.

"Okay. Marisol Alvarado. Jaromir Ambrosevich. DS9. And don't mention King Asshole."

"What…? Oh. You mean Kolya. Correct."

Her foot slipped again. It was only a tiny skid, but enough to start her heart pounding given the dark gash that was now visible at the bottom of the hill. "Listen, I need to stop talking for a bit. Getting down this hill is going to be tricky. It looks like there's a ditch down there, and I'd rather not lose my footing and slide straight into it."

Now that she'd found the visor's zoom, she used it to chart out the best path down the hill and then began a very cautious descent. She managed to stay upright *most* of the way. When she slipped for the third time, she decided to take the last fifty meters or so seated. It was too dark to see exactly how deep that ravine was from here and it was much easier to control her speed on her butt.

It turned out to be a very smart decision.

"We have a problem," she said to Macek. "Remember that ditch I mentioned? It's more of a chasm. There's no way to cross. I'm going to have to go around."

"Great. Can you tell how far it goes?"

"Not unless you've got a map with more detail. I'm just going to pick a direction and start ... What the hell?"

She scooted backward as a large black disc rose up from the ravine and paused in front of her. Three amber lights flashed along its rim.

"What's wro—" Macek's voice cut out abruptly as an alarm began sounding inside her helmet. An instant later, the drone's spotlight flicked on and pointed directly at her.

"This land belongs to Lyot Excavation." The man's voice came from inside her helmet and given that it cracked audibly on the word *belongs,* she doubted that it was automated. "You're trespassing. This drone is fully armed. Identify yourself."

"Did you hear that?" She whispered the question, hoping that Macek might have heard it, but the other guy answered.

"What I *heard* was me telling you to identify yourself. Which you need to do right now if you don't want this drone to start shooting."

Claire debated whether to use a fake name, but there was a decent chance that someone would recognize her, due to her very public role in unveiling the Icarus chamber. She might go undetected given that she was wearing no makeup and probably had a severe case of helmet hair. But if they *did* recognize her, they'd undoubtedly connect her to Kolya. Either way, starting with an outright lie didn't seem like a good idea when she was asking for help. But a little strategic mispronunciation? That could be easily explained away, and it might at least give her a bit of time before the situation got bogged down in Martian political rivalries.

"My name is Kara Cole. Our shuttle was on the way from Noachis to Elysia when it malfunctioned. I need to get a message to Marisol Alvarado at Elysia that shuttle DS9 piloted by Jaromir Ambrosevich has crashed. We have two wounded. If there's any way you can patch a call through or send that message, I'd be very grateful. In fact, I can promise a *substantial reward* for your help."

A pause, and then the man's voice came back. "So … why were you going to Elysia in the middle of the lockdown?"

The question struck Claire as highly hypocritical, coming from a guy who was obviously part of an entire mining crew that was currently operating in violation of the lockdown rules. This didn't, however, seem like the best time to raise that point.

"Medical emergency," she said, thinking back to something Kolya had told her when she asked what would happen if there was an emergency at Doba or Ehden while the planet was on lockdown. He'd said that they'd be evacuated to Elysia, so maybe the excuse would fly. "My husband shattered his shoulder. We don't have anyone in Noachis who can handle the reconstructive surgery he needs."

"So, why didn't you go to Daedalus? Aren't they closer?"

Great. She had no idea where Noachis was, or where they fit into the tapestry of Martian politics. That seemed like something Macek should have considered when concocting their cover story. On the other hand, he'd specifically said to avoid mentioning Nepenthes, so he probably wouldn't have suggested Noachis if they were closely allied with Kolya.

"Bastards wouldn't take us," she said. "Told us supplies were low due to the lockdown."

He huffed. "Typical. You said somethin' about a reward. How much are we talking?"

She nearly mentioned a dollar amount but caught herself.

"Enough credits for a week at Elysia. Or Daedalus, if that's more to your liking."

"That would be two thousand," he said. "I got expensive tastes. But how do I know you're good for it?"

"I guess you really don't," Claire admitted. "But I swear to god—"

"Yeah, that ain't gonna cut it. And it's actually gonna cost you *six* thousand, because I need to bring a few buddies in on this deal if we're gonna make it work. Think you can handle that much?"

Assuming the exchange rate was roughly what it had been on her last trip, the amount they were talking about wasn't much more than two nights at a decent hotel in New York, so she could handle it about a million times over. But she had no idea what average pay rates were on Mars, so she waited a few beats before answering. "Yeah. I think between the three of us we can cover that much."

"Okay, then. What was that name again?"

"Marisol Alvarado."

"I *know* that one," he said and she could practically hear the man's eyes rolling. "I'm not an idiot. The *other* name. Your *pilot*."

"Jaromir Ambrosevich, pilot of shuttle DS9."

"Spell it. And give me the coordinates of the crash."

She did both.

"Let's hope she's willing to forward you that six grand up front," he said. "Because that's the only way this is gonna work."

There was an audible click on the other end. The drone was still there, though, still staring at her with its three amber eyes, so she didn't move.

Seven minutes of complete silence followed, and then she heard another click. She waited a moment, then said, "Hello. Are you there?"

"Oh, yeah, I am definitely here. Stay right where you are. My guys will pick you up shortly."

FROM THE RED PLANET

SUNDAY, 547/69

Jurisdiction Questions Plague Ljubic Trial

ACCORDING to our sources at Kolya International, Stasia Ljubic, former chief operations officer for the company has been apprehended on Earth and is currently in transit to face trial for the bombing at Icarus Camp that killed three people and injured several others earlier this year. Ljubic is also suspected of involvement in several additional attacks, including the bombing at Millex a few days prior to the Icarus attack, and last week's destruction at the KTI facility at Nepenthes, which resulted in a combined total of at least fifteen deaths.

The leaders of all five colonial councils held a virtual meeting this afternoon to discuss jurisdictional issues surrounding the case, which is complicated by the fact that only one of the attacks —the one at Icarus—occurred within colonial borders. Käthe Vogt, chair of the Daedalian Council, argued that Daedalus has a preemptive claim, based on the fact that all of the attacks occurred on land leased by Kolya International. Arthur Palisin, the Tharsis colonial chair, had initially agreed to cede the Tharsis claim, despite the fact that one of those killed in the Icarus attack was a Tharsan citizen. He noted today that the Tharsan Council is reconsidering that position due to outcry among their citizens over the fact that Daedalus is one of the only two colonies that does not have a death penalty.

The leaders also heard testimony from two whistleblowers who are demanding that the council launch a full investigation into the deaths of more than fifty workers at Millex Camp, during the third month of lockdown. A statement from Millex, which was read into the record, repeated their assertion that the barracks collapsed due to being built over an undetected sinkhole. The witnesses, whose identities are being protected, presented evidence supporting their claim that individuals in the barracks died as a result of exposure to *Azospira oryzae*, and the barracks was destroyed in an effort to hide the evidence of a containment breach. The matter was handled as separate from the Ljubic case, but one of the witnesses and several council members expressed concern that the incident might be related to the attacks by Ljubic and other members of the Earth Watch Alliance.

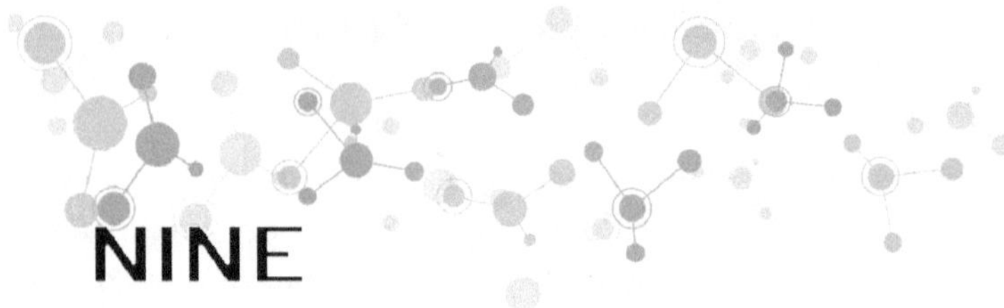

NINE

Wednesday, October 4
Daedalus City

BECK RELEASED the breath he'd been holding as the *V2* made a perfect, featherlight touchdown at Daedalus Station. Stasia, however, continued to clutch the armrest, maintaining a death grip even as the ship came to a stop and they heard the slight sucking noise of the airlock tunnel attaching to the ship. She didn't let go until the *V2*'s smooth-jazz AI came over the speaker telling them to prepare to disembark.

Wyatt remained strapped in, finishing a response to a message from Claire that had hit his phone as soon as they were within range of Daedalus.

"Are they at Nepenthes yet?" Beck asked.

Wyatt shook his head. "I don't know. The timestamp is from when we were still at Ares Station, just after the explosions. She was asking if we were safe. The message I sent in transit doesn't show as delivered. I just sent off another one to let her know we've arrived." He leaned forward toward the captain's chair, where Paul was glued to his armscreen, scrolling through a log of some sort. "Hey, Paul. Was the trip to Nepenthes longer or shorter than the one here?"

"A bit shorter. But the shuttles are also slower than these raptors. They *might* be there by now, but I wouldn't guarantee it. I'm looking at the Ares Station logs, and they did enter a flight plan to Nepenthes, so I'm pretty sure they got away from the station. No flight plan for the *Velox One*, however, and…" He nodded toward the viewscreen. "They're clearly not here."

Stasia, who was standing near the bulkhead, turned back at the mention of the *V1*. "If communications are back up with Ares, see if they can access the data from the cameras in Bay Five. Maybe they got footage of the theft."

"I'm working on it," Paul said through clenched teeth, clearly not happy with Stasia telling him how to do what had once been her job but was—at least for now—his. "I thought you were all convinced that Durav stole it."

"Either Durav or someone he gave the code," Stasia said. "There's a big difference."

Paul continued scrolling. "And why is that? Does Durav shoot lasers out of his fingers? Or maybe he has Jedi mind powers?"

Stasia caught Beck's eye, probably thinking back to their earlier joke about pulling Paul over to the Rebel side. "No Jedi powers that I'm aware of. But Durav does have at least a hundred lifetimes of experience over any mercenaries he may have hired. And he'll have far fewer qualms about killing any Earthers who happen to get in his way."

"That's actually saying something," Wyatt said. "Boudreaux was with Lone Star when they released sarin at that concert in LA back in '58 and when he has a drink or two, he's been known to brag that he was the one who planted the canisters into the HVAC system."

Beck remembered that attack. He'd been at his cabin in Maine when it happened, taking a few months' sabbatical between his assignment at VersaBio and his graduate work in Ireland. He'd been avoiding the news for the most part and just happened to tune back in the day after the attack. Video coverage was everywhere you looked and it had been horrific. Most of the victims were under sixteen. A few thousand *teenyboppers*, as they'd called them back when he first arrived on Earth, had crowded into the Dome to see some boy band. Over a hundred and fifty dead.

Nearly a thousand others seriously injured, many with permanent nerve damage.

"That was more than twenty-five years ago," he said. "He doesn't look that old."

"Yeah, it might not be true," Wyatt admitted. "The attack was never officially pinned on the group. But Boudreaux's sniper skills got him into the group when he was barely old enough to shave. And there are images of someone who looks a whole lot like him in the lobby just before the concert. Either way, it says a lot that he'd go around bragging about something like that."

"A homicidal maniac," Stasia said, "is still preferable to one of the genocidal variety."

Paul sighed. "Fine. I'll send a message to Wheatley asking her to check the footage. It may be a while, though. I'm guessing she's a little preoccupied right now, making sure the station is still in one piece and that the two thousand people currently docked there are safe."

"Of course," Stasia said. "Any idea how many casualties we took?"

Paul looked like he was going to object to her use of the word *we*, but he ignored it. "We got lucky. Only two deaths. A few dozen with injuries, but none serious enough that they can't be treated at the station. Exterior damage was mostly confined to the docking bays and thankfully, there was no damage to the laser array."

Beck followed Stasia into the bunkroom to retrieve his bag. "Are you okay? I thought you were going to break the armrests a few minutes ago."

"I'm okay. But…" Stasia raised her voice slightly to include Wyatt and Paul who were now in the corridor. "Looks like I won't be joining you on the trip to Nepenthes. As I said earlier, when I logged in using Kolya's credentials, I combed through a few of his recent messages. The one to KTI Security that revoked Paul's override authority also instructed them to take me into custody immediately upon landing and to hold me at Daedalus until he returns. Although, maybe it's for the best. I doubt either Shepherd or Dr. Monroe would welcome me with open arms."

Paul gave her an incredulous look. "Staying here is much worse, believe me. You were logged in as Kolya. Why didn't you send them another message saying you'd changed your mind?"

"I considered it," she said. "But it would have raised suspicion. We stand a better chance of securing the plane and getting the three of you out of here if I stay behind. And ... it's not that big of a deal, really. I mean, it's not like they're tossing me into a holding cell. Kolya explicitly instructed them to confine me to my old quarters at the Red Dahlia, and on the bright side, those accommodations are much better than anywhere the three of you will be staying in Ehden. Even if they put me on bread and water, I'll be fine. I could live happily for weeks on Chef Andrea's focaccia. I'm exhausted, anyway. I'm just going to think of this as a much-needed vacation—sleep, soak in the tub, then sleep some more."

Beck found the part about her being happy to return to her room at the resort quite convincing. But given her white-knuckled grip on those armrests, she was worried about something. He just wasn't sure whether it was fear of being mistreated in custody or simply that she dreaded facing the crew at Daedalus. The security staff and workers were undoubtedly people she knew, people she'd worked with. People who now believed she was a traitor and a murderer. And she wouldn't be able to explain to them why she'd done any of it. Even if she tried, no one would believe her.

"At least one of you, however, should object a tiny bit when they drag me off, since Kolya told them you probably would. We don't want it to look like we're expecting this. I nominate Wyatt."

"Why him?" Paul's voice was slightly muffled as he rummaged inside a closet in the hallway. "He seems the least likely, given that you nearly got Claire killed."

"They probably don't know about his relationship with Claire," she said, "and..."

"And I'm the one who's most expendable," Wyatt said,

without looking up from his messages. "If it turns out the guards are in the mood to lock up *two* people, instead of just one, it can't be either of you. Beck is needed at Ehden to help Claire, and I can't fly the plane to get him there."

Paul handed out biosuits and helmets. "Maybe you can duck past security if you're in this?" he said to Stasia. "You could go straight to the departure dome. I doubt anyone is on duty over there yet, since they said they'd have to pull people off furlough. You could just wait around inside the hangar."

She shook her head as she took the suit from him. "It's not going to work. But it will probably look odd if I don't at least try, given that Kolya set this up to be a nasty little surprise."

"What I find odd is that it would be Kolya issuing the order, rather than Macek," Paul mused as he began pulling on his gear. "Going over Macek's head and giving orders to a security team is the only thing I've ever seen Kolya do that pissed him off to the point I thought they were going to go at it. You remember that incident at Deuteronilus?"

Stasia nodded but didn't comment.

"You think maybe it's because Macek didn't make it off the station?" Beck asked.

"No," Paul said. "Macek's fine. I'm sure of it. If he wasn't on the *V2*, Kolya would assume Stasia was still back on Ares Station. He wouldn't know that I broke the rules to get her out."

"Sorry…" Stasia said.

"You should be." Paul tightened the strap on his boot, then sighed. "No, that's not entirely fair. Don't get me wrong. I'm still mad at you for not telling me about all of this. You lied to me for *years*. But I should probably thank you. Now I can turn in my resignation without stressing over the decision or wondering if Ayman will think I'm doing the right thing by leaving. And … if Kolya's actually going to fight us on this, I don't want to work here anyway."

"Pretty sure Ayman has wanted you to quit for the past few

years," she told him. "Maybe even longer. He just knew that you needed to be the one to make that decision."

Beck was the first to exit. Sure enough, three uniformed guards were waiting outside, dressed in suits identical to his own, except for the words KTI SECURITY stamped on the left side of their chests and just above the visor of their helmets. A maglev tram was parked on the charging pad about twenty meters behind them, just outside one of the three entrance tunnels to the dome. It was probably a service entrance, since no one had bothered to landscape the area around it, and it lacked the animated *Welcome to Daedalus City!* signs that flashed in vivid colors above the two entrance tunnels situated off to the right.

Whether accidentally or on purpose, the guards had lined up in order of height and the effect bordered on comical, almost like Russian nesting dolls. The woman on the left was the shortest, about Paul's height. The man in the middle was almost exactly a head taller, and the guy on the right, a head taller than the one in the middle.

The others were filing out of the ship now, with Stasia behind Wyatt, and Paul bringing up the rear. Even with the helmet partially obscuring her face, the biosuits fit closely enough that there was no doubt which of them was Stasia. Before her foot even hit the tarmac, the female guard pulled a weapon from the holster at her side and aimed.

"Whoa," Beck told her. "You don't need that."

"Yeah," Wyatt said. "What the hell?"

The tallest guard pulled his weapon, too. Wyatt raised his hands slightly and he and Beck both took a step back.

"Stasia Ljubic," the woman said in a thin, reedy voice. "I have direct orders from Anton Kolya, CEO of Kolya International, to detain you on suspicion of terrorism and the wanton destruction of KTI property. You are to be held here until he returns, at which time he will call a meeting of Daedalus's elected leaders to determine when judicial proceedings against you will begin. At that time, you will be provided with legal counsel and the opportunity to state your case. In the interim, anything you say can and will be used against you in those proceedings, so you would be advised to—"

"To keep your bitch mouth shut." This was from the middle guard, who stepped forward abruptly and grabbed Stasia's right arm. He twisted it, spinning her around roughly so that he could cuff her hands behind her back.

Before Beck or Wyatt could react, Paul was in the guard's face. "Watch it, mister. You are *seriously* out of line. I get that you need to take her into custody. But in case you haven't noticed, she's not resisting. She's going to go peacefully. Right, Stasia?"

"Right," she echoed, but there was a hitch in her voice. "I'm not resisting."

Paul turned to the woman, who Beck thought must be the one in charge. "Your orders said to detain Ms. Ljubic and keep her in custody at the Red Dahlia until Kolya returns. Correct?"

"Correct."

"That was my understanding as well," he said. "You're going to follow those orders to the letter, and I'll be right behind you to make sure that you do. You are to take Ms. Ljubic to her quarters. You will post a guard outside her door. She will be allowed to order three meals a day. You will *not* use force of any kind against her unless she attempts to escape, to harm herself, or to harm another individual. In that event, you will use the minimum force necessary to contain the situation. Do you understand?"

The woman gave him a curt nod.

He turned to the other guards. "How about you? Did you follow all of that or do I need to go over it again?"

"I got it, *sir*." The middle guard's tone was clipped and precise, with a faint touch of sarcasm on the last word. The other one also mumbled an affirmative, and then the three guards headed with Stasia toward a tram waiting a few meters away.

"Come on," Paul said. "That's our ride."

Beck glanced at the tram, which wasn't much bigger than a golf cart. "Are you sure they have room for all of us?"

"No. I'm sure they *don't*. It's a six-seater and there are seven of us, which means the guard who twisted her arm will be walking back or calling for another ride. Kolya may have reduced my authority, but I'm still way above that bastard's paygrade."

TEN

BECK HAD SEEN videos of Daedalus City for well over a decade and had tracked its metamorphosis from a basic colony to a tourist mecca. He'd even watched an action movie filmed in Daedalus a few years back where the hero was chased down this very strip. None of it prepared him for how big—or how busy—the place was. Maybe it was the juxtaposition of seeing the dome from above only a few minutes earlier, where it had looked like a small, garish still life, aside from the blinking lights. Now that he was inside, though, everything around him was in motion, even the buildings. Most of the structures had their gravity rotations synced up, but it was still a bit dizzying for the uninitiated.

Another surprise was how many people were on the streets. He knew that Kolya had allowed some tourists and researchers to stay during the lockdown and the dome was also housing a good number of workers who usually lived at the mining camps. But it was after eleven now, and even in a resort town, you wouldn't expect this many people out. As they drew closer, he realized this wasn't the typical late-night crowd. The Daedalus City grapevine was apparently in perfect working order, because most of these people were gawkers. It reminded him of trying to get through the throng of Flock members and Gates of Destiny protesters outside Jonas Labs.

People lined the street like spectators at a parade, craning their necks to catch a glimpse of the traitorous Stasia Ljubic. Some held signs—*KTI Shelters Terrorists, Justice for Millex,* and *Send Her to Tharsis*. He didn't really get the last one, but asking what it meant with Stasia right there in front of him seemed a bit churlish.

An assortment of jeers and boos sounded as the security tram passed by, with many of the crowd clearly disappointed that all they could see aside from the two security guards were four people still wearing biosuits and helmets. He was now glad that Paul had insisted they leave the helmets on, even after the tram's AI announced that it was safe to remove them. At the time, he hadn't understood why. Now it made sense. Stasia was easily the second most famous person in Daedalus after Kolya. Given how extensively they'd used her avatar, people might even be more familiar with her face than with his.

"We'd have been there already if you'd taken the back way," Paul said as the tram slowed yet again for a cluster of people pressing into the street.

The female guard gave him a tight smile. "I'm sorry, sir. But we have two first time visitors to Daedalus City onboard. I'm following standard protocol."

"Protocol for *registered* guests. We'll be leaving in—"

Stasia interrupted him. "It's okay, Paul. Even though they're not registered to stay at the resort overnight, Mr. Beckett and Mr. Garcia are KTI and Kolya's *personal guests*." She stressed the last two words to remind him of their cover story. "I'm sure he would want them to see Daedalus City at its best. Captain Jenkins is entirely correct to follow the protocol."

Beck, who was seated across from Jenkins, saw the woman's body visibly tense up at Stasia's compliment.

"What exactly is the protocol?" Beck asked Stasia, who was between the two security guards. The third guard—the one with the extra surly attitude—was riding back on the separate tram that Paul had paged to transport their bags.

"You are currently experiencing the VIP introduction to Daedalus City," Stasia said, keeping her eyes focused on the floor of the tram. She used the same perky tone as the avatar he'd seen at Ares Station, which was a bit disconcerting. "Escort all guests of the Red Dahlia down the Strip, and around the Circle. Engage the noise filter once you go through the gate to highlight the tranquility of the gardens surrounding the resort. Cross the lake, and approach the Red Dahlia from the front, so that they can take in the full magnificence of its architecture." She dropped her voice to a more normal range. "In case you haven't noticed, Kolya is a big fan of shock and awe."

They left the main drag a few minutes later and Beck realized she wasn't wrong about the effect. As soon as the tram pulled through the gate, which was lined on either side by a tall privacy hedge, the crowd noise dissipated. It was replaced by silence aside from the faint chirping of crickets and various night noises. And the cricket sounds had to be fake. From what he'd heard there were no insects or any other animal life roaming freely inside the dome.

The tram, which was the only vehicle in sight, picked up speed as it zipped along the tree-lined lane toward a massive lake at the bottom of the valley. Perched at the center of that lake on a stationary platform was the Red Dahlia, a massive, spinning blossom with each petal outlined in sparkling lights.

When the path ended abruptly at the edge of the lake, the tram continued, zipping across the water toward the resort. He still saw no other vehicles, but a few dozen people were waiting at the main entrance.

"*No*. Take us around back," Paul said when the tram began to slow and they heard the sound of booing. "Let's go in through the executive pavilion. And tell one of your people to clear that crowd."

"There's not much we can do, sir, assuming they're guests of the property and not trespassing. People do have the right to assemble."

The tram veered out over the water again, taking a wide path to avoid startling guests on the patio overlooking the lake. A few minutes later, it pulled onto a drive where two other trams were parked. Thankfully, there were no crowds here. It was completely empty aside from a guy vaping on a bench. As they got out of the tram, Jenkins informed them that they'd need to remove their biosuits before entering, nodding to a sign near the entrance as confirmation. It also said *business casual,* which Beck's khaki pants might satisfy, but Wyatt's jeans and band tee probably would not.

"Just leave the suits out here," Paul said, and then told the two guards to wait up. "Listen, I need to get Stasia settled and then I'll see if there are any empty rooms. There may not be. We took on about a quarter of the mining crews and outside workers as part of the labor settlement to keep Stage Six on schedule. They were in temporary housing, but there was an … issue a week or so back, so we had to reorganize. All of the paid guests were moved here, so that the smaller resorts could take in some of the workers. They rotate staying at the temporary settlement and here in town. If nothing is open, you can use my apartment to shower and change. Go ahead and grab a drink and something to eat. Assuming Kolya didn't revoke those privileges, too?" He added the question in a lower voice, and glanced at Stasia, who shook her head.

"Any chance you could arrange for me to bring in a guest for an hour or so?" Wyatt asked, looking up from his phone.

Paul frowned. "What?"

"There's a professional colleague I need to talk to about *another matter."* He emphasized the last two words, clearly not wanting to say too much within earshot of the guards.

"Yeah, I guess. Give me the name and I'll ask the host to let them in when I tell them to overlook your … wardrobe deficiency."

"Jordan Mercer."

He winced. "I should have known you two would be in contact. What time will she be here?"

"As soon as they let her in. She's out front."

Paul sighed again and headed off after the guards and Stasia.

"Who is Jordan Mercer?" Beck asked.

"Editor of *The Red Planet.* The only *official* news outlet in Daedalus. She does a decent job of keeping it from devolving into a corporate newsletter for KTI, given that everything other than op-eds and letters to the editor have to go through Kolya's censors. Which is probably why Paul's not a fan."

"And she was in the crowd waiting at the front entrance?" Beck asked.

"Yes," Wyatt said, apparently picking up on his disapproval. "*Reporting,* not participating. Stasia's return is headline news. Jordan is just doing her job. I don't know her personally, but we have mutual acquaintances, including the guy I'd be talking to at Nepenthes right now if Kolya wasn't such a duplicitous ass."

As the door closed behind them, Beck saw Paul speeding up to join the two guards and Stasia in an elevator at the back of the massive, multipurpose room. The left side of the pavilion included a business center, with stock tickers and conference rooms. A slightly larger area on the right was designed for socializing. The highlight was a floral-shaped sunken lounge decorated in muted shades of red. It faced a stone fireplace and held an assortment of sofas and chairs clustered into small conversational groups. A curved staircase led up to the mezzanine level, which housed a bar and, presumably, the restaurant that Paul had mentioned, along with tables, a few booths near the back, and a crimson piano. The most notable thing about the place was how empty it felt, especially after driving through the crowds to get here. One guy was at a desk in the business area, and a lone couple sat at a table near the bar, but that was it.

"Since you have a meeting, should I..." Beck motioned upward to the bar.

Wyatt considered for a moment and then shook his head. "No. I'd like to get your feedback."

They found three chairs on the edge of the conversation pit that were easily visible from the door. A realistic avatar of a curvaceous young woman with auburn hair popped up from the center of the coffee table as soon as they sat down. The hologram was maybe half a meter tall, and aside from the flower in her hair and the addition of a very short skirt resembling dahlia petals, the costume reminded Beck of the Playboy bunny getups from the mid-twentieth century.

The avatar flashed a sassy smile. "Welcome to the Red Dahlia, gentlemen. My name is Aria. May I take your order?"

Wyatt stared at her for a beat, with his head cocked to the side like something was puzzling him. "We're ... expecting a third person. Can you check back then?"

"That will be no problem at all, sir."

Beck gave a short chuckle when the avatar was gone. "You're not imagining it. That was definitely Stasia's voice. At least they changed the visual. You almost have to wonder if Kolya left all of these on purpose, just to remind people of what she did in order to keep their anger at full tilt. I mean, she's been the face of Daedalus since they started making the big push for tourism. People here have to be feeling like Minnie Mouse went rogue, blew up Cinderella's castle, and killed off a bunch of people in Adventureland."

Wyatt shook his head in amusement. "Claire is right, you know. You really do need to update your analogies."

"Nope. I realized earlier today that there is one undisputed bright side to all of you knowing the truth now. I can stop weighing my words before I speak. If you don't get my cultural references, you can look them up. And you do have to admit this place feels like a theme park. Minus the kids, I guess. There don't appear to be very many of those."

"True," Wyatt said. "That's a key plank in the proposed constitution, by the way. Kolya is adding lots of incentives to make more little Martians. That's one of the more popular proposals, actually."

"You know more than I would have thought about the politics of Mars. Aren't there enough conflicts on Earth to keep you busy?"

Wyatt shrugged. "I've been assigned off-planet on a few occasions. Mostly labor disputes. And only Lunar and satellite issues prior to this. To be honest, I really hadn't paid much attention to Martian politics until this year, aside from the connections to some of the militia groups I follow. But when I found out Claire was going to be traveling with Kolya, I did a deep dive in order to get up to speed." He glanced at the phone again and shook his head. "She should have reached Nepenthes. And she knows I'm worried. She'd have messaged back by now. Something's gone wrong."

"I'm sure she's fine," Beck said, even though he was also beginning to worry. "I wouldn't be surprised if Kolya just blocked her communications so that she doesn't find out for sure that he sabotaged the plan for me to join her in the negotiations."

"Yeah, well then you also shouldn't be surprised if I punch him square in the face if we're ever in the same room together. Manipulative son of a bitch."

Beck gave a wry chuckle.

"What? You think that's an exaggeration?"

"Oh, no. He's definitely manipulative. I was just considering the irony of that statement given that you're the one who extorted him into transporting us to Mars."

ELEVEN

THE WOMAN WAS TALL, dark, and thin. Judging from her dress, Beck suspected she had a flair for the dramatic. A flowing daisy yellow skirt fell to midcalf, over black leather boots. She wore a matching scarf, with a crisp white blouse. The ensemble was topped off by a wide-brimmed yellow hat. A gold cuff that was probably an armscreen extended from her left wrist to just below her elbow. As she drew closer, he could see that she was at least a decade—and possibly even two or three decades—older than the mid-thirties he'd estimated when she entered the room.

"Jordan Mercer, with the now sadly misnamed *Red Planet*." She extended her hand to Wyatt. "I recognize you from your byline photo at the *Atlantic Post*, but who is *this* young man?"

Beck rose and offered his hand. "John Beckett." Leaving it at that felt odd after so many decades of appending a company name after his own, but he was no longer employed at Jonas Labs or anywhere else. He was no longer even a member of the Watch, not that he'd ever added that to his introductions. "Pleased to meet you."

"He's traveling with me," Wyatt said. "You can count on his discretion."

Jordan arched one sculpted brow. "Given that you're traveling with Kolya, I have serious reservations about whether I can even count on *your* discretion."

"Believe me, bringing us along was *not* Kolya's idea," Wyatt said with a glance toward Beck. "It's a long story, almost none of which I'm at liberty to share at the moment, but as Beck reminded me a few minutes ago, it involved a touch of extortion on my part."

Jordan laughed, a full-throated chortle. "Really? You'll have to share your technique once you're free to talk about it. I've tried to extort that man on multiple occasions and failed miserably each time."

The waitress avatar popped up again as soon as they sat down. "Welcome to the Red Dahlia. My name is Aria. May I—"

"Could you give me a second to catch my breath, please?" Jordan said. When the avatar vanished without a word, she chuckled. "Kolya certainly wastes no time before he goes after your money."

"That does seem to be his primary personality trait," Wyatt agreed. "If you'd like to extract a bit of revenge, though, we're on KTI's tab. Feel free to order whatever you'd like."

She made a sad face. "I ate dinner hours ago. But no one in her right mind ever passed up dessert at the Red Dahlia."

The avatar returned while Jordan was speaking, as if it had been summoned when Wyatt said the word *order*. Beck would have wagered a considerable amount of money that every single one of these tables was monitoring—and most likely recording—the patrons' conversations. He wasn't particularly hungry, so he just ordered a bourbon and ginger. Wyatt ordered a sandwich and a beer. Jordan, who had clearly been to the Red Dahlia before, opted for a coffee martini and asked if it was possible to order off the dessert menu from *Della Marta.*

"Of course," the avatar chirped. "Would you like to see tonight's selections?"

"No need. I'll have the *galaktoboureko*—chocolate, if you have it, but whatever flavor Andrea has prepared today will be fine. Oh, and a double order of the custard *loukoumades* for the table." When the avatar was gone, she said, "One of the nicer perks of this job is that we get commissions to review restaurants for Earth travel publications a few times a year. It's the only time anyone is allowed to dine at the Red Dahlia if they're not staying at the resort—which is seriously outside of our price range—so the three of us take turns. I'm very generous with my employees, but that's one benefit I'd really prefer not to share. You'll see what I mean when you try Andrea's *loukoumades*. Are you familiar with Greek pastries, Mr. Beckett?"

"Um ... not really. Baklava and those little finger-shaped things. That's about it. And please, just call me Beck."

"Of course, Beck. What kinds of desserts *do* you like?"

Beck gave her a confused smile. He wanted to tell her that she really didn't need to try so hard to pull him into the conversation, but that seemed rude, so he just said, "I like pie."

"What sorts of pie?" she said, making a hand motion to encourage him to give her more.

"Uh ... pecan? Apple, cherry, lemon custard, coconut. Pretty much any kind of pie."

Jordan gave him a nod, apparently satisfied with the rundown of his favorite desserts. Then, she tapped her arm cuff, which did indeed turn out to be a phone. After scrolling through for a moment, she tapped again, and pulled the screen off of her arm, placing it on the table. "You might want to do the same," she told Wyatt. "Kolya's hired ears are exceptionally active in here. But just go with white noise. I'm running a conversation emulator. Which is why I had to coax a few extra words out of you, Beck. You'd been rather quiet, and the program didn't have enough to work with."

"Will an emulator fool the censors?" Beck asked.

"Not entirely. They'll probably pick up on the fact that our conversation is far too anodyne to be real. But they won't know what we actually talked about and that's the most important thing. I'm also recording this conversation, just so you're aware. My memory isn't quite as sharp as it once was." She turned to Wyatt. "Before we get into the Millex case, I need you to answer two quick questions for me. First, what is the current situation at Ares Station?"

Their drinks arrived. Wyatt downed about half of his before

answering, and Beck suspected he was using the time to consider what he could say without totally pissing Paul off if it showed up as breaking news.

"Um … this isn't official," he said finally. "But from what I overheard, the station suffered minor damage, mostly to the docking area. Two fatalities and some injuries, but they're all being treated on the station."

"Any suspects?" she asked.

Another pause, then Wyatt nodded and began searching for something on his phone. "Two individuals who stole a ship belonging to Kolya. A raptor, which is the twin of the one we just arrived in. You've probably already seen these." He tilted the phone in her direction to show the images of Boudreaux and Durav. "Nothing certain at this point, but we had a tentative sighting of the guy on the left about an hour before the explosions. Someone is with him, but it may or may not be the guy on the right."

Jordan's dark eyes widened. "Aren't those the men suspected in Janelle's murder?"

"They are," Wyatt said.

"Which leads directly to my second question. How is Stasia holding up?"

This seemed to catch Wyatt off guard, although it may have been less the subject than the concern in her voice. "Uh … fairly well, I guess. Although Beck could probably answer that better than I can. I don't really know her all that well."

Jordan nodded and turned to Beck. "And how are you and Stasia acquainted?"

He was about to say they were colleagues at a previous job, but his mind went blank and he couldn't remember any of Stasia's employers prior to KTI. And something about the woman's expression suggested that she might know Stasia well enough to tell if he lied. So, he said that he knew her at university, which was true if you counted their training at the Academy.

"And yes, she's definitely shaken," he added quickly, hoping to forestall any follow-ups that he couldn't answer. "Which shouldn't be surprising, given the crowds booing her on the Strip and the security guard yanking her around."

"Which guard was it?"

Beck shook his head. "One of the men. I only caught the name of the woman, so…"

"It was probably Hurst. His brother-in-law was killed a few weeks back after what I'm fairly certain was a botched rescue attempt at Nepenthes. Stasia hasn't been officially charged with that, of course—she wasn't even on the planet—but I'm afraid she's already been convicted in the court of public opinion. For today's incident on Ares Station, too. Between tourists and researchers, we got a few hundred people visiting here who are convinced that she damaged the laser array and they'll be stuck here even after lockdown ends."

"Pretty sure that part wasn't damaged," Beck said. "And Stasia was locked up when the attacks happened."

"Did Kolya have the key?" Jordan said. "If so, that's not going to convince the crazies. Most of them think he's in on it. To be clear, I don't think either of them were involved, but…"

"I take it you and Stasia are friends?" Wyatt asked.

Jordan considered the question for a moment. "Yes, I'd say we are. At the very least we're friendly. She was always very helpful when I had … difficulties with Kolya. Caruso is nice enough, but he's nowhere near as good at pulling his boss over to the freedom of expression side whenever we clash with KTI's censors. And I was close to Janelle, which sort of carried over to Stasia when she joined the operation. The three of us often lunched together before Janelle grew tired of Kolya's obsessive need to manage every little detail of every little thing at KTI. None of this adds up, though. It was hard enough to imagine Janelle taking over the Flock. She was always so supportive of Kolya's work, and I cannot begin to imagine her living on a farming commune let alone directing terrorist attacks. She liked her creature comforts. So does Stasia … and she's *not* a murderer. It's hard to picture her willingly hurting anyone. Yes, yes, I *know* they're saying she merely ordered the killings so it's not like she had to get her hands dirty. But like I said, it doesn't add up. Not to anyone who actually *knows* her." She looked to Beck for confirmation. When he nodded, she continued. "The masses out there, though? Did you know they destroyed or at the very least vandalized all of the outdoor information kiosks? Anything bearing Stasia's likeness has been fair game for the past six months."

"Huh," Beck said. "Now I'm wondering if that was what happened on the station. From where we were, it looked like a fight broke out in the concourse, but maybe they were just targeting the information kiosk."

"I wouldn't be surprised," she said. "And as I mentioned a moment ago, Kolya's popularity has hit the skids as well. With both his chief operations officer and his ex-wife implicated, people think either he was in on the entire operation or he's a damn fool. The crowd you saw coming through town began gathering about an hour ago because someone leaked the fact that Stasia's going to be held *here* instead of at the city jail. And a good quarter of the folks here say even jail is too good. They want her extradited to Tharsis."

"I saw that on one of the signs as we were coming in," Beck said. "Why Tharsis?"

"The man who was killed in the explosion at Icarus was from there, so they have a claim against her. A more pressing claim, one might argue, since no Daedalian citizens were killed. The charges here are terrorism and property damage. And ... Daedalus doesn't have the death penalty. Tharsis is one of the three colonies that *does*, and they use it at the slightest provocation. I can't believe Kolya was stupid enough to bring her back here. He should have left her on Earth."

Wyatt glanced at Beck, and then said, "I had the impression that Kolya—or at least, Macek—thought she might be *safer* here than if they turned her over to the US authorities. I mean, the US has the death penalty, too. They may not use it as often as they used to, but it's probably not off the table if they can connect her definitively to those attacks."

All of that applied to Beck, as well, which explained the look that Wyatt had given him. He was only connected to one of the attacks and he'd tried to save lives, so they'd probably go easier on him. There was even a chance that he'd avoid legal trouble entirely, depending on how much Joe, Kai, and Wilson decided to share with the police. Either way, the odds were exceptionally good that none of it mattered in the slightest, because by the time the case made it through the legal system, there would be no one left on Earth to serve as judge and jury.

"Which begs the question of why the authorities would let Stasia leave," Jordan said.

"I don't think they were given an option," Wyatt said. "I'm not even sure when Kolya informed them, except that it was almost certainly after we left Tranquility. Caruso says Kolya's lawyers are claiming Daedalus has priority for prosecution because they were the first to charge her with a crime."

"Are you sure that it's not because he wants to be the one to extract his pound of flesh?" she asked. "Metaphorically, of course. The man's ego is gargantuan, and he's not the type to take it kindly when someone screws him over."

"Maybe. But he and Macek are aware of some … potentially mitigating circumstances." Wyatt held up a hand to forestall the question that was clearly coming. "Which I absolutely cannot talk about at the moment. Sorry. But yeah. There's reason to believe she wasn't responsible. Certainly not to the point where she should get the death penalty."

"So, we're back to the Kolya is an idiot thesis," Jordan said. "I doubt that either of you have been keeping up with the situation here during the lockdown. But Kolya gets daily updates. He knows that Daedalus is a tinderbox, mostly because he took on a few hundred…"

She trailed off as the cart arrived with their food. After a bite of a concoction with flaky layers separated by several inches of dark chocolate custard, she continued. "Kolya took on a few hundred more of the mining and bamboo crews than we could easily handle, especially given that he'd already decided to let in tourists and researchers during the lockdown. The temporary housing units they constructed are crap—admittedly better than some of the camps where these workers are normally housed, but out there, everyone is in the same boat. There's nowhere to go, nowhere to spend the money they're earning. Work, eat, sleep, repeat, with a week off every six months if you haven't pissed your bosses off too badly. Here, though? You're got nearly five hundred men, most under twenty-five, and they're about a forty-minute walk from the Strip. No job, nothing to do. Kolya loosened the odds at the casinos considerably during lockdown, but far too many of them gambled and drank away their credits in the first two months. They're constantly faced with the fact of how much better the conditions are here than what they're used to. And I don't know who handled the housing assignments, but they needed to be a lot more careful about which groups they shoved together. Tharsan miners don't always play well with others."

"Not too surprising," Wyatt said. "From what I've heard, Tharsis and Lyot are lawless."

Jordan shook her head, swallowed her bite of pastry, and then said, "That's not entirely true. They do have a code of sorts. And if someone breaks that code, then you get a group of your friends together and you go break *him*. We had a case a few weeks back where there was a theft in one of the temporary units. Somebody reported seeing the thief with the goods—some opals the other guy may well have stolen himself. Anyway, the thief was arrested, the goods recovered, and after a few days, he was released pending trial. That night, the victim and a few of his buddies found the thief and beat the living hell out of him in the middle of town and left him for dead. Someone called the hospital, but he was dead not long after arrival. In Tharsis, they wouldn't be prosecuted at all. Here, they're facing a manslaughter charge. The other Tharsans are all pissed, and our police are in over their heads. Daedalus City police normally spend their time giving directions and occasionally ushering a drunken tourist back to their hotel. We've had four other assaults in the past six months, and dozens of home break-ins. City moved the tourists and researchers out of the lower cost hotels where many of them were staying and into suites here at the Red Dahlia for security reasons. That further pissed off the workers. Daedalus residents, too, because *our* homes are outside the safety of these gates. That crowd you saw earlier was mostly residents, but I'm guessing the mining crews are hitting the casino and bars in full force by now. When they learn that one of these lovely suites is now housing a woman they suspect in the murder of dozens of Martian workers, they're not going to take it well."

"But KTI Security handles the Red Dahlia," Beck said. "They're separate from the local police, and I would assume they're better trained, too. Even if they manage to get up a mob, this seems like it would be a pretty easy spot for Kolya's security to defend. So … Stasia should be okay here, right?"

"She *should* be," Jordan said. "But you're assuming KTI Security actually *wants* to keep her safe."

SELECTED CORRESPONDENCE

From: Davina Monroe <dm@KTINepen>

To: Kolya <K@KTICentr>

Subject: Your damnable ego

What did I tell you? What did I specifically and in no uncertain terms tell you about your idiotic plan for Ehden?

But no. You come up with these wild harebrained schemes and think they will always work. Just because a handful of your crazy ideas have flourished, you forget the many, many times that they failed utterly and completely.

Remember the clusterbùrach at Deuteronilus? If you don't, if it has conveniently slipped through that sieve that serves you as a conscience, ask Macek. Because I can promise you that he remembers.

This was a horrendous idea from the start, Anton. I never trusted Shepherd and his brain-dead religious fanatics. Now they've killed fourteen of my people and god in heaven only knows how many of my creatures we will find under the rubble.

You and Macek need to get your miserable asses back to Nepenthes ASAP and help me deal with this. We have detained the Flock members we captured fleeing from the entrance to the lab tunnel. They are suspects, obviously, and we are well within our rights to hold them, but Shepherd has retaliated by holding an equal number of our people hostage, including Idi and his family. We have agreed on the proper treatment of our respective "hostages" as he insists on calling them, although I would argue that ours are legally detained as suspects, and Shepherd has tentatively agreed to release the children. He insists, however, that any other negotiations are predicated on a full prisoner swap, which we obviously will not do.

One other thing before I go. I absolutely do NOT care that we are under lockdown protocol—you need to send me some reinforcements. My security team was already understaffed and now one is among the dead and one is missing.

From: Davina Monroe <dm@KTINepen>

To: Kolya <K@KTICentr>

Subject: Make that TWO dead security guards

I told you they were mindless animals. You want proof? See picture #1, the missing security guard. It wasn't enough to simply kill the kid. They mangled his body. He was twenty-two, Anton.

Shepherd sent a rambling message telling us where we could find his body. He implied that the boy was killed because KTI violated the agreement I made with him when he released the children. I have no idea what he's talking about, and I sincerely hope that the same can be said for you and Macek.

From: Kolya <K@KTICentr>

To: Davina Monroe <dm@KTINepen>

Subject: Re: Make that TWO dead security guards

You SAID you wanted reinforcements ASAP. This seemed like the best way to provide them. Unfortunately, someone slipped up, and now we have more people dead.

From: Davina Monroe <dm@KTINepen>

To: Kolya <K@KTICentr>

Subject: Re: Re: Make that TWO dead security guards

Would have been nice if someone had checked with me first. Things seemed to be stabilizing before this. They sent us fresh food, saying we could test it first on the detainees. I didn't eat it, of course—I've lived on floater rations for a year or more at a time, so this is no big deal. But once we let them talk with Shepherd, the mad bombers we're holding were happy to gobble it up and I didn't stop any of my people who wanted to join in, even though I think they're damn fools.

Speaking of, we seem to have a bit of Stockholm syndrome developing in Ehden. Shepherd keeps sending me videos of our people claiming they're convinced that no one in Ehden was involved in the bombing. Even Idi and his wife, which defies explanation. Both of them are too smart to let themselves be swayed by a charlatan like Shepherd.

And what in the name of all that is holy is going on in your little Disneyland? The Red Planet is saying your Tharsan guests just dragged one of the other miners into the street for a public execution over a theft. Maybe it's just as well you didn't siphon off any more KTI Security to send my way. Sounds like Macek is hiring bloody incompetents.

TWELVE

Wednesday, October 4
Near Hyblaeus Mining Camp

NEARLY HALF AN HOUR after the man said his guys would pick her up *shortly*, Claire was still waiting, still staring at the blinking amber lights of the drone hovering over the chasm. His definition of *shortly* was clearly quite different from her own.

Either that, or he'd changed his mind.

Both of her legs were asleep, and her arm muscles were twinging from holding the same position for so long, a situation that wasn't helped by the rigid casing of the suit. Moving to a different position was out of the question. The drone shrieked and went to code red if she moved at all beyond taking shallow, measured breaths. She had tried twice to reach the external pouch that held her phone, thinking maybe she was close enough to piggyback off whatever system they were using at the mining camp. But each time she moved her arm more than a couple of centimeters, the drone made it clear that she was on shaky ground.

If they didn't show up soon, her muscles were going to give out, and the drone would just have to shoot her. Hopefully, it wasn't set to kill.

Two or three minutes later, she detected lights from the corner of her eye. When she tried to turn her head toward it, however, the drone squawked again and its eyes went to red alert.

"Ooh. Looks like you done made your babysitter mad." The

voice coming over her helmet had a lilting accent that sounded vaguely Caribbean. "Hold still, I'll get rid of it."

A second later, the drone's lights turned green. Then it sounded four cheery notes and disappeared back into the trench.

"Thank you." Claire sat up straighter, rolling her shoulders and arching her back to release the built-up tension. Then she turned toward the vehicle. It looked a bit like a dune buggy—with extra-wide tires and a completely open frame, aside from the roll cage. Both of the passengers were in bulky Stay-Puft suits, and they took up most of the space inside the vehicle.

"You Kara?" the guy asked.

"Yes."

"Just makin' sure," he said with a chuckle. "Wouldn't wanna get all the way back to camp and find out we'd picked up the wrong passenger."

Claire flexed her stiff legs and decided it was a bad idea to trust them so close to the edge at the moment. She crawled a few meters to a spot where there was a wider ledge of flat ground before slowly getting to her feet.

"You okay?" the man in the buggy asked.

"Yeah, just trying to get the blood flowing back into my feet."

The guy on the right was out of the buggy now, motioning toward a small jump seat in the back. He was saying something, too, but she couldn't hear him. Apparently, whatever they were using to tap into the frequency of her helmet's comm system only allowed transmissions from one person.

As she drew closer, she was kind of glad she couldn't hear the second guy. Even though she couldn't see his face clearly behind the helmet, something about the way he was standing gave off bad vibes—one foot on the rim of the tire, his arm resting casually on top of the buggy. Was he actually trying to give off swagger vibes in a puffsuit?

The guy who was still in the buggy pointed to a towel on the empty seat. "Use that to wipe the creeper grass off your suit and shoes before you get in. Otherwise, it'll cover the whole damn floorboard before we get back to camp and then I'll have to spray down the inside as well as the outside."

She took the towel and followed his instructions. Swagger-Guy was standing a little too close for her comfort, watching her intently.

"Just drop the towel out there," the first man said. "It will disintegrate. I'm Ajay. And that's Bowen. Ignore his bad manners. He's imaginin' what you look like underneath that suit even though Carson told him you are married and said we better not do anything to piss the princess off."

She was close enough now that she could hear the other guy tell Ajay to shut the hell up. Ajay ignored him, but the princess remark unnerved her. It seemed like the kind of nickname they might use if they'd pieced together who she was, and while it wasn't likely, it also wasn't impossible. The trio in the concourse on Ares Station had recognized her. Other people may have, too, and they could easily have posted on one of the Martian social media sites. And if these people knew who she was, they probably weren't going to be satisfied with six thousand credits. She'd be willing to pay more, but this could easily deteriorate into being in a hostage situation herself rather than heading to Nepenthes to resolve one.

"Gonna be a tight fit," Ajay said. "But this is all we could sneak out of the motor pool without raising red flags. And Carson didn't say nothin' about you being in a hardshell suit. I thought those were only for like … maintenance crews at Ares Station?"

"Maybe. It was the only kind of suit on board. Guess they got it cheap as surplus or something. God, I hope it's not defective." She added a nervous laugh as she climbed into the back and wedged her legs behind Ajay's seat.

Ajay instructed the buggy to head back to base. "We got a bit of a drive ahead. Gotta go all the way back around that big ditch you nearly tumbled into. And then we're gonna have to wait at the motor pool until Carson gives us the all clear. You picked a bad time to crash. Hyblaeus is hoppin' tonight. We had nobody here for like the whole month since we came over from Lyot but now it's buzzin' like Tranquility Base. You got enough room back there?"

"Yes," she lied.

"Good, 'cause otherwise we'll have to make Bowen ride on top. Hey bug lights out."

He didn't pause at all before the last part, and the words ran together. While her brain was trying to figure out if she'd heard him correctly, the buggy's lights flipped off. She opened her mouth to ask whether that was a good idea this close to the edge of the trench, but Ajay either anticipated the question or caught her expression from the corner of his eye.

"We gotta run dark. Otherwise, we're likely to get caught. I only turned on the lights so we didn't sneak up on you. This little bug don't need the lights, anyway. She knows the way home. So, Carson says you were headin' to Elysia from Noachis. What do you do there?"

Her mind went blank for a moment, as she tried to think of something she could tell him. Mining was out, since she knew very little about the job, and even less about Noachis. Paul had told her that Pada, the company that owned Icarus Camp, was one of the few that hired women for the actual mining jobs, so she probably needed to make it a support role. "I'm a cook. Sort of. I mostly make sandwiches for the grab-and-go case."

"See, that's the kind of thing we need here at Hyblaeus. We had fresh food the first week we were here, but all we've got now are floater rations like we ate on the worker transport. They say it will be better once lockdown ends, but I'm not holdin' my breath, you know?"

Ajay kept up an amiable patter for the next few minutes. He seemed like a nice enough guy, and Claire didn't want to be rude. He'd said he was a relative newcomer, having arrived on Mars only a few months before lockdown, but if the conversation kept going there was a chance one of these guys would realize she was making everything up as she went along. So, she closed her eyes part way and leaned her helmet against one of the bars behind her as if exhausted, which wasn't entirely a lie.

After a few of her mumbled responses, Ajay switched the helmet over to talk to Bowen. Claire could still hear them, although it was more like a conversation in the next room, instead of having Ajay's voice inside her ear.

"I'm startin' to get worried, man. We shoulda seen the plane take off by now. You think maybe we missed it?"

Bowen ignored him.

Ajay shook his head, clearly annoyed. "Man, you need to quit sulkin'. I was doing you a favor, 'cause I *know* you. You were two seconds away from runnin' your mouth, or worse. Then this lady tells the princess, who cancels payment, and you've ruined the whole damn thing."

Okay. So, the *princess* quip was directed at Marisol Alvarado, not at her. Which probably meant they'd convinced her to put up the promised six thousand credits in advance.

Bowen waved a dismissive hand. "She's not a princess, dumbass."

"Might as well be," Ajay countered. "They may have elected titles, but her mama owns Elysia every bit as much as that Kolya guy owns Daedalus. She's next in line. That sounds a whole lot like a princess to me."

"Yeah, well, like I said. You're a dumbass."

They continued in silence for about ten minutes. If the terrain hadn't been so bumpy and the chasm off to their right so ominously close, she might have been able to doze off.

When the buggy finally cleared the edge of the gorge, it made a sharp turn to the right.

"Welp," Ajay said, "guess we didn't miss it. Still on the damn runway."

Bowen let loose with a string of curses. "Remind me to kick Carson's ass. He *said* they'd be gone by now. Pull into the *back* hangar. They'll be less likely to see us out there. Maybe we can just wait it out."

"Way ahead of you, man."

Bowen cursed again and banged his fist against the side of the buggy. "I shoulda known. We're gonna get caught over this piddly two thousand credits and they'll bump me off the away team."

"You really plannin' to take them up on that?"

"Sure. Why the hell not? You seriously telling me you're gonna pass up 10k? That would almost make up for what Wes cheated us out of in bonus money due to the lockdown."

The bonus payments had been a huge sticking point in the labor negotiations Kolya mediated at Daedalus before the lockdown began. Bonuses made up a major percentage of the money that the two-year workers made on their contracts. And workers couldn't stay beyond two years unless they decided to become permanent residents. Mine owners had initially said the bonuses wouldn't be paid at all for that period, just base pay, but the fledgling Mars Federation of Labor had threatened a strike. Claire didn't know the exact terms of the agreement, but they'd settled somewhere near the middle, with the workers getting partial bonuses for the time they were in lockdown—which, in the case of Hyblaeus, had apparently only been around four months, rather than the full six. And did Bowen mean they'd only gotten the agreed-upon amount or had Westmoreland refused to cover even that much?

Something began rattling against the hard seat of the buggy. It took a second for Claire to realize it was her phone. They must have moved within signal range. She shifted in her seat until the noise stopped, but the two guys up front didn't seem to have noticed.

Ajay sighed. "I don't know. If I wanted to carry a gun for some rich asshole, I coulda stayed on Earth. I came here to get away from all that. The money would be nice. Give me a bit more to send back home. But … you tellin' me that one guy don't give you the creeps?"

"The one with the face tats?"

Claire's breath caught in her throat. There were plenty of people with face tats, though. It didn't necessarily mean…

"Yeah, he's weird, alright. But he ain't in charge. And the other guy seems okay."

"If you say so. Personally, I don't trust nobody who walks around in cowboy boots."

"My view is, it's good money. They're a bunch of freaks anyway. Pacifist freaks, on top of that. They're not gonna put up any resistance. Honestly, I don't even think they need to worry with getting people from Lyot. We probably got enough volunteers here that they'll cave in thirty seconds flat." Bowen lowered his voice to the point that she could barely make it out. "And most of them are *women*. They ain't gonna fight us. Some of 'em might even be glad to see a real man for a change."

Well, that confirmed it. They were talking about Ehden. Claire sat up as best she could and arched her back a bit, as if she'd been sleeping, hoping it would prompt Bowen to shut up. The last thing she wanted was to hear this guy fantasizing about the spoils of war.

She had a clear view of the hangar now. It blocked part of the landing area, though, so she couldn't see the smaller of the two planes she'd noticed when she zoomed in on the camp.

The rear of the second craft—which was much, much larger—wasn't visible either. But she'd just spent nearly three weeks onboard a raptor. She didn't need to see the KTI logo on the back half to know that she was looking at the *Velox One*.

THIRTEEN

JUST BEFORE THEY reached the dome at Hyblaeus Camp, the buggy dipped down into an airlock tunnel. It continued for maybe a hundred meters, eventually emerging inside a hangar, where it squeezed past two larger vehicles, and parked on one of the two remaining charging pads. The building seemed smaller than it had appeared from the outside, although Claire thought that might be because it was packed pretty much from wall to wall with other vehicles, assorted maintenance equipment, and storage crates that took up more than a third of the space on the left.

Ajay and Bowen remained inside the buggy when it stopped. They seemed to be listening for something. Neither man spoke, which seemed out of character, at least for Ajay.

After about a minute of silence, she asked "Is there a problem?"

"Yeah." Ajay's voice didn't come through her helmet speaker this time, so it was more muted. "We gotta wait for the all-clear from Carson. That plane out there should have already left fifteen, maybe twenty minutes ago. But ... I'm thinkin' now that me and Bowen should maybe head into the dome. Find Carson, see if he knows what's up. I would just call him, but we obviously can't have this conversation over the normal channels. They check every damn thing. You wait here, okay? We'll be back in five, maybe ten."

"I can wait with her," Bowen said.

"The hell you can. And don't give me that look. You wanna

get caught out here and screw up your chance at those big bucks you mentioned earlier?"

"No."

"Then move your ass." Ajay motioned Bowen toward the tunnel entrance, then turned back to Claire. "How's your air?"

"Sixty-eight percent, but the light just went on saying it's pulling in external at the moment."

He nodded. "Yeah, you'd be fine without the suit in here, but I don't know what sort of transport they'll be sending or how soon it arrives so probably best to stay in your gear. Like I said, shouldn't be long. I'm guessin' the delay is because Little Stevie made the techs doublecheck his plane. His dad's shuttle crashed a few months back. Some mechanical issue, but he's convinced it was tampered with so he's like super paranoid. Makes a big show of having two or three different techs check the plane out. Carson says he even repacks his own parachute before each trip."

"That makes sense, I guess. How far is he flying?"

She knew it might be a weird question to ask, and judging from the slight tilt of Ajay's head, he agreed. Still, he answered. "All the way to Lyot. So you can't really blame him for wantin' to make sure everything is in order. Anyway, this is mostly a storage shed, so I doubt anyone will come in. But stay in the buggy and try to keep outta sight, okay? Just in case."

Claire slunk back down onto the seat. She gave it a couple of minutes to be sure the men were gone and then unfastened the side pocket on her suit and pulled out her phone to see if she still had a signal.

The small green light flickered once, then steadied. Sending a message was risky. Her encryption apps were solid enough that she wasn't worried about anyone reading the messages, but they might be able to tell that a call was going out from the hangar. Still, she had no way of knowing when or even if she was going to make it to Elysia. This might be her only chance to get a message to Wyatt, so it was a risk she had to take.

Crashed near Hyblaeus Catena. K & M injured, shuttle leaking oxygen. They have suits but they need help ASAP.

I'm okay. Hiked to mining camp. Open despite lockdown but owned by Wes Jr. I bribed someone to contact Elysia—only a few hundred klicks from here. Macek has a friend in high places there. I've been told Elysia is sending a shuttle.

VELOX ONE is here at Hyblaeus. Probably NOT Durav. Boudreaux and an ipret-tai, from what I overheard. I think they're planning to attack Nepenthes. Some of the mining crew agreed to fight with them. Going to Lyot first, though.

She started to type more, but Wyatt could read between the lines. He'd understand what to do with the information—get it to Paul, so that Paul could pass it on to the people at Nepenthes and anyone else who needed to know. She ended by adding the location marker she'd recorded before leaving the shuttle and posted a second marker with her current location.

And then she waited, hoping for the sort of immediate response she always got on Earth. But she already knew that wasn't the norm on Mars. It would be several minutes, at a minimum. If by some miracle they'd managed to convince Paul to break the lockdown protocol, they could even be on their way to Nepenthes Station, in which case it might be hours. Then she remembered the messages that had come in earlier, when the buggy first rolled into range of the Hyblaeus comms network. There were three, all from Wyatt.

She opened the most recent message. The first three-quarters of the text was straightforward—*why aren't you answering, you should have arrived by now, WORRIED, please message me back*. He added the troubling but not entirely surprising news that Kolya had ordered his security team to place Stasia under house arrest at the Red Dahlia, and the surprising but very welcome news that

Paul and Beck would be leaving shortly for Nepenthes. The last part, however, was mostly in code, reminding her of their conversations during her previous Mars trip.

> Unfortunately, I need to stay behind. Paul says the connectivity sucks at Ehden, and I have a colleague here in Daedalus who has offered desk space. Erika is pushing me to submit my draft article about the Idaho trial ASAP. Trying to avoid a situation where she ends up in the crosshairs again. I'm afraid Andrus (and the rest of the editorial mob) will drag her to the gallows and there's nothing I can do to take the heat off when I'm so far away. Love you—and again, WORRIED. Message me back NOW.

Erika was his editor. There was, however, no upcoming article about a trial in Idaho. That part could only refer to the Boise Bois trial that took place a few years back, not long after she started work at the *Post*. The phrase *in the crosshairs* was an obvious reference to the threats that most of the reporters received during that trial with their byline photos printed from the website with crosshairs over their faces. Wyatt, who had written the article that enraged the group, had told her a few months back that he received *two* photos in his envelope—one with his face in the crosshairs and one with Claire's.

There was no one named Andrus or any *editorial mob* above Erika in Wyatt's chain of command at the *Post*. But she recognized the reference. Members of the Boise Bois militia had dragged two lawmakers who were in favor of the state rejoining the US into Andrus Park outside the state capitol and shot them. Four of them were arrested, put on trial, and convicted. Two months after the verdict was handed down, however, Idaho voted against returning to the union and elected one of the Boise Bois loyalists as governor. As soon as he was in office, he not only pardoned those who were convicted, but issued a commendation for everyone who took part.

All of this was several years in the past, though. Wyatt could be referring to Boudreaux's connection to militias outside his own Lone Star group, but the specific reference to Andrus and the mob seemed to point more toward the lynching.

Her translation: Wyatt believed Stasia was at risk of mob violence and he was staying behind to either keep an eye on the situation or to help the colleague he mentioned try to douse the flames of public sentiment. Possibly both. And the fact that he was speaking in code to avoid the KTI censors, meant that he thought Kolya's security forces were involved. Maybe even Kolya himself.

FOURTEEN

CLAIRE WAS SO focused on trying to piece together the clues that she didn't hear the tunnel hatch open. Neither of the voices belonged to Ajay or Bowen, so she turned off the phone and shoved it into the pouch, then flattened herself as much as possible against the floorboard, praying that they hadn't noticed the light from her screen.

They were talking about a recent shipment of guns, with one of the men ticking off a short list of what she assumed were rifles. "And we got one dozen M41As, as requested. You wanna look at those? They're right over here."

"I guess," the second man said.

She held still, taking shallow breaths. From her vantage point, she could see the men from their knees up. One was dressed to impress, with polished loafers and creased trousers that seemed a bit ludicrous at a mining camp. The second guy wore jeans and cowboy boots. His voice was deeper than the first man's and while their accents weren't identical, they had a similar twang. A *Texas* twang, which pretty much confirmed their identities. Boudreaux had been with Lone Star, and one of the men she eavesdropped on at Kolya's ACON dinner had said that Westmoreland Sr. pissed off half of that state before relocating his business to Mars. As the men drew closer, she spotted a third set of feet a few meters behind them, wearing white hi-tops with a black swoosh on the side. He seemed to be observing rather than joining in. Was that the *ipret-tai?*

She heard the scraping noise of something being dragged

across the dirt, then a beep, followed by a slight popping sound that must have been the crate opening.

"I've got two more boxes of these babies with the drones at Claritas," Westmoreland said. "This whole stash is maybe a quarter of what we've got there, but it's serious overkill for your little project. You need fifteen, twenty men, max. Maybe not even that if we bring a bunch of drones back. My source says your target's got a couple guns they liberated from security guards, but that's it."

Boudreaux made a non-committal huffing noise. "Are we taking these weapons with us?"

"Nah. Not enough room. I'm in a four-seater. I'll have the volunteers bring what we need on the personnel transport."

"And you're sure you can trust your people to keep an eye on all this? Because you just said—"

"What I *just said* is that we didn't need to have this discussion in the bar with half the workers in that dome, any one of whom might have overheard us. And yeah, I got people I can rely on, but like my daddy always said, trust but verify. And personally, I lean toward the latter option. Every damn one of these crates is sealed with a biometric lock and a shock guard. Same at Claritas. I'm the only one who can open them, and I can assure you that anyone else who tries won't be messing with my things a second time." Westmoreland hesitated for a moment, then continued. "There's only one thing we're still waiting on and that's the sarin. It probably won't arrive until after they lift the travel ban. They don't make the stuff here, and what with the lockdown and all, off-planet contraband is hard to come by. We've got plenty of explosives, though, or I got a local—"

"I told you already," Boudreaux said. "Explosives aren't gonna cut it. I need the buildings intact. Otherwise, we gotta comb through tons of rubble and I want us out of there before Kolya sends in reinforcements."

"Oh, reinforcements ain't gonna be a problem, my friend," Wes said with a dark chuckle. "Kolya's gonna have all of his reinforcements in Daedalus City. They're probably already in route."

He didn't elaborate, but Claire's confidence in her interpretation of Wyatt's message grew tenfold at the tone of the man's laugh. It also had her wondering if Westmoreland had people in Daedalus stirring up trouble.

"But," Wes said, "you didn't let me finish. You don't need the sarin, and you don't need explosives. I've got a homegrown alternative that we collected at the beginning of stage six. That lime green *Azo* shit KTI cooked up will do exactly what you want. The structures will remain intact, minus the inhabitants. We've already seen how fast it can zip through a dome, and as for the lab, my source says KTI's got all of their people, including security, in the underground section of the lab due to the damage above and the hostage situation."

That tracked with something Kolya had told Claire earlier, and it made sense, anyway. The upper section of the lab had taken a serious hit.

"All you gotta do is prep one of the tunnels to the lab. Blast it with perchlorates, then we pipe in a bit of the *Azo* and wait. Only takes a few people inhaling it and an hour or so later, all of them will be coughin' up green snot and droppin' like flies. Once the KTI crew has cleared out, we can fan out into the buildings until you locate your man. Any of our folks who go in after that will need biogear, but that would be the case with your sarin, too, right?" There was a snap, and another scraping sound, as he moved the crate back into place.

The two men began walking, but the Nikes remained in the same spot. Had the *ipret-tai* seen her?

"Personally," Wes continued, "I'd have used *Azo* for the Nepenthes lab hit if I'd been handling it. Woulda been poetic justice, in my opinion, to hit them with their own creation. But Berger said they needed the visual to sync up with the Earth attacks and they were picky about limiting the number of casualties. Since you're less squeamish in that regard, we should be fine.

But again, if you want the most bang for your buck, we need to flip the script so you can get in on both. I could really use your skills on the personal project. Shepherd's not going anywhere right now and timing is everything, man. Once lockdown ends we lose our advantage. I'm tellin' you, we pull this off, we've got the whole planet under our thumb."

"Really?"

"Well, most of it. I don't think Elysia will back us, but the others will. We're not gonna get a better opportunity..."

Their voices faded out. The Nikes still didn't move, but they shifted slightly to the right. Maybe Wes and Boudreaux were examining another crate out of earshot?

Finally, the Nikes headed off in the same direction. Claire took a deep breath for the first time since they entered. She didn't move, though. There was no way to tell whether the men had left the hangar, and she still half-expected the *ipret-tai* to creep around to the other side of the buggy and grab her by the boots.

So, she just lay there, her mind spinning at what she'd heard. They weren't just attacking Ehden. They were planning to take out the lab, too. A nasty little voice inside her head pointed out that their plan to wipe out the Nepenthes lab would solve the whole problem of Kolya's exoplanet project, or at least seriously delay it. But at what cost? She couldn't even stomach the idea of sacrificing Davy, Idi, and the other hostages. But there were dozens of other scientists assigned to that lab. Families, too. And they'd be hitting Ehden, as well. She needed to get another message to Wyatt, so that he could warn Paul. Even though Paul didn't handle security, he could contact Davy and give her a heads-up.

And the Berger guy that Wes mentioned. The name didn't ring a bell for her, but maybe it would for KTI security. It still didn't fully absolve Drex and Stasia, since the Flock contracted with the man, but it might give the mob that was apparently forming—possibly with Westmoreland's help—an alternative target for their rage.

When Ajay's voice sounded inside her helmet a few seconds later, it startled her so badly that she whacked her head against the jump seat.

"Hold tight just a little bit longer, okay? We'll have you outta there pronto."

He was gone before she could respond. All she could do was lie there and wait, watch the seconds ticking away on her visor, and hope that he was right.

Four minutes and twenty-three seconds later, the buggy began to shake. It lasted less than a minute, and then everything went quiet again until she heard footsteps.

"Okay, they're gone." Ajay, still in the puffsuit, dropped himself back into the driver's seat. "Carson signaled to your ride that the coast is clear. Should be here in two minutes, maybe three. Although I got no idea how he's gonna explain a skimmer takin' off with a passenger to the two techs out there strippin' down that raptor. Bowen's gonna be pissed if we have to split the credits five ways instead of three. Six ways most likely, since you know Carson. He's gonna keep a full share for himself."

Claire, who didn't really know Carson at all, was still certain that Ajay was right. "So, it's safe to sit up now?"

"Yeah, yeah. Li'l Stevie's plane lifted off a couple minutes ago. Carson says that man ain't come here twice the whole time he's worked at Hyblaeus, and suddenly he's givin' guided tours. It definitely makes you wonder what he's hidin' in those crates."

She was tempted to tell him that it would be a very bad idea to go poking around. But did she really want to let him know how much she'd overheard?

"Come on," he said, extending a hand to help her out of the jump seat. "We need to get closer to the hatch so I can listen for Bowen's signal."

Claire stood and stretched as best she could. Her left foot had gone pins-and-needles again, so she limped slightly as she followed him toward a hatch beyond the maze of around twenty crates. Westmoreland had said this was only about a quarter of the weapons. She wasn't a munitions expert by any means, but it looked like far more weapons than they'd need to kill everyone in Ehden, Doba, the lab and any other dome at Nepenthes Station.

Someone was already tapping on the wall when they got to the hatch. Ajay entered something into the control panel. When the door opened, they stepped into the airlock. A few seconds later, the outer hatch opened to the landing strip. Sure enough, two men in puffsuits were standing next to the *Velox One*, apparently overseeing the four robot mechanics that were pulling parts from the ship. The two men nodded in their direction, and one pointed at the vehicle waiting off to the left, seeming to confirm Ajay's speculation that they were being paid to keep quiet.

Her ride was a single-seat skimmer. It was enclosed, thank god, but still not much wider than a motorcycle. Having just lived through a crash, her first thought was that it offered absolutely no protection from impact. But what choice did she have?

Ajay laughed, seeming to pick up on her reaction. "Yeah, the princess really rolled out the red carpet for you, didn't she? No life support in these little buggers so you're gonna have to stay in that suit all the way to Elysia."

"That's okay," she said. "At least, she was willing to help. And Carson confirmed that she was sending a rescue team to the crash site, right?"

Ajay shrugged and tapped on the side of the skimmer to open the door. "I guess? All he said was that they transferred the credits to his account. Which I can promise you is the only thing he was worried about. Money is that man's only motivator."

Of course, Ajay was one of the two people Carson turned to as likely assistants for his scheme, which suggested that money was probably pretty high on his list of motivators as well. But that could be said about the vast majority of people inside that dome. On the entire planet. Earth, too, for that matter.

"You have a good trip now, okay?" Ajay grinned at her, his face slightly green inside the visor. "And try not to crash this thing."

The door began to close, but Claire waved her hand to stop it. Kolya wasn't entirely wrong in his observation that growing up with money skewed your perspective. And growing up without money might increase the temptation for Ajay to peek inside those crates. Probably not, given that they belonged to the boss, but the note of curiosity in his voice had been clear. He'd also been nice to her when he didn't have to be, and that wasn't a given.

"Hey, Ajay? You shouldn't go poking around in those crates back there. Your boss has them booby-trapped."

FIFTEEN

CLAIRE'S AIR indicator dipped to amber about twenty minutes west of Hyblaeus, but she wasn't worried. She'd be at Elysia in less than half an hour, and the rescue team should have already arrived for Kolya and Macek. She browsed through her messages from Wyatt again, mostly for comfort, since the skimmer had no service and there was nothing new from him. She noticed the files Kolya had given her earlier containing his correspondence with Davina Monroe, and opened the first one, but she couldn't focus. After a while, she put away her phone and simply allowed the shapes in the viewport to float past her eyes. They were just dark blobs of varying sizes, barely even distinguishable as geographical features in the faint light of the distant stars and the one minuscule Martian moon that the Ares Consortium had left intact.

The effect was hypnotic, and she might have dozed off, despite the rigid discomfort of the hardshell suit. But each time she closed her eyes, she found herself back in the shuttle as it crashed and bounced. Or she saw Macek slumped against the wall, his face pale and sweaty inside his visor. Or Kolya pinned beneath the console. The entire day seemed surreal, even in the context of the past six completely insane months of her life. First the explosions at Ares Station, then the crash, and the hike to Hyblaeus. Add in the fact that she'd just bribed a man she'd never met into sending an encrypted message to a leader of the Elysian government, and it felt a bit like she'd been dropped into a poorly plotted spy novel.

As Elysia grew larger and brighter in the viewport, she kept waiting for her phone to buzz again. Surely she was closer now than she'd been in the shuttle. The four pods had barely been more than tiny points of light. But whatever access Macek had given her earlier was either temporary or required his phone to be nearby.

In a final assault to her frayed nerves, the skimmer bypassed a perfectly serviceable landing field and seemed to be aiming at a tiny mousehole near the bottom of the base supporting the four colossal cones—each of which had to be nearly a kilometer across—that housed the colony. Her stomach lurched at the sight, so she focused on the other pods off in the distance.

They reminded her of giant wine glasses, with the spinning cones as the bowls. Surrounding each bowl was a silver mesh frame, with a single wider thread of the same material wrapped around the bowl in a spiral. The frames narrowed at the bottom to form the stem of each glass. All four cones sat on a base that looked like it was about the height of a New York skyscraper. Each cone—or pod, as they were apparently called by the residents—stretched upward for what looked like hundreds of meters from base to rim, not counting the stem. Some sections of the pods were transparent, but they were spinning too rapidly for Claire to make out anything inside. Just three blurry goblets. Two were slightly muted, marbled in shades of navy blue and dark green, with occasional blips of light, while the third looked as if someone had filled the bowl with multicolored Christmas lights before they set it spinning.

When she had flown by with Kolya on their trip from Daedalus to Nepenthes, he'd told her that the colony had originally been enclosed in a dome, and they'd made some attempts to cultivate the land. At some point, though, they'd abandoned the dome and simply relied on tunnels to move between the pods. Now, the colonists rarely ventured outside. He'd said they used the tunnel-like base to navigate between the pods, but she could also see bridgeways between the frames surrounding the pods, so perhaps they had a shuttle system, as well.

Claire didn't think she'd ever want to live anywhere on Mars, but she could at least imagine life inside a domed habitat like Daedalus, Ehden, or even the two mining camps. The sky might be different from the one on Earth, but at least you could *see* it. Here, though? She couldn't fathom why anyone would choose to spend their entire lives within the confines of four spinning cones.

The skimmer was now entering the base of the closest pod. She squeezed her eyes shut and felt a moment of panic as the vehicle dipped downward into the tunnel and kept going. Finally, she felt a tiny jolt as its landing skids hit the surface. When she opened her eyes, she found herself in complete darkness. Then a bright, almost blinding light filled the narrow cabin, and an annoyingly cheerful female voice began an announcement. Claire frowned, trying to piece together what was being said with her two years of college Spanish, but then the voice switched to English.

"Welcome to Elysia. We hope you enjoy your visit. Please be sure to gather all of your personal items and exit through the door on the left."

"Like I have a choice," Claire muttered under her breath as a mechanical click sounded and the door on the left—which was the *only* door—slid upward. She unlatched her seatbelt and slipped out into a tunnel and followed the arrows to the decontamination chamber. She'd gone through a similar process at Icarus Camp when moving between the dome and the mining area, but it was part of the airlock tunnel and only took about a minute. This was a glaringly white cylinder, and there were four separate cycles of about ninety seconds each. When the final light turned green, she entered a dimly lit chamber.

As her eyes adjusted, she saw a small figure emerge from the shadows. A girl, no older than eight or nine. She had an oval face and long dark curls and wore a shapeless blue dress that clung to the thin bones of her shoulders.

The girl cast a wary look at Claire, then gave a polite half-bow and said, "You'll need to leave your suit in the *vestíbulo*." Her voice was slightly husky and her English was precise. Claire didn't think it was her native tongue, though, given the way she rolled the *v* into a soft *f*.

The vestibule was a small hexagonal chamber, lined on three sides with lockers and benches. Claire removed her phone from the suit's external pocket.

"Is there any chance you could connect my phone? I have friends who will be very worried by now."

"Sorry," the girl said with a helpless shrug. "I don't have authority. You'll have to request permission."

Claire nodded, then stripped down to the tee and shorts she'd chosen that morning simply for their comfort. She'd planned to change into something slightly more formal when she reached Nepenthes, but that was no longer an option since the bag with all of her other clothes was floating somewhere in space. Her shirt and shorts were both drenched now, and her feet were bare aside from a pair of thin cotton footie socks. She shivered in the frigid air, feeling woefully underdressed. The servant girl seemed to agree, judging from the slightly pinched look on her face as she watched silently from the corner.

"I don't suppose you could point me toward a bathroom?"

The girl blinked and tipped her head toward a smaller tunnel on the right. "There's one where we're going."

Thankfully, the air grew warmer as they continued into the tunnel, which smelled faintly of antiseptic. She kept expecting them to enter a docking cube like the ones at Ares Station or the Red Dahlia that would get them up to the same velocity as the pod above them so that they could enter, but they remained at ground level, or slightly below, winding through several narrow hallways until they finally arrived at a large, softly lit office. It was empty at the moment but clearly used regularly. A desk near the center of the room was covered with assorted devices and gadgets. Only a small area was clean near the center. It held a sketch pad and an oversized coffee mug with a logo shaped like one of the pods and the word ElyCorp. Claire had a vague memory of Kolya speaking the word. Maybe it was the colony's mining operation?

"The bathroom is at the back," the girl said. "I will tell *la vicepresidenta* that you are here."

Claire nodded again, too exhausted to process more than the immediate relief of a real toilet and running water. She rinsed her face, using cold water at the end to wake herself up, and then stood for a few seconds in front of the mirror. Her dark hair was a tangled mess, her cheeks bore angry red splotches from rubbing against the inside of the helmet, and her left collarbone sported an angry bruise that she didn't even remember getting. She ran her fingers through her hair a few times and decided it was the best she could do under the circumstances.

The girl in the blue dress was waiting in the office, but she was no longer alone. In fact, she was barely noticeable due to the new arrival, whose presence seemed to fill the room. She was tall, with an athletic build and rigid posture that was somewhat at odds with the long black hair that fell in soft waves nearly to her waist.

The woman spoke first to the girl, her voice resonant and slightly husky. "It seems that you were correct, Angelina. This does indeed appear to be the reporter who covered the Icarus discovery." She sat in the desk chair and shifted her gaze to Claire. "I don't believe that Claire Echols was the name I was given by her friends at Hyblaeus Camp, however."

"They're not my *friends,*" Claire said. "I hiked to Hyblaeus after our shuttle crashed. Given the lockdown, I didn't expect anyone to be there. My instructions were to find the communications system and get a message to you. When I realized the camp was occupied, it seemed unwise to give the man my actual name. If he'd known he was dealing with Kai Jonas's daughter, I doubt that he'd have settled for a mere six thousand credits."

"Six thousand?" Her brows, dark and thick, creased in annoyance. "I paid him *twelve*. Which, I suppose, more than proves your point."

"I'll reimburse you for that as soon as I can contact my bank."

Marisol waved a hand as if the money wasn't important. "The little weasel who called also gave me a second name. He said that it was your shuttle pilot. Could you repeat that name for me?"

"Yes. Jaromir Ambrosevich, captain of the shuttle DS-9. His last name is actually Macek, but he felt that it might be best to withhold that, since it could tip them to the fact that the third person on the shuttle—the one who was flying it, actually—is Anton Kolya."

"What a surprise." Her tone conveyed absolutely *no* surprise, however, and her mouth twisted slightly as she spoke.

Claire couldn't tell if her expression was amusement or annoyance, so she pressed on. "Have you heard back from the rescue team yet? Were they able to get them out safely?"

"I'm afraid not. I sent an unpiloted skimmer to the coordinates I was given. They'll have to take it from that point, because there's nothing more I can do."

SIXTEEN

CLAIRE SUCKED in her breath and tried to think of what to say next. She'd assumed that Marisol understood the stakes and would have sent a rescue team to the crash site at the same time the skimmer was sent to pick her up at Hyblaeus. Or even before, given what she'd told Carson the Conman.

"But *why?* Didn't he explain to you that they are injured?"

"He did. But the message came from *Hyblaeus*, Ms. Echols. That's a Lyotian camp. I don't know how well acquainted you are with Lyot and its leadership, but there was an excellent chance that this entire thing was a hoax. Not for the money—that's a trifling sum for Westmoreland's *cachorro*, who is every bit the scum his father was. But he knows he's facing some major fines and ... *cómo dices* ... diplomatic blowback, I guess, for breaking lockdown rules. It would make his life much, much easier if he could goad another colony, especially one like Elysia, into violating the rules, as well. Technically, I've already broken the lockdown protocol by accepting you without a proper declaration of medical emergency. I simply don't have the authority to send an entire rescue team. The best I could do was send that unmanned craft."

"The shuttle—Kolya's *personal shuttle*—released an emergency flare when we crashed a few hours ago. Check your logs. There's also hull damage and we vented even more air when Macek had to open the hatch to let me out. They're well into the reserves from their suits, by this point. And I'm telling you there are two *medical emergencies* on board. Macek's shoulder is broken, possibly shattered, and Kolya was unconscious when I left."

It was true. Mentioning that he seemed to be coming around didn't help their cause, so she edited that part out.

"It's going to take several people to extract them from that wreck," she continued, and then thought back to the creaking noise the panel made as she ascended to the top of the bulkhead. "They'll probably need a hoist of some sort, too, because even if Kolya is conscious now, the panel I climbed up to reach the hatch won't hold his weight. And it definitely won't hold Macek."

Marisol's expression didn't change, but she made a sound that might have been a laugh. "True. He's never been *un hombre pequeño*." She fell silent for a moment, then tilted her head and gave Claire an appraising look. "I assume Kolya and Macek were headed to Nepenthes to deal with the hostage situation. But I don't understand why *you* are here. Does Kolya have a dedicated press team following him around the clock now? Or are you accompanying one of them for *personal* reasons?"

The emphasis on the word *personal* left little doubt as to what the woman meant, but Claire ignored her implications. "I've been drafted to help negotiate with Shepherd. It's a long story." Claire hoped Marisol would take the hint, but the woman simply raised her eyebrows and waited. "I will *happily* give you all of the details, but I don't know how much time they have left. Do you seriously intend to let them die out there?"

The woman closed her eyes and heaved a loud sigh. "No. But unfortunately, we've reached the bounds of my authority. I was able to send out the unmanned craft during lockdown without further approval, but I'll have to ask my mother to clear sending out a rescue crew. I just hope she's still awake."

Claire didn't respond. Had Marisol added the last part because she didn't enjoy the prospect of waking her mother or because waking the woman wasn't even an option?

Marisol reeled off some instructions in rapid-fire Spanish to the girl, who was still standing at attention near the door. Claire thought she picked up the words *sopa* and *vestido*, but that was all she could make out.

The girl bobbed her head, shot a last nervous look at Claire, and vanished into the corridor. Marisol followed. Claire reached for her phone and then remembered she'd never asked about getting it connected. So, she simply waited in the chair facing the desk—the supplicant's chair, as she and Joe had always called it when summoned to Kai's office.

When the door opened about ten minutes later, it wasn't Marisol, but Angelina. She placed a tray on a small table near the window. At the center, a steaming bowl sent up the mingled aromas of simmered chicken and lime. The girl poured a glass of water from the pitcher, then laid a neatly folded dress over the back of a highbacked chair. "There is a brush in the pocket. And you should change before *mi abuelita* arrives. The *pozole* is still very hot anyway, too hot to eat."

Abuelita. She wasn't sure whether this meant Angelina was the grandchild of Marisol or of Marisol's mother. Either way, the girl clearly wasn't a servant, as Claire had assumed.

She returned to the bathroom, stripped off her T-shirt and shorts, and used the brush to repair some of the damage to her hair. It was still damp and flat, but there wasn't much she could do about it. The dress was a soft yellow shift that fell below her knees, with a cloth belt, loose sleeves that gathered at the wrists, and a single row of buttons down the front. The fabric was almost toasty, reminding her of chilly mornings as a small child when her father had tossed her clothes into the dryer to warm them before waking her to run errands with him or tramp off to one of his building sites.

"Better?" she asked the girl after she was done.

Angelina nodded. "*Abuelita* will be more likely to consider your request favorably now. She would find your short pants … *indecente.*" She said the word with an apologetic smile.

So, she was the *president's* granddaughter. Claire wondered if this was a typical chore for her, or if she'd been pulled in specifically because they needed someone they could trust not to gossip about this breach of the lockdown protocol.

"You should eat now," Angelina said, nodding toward the bowl. "I think they will be here soon."

Claire did as she was told. The *pozole* was rich and silky, with a touch of spice in the broth that was studded with hominy and shredded chicken. It burned the side of her tongue, which was still swollen from her chomping into it when the shuttle crashed, but she ignored the discomfort. As she ate, her thoughts went back to the girl's commentary on her cargo shorts. The hem hit around mid-thigh, far from what most people considered indecent. And given that Kolya, Paul, and others had mentioned that Elysia was heavily involved in the sexbot trade, the whole propriety thing struck her as odd. You'd think the leader of a colony that courted sex tourism would be a bit more relaxed.

Angelina stood by, silent and watchful, until the bowl was nearly empty. "They are coming now. I must clear this away."

The girl scurried out of the room with the tray, closing the door behind her. Claire heard voices outside, but they were muffled and speaking Spanish, so she couldn't understand anything. Then the door opened and the leader of Elysia entered, followed by her daughter.

The president was small and frail, dressed in a sheath of purple silk, buttoned to the throat. Her silver hair was piled into a bun held in place by opal-studded combs and her skin was creased with a mosaic of fine lines that reminded Claire of the marbled tea eggs that a friend of Rowan's once brought to a potluck. The woman walked without assistance, but each movement was measured and deliberate.

She took the chair behind her daughter's desk and once she was seated, cocked her head at Claire and motioned for her to sit. "I am María del Pilar Alvarado. *Explíqueme*. How bad is his injury?"

"I'm … not sure, ma'am. He was unconscious when I—"

"Not Kolya," Marisol said, looking somewhat embarrassed. "She authorized a rescue team to extract Kolya before we left her quarters. They should arrive at the crash site within half an hour and Kolya will receive any medical care he needs. Her question is about Jaromir."

"*Jaromir.*" The older woman repeated the name, making it sound like a curse.

Macek's comment about not being welcome in Elysia was beginning to make a lot more sense. She hesitated for a moment, thinking how annoyed he was likely to be at her revealing his weakness, but this didn't seem like the time to play down the extent of his injury.

"At first, he thought the shoulder was dislocated. He tried to reset it himself. But it's clearly broken, maybe even shattered. The pain was so bad that he passed out."

A tiny smile creased the corners of the president's mouth. "*Good.*"

Marisol sighed, her eyes shooting upward as if praying for patience.

"I don't think you understand," Claire continued, trying to contain her anger. "Macek's air will run out before anyone else could reach him. He will die if you don't help him!"

The smile widened, and the old woman opened her mouth. But before she could repeat the word *good,* Marisol interrupted with a long, angry stream of Spanish.

They went back and forth, voices rising, for nearly a minute. Finally, the older woman yelled "*¡Basta!*" and rolled up her sleeve to reveal an armscreen. She tapped something in, and then narrowed her eyes, looking first at Claire and then at her daughter. "There. Are you happy now? We will bring him here and we will treat him. And then he *leaves*. Do you understand me?"

The question was clearly intended for Marisol, but when she didn't answer, Claire filled the silence. "Yes. Thank you. Thank you so much, President Alvarado."

The old woman waved a dismissive hand and muttered several things Claire didn't understand. Then she stood up and turned toward the door. "Just be sure you keep that *pendejo* out of my sight."

PART III

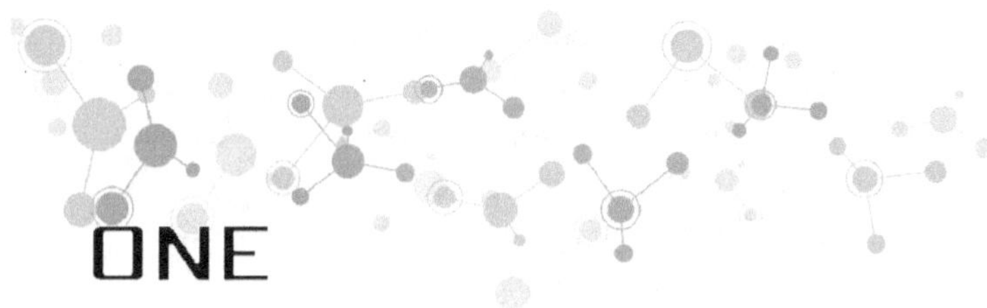

ONE

Wednesday, October 4
Topsfield, Massachusetts

ALICE STARED bleary-eyed at the menu screen on the table for several seconds, before realizing that her brain wouldn't be able to handle weighty decisions like what to have for breakfast without a jolt of caffeine. She took a mug from the rack, slid it beneath the spout, and filled it with coffee. It was lava-hot, even after a hefty dose of milk, but at least it didn't smell burnt. After pouring a second cup for Housen, who was connecting the rental car to the charger, she carried both mugs back to the booth. She settled into the padded bench, held the coffee to her face, and breathed in the aroma.

The diner, a tiny little dive just off I-95 called the Topsfield Hat, was practically empty at just after six on a Wednesday morning, and she'd managed to scurry in quickly enough that no one noticed she was barefoot aside from her tights. There were a few people in line at the takeout counter, though, so maybe the food was decent. Either way, they had a couple of hours to kill. She'd messaged Claire's brother around two a.m. to explain her situation, assuming that he would answer when he woke up. But he'd responded a few minutes later. *OK. Everly at 11. Careful running gauntlet.*

Either he was as much of a night owl as she was or—more likely given the terse message, she'd woken him up. She wasn't sure what he meant by the gauntlet remark, but Everly Estates was the neighborhood where the drone video had been taken.

Housen slid into the other side of the booth. He gave the mug a dubious look, then pushed it away and began scanning the menu. "Hope you're in the mood for a second cup, because no way am I drinking that."

"Hmm. Coffee aversion. Is that an alien thing, or…?"

"No, it's a *me* thing. I prefer tea."

"Weirdo," she said with a slow shake of her head. "But yes, I will absolutely be drinking a second cup, assuming it ever cools." The caffeinated steam had cleared her head enough to order, so she selected the pancakes when Housen turned the menu toward her. "I thought you might have decided to take off without me."

"I considered it. Not as retaliation for your own … surreptitious exit in New York, but as self-preservation."

After she'd shown Housen the video and gotten confirmation that the individual in the pool was almost certainly Sandjeel, she'd expected that he would be all onboard for contacting Joe Echols, but he'd greeted the idea with a surprising lack of enthusiasm. When she asked why, he'd spent the next half hour or so explaining his connection with the Flock and the role that he'd played in setting the bombs that had destroyed the Jonas Labs campus. She understood why the Flock had decided to take those actions, and even why Housen had agreed to help. But she'd be lying if she didn't admit that it lowered her trust in the guy a few notches. People had died in those explosions. Not many, because they'd been given advance warning, but…

"This still feels like a bad idea," he said. "I mean, we're not even sure that Sandjeel is there. And they almost certainly have footage of me in the building or on the grounds that day."

"If they had footage of you, why didn't they release it? You said they put out a sketch of the other guy, so…"

"One of them, yeah."

"Plus, if this Sandjeel guy is under lock and key, he's been lucky enough to land in a jail with a pool. Hanging out with what sounded like a small child. And Beck was at the lab that day, too, right? Now he's with Claire, on his way to Mars, so…"

"I know. It still makes me nervous."

He poked around on his phone for a bit after that. She normally didn't mind, but it felt rude when she had no device of her own with which to retaliate.

"You could get a hotel room and let me talk to him first," she suggested when their food arrived and he finally looked up from the screen for long enough to grab his omelet and hashbrowns from the cart.

"I considered that, too. But … I think I know what Echols meant with his comment about running the gauntlet. The Flock has had one or two chapters hanging out around here on rotation, protesting both at the main lab and at their neighborhood pretty much non-stop since the Rejuvesce announcement. A group of them blocked the car before Reese and I…" He trailed off, clearly not wanting to say *before we blew up the building*. "I just think you may have an easier time getting past the roadblock if I'm with you."

"You know a secret Flock handshake?"

"Something like that. Although, they've splintered even further in the past few weeks given Shepherd's absence and Drex's death. I have no idea which faction might be out there protesting today."

She poured some syrup on her pancakes, took an experimental bite, and then added another splash. "To be honest, I'm not worried about the Flock. I've dealt with them before. They had groups on campus on and off for the past few years. I even ran into them when I was studying in London."

"Okay, but … there are *other* groups picketing Jonas Labs, as well. A few of them could be even more capable of stirring up trouble."

The hesitant tone he used sent up warning signals. "Such as?"

"Gates of Destiny," he said around a bite of toast.

She struggled to keep her face neutral. "And why do you think they might be a problem?"

He lowered his voice. "Don't freak out, okay? I'm not going to give up your secret, and it doesn't necessarily mean you need to change anything. Whoever put together your papers did a good job. It's just … we needed new backgrounds frequently as Watchers. I helped create them, so I'm very familiar with the markers of a forged identity. I just pulled at a loose thread and eventually got to the info about your—or rather, Cecilia Cooper's—relationship with Mitchell Morris, her arrest warrant, and her supposed death." He shrugged. "I don't know how diligent you need to be about avoiding the group, but I thought you should know they've been maintaining a steady protest at the lab, so they'll likely be outside Kai Jonas's neighborhood, as well."

She sliced off a triangle of pancakes and stabbed it so hard that the fork vibrated in her hand. "To be clear," she said in an even lower voice. "I didn't steal *anything* from that bastard. When I was finally able to set up an escape, I left everything of his, including the engagement ring, in his apartment. His father no doubt collected the insurance money and then sold the ring under the table. The statute of limitations is up anyway, but I was never as worried about the actual police as I was the Gatekeeper's own enforcers. I've changed some aspects of my appearance. I actually *eat* now"—she nodded toward the pancakes and bacon—"instead of starving myself. Different hair, different style of dress. I have perfect eyesight, so the glasses are just for show. But yes, I avoid them. They've got an intel network like the frickin Mossad. And here's what wasn't in any police report because his daddy paid to keep it out. Mitch *shot* me in the leg during an argument that started because I embarrassed him by disagreeing with him in public. I'm sure he was even more embarrassed when I vanished a few weeks before our wedding. He'll probably aim much more carefully if he ever gets a second shot at me."

"I'm sure you're right. I've dealt with his kind before, and they don't mellow over time. Which, as nervous as it makes me, is why we should go in together. If we get stopped by the protesters, I'll take the lead. You can do the same with Jonas Labs security. I do need to figure out something to do with my gun, though. I'm sure they're scanning visitors, and it won't help our case if we roll in armed."

By the time they finished breakfast, the other booths were beginning to fill up. They still had a few hours until eleven, so they found a department store a few miles away where Alice picked up a pair of shoes, a replacement for her armscreen, a serviceable change of clothes, and an array of travel-size toiletries, since who knew when she'd be back at her apartment. Housen bought a waterproof bag and then hiked out into the woods near the shopping center to stash the gun.

The route to Everly Estates followed a narrow and winding two-lane road, with occasional glimpses of the Ipswich River through the trees. As they approached a curve about three hundred meters from the entrance, the car slowed.

"Reported lane closure ahead. Proceeding with caution."

"Could be road repair," Housen said. "The protesters generally don't block the roads because that gets the police involved. Well, the Flock doesn't do that, at least. It's in their rulebook."

"The Flock has a rulebook on protests?"

"Yeah. Rules for pretty much everything. Shepherd is a bit on the OCD side."

When they eventually rounded the corner, they found that the lane wasn't actually blocked. The road was partially obstructed on both sides by vehicles parked along the shoulders, leaving just enough room for them to squeeze past another two-seater heading toward them. The cars parked along the road seemed to be overflow from an undeveloped plot of land on the right, which she could now see was filled with protesters. Some held signs and banners. The steady rhythmic roar of their chants was audible even from inside the car.

"Guess Echols was right about running the gauntlet," Housen said.

It was a motley assortment of people. Some were Flock members, as Housen had predicted. A refurbished school bus with the Earth Watch Alliance logo—a garishly painted human eye with a globe in place of the iris—was parked at the back of the lot, under the shade of some overhanging trees.

He was right about the Gatekeepers, too. A tiny blossom of fear sprouted in her stomach, as it always did when she came face to face with any members of the Gates of Destiny. It wasn't the first time that she'd encountered one of their buses, although they were fairly uncommon in New York City. A branch operated in the Buffalo area, but the NYC franchise owner had been convicted of racketeering and fraud shortly before Alice took the job at Columbia. There had been talk the previous year of a prospective franchisee knocking down the old Javits building and constructing a worship center there, but the state decided to hold onto the property a bit longer so that they could use it as a Rejuvesce distribution center. That was probably another reason the Gatekeepers were pissed off about the new drug.

She wasn't actually worried about running into Mitch. His parents owned the Denver franchise, halfway across the country. None of their followers would be protesting in Boston. Aside from some joint national—and, in recent years, international—marketing and the massive annual gathering for the Gates of Destiny Jubilee, they tended to stay within their own borders. They certainly didn't proselytize outside their territory. There were plenty of sinners to go around, after all. No need to feed from your fellow Gatekeepers' troughs. The smiling couple whose picture was on the side of the bus did seem familiar, but that was probably because she'd seen them on a billboard the night before as they drove through the Boston Metro area.

"When did the Gatekeepers start tag-teaming with the Flock?" she asked.

"When Jonas Labs launched Rejuvesce," he said. "Opposition to longevity drugs makes for strange bedfellows, I guess."

"Maybe not so strange. Shepherd directs his followers to turn over all of their worldly goods, but they get room and board, right? The Gatekeepers only take ten to twenty percent, but all they give back is a big song and dance extravaganza once or twice a week. It probably balances out."

"Shepherd also used the surplus for environmental mitigation programs," Housen said. "While the Gatekeepers seem to spend theirs on mansions and private jets."

"Don't forget the small but vigilant army of spies and enforcers."

One of the two security guards posted at the intersection tapped on her window. She expected Housen to lower it—this was his rental car, after all—but then she remembered she was supposed to take the lead on dealing with Jonas Labs.

She pulled out her university ID and lowered the window just enough to hand it to the guard. "Alice Dobroski, Columbia University Archeolinguistics Department. I have an eleven o'clock appointment with Dr. Echols. He asked me to meet him here."

The man crouched down to peer through the window at Housen. "And you are?"

"My graduate assistant," Alice said. "Howard Senn. His English is seriously limited, but you should see what the man can do with an ancient Etruscan rune." She gave the guard her very best smile, which was probably only half as effective with dark circles under her eyes from a night with very little sleep. But it still had at least a hint of its usual oomph, apparently, because he gave a small monosyllabic chuckle as he handed back the ID and then stepped away to speak into his phone.

"You've seriously oversold my skill at translating ancient Etruscan," Housen said.

"Oh, no," she said with mock horror. "Whatever will we do if he comes back with a fragment from a funeral stele and gives you a pop quiz?"

The guard didn't come back to the window at all. Instead, four menacing drones rose up from the ground along the wall and circled around behind the car. Once the sentries were in place, the guard opened the gates and motioned their car into a narrow tunnel, where it braked instantly in response to the red light above the exit.

"What did I tell you?" Housen said. "A weapons sweep."

A few seconds later, the light began to flash, accompanied by a blaring sound.

"I thought you got rid of the gun," she hissed.

"I *did.*"

The guard was back at the window now. "I'm going to need both of you to step out of the car. Leave your belongings and keep your hands where I can see them."

TWO

"IS THERE A PROBLEM?" Alice knew it was a stupid question, given the wailing alarm and the man's expression. But it was exactly the thing someone would ask if she believed there shouldn't be a problem.

And there *shouldn't* be a problem. She'd searched her bag carefully and the taser was definitely not inside. Unless they'd somehow picked up the nail file she carried, or Housen had a second weapon that he'd forgotten to ditch, they were clean.

Whatever the problem was, it seemed to be with her, rather than with Housen. The guard told her to stand still, then pulled a scanning device from his pocket and strapped it to his palm. He crouched down in front of her and ran the scanner slowly along both sides of her skirt, keeping the device a few inches away from her body. It chirped softly at first, picking up in both speed and pitch as he moved upward. By the time he reached her temples, it was emitting a steady, metallic whine.

"Take off the glasses and hand them to me, please."

She did as she was ordered.

The guard examined them for a moment and pulled something off the inside of the frame. "Stay there, both of you. I need to call this in."

Alice could only hear his end of the conversation but gathered that the thing he'd pulled off of her glasses was a tracking device and that it was currently transmitting. Eyebrows raised, she stared meaningfully at Housen. She'd only fallen asleep for a few minutes in the car, but he'd tagged her pen at the club. It seemed reasonable that he might have done it a second time. But he shook his head firmly.

"Care to explain why you're wearing this tracker?" the guard said when he walked back over and returned her glasses.

"I didn't know that I *was* wearing it. But ... it's probably connected to the matter I need to discuss with Dr. Echols. Can I see it?"

The guard narrowed his eyes. "Sorry. That's not possible."

"Of course, it's *possible,*" Alice said. "All you have to do is open your hand. It was on *my* body. I want to know what I've been carrying around."

"Sorry. I have my orders. Get back into the vehicle. Tell it to take a right at the intersection and continue to the third house on the left. Someone will be waiting at the gate." He then turned to Housen. "You understand what I said?"

Housen nodded vigorously. "*Ja, ja, danke.*"

For a second, Alice wondered what he was doing and then remembered the story she'd given to the guard a few minutes earlier. Damn, she *really* needed sleep.

"*Mein pleasure.*" The guard glared at Housen as he spoke, packing the two words with more venom than Alice would have thought they could hold.

"Well, so much for our cover story," Housen said as the car pulled away.

"Yeah. Think you may be right that they have footage of you. Between his sudden change of attitude and that tracking device, whoever meets us will most likely be carrying handcuffs."

"And they'll probably be accompanied by more of those security drones."

Most of the homes in the neighborhood were barely visible from the street, set back on several acres with tree-lined gated driveways and towering hedges. The third drive on the left was 11 Everly Place, and the gate was closed.

Two people stood on the other side. Neither appeared to be carrying handcuffs and there were no drones nearby. Joe Echols was taller and more muscular than Alice would have guessed based on photos she'd seen. He had long dark hair and the same bronzed coloring as his sister.

The woman standing next to him was also exceptionally tall, with a willowy build, pale skin, and black hair that fell nearly to her waist. As soon as Housen lowered the window, she said, "Where the hell have you been? They found a body buried near the gift shop and given that it's been nearly three weeks, we'd pretty much decided it had to be yours."

A body near a gift shop? There was clearly a story there. Alice filed it away as something to ask later.

"No," Housen said. "I made it back from Arizona without any problems. *Mission accomplished.* The rest is a long story. I've mostly been running and hiding out from Durav. And now Alice is doing the same."

"Go ahead and send the car back," Joe said to Housen. "Sorry to make you hike up the drive, but I'd rather not give out the entry code to a rental."

"No problem," Housen said as he opened the app to release the car. "I've been sitting for most of the past twenty-four hours anyway."

"I'm just relieved that you're safe." Arbet pulled Housen into a hug once he was through the gate, then slipped something into his hand. Alice only got a brief glance, but it looked a bit like a flattened egg. Whatever it was, it clearly meant a great deal to him because his expression changed. It almost looked like he was going to cry.

Alice followed him through the gate, then glanced back at the car, which was now heading out of the neighborhood.

"Something wrong?" Joe asked.

She started to say no, but the disconnect between this welcome and the attitude of the guard bothered her. "It's just … I got the feeling from your guard that we should expect a very different sort of greeting when we got here. Because of the tracker?"

Joe nodded but didn't say anything.

"Not that the man did anything wrong exactly," she added quickly. "It was more that his tone was off when he spoke to Housen at the end."

"Huh. No surprise there."

"Because...?" she asked, not wanting to give up any information they didn't already have.

"Because he recognized Housen from our security footage."

"Okay. But ... what did you tell him? Is he calling the police? The *actual* police, I mean?"

"No. He knows to keep things in house."

Alice didn't like the sound of that. She stared at him for a moment, eyebrows raised, hoping he'd take the hint and explain further. But he didn't. Fine, then. Challenge accepted. She was an academic. She'd dealt with more than one professor you had to drag information from word by word.

"So ... what exactly does that mean?" she prodded. "Keeping things *in house* encompasses a pretty wide range of options, including ones that end with a burial in the woods behind the house."

"The guard probably thinks we're placing him under house arrest."

"Are you?"

He shrugged. "It's not too far from the truth. We're all in a holding pattern until we know whether Claire and Beck are successful in securing that beacon."

"But ... aren't the police curious about what's going on here?" Alice asked, gesturing to the other houses in the neighborhood.

"Local cops have been told we're holed up *here* in response to the protests out *there*," Joe said. "Plus, we said we temporarily relocated some projects while we rebuild the lab."

"They've got fifteen acres, plenty of money, and a private security force," Arbet said. "You'd be surprised how *uncurious* local authorities can be when they think a problem is being solved privately and they don't have to throw resources at it. And I suspect that Dr. Jonas is a generous donor to the police benevolent fund."

"Both the public and under-the-table versions," Joe said. "Everly had private security for as long as I can remember. Cops didn't worry much about it when it was an enclave of mostly retired CEOs. Not much has changed now that it's a safe haven for refugee aliens."

"Not *just* aliens," Arbet said. "We also have a fledgling doctor, a kindergartner, and now, an archeolinguist."

Alice wanted to argue the point, wanted to tell her that she would be heading back to New York, that she had classes to teach and tenure to chase. But who was she kidding? This was the same sort of crossroads she'd faced when she left Mitch. When sticking with your old life brought with it the very real possibility of you ending up dead, change was the only viable choice. If Claire and Beck weren't successful, it might only buy her an extra few months, but even so…

Arbet and Housen were talking about something, so she turned to Joe. "Have you heard anything from Claire? She was supposed to contact me during the trip and explain all of this in more detail. But I haven't heard a thing since she left."

"Yeah. About an hour ago. First time in ten days. That's … not like her."

"Where are they?"

"Ares Station. KTI censors seem to be blocking both ways. Stuff they consider sensitive. Or secretive." Joe nodded toward Arbet and Housen, who had slipped into Ufretan.

Alice's ears perked up instantly. They seemed to be talking about communication problems, too, with Housen explaining why he hadn't been able to contact Arbet. It occurred to her that they might be using the language to keep their conversation private, but that only made her even more curious to know what they were saying, given that her fate was intertwined with all of this. Even if she hadn't understood the language at all, though, she'd have been able to tell that their conversation had taken a serious turn from the slump of Housen's shoulders.

"Someone ... died?"

"Yeah," Joe said. "Reese. The other guy who set the bombs at the lab. Although, she could be telling him about Sandjeel. He's not *dead*, but ... the Triad had a replicator for a few key nutrients he needs and I'm having a tough time coming up with substitutes. So, you actually understand what they're saying?"

She shrugged. "Bits and pieces. I'd be able to eavesdrop a lot more effectively if they'd speak in *ancient* Ufretan."

"You're ahead of me, either way. I've only picked up a few words. Jemma, on the other hand, soaks it up like a sponge."

"That's the daughter of Claire's roommate, right? Was she the child in the swimming pool in that drone footage?"

"Yeah." His expression clouded at the thought of the viral clip. "Did my sister ever say anything to you about Bryce Avery?"

It seemed like an odd non-sequitur, but she thought back to her conversations with Claire. "Maybe? The name seems familiar, but I can't place it."

"Another science reporter at the *Post*. I listened to Claire complain about him for years. Always thought she was exaggerating. Now, I get why she hates the son of a bitch."

"You're saying that video was captured by the *Atlantic Post*? But ... that's illegal."

"It's absolutely illegal," Arbet said, speaking English now. "But it wasn't the *Post*. Or at least not directly. It was recorded by one of the protesters. We could probably have gotten the thing pulled down, though, or at least stamped as an AI-fabrication. But before we could even get moving on that, Avery had fact checkers at the *Post* confirm that it was actual unedited drone footage."

"He's got connections to some of the crazies out there. The Bible-thumpers, not the tree huggers. Wilson, our security chief, thinks he knew about the video before it ever hit the internet. Maybe even put them up to it. We've increased security since then."

"Don't even think about trying to get food delivered," Arbet said. "Delivery drones give this place a wide berth now, because they've got some heavy-duty drone blockers that would undoubtedly land them in trouble if Dr. Jonas didn't have friends in high places. That's one reason I suggested the two of you stay here with me, Dora, and Denny. That way, there are fewer houses they'll need full security on."

"Are you sure?" Alice said. "I hate to intrude."

It was true, but also pointless. Where else was she going to go?

"You might not even see each other." Joe nodded toward the huge brick colonial directly in front of them. "Houses in this neighborhood were built to support CEO-sized egos."

Arbet pressed her palm to the front door. When it opened, they stepped into a large, empty foyer. A glance to the right showed a furnished living room, but there was nothing on the walls and none of the other items that would make it look as if anyone actually lived there. The same was true for the adjacent dining room, which had a dinner table for twelve and an ornate sideboard with glass doors that revealed empty shelves.

"He's right," she said, "The house has eight bedrooms, each bigger than your average New York apartment. And that's not even counting the guest house out by the pool. You could easily wander around for half an hour inside this place and not bump into anyone else. Plus, Dora and Denny swap out shifts caring for Sandjeel, so it will really just be four people. Are the two of you…" She made a vague waving motion with her hands.

It took a moment for Alice to figure out what she was asking. "Oh, no," she said, almost at the same time as Housen.

"We met less than twenty-four hours ago," he said. "And she ditched me the first chance she got. Separate rooms are definitely in order."

"Okay, then. The rooms are mostly furnished—the family who lived here apparently left in a hurry. They seem to have just taken clothes and personal items."

"Kai paid them enough to buy new furniture," Joe said, as a

large gray cat rubbed against his calf. "I think most of them were so tired of the chaos out there that they literally took the money and ran. Do you have food here?"

Arbet frowned, looking a bit confused. "For you or the cat?"

He grinned. "Both. I just woke up."

"Crichton still has kibble in his bowl. But there should be something in the kitchen that we can wrangle into a meal. Have you two eaten? I'm afraid we keep rather odd hours here at Camp Ufrete."

Housen told her that they'd had breakfast, but it was hours earlier.

"Brunch for all, then," Arbet said. "I'm sure you'll want to freshen up and get settled a bit first, so I'll let Denny show you to your rooms."

She nodded toward the foot of the stairs, where a man who looked to be in his early thirties was waiting. He was tall like the others, and his smile was pleasant enough. But all Alice could see were his blank, expressionless eyes … and the tattoo on the right side of his forehead.

THREE

ON CLOSER INSPECTION, Alice noticed that there was only *one* tattoo above the man's eye. No Ufretan number, just that odd symbol that looked a bit like a musical note inside a crescent.

Housen grabbed her by both shoulders, as if he thought she was about to faint. Or maybe go on the attack. Neither was true, but running for the door had certainly entered her mind.

"Take it easy," he said. "Denny's cool. Remember what I told you earlier? Not all of the *ipret-tai* are with Durav. Denny, this is Alice. She had unpleasant encounters with both Ren'djat and Do'djat last night."

Denny nodded. "I'm sorry. I have also had unpleasant encounters with Durav's *ipret-tai*. Do you have other bags?"

"No," Housen said. "Neither of us really had time to pack."

"Very well. Follow me." They followed him up to the second floor. "I'm afraid we didn't have a chance to air these rooms out so they may be a bit musty. Someone is bringing bedclothes from the other houses, and we'll have them made up soon."

Bedclothes. Alice wasn't sure she'd ever heard that word spoken aloud. It was more of a word that you read in books from Jane Austen's time.

She thanked him, and he started to head off with Housen. But then he turned back, tilting his head at a quizzical angle.

"Would you sleep more comfortably if I installed a latch on the inside of your door?"

"What?" she stared at him for a moment, wondering if he were psychic. "No. Thank you, but that really won't be necessary."

Alice stepped inside and closed the door behind her. *Of course,* she'd be more comfortable with an inside latch, and not just one, but four or five. It wasn't because of the *ipret-tai,* though, or at least not entirely because of him. She'd spent the past eight years sliding multiple locks and setting alarms as soon as she entered her apartment ... and double-checking them all before bed. It wasn't something she felt comfortable admitting, though. She just hoped the dresser wouldn't make too much noise when she moved it in front of the door before going to sleep.

After plugging in her new armscreen, she undressed and spent the next twenty minutes in the shower. On the one hand, she was glad she couldn't remember being carried to the car and searched by Do'djat, but another part of her wished that she *could* remember. The tracking device the guard found had been a harsh reminder that she didn't know anything that happened during that hour-long gap, and that was its own kind of torture. She felt okay physically and the *ipret-tai* didn't seem like sexual creatures to her, but she didn't really know any of these people and that wasn't the sort of thing she felt comfortable asking. So, she just scrubbed her skin nearly to the point of chafing and double lathered her hair, then let the steamy water wash away the suds and every trace of the previous night.

There was no hair dryer, so she toweled her long curls dry as best she could and changed into the clothes she'd bought earlier. The armscreen had finished charging, so she took a couple of minutes to connect it to her service and start the transfer of apps and data from the backup server before heading downstairs.

Joe hadn't been joking about the size of the house, but she was able to find the kitchen by following her nose. She was only mildly hungry, but the coffee smelled incredible. Still, she needed to hold herself to half a cup until she knew whether sleep was in the cards over the next few hours.

As she was debating which pastry to grab from the tray on the counter, her screen pinged with an incoming message to her university account. The subject line was blank, and the number wasn't one that she recognized, so she ignored it for the time being and carried her coffee and cheese danish into the adjoining dining area. No one was there. She listened for a moment and picked up voices, eventually tracking them down to the patio that overlooked the pool and beyond that, a lush and very overgrown yard. Housen, Joe, and Arbet were seated at an oval table with a middle-aged black man who wore the same uniform as the gate guards. Joe introduced him as Demar Wilson, Chief of Security for Jonas Labs.

"Alice Dobroski." She gave him a weak smile and took the empty chair next to Joe. "I swear I didn't know I was carrying that tracker."

"Not a problem," he said, returning her smile. "I hear you had a bit of trouble last night. You doin okay?"

She nodded. He seemed genuinely concerned, and she was surprised to feel tears pricking her eyes. "I'm fine. I *am* curious about that tracker, though. I heard the guard say it was transmitting, and I have a signal blocker in my bag that is configured to disrupt anything on the market. So..."

"So, you're wondering if it's alien tech?" Wilson reached into the breast pocket of his shirt, then held out his hand, palm up, to reveal a tiny silver dot. "Sure looks like it to me."

The device seemed identical to the tracker she'd pried off her pen in the car the night before. She gave Housen a questioning glance.

"I've already caught them up on everything that happened last night," he said. "And yeah, it's the exact same device. That's at least a bit of good news, since we already know your signal blocker jammed the audio feed on the one I planted, just not the location. Drex bought five or six trackers and a few other odds and ends off Maela a few years back when she first went undercover with the Flock. Maela works for Durav, but she isn't averse to making a bit of extra money on the side, especially when she's pissed at him."

"She *worked* with Durav," Arbet amended. "Beck found her

body with Drex's in the Triad's chambers just before the fires started."

Housen was quiet for a moment, then shook his head and gave a harsh laugh. "I'm not even going to pretend to be sad about that. You weren't there when he killed Sarah. Maela was a gleeful little ghoul."

Alice was going to ask who Sarah was, but something in Housen's eyes told her she might not want to go there. Maybe she was another member of the Watch? Or one of the *ipret-tai?* Housen had said something the night before about Do'djat being aware that his kind didn't live long if they crossed Durav.

"Anyway," Wilson said, "the only thing the tracker really changes is that Durav knows the two of you have arrived. Pretty sure he already knew that Sandjeel was here. If Sandjeel's body had been found in that fire he set at their headquarters, emergency workers would have had a hard time mistaking him for human, so Durav may have guessed even before the drone video went viral. Either way, I'm sure we've got more people guarding this place than he wants to deal with."

"Maybe." Housen removed his teabag, pressing it against his spoon to extract the last drops. "I mean, you've definitely got more than the three or four *ipret-tai* who went with him and the mercenaries he had hanging out at HQ. But he's got money. There are always people willing to sign on as hired guns. I don't think he's pulled in extra people yet, otherwise he'd have paired one of the mercenaries with the *ipret-tai* who were following us in New York. He usually doesn't send them out alone. But he can get more and he will if we don't act soon. Unfortunately, he has the advantage since he knows where we are, and all we know is that he's somewhere within an hour or so of Manhattan."

Alice frowned, trying to remember exactly what the Pulsar's AI had said after Do'djat issued the override command. It had given a street address, but had it said the city? If so, she couldn't recall. "The car said that it was resuming course to 167 Riviera Drive. We were set to arrive about half an hour from where you picked me up. It didn't mention a city, at least not that I recall, but there can't be that many Riviera Drives in New York, right?"

Housen gave her an incredulous look. "You knew the *address*? Why the hell didn't you say something earlier?"

"Because this is the first time you've mentioned going after him."

"I explicitly remember telling you that I'd been trying to track Durav's *ipret-tai* back to their boss."

That *did* kind of ring a bell, but she was pretty sure he'd said it well before she was abducted and she hadn't really connected the two things. "Okay. Sorry for not mentioning it. But ... what exactly were you planning to *do* with the information? Go into a place with who knows how many armed guards and try to take Durav out on your own?"

FOUR

ALICE WAITED for Housen to answer, but it wasn't really necessary. His expression left no doubt that storming into Durav's place on his own was exactly what he'd been planning.

Joe seemed to pick up on the same thing, because he chuckled softly. "Sounds like we're in need of an *actual* plan rather than a suicide mission. Ideas?"

They were all silent for a moment, then Arbet said, "Durav suspects Housen either has the backup beacon or knows where it is. Maybe we could stop blocking the listening device and let him overhear a plan to get rid of it. Assuming Alice is a halfway decent actress, that is."

"Two summers of improv theater in college," she replied. "I'll be fine. But don't you think he'll be suspicious if the audio suddenly starts working?"

"He might be," Arbet admitted. "But I don't think he'll be able to resist. I'm guessing he'll send a few people a couple of hundred miles north in search of the backup, given that he sent two of his people all the way to Mars simply because he thinks Shepherd has the one Uden took from the Triad's office."

"Wait," Alice said. "Did I miss something?"

"I got a message just now from Beck," Joe said. "Came in while you were upstairs. He spotted some militia guy named..." He shook his head. "Blanking on it, but it's a French name."

"Boudreaux," Wilson said. "Beck thought the other person with him might be Durav, but I sent something back to let him know that seems unlikely based on the conversation Housen says you overheard last night. You're sure it was Durav on the other end of that call?"

Alice nodded. "The *ipret-tai* said his name. Twice. Maybe three times. And I understood enough of the conversation to piece together that it was the name of the guy on the other end who was issuing his orders."

"I could have told them it wasn't Durav," Arbet said.

Housen snorted. "Yeah. Not unless he was able to book passage on one of Kolya's luxury ships. So … are you thinking that we lure them here?"

"Not here," Wilson said. "If we're going to do this, it needs to be isolated." He turned to Joe. "What about Beck's place in Maine? We can make them think Alice and Housen are planning a little boat trip to dump the beacon he believes they have."

Joe considered for a moment. "The bed and breakfast? Could work. I could even reserve a boat like I did last time in case he has someone dig into the story a bit."

"The reservation is a good idea," Wilson said. "But no, I'm thinking his cabin. Middle of nowhere and much easier to set up a trap. I still have the gate code from when we sent in that cleanup crew. I'd prefer a location his people aren't familiar with, but that would take more time to arrange, and it might be hard to find another spot as isolated. When they arrive, they'll find a bunch of our people. We bring Durav and the *ipret-tai* back here. Charge any others with trespassing. I'm guessing at least a few of them will have outstanding warrants, so maybe I can throw that FBI agent a bone and get him off our backs."

"Not a bad idea overall," Housen said. "It could definitely work to draw away some of his security. But Durav won't be with them."

"Not the type to get his hands dirty?" Wilson asked.

"If by dirty you mean *bloody*, he's more than willing," Arbet said. "But he's not going to do anything that involves personal risk or discomfort. He's not even a fan of inconvenience. He does have an ego, though. Taunting him about his cowardice might draw him out. But we'd have to be careful not to make it too obvious."

"No," Housen said. "The better course would be to hit on two fronts. Draw his forces up to this place in Maine and then hit the location where he's holed up and take him out."

Wilson frowned. "Take him out? Sounds like you're saying we kill him. If so, I'm not down with that. I've got issues with the death penalty to begin with, but without any sort of judicial process? No way."

"Would you still feel that way if the man in question was a serial killer?" Arbet asked.

"Biologically immortal serial killers," Joe mumbled. "Yet another moral conundrum we should have taken into account when developing Rejuvesce."

"And you're missing an important point," Wilson said to Arbet. "How are we supposed to know for certain that he *is* a serial killer without a trial?"

"You can never know for certain, even *with* a trial," Arbet said. "But in this case, a trial simply isn't feasible. The last thing we need is the authorities adding Durav's DNA to their database. Absent an official trial, you have to fall back on the evidence and witness testimony. Both of us—three if you add Sandjeel, four if you contact Beck—will all tell you that Durav has killed dozens of people."

"Don't forget Denny and Dora," Housen said. "They're witnesses, too."

"Right," she said. "So that's six witnesses, in all, to dozens of murders. You have all of the dead bodies discovered in the fire, but even if you choose not to count Watchers or *ipret-tai,* there are multiple corpses buried on the grounds at Triad HQ." Her eyes flitted briefly toward Housen. "There are also several people buried at an abandoned ranch near Houston. Several more—fairly recent—who were killed near a tourist town outside of Kingman, Arizona."

"And you know for certain that Durav personally killed all of those people?"

"Not all," she admitted. "He's always taken pleasure in handling such matters himself, but I'm sure there were plenty of cases where he simply ordered the *ipret-tai* to kill someone. But orders to an *ipret-tai,* are the same as pointing a gun or programming a drone. They had no choice but to obey his orders, and they would never take initiative on their own that went against their code of conduct. Either way, Durav is responsible."

Wilson cast a nervous look toward the house. "You're saying if you told Dora to kill me, she'd do it?"

"Yes. So would Denny. I'm sure that they would ask me several times for clarification, given our discussions on morality, but they only understand those concepts in the abstract. In the end, it wouldn't override their duty to obey me. And Durav's *ipret-tai* have never been instructed on such niceties, so…"

"Okay, let's break this down," Wilson said. "For argument's sake, I'll take it as given that this Durav is a serial killer, as you claim. Doesn't matter. It's enough of a risk handling the cleanup, but I don't think we can go beyond that. Even if I was comfortable giving a kill order to my people or doing the job myself, I can't bring that kind of … culpability on Jonas Labs." He glanced at Joe. "Especially without explicit approval from your mama, and I doubt you want to go there."

"You don't have to order anyone to do anything," Housen said. "If you lure enough of his security forces away, I'll take it from there."

"By yourself?" Alice asked. "That doesn't seem like a good idea."

Arbet nodded, frowning. "I … could ask Denny. He's had the same standard security programming as the other *ipret-tai*."

"No," Housen said. "As you just pointed out to Chief Wilson, he'd have no choice but to obey. You want to give him an order that could get him killed?"

Arbet's face flushed. "First, it wouldn't be the only time he's had to do something dangerous. And second, I said I could *ask*, not *order*."

He shook his head. "That's a distinction without a difference. You know he would see it as the exact same thing. I wouldn't mind having a lookout, but I'd rather do it on my own than involve someone else, especially someone who's incapable of saying *no*."

Everyone was quiet for a moment, and then Joe asked the question that Alice suspected all of them had been thinking. "Are you sure you're capable of killing a man in cold blood?"

It was clear that Housen didn't care for Joe's phrasing, but he didn't hesitate with his response. "If that man is Durav? Absolutely." After holding Joe's gaze for a moment, Housen grabbed his cup and went back inside.

Arbet watched him go, waiting until he disappeared into the kitchen. He'd only closed the screen door behind him. She got up, apparently intending to close the glass door as well, but Denny appeared and closed it when she'd only taken a few steps in that direction.

When she was back in her chair, Joe asked if he'd touched a nerve with Housen.

"You could say that. Do you think avenging a murder counts as killing *in cold blood*?"

Joe and Wilson exchanged a look, and then Joe said, "I don't know. It would depend on the circumstances of the murder."

"Exactly," Wilson said, nodding in agreement. "How long ago it happened. Maybe how close you were to the victim. Or victims."

"One specific victim in Housen's case," Arbet said. "And while it happened about seventy-five years ago, I would caution that you probably consider that a much more substantial period of time than we do. Sarah was his wife. That's not common knowledge, even among the Watch, although I think everyone knew he was in a serious relationship."

"I wouldn't have thought that was something you were allowed to do," Alice said. "Get married, I mean."

"Serious relationships with Earthers weren't encouraged," Arbet said. "But we were supposed to blend in, so keeping to yourself entirely wasn't the best idea, either. Housen was far from the only Watcher who ignored the caution against getting too close. They'd only been married for a few years, and I guess she stumbled on something that made her suspicious. He said later that she was worried about him, that she'd overheard something that had her thinking he was in some sort of financial trouble with the mob. Anyway, she followed him to a Conclave."

"And Durav killed her for that?" Wilson asked.

"Again, I don't know if he did it personally or had one of his *ipret-tai* do it. I do know—and so does Housen—that it would have been *highly* unusual for Durav not to have taken liberties with her beforehand. I'd say the odds are very strong that he tortured her as well. Probably justified it by saying that he needed to find out how much she knew and whether she'd told anyone, but he takes great pleasure in dishing out pain. Eventually, either Durav or one of the guards showed Housen her body in the back of a Jeep, handed him a shovel, and forced him to bury her in the back pasture. Personally, I think it would take *well* over seventy-five years for avenging that kind of murder to be called a *cold-blooded* killing."

TALES FROM THE AVEEZI FOREST

THE POISONED PELA

Translation by Nathaniel Everett

AS EVEN THE smallest child knows, the Aveezi Forest is a place that you should never, ever go. Dark and wild, the forest teems with creatures that snap and snarl. They will happily gobble up any youngling so foolish as to enter.

But even in the Aveezi Forest, light and dark must find a balance. Deep, deep inside the forest—where, I must again caution, you should never, ever go—there is a wide glade called Alestria, where gloom and danger may not tread. Here, the trees hang lush with ripe babda and usimi fruits, the waters flow sweet and cool, and the wind hums a soothing song. Here, the suns shine brightly in the daytime, the sky shimmers emerald and violet as they set, and the creatures live (mostly) in harmony.

It is here in lovely Alestria, on a bright morning in second autumn, that we find Motz and Tibbo—the very best of best friends—on their way to the babda orchard near the lake. The village had harvested most of the babda fruits the week before, but there were always a few stragglers that ripened late. These were usually smaller than the early harvest fruits, and a paler shade of blue, but they were still tasty. Ossa had asked them to bring back as many as they could find, promising a babda pie with their evening meal if they found more than a dozen.

Babda pie was Motz's favorite, so she hummed a merry tune and there was an extra spring in her step as they headed down the hill. Tibbo was in his usual perch on her shoulder, his tiny orange body bouncing so high with each of Motz's steps that he had to tighten his grip on her shaggy blue fur to keep from tumbling off.

When they reached the lake, Motz placed the smaller bag with their lunch on the flat stone that stretched out over the suns-dappled water. The lake *looked* warm and inviting, perfect for a morning swim, but Tibbo knew better. It had been so icy that he got the shivers just dipping his toes in last week, and the temperature had fallen rather sharply since then.

Too bad. He loved swimming. But babda picking was fun, too. And the good thing about harvesting babda was that they were only tasty once they were cooked. It wasn't like picking wesselberries, where Motz popped more into her mouth than she did into her basket and it took them all day to fill even a small pail. He was relieved to see that there were still plenty of babda on the trees today. Far more than a dozen and his tummy smiled happily at the thought of the pie.

Motz was tall enough to reach most of the fruits, but occasionally a ripe babda was just a bit too far up the tree. When that happened, Tibbo would hop up from his spot on her shoulder and scurry to the high branch so that he could shake it loose. It was kind of fun, as long as he didn't have to go *too* high. The branches near the top grew rather thin, and the winds were unpredictable this time of year.

Tibbo breathed in the heady aroma of the orchard. It reminded him of the shed where they made the special cider that younglings weren't allowed to drink. Ossa said the scent was from fruits that had fallen and fermented in the sun. It wasn't a bad smell, except for occasionally when someone stepped on a rotten piece that was hidden beneath the leaves.

Motz kept count as they went along, dropping the ripe fruit into their bag. One, two, three. Four. Five.

The next babda they found was a little *too* ripe, though. Worse yet, Tibbo spotted something wriggling out from a hole near the stem.

"Six!" Motz said.

Tibbo pointed to the bright green worm. "Do you want *that* in your pie?"

Motz flicked the tiny creature away, then dropped the brownish-blue globe in with the others. "Six."

"No!" Tibbo said. "That one is *rotten*. There could be other worms inside and they could ruin the other babda."

Heaving a very dramatic sigh, Motz fished out the too-ripe fruit, tossed it aside, and moved on to the next tree. She plucked another babda and turned it very slowly in front of Tibbo's tiny face.

"Does *this* one meet your standards?"

Tibbo did not particularly care for her sarcastic tone, but he ignored it and simply checked the fruit for flaws. "Yes. It looks *very* good."

"Six," she said, and dropped it into the bag.

The next babda was on a high branch. Tibbo climbed up to shake it loose and spotted two more even higher up. Seven, eight, nine.

Or it *would* have been nine. Motz didn't catch the last one. It splatted on the ground, and she kicked it off into a pile of leaves.

They continued on. Nine, ten, eleven, twelve…

As soon as the thirteenth babda was in the bag, Motz turned and headed back toward the lake.

"What are you doing?" Tibbo asked. "We're not finished!"

"Yes, we are," Motz replied happily. "We get pie!"

"Well, yes, but there are still at least two dozen more on the trees. Maybe even three dozen."

"But Ossa said—"

"Ossa said to pick as many babda as we can find."

"No. He said if we pick more than a dozen, we get pie. Thirteen is more than a dozen. Now we can sit by the lake and skip stones before we eat lunch. And then take a nice long nap." She added a wide, loud yawn at the end.

Tibbo sighed. Motz was stubborn and her memory could be very selective, especially when remembering fully might require her to do extra work. The only thing that overpowered her laziness, however, was her love of food.

"We have to pick *all* of the ripe fruit first," he insisted. "If there are extras, maybe we'll have enough babda jam to make popkins even in the summer. Remember how sad you were when we ran out of jam last year?"

Motz thought for a moment, then her big blue shoulders sagged. "Fine."

They trudged along to the next row. Motz was silent now, but Tibbo kept count in his head. The eighteenth babda was just out of reach, so he shook it loose and was about to climb down when Motz said she saw another one, even higher up.

Tibbo followed her directions and climbed higher.

"Where?" he asked after reaching the branch he thought she'd pointed to. "I don't see it."

"No. It's higher. Just keep going."

He went up a bit further, choosing his branches carefully to make sure they would hold his weight. Finally, he said, "I still don't see it. I'm coming down."

Just then, a chilly gust of autumn wind whipped across the lake, whistling in his ears and shaking the top of the tree. Tibbo clutched the trunk tightly, very nearly losing his grip. When the wind eventually died down, he picked up another sound from below.

Motz was laughing.

"You dirty liar!" These were very harsh words for Tibbo, but he was very mad.

"I'm sorry, Tibbo. It must have been a trick of the light. I really *did* think I saw one up there."

"I nearly fell!"

Motz shrugged. "Then I would have caught you. You know that."

Tibbo knew that she would have tried. But he couldn't help remembering the babda she'd missed a few minutes earlier and the jammy blue stain it had left behind on the ground when she kicked it into the leaves.

They continued to the other three rows. Motz, who could tell he was still quite angry, didn't play any more nasty tricks, but that didn't stop her from complaining every few minutes. Tibbo would then mention the alluring prospect of lakeside picnics next summer with babda popkins in their basket, or maybe even babda ice cream for her birthday, and she would keep going.

By the time they were finished, their bag was nearly full.

"See?" Motz said, as they unpacked their lunch. "There's no time for skipping stones now."

It was still far too early for lunch. They could have skipped stones for an hour—long past the point where they usually grew bored with the game—and there would still have been time to eat and for Motz to take her inevitable after-meal nap before they headed back for lessons. But Tibbo didn't argue. He'd known there would be a price to pay when he kept pushing her to pick the rest of the babda, and this was apparently it.

While Motz slept, Tibbo lugged each of the babda fruits down to the lake one by one. They were heavy, and he was very small, so he had to be careful not to drop them. He washed each one and then set them out to dry in the light of the suns. After he finished, he skipped stones for a bit, but it wasn't much fun on his own, so he placed their lunch bag and the clean babda back inside the sack and waited.

When Motz finally awoke from her nap, they headed back uphill to the trail that led into the village. Shortly after they turned onto the path, Tibbo spotted a strange figure at the edge of the forest. He had a long thin neck like Ossa and wore a hooded cloak that shimmered like the scales of a porelfish in the light of the noonday suns.

The stranger bowed low and smiled.

"Hello, younglings. I come from a village on the other side of these woods seeking friendship and trade."

"We have nothing to trade," Tibbo said.

"Well, we do have some extra babda fruit," Motz said, even as Tibbo tugged at her fur to urge her to keep moving.

"No," he whispered into Motz's shaggy ear. "He came from the forest. It isn't safe."

Motz nodded, and Tibbo was relieved that she'd listened to reason. But then the stranger reached inside his cloak and pulled out two orbs. They were emerald green, with smooth shiny skin, and easily three times the size of the largest babda in their bag.

"This is our pela fruit," the stranger said. "We have a surplus this season. Most seasons, truth be told. They are delicious when ripe, but hard to preserve." He took a bite from one of the fruits. It was red and juicy inside, much like a wesselberry, and even though Motz had eaten a very big lunch barely an hour before, her big tummy rumbled at the sight.

Tibbo jumped in quickly, because he could see exactly where this was going. "I'm very sorry, good sir. These babda belong to our village, so we cannot trade with you. Safe travels and may the suns be ever at your back until your return." He wasn't entirely sure that he wanted the stranger to come back at all, but this was something he'd heard Ossa and the other elders say on the rare occasions when an outsider came into their village.

The stranger laughed. "Very well, my tiny young friend. Keep your babda. All that I ask is that you take this sample back to your elders as a gesture of my goodwill." He tossed the other pela fruit to Motz, who caught it easily in her big blue paw.

Without another word, the stranger popped the rest of the pela he was eating into his mouth and slipped back into the woods. They caught a few glimmers of his robe in the shadows, and then he was gone.

"Well, that was kind of him." Motz held the fruit up for closer inspection, then drew it close to her nose so she could sniff it. "I've never seen a pela fruit. Isn't it beautiful?"

"Yes," Tibbo said. And it *was* beautiful. Perfectly round, with skin that was unmarred by even the slightest blemish. But it also gave him an uneasy feeling that he couldn't explain. "Don't eat it!"

"I wasn't going to," Motz said, even though Tibbo knew perfectly well that she'd been thinking about doing precisely that. "It almost looks too pretty to eat. *Almost.*"

She opened the bag with the babda and was about to drop it inside.

"Stop!" Tibbo yelled. "You can't put it in with the other fruit."

"Why not?"

"I ... I don't know," Tibbo admitted. "Just put it in the bag that held our lunch."

For a moment, it seemed as though Motz was going to humor him. That was unusual, so maybe she was uneasy about the stranger, too. But then she realized the lunch bag was beneath the dozens of clean babda fruits.

"You're being silly, Tibbo. Unless *you* want to carry it, it's going into the sack."

Now it was Motz who was being silly. The pela fruit was nearly as big as he was.

"You know I can't. Maybe we should just throw it into the forest?"

"That sounds like a bad idea. What if we hit a naidar? Or a vurga? We need to show it to Ossa. He'll know what to do."

"Fine," Tibbo grumbled. "Let's just go, then. We're going to be late for lessons."

As they passed the path that led to the village storehouse, Tibbo caught a whiff of the winey odor he'd noticed at the babda orchard. Had they accidentally picked a fruit that was too ripe?

The smell grew stronger as they continued, and by the time they reached Ossa's cottage, it was pungent enough that even

Motz noticed it. Tibbo scurried off her shoulder and once he landed on the ground, he saw the stain spreading across the bottom of the sack. A dark liquid was now seeping through the coarse weave of the fabric.

When he pointed this out, Motz made an odd squeaking noise and flung the sack to the ground. The babda they'd picked earlier tumbled out onto the path—now blackened and mushy, with a stench like rotting meat. And there in the center, completely unharmed, was the brilliant green pela fruit the stranger had given them.

"Oh, my," Ossa said when he opened the door and spied the mess outside. "What happened to the babda? And what in the stars above is that?" His long forefinger pointed directly at the pela fruit.

One of the babda at the edge of the pile throbbed as a large blister formed on its skin and then popped. The fruit deflated, leaving behind a mound of dark gloopy pulp. Ossa disappeared into the cottage and came back with a large bucket, which he placed over the pile.

"Well?" Ossa prompted.

When it became clear that Motz had no intention of answering, Tibbo took a deep breath and began. "After we picked the babda—"

"*All* of the ripe ones," Motz added. "Just like you asked."

Tibbo waited for her to keep going, but she didn't. "Anyway," he said, "after lunch, we started home and we met a stranger—"

"On the trail!" Motz said. "Right in the middle of the trail, blocking our way."

That part wasn't at all true. The stranger had stayed near the edge of the forest the entire time. But maybe Motz was trying to keep the two of them from getting into *too* much trouble. And it was only a tiny lie, so...

Tibbo nodded. "Anyway, the stranger wanted us to trade our babda for that green thing, which he called a pela fruit. And I told him no—"

"So did I," Motz said. "And then he got very angry and threw the pela fruit at me. He threw it straight at my head. And then he ran back into the forest."

That was also not true, but Motz had apparently decided to tell the story now.

"I wanted to throw it right back at him," she said, "but Tibbo told me to put it in the sack. He said that we should bring it back to the village, to see if you knew what it was."

This was the final straw for poor Tibbo. "Not true! I'm the one who said to throw it back. And I definitely didn't say you should put it in the sack with the—"

"Tibbo!" Ossa's voice was sharp. "What have I told you about arguing? Especially about something so petty. I don't *care* who said what. I care that the two of you have brought such a dangerous thing into our village. What if I'd told you to take these fruits straight to the storehouse like we did last week instead of bringing them here?"

It was a fair point. They often dropped off bags of sperza, usimi, and other crops on the way back from the fields.

"The entire harvest might have been ruined," Motz said. "Even worse than adding a wormy babda to the sack."

Ossa nodded. "Exactly. As it is, we'll have very little babda jam this year. And obviously there will be no pie with our evening meal tonight."

Motz's shoulders slumped, but Tibbo really didn't care about the pie. After seeing and smelling all of the rotten fruit, he doubted that he'd have much appetite for anything made from babda for quite some time.

Ossa was not finished, however. "What worries me far more, however, is that you did not pay attention to my teachings about danger." His voice was very sad now. "I fear I have failed you as a teacher if you ignore the one lesson I have stressed above all."

"But … we didn't go *into* the forest," Motz said.

Tibbo nodded. "She's right. We didn't ignore your teachings, Ossa. We stayed on the path."

"Ah, but that means you have only learned the words, Tibbo, not the meaning behind them. It is, of course, very important that you never, ever go into those woods. But you must also stay far, far away from anything and anyone outside of Alestria. The evils that lurk in the world beyond will tarnish our treasures, twist our minds, and poison our blood. No matter how bright and tempting the fruit, if it comes from the Aveezi Forest or beyond, it is rotten to the core."

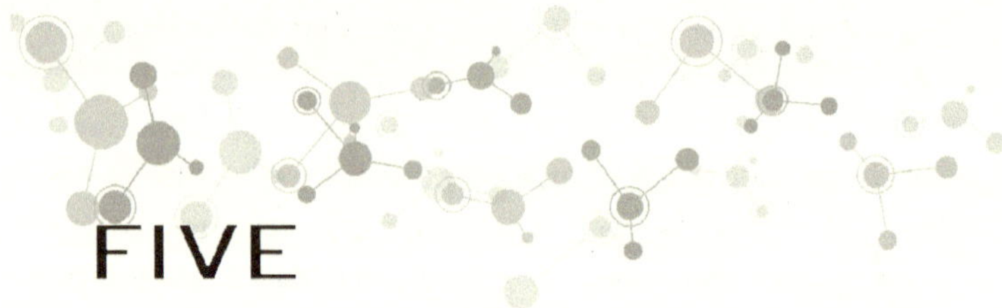

FIVE

Thursday, October 5
Capullo del Sur, Elysia

CLAIRE WAS WAITING in the vestibule outside the landing bay of the hospital when the rescue shuttle arrived. It was well after midnight—halfway into the odd, nearly forty-minute "time slip" where clocks simply stop in order to keep Martian days in sync with those on Earth. Marisol had taken her to a guest room in the first family's living quarters around eleven and strongly encouraged her to sleep, since they still didn't know how long it would be before the shuttle arrived. But she didn't argue when Claire said she wouldn't be able to relax until she knew Kolya and Macek had arrived safely.

So, Marisol assigned a young man to escort her through the tunnels to North Pod, or as they called it, *Capullo del Norte*. He carried a side arm, and Claire wasn't sure if he'd been sent along as protection or to keep her in line. Maybe both. He waited with her, but his English was as limited as Claire's Spanish, so she'd spent most of the past hour sending carefully worded messages to Wyatt and Paul, filling in what blanks she could beyond the hastily written text she'd sent from Hyblaeus. There was also a long message from Ro, written a few days earlier, with a picture of Joe and Jemma around an odd game board. Ro had wisely cropped it before sending so all that remained of Sandjeel was an extra hairy arm that could easily have been an oversized stuffed animal.

Claire had just started composing an answer to Ro when the

emergency shuttle finally arrived. The hatch opened a moment later and she watched as the rescue team extracted first Kolya and then Macek. Both were on stretchers and neither of them seemed to be conscious.

"Excuse me," she said to one of the workers. "I'm the passenger who hiked out to send the SOS. Can you tell me how they're doing?"

"We won't know for sure until they're checked out thoroughly at the hospital," the woman said. "I can tell you that Mr. Kolya slipped in and out of consciousness a few times in transit, but he was speaking fairly coherently. The other man was alert until we gave him something stronger for the pain in his shoulder and leg."

"His leg?"

"Yes. I believe it's broken. Check back in the morning and they should be able to give you an update."

That didn't make sense. Macek hadn't been getting around as well as normal when she left, but that had clearly been due to the fact that his shoulder hurt every time he moved. She was certain that he'd been putting equal weight on both legs.

Claire thanked the woman. There was nothing else she could do at that point, so she asked the guy assigned as her escort to take her back to the guest room.

Once she was back in her room, she took a quick shower and pulled on the nightgown that had been left at the foot of the bed. The room was nice, but it felt a bit claustrophobic—not because it was especially small, but because there were no windows. She was wondering why the first family of Elysia would choose to live in the basement tunnels rather than in the pods when she finally dozed off.

She was awakened a little before seven by a young woman carrying a breakfast tray with bread, cheese, fresh fruit, and a hot oat drink flavored with chocolate and cinnamon. A note was on the tray as well, engraved with the words *Oficina del Vicepresidente de Elysia*. Marisol informed her that Kolya had a hairline fracture at the base of his skull and a concussion. They were monitoring him to see if they could reduce the swelling without surgical intervention. Macek had come through surgery without any problems and was now fitted with a new shoulder and a boot for the minor fracture in his leg. Neither man would be leaving Elysia for at least a few days.

That would probably not sit well with either of them—or with Maria del Pilar, in the case of Macek—but it was very good news for Claire. No matter how much Kolya might prefer to be in on the negotiations with Shepherd, there was no way he could afford to delay the meeting and further postpone ending the lockdown. Paul and Beck were set to arrive by early afternoon to take her to Nepenthes, which was about two hundred kilometers outside the range of the automated skimmer that had picked her up the previous night. That was good news, too. The half-hour ride from Hyblaeus had been borderline intolerable. She couldn't imagine being stuck inside that tiny cabin for more than two thousand klicks.

She resurrected the yellow dress from the chair where she'd dropped it the previous night and had just finished buttoning it up when she heard a soft tap at the door. It was Angelina. She wore a more modern-looking outfit today and Claire wondered if the shapeless blue dress she'd worn the night before had been her nightgown. The girl was still fully covered, though, with a form-fitting body sleeve in a vivid geometrical print under her black jumper.

"I'm supposed to take you to del Norte. Mr. Kolya wishes to see you." She held out the sandals. "Do you think these will fit?"

"Maybe." Claire sat on the bed to try on the shoes. "Kolya is doing better, then?"

"I guess so. Tia Marisol just said for me to bring you."

"Oh. Marisol is your *aunt*?"

Angelina grinned, clearly more at ease than she'd been the night before. "Did you think she was my mother?"

"I did," Claire admitted. What she didn't add was that she'd also wondered if Macek was the girl's father, since that might have solved the mystery of why Marisol's mother hated him so much.

"A lot of people make that mistake. I was the first baby born in Elysia, but my mother's health wasn't good here. She couldn't adjust to the spin from the *capullos*, which is why I was born down here. There were other health issues, too. She and Papa went back to Earth just after my second birthday."

Claire wasn't sure how to respond to that. The girl didn't sound particularly sad about it, just very matter of fact, so she gave her a sympathetic smile before standing up to test the shoes. They were a bit loose, but serviceable.

"So … that would make you one of the first babies born on Mars, right? Baby Marta is … what? Six or seven years older than you?"

"I was number four. It was slow at the beginning, but there have been a lot of babies born here recently. We had three in Elysia last year, and two more are on the way. And *Baby* Marta?" Angelina rolled her eyes. "She is no baby. She's sixteen now. So, only *four* years older."

Well, that explained why Angelina had seemed unusually mature for the eight or nine years that Claire had assumed. She was simply small for her age.

"I met Marta last year when my parents visited and took me to Daedalus City. She was born in Olympia, but her family lives in Daedalus now." Angelina wrinkled her nose in distaste. "She's not very nice. Tia says all the publicity made her *chiflado*. That means like a spoiled brat."

Claire laughed, thinking back to the publicity swirl around the first Martian baby, who was conceived by accident when one of the contract workers either didn't realize she was pregnant or didn't want to admit it to her employer and risk being shipped back to Earth without her bonus. The woman was nearly seven months along when her condition was discovered and given that she was in the second year of her two-year contract, the pregnancy had to have originated on the planet. By that time, transporting her back to Earth was riskier than allowing her to have the baby on Mars. The delivery went smoothly, and Marta was something of a celebrity on two planets for the first few years of her life. Once it was clear that she was developing normally, the Ares Consortium authorized a test program for permanent colonists who wanted children. The only catch was that children born on Mars had to stay on Mars. No one really knew what effect the higher gravity of Earth would have on their bodies, and no parent was crazy enough to let their child be the guinea pig.

"So that's why your family doesn't live in the pods." Claire tapped one of the girl's brightly colored sleeves. "Are those for compression?"

"Yes. I can spend about three hours each day in the pods now, as long as I ride my scooter. If I try to walk or I stay much longer than that I get really tired. I'd kind of hoped they'd get me to the point where I could travel to Earth, but my progress has … I don't know the word." She held out her hand, first positioning it at a steep incline and then tilting it down until it was nearly flat.

"Plateaued?" Claire suggested.

She nodded.

"Do your parents visit often?"

"Every year or two. I think Papa wishes they could have stayed on Mars, but now I have a brother and sister on Earth, and they are too young to make the move. I will be glad when they are old enough to visit, though." She shrugged as if to say *it is what it is*, then paused as they turned into a larger hallway. "Do you want to take the tram straight to the hospital, or would you like to go on foot through the pods? It's only about half an hour's walk. Tia said it would be okay as long as we only walk through Capullo del Sur. And I can also show you Capullo de Jardín, on the way. That's our farm."

"Walking would be nice. But are you sure you'll be okay?"

"Oh, yes. You will be the only one walking. I will ride my

scooter. I often use it to give tours of the pods when we have visitors. Well, except for Capullo Oeste. I'm not allowed there."

"That's the ... West Pod?" Claire asked, uncertain of her translation.

"Yes. The tourist pod. All the workers we're housing for lockdown are there and Abuelita says they are *ruidosos* ... like troublemaking." Her mouth pressed into a prim line. "Even in usual times, Oeste is not a good place for young ladies."

Claire nodded, thinking that she now had a pretty good idea where the sexbot tourism happened.

"I wouldn't want to go through there anyway. Capullo Oeste is just bright lights and loud noise. It makes money, though, and that helps pay for upkeep on the other pods. But you really do need to see the garden pod. It's beautiful. Especially the orchards."

"I remember Kolya mentioning that you had orchards here. Apple trees, right?"

"Apples, yes. But others, too. The cherry trees are my favorites. They were planted the same year that Elysia was founded, in our underground gardens, but they brought them with us when we moved to the pods."

They walked in silence for a moment, and then Angelina slipped into tourist guide mode. "Did you know that Elysia was the first permanent colony? Not the first mining colony—that was Tharsis. But we were the first where people came as settlers."

"I actually *didn't* know that," Claire said, amused at the girl's enthusiasm. She was practically bouncing on her heels. Either she'd been tired the night before or else nervous about her aunt's breach of protocol. Now, she reminded Claire a bit of Jemma, or at least how Jemma might be if she got the chance to make it to age twelve—the same dark eyes and hair, although Angelina was thinner and her curls were longer and less wild.

"Abuelita founded Elysia back in 2061, with my grandfather. He died before I was born. Everyone lived underground at first, and then inside a dome. Papa would have been the next in line to lead, but since he is not living here now, that means Tia Marisol will take over when Abuelita is gone."

"And then the job falls to you?"

"Oh, no," she said, looking somewhat horrified. "*Menos mal!* We're nearly halfway to the *semicentario*, and after that, the Elysian Council will select *la presidenta*. Or *el presidente*, I suppose, since it could be a man."

Claire started to ask what the *semicentario* was, but then she pieced together the cognates and decided it must mean *half-century*. "And who selects the Elysian Council?"

"The people. Everyone has equal say, beginning after we finish *bachillerato*. That is required, because otherwise, we don't understand our history and our government and might make poor choices. I'll be glad when I can help vote out the members who give Abuelita so much trouble."

"How old are you when you finish bach…"

"*Bachillerato*," she said with a laugh. "Is like high school. Most finish at sixteen. I *think* I will finish at fifteen. Then I will start to train at the hospital, although I will have to go slow since I can only be there a few hours at a time. Maybe four hours by then."

"You want to be a doctor?"

They were at the end of the hallway now. Angelina pressed her palm against an access panel. "Not exactly. I like better using the computers to help diagnose what is wrong. It's like solving a mystery. And I can do some of that from our quarters at ground level."

"That's kind of what my brother does." Claire started to add that if the girl was ever near Boston, she'd arrange a visit to the lab, before remembering that Angelina was tied to Mars … and Joe didn't even have a lab at the moment.

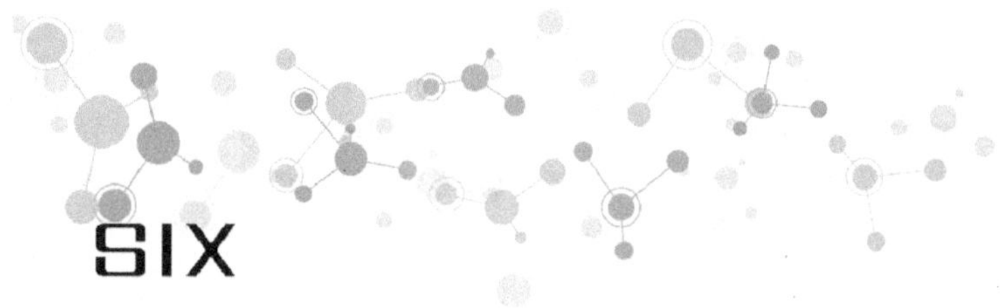

SIX

WHEN THE DOCKING CUBE OPENED, Angelina stepped inside and gripped the handrails. "Hold on tight. This moves pretty fast."

The cube shot off to the left, gaining speed as it moved upward along the spiral track that Claire had noticed the night before. She was surprised to find that the walls of the cube were transparent. The inner wall, which looked into the pod, was still a blur, but if she looked to her right, she could see the land around the colony. She even caught a glimpse of Elysium Mons off in the distance, where they'd soon be starting construction on a second hyperlift like the one near Daedalus City. When they were about halfway up, the terrain around the pods began to blur and the view on the left gradually came into focus. She could now make out distinct features inside. At first it was just larger areas like a park and a lake, but as the cube gained speed, she could see a rowboat on the lake that clung firmly to the inner wall of the *capullo,* even though it looked like it should flow to the bottom. Streets surrounded the park. Shops lined the streets. Two people strolled along a trail. It all looked quite normal, aside from the fact that the entire scene was concave and wrapped around the inside of the pod.

Near the end of their ride, the cube tilted slightly forward, and when the door opened again, they stepped out into an apartment with a terrace overlooking the lake she'd seen. It appeared less curved now, but the boat was still floating slightly uphill and the sky … well, it was sort of slanted off to the left.

"This is going to take some serious getting used to," she said.

Angelina laughed. "That's what everyone says. Just keep your eyes on your feet when you're walking and it's easier. If you want to look at something in the distance, stop first so that you don't get dizzy. People who live here say they don't even notice anymore." She sank into the high-backed seat of a mobility scooter parked a few steps away and pulled on a pair of tight black gloves that were stashed in the side pocket. "Are you ready?"

Claire nodded, even though she wasn't entirely certain that was true. They headed out to a street with about a dozen houses facing the lake, their facades painted in an assortment of creamy pastels that reminded her of the week she'd spent in Villajoyosa with Wyatt and some college friends. There was even a small strip of white sand bordering the lake. A couple lounged beneath a tree, and other people walked along (*up*) the sidewalk or sat at small tables near the shops. And the sky wasn't the grayish shade she'd seen from the docking cube. Aside from the fact that it wasn't directly overhead, like it was supposed to be, it appeared as a normal blue sky, with a few wispy clouds—which meant it had to be a simulation.

"We'll go through the park on the way there," Angelina said. "And then maybe we can visit the shops on the way back. Do you like gelato?"

"That sounds like an excellent plan. And I've never met anyone who doesn't like gelato."

Angelina laughed. "Abuelita says it hurts her teeth. But she still eats it."

They entered the park, continuing along a paved walking trail. Capullo del Sur reminded Claire a bit of Daedalus, but even though it was in some ways more artificial, it actually looked more like a functional community. It was weird, and she'd never have imagined it from the outside, but she could kind of see why people might prefer this to the domes. Aside from the curvature and, at least so far, the lack of any cars, it reminded her of many planned communities on Earth, well-maintained and carefully designed. Kolya's Daedalus City, on the other hand, felt more like a façade, with its spinning hotels and flashing lights. Much of the appeal lay in the contrast between the luxury inside the dome and the barren terrain that surrounded it. Terraforming would change that—had *already* changed that—and she couldn't help but wonder if tourists would find Daedalus more or less appealing when the backdrop was green and fertile instead of craggy red rocks.

Of course, that was also true for Elysia. If all went according to plan, the air outside would be breathable within five years. The temperature would rise to a tolerable range within the next decade, and eventually, the only functional difference between living in the pods and living on the surface would be the lower level of gravity outside.

"Do you know what the plan is for Elysia as terraforming proceeds?" she asked. "I mean, is all of this temporary?"

Angelina shook her head. "For now, the plan is for Elysia to stay in the pods indefinitely. People can always move away if they decide they want to live on the surface. But who knows? At some point, maybe the citizens will take a vote and close down the pods, if we find that living on the surface uses fewer resources. But living inside the pods gives people more flexibility. They can visit Earth without risking their health. Maybe even move back if they want. That's not an option in the other colonies, unless they live in one of the more expensive buildings that have to spin even faster than the capullos."

"True," Claire said, thinking of Davina Monroe. She'd had a fairly strong incentive for deciding to stay on Mars, given the laws against the sort of genetic modification that she practiced, but returning to Earth hadn't been an option for her after so long away. Kolya had even said he'd probably make the same choice eventually, and retreat permanently to his cabin at Ehden, which he visited when he wanted a break from artificial gravity.

Angelina led Claire along a path that curved upward around the lake, taking the left fork which led to an arched bridge. Most of the terrain had *felt* level up to that point, even if it didn't look that way. But as they began the slight uphill, she was surprised to find that her injured leg wasn't twinging the way it had at Ares Station.

"Is this *full* Earth gravity?"

"Not quite," Angelina said. "We keep Sur, Norte, and Oeste at eighty-seven percent. The only spot in Elysia that has full gravity on some levels is Capullo de Jardín. Some plants don't grow as well, otherwise. Almost everyone volunteers in the gardens during harvests, but that's one job that I can't do. It tires me if I spend too much time there. That's why Tia said we shouldn't go in but just take a peek on our way to del Norte."

About a hundred steps on the other side of the bridge, they exited the forested area and found another row of houses. They were so similar in color to the ones on the other side of the park that Claire wondered for a moment if they'd somehow made a complete circle. But these buildings were smaller and looked more like modest single-family homes, with small yards in the back.

They continued down a narrow path between the houses and eventually arrived at another shuttle entrance. Angelina parked her scooter in an alcove on the right and then they entered the clear capsule. She tapped something into a pad on the wall and then they zipped off toward the next pod, moving at a much faster speed than the last time. Which she supposed made sense. The pod itself was already moving at a rapid clip in order to maintain gravity and they'd just been ejected from the side. Still, it was unnerving how quickly they were moving toward Capullo de Jardín.

Angelina caught her expression and laughed. "Don't worry! It's all perfectly timed. Our tram system has never had a crash in the entire history of Elysia."

"Always a first time," Claire said under her breath. She squeezed her eyes shut to wait for the little dip she'd felt when they docked at Capullo del Sur, but it never came.

"You can look now. We're not stopping, remember? Just taking a quick spin around and then we'll shoot off to del Norte."

Claire slowly opened her eyes, and they instantly filled with tears as she stared down at the scene inside the pod.

"Are you okay?" Angelina's voice was softer now. "I'm so sorry. I cannot believe I forgot that you crashed last night. No wonder you are so—"

"Oh, no, no. It's not that." Claire nodded toward the window, which displayed the lush garden that lined Capullo de Jardín. Most of the area along the sides was devoted to farming, but the area at the bottom of the pod was a wild space with trees and a stream that cascaded over large rocks into a small lake. They were red rocks, not the slate-gray of the ones in the biodome back home, but it still stirred a deep sense of longing. "I was just wishing that my father had lived to see this. Capullo del Sur, too. He would have been amazed. Does this pod provide all of the food for Elysia?"

"Most of it, yes. There's also a vat meat factory in Norte, and we do import a few spices and other things from Earth. But we grow enough food here to feed all of our citizens. We also provide food for the workers in our mining camps. And if there's enough left over, we sometimes trade with the other colonies, too."

Claire was quiet for a moment, thinking about the distinction the girl had made between feeding the citizens and feeding the workers in the mining camps. Was it Wyatt or Kolya who had mentioned that the Mars Federation of Labor formed in Elysia? She couldn't remember.

"What percentage of your people live in the mining camps?" she asked.

Angelina shook her head. "Our citizens only live in the pods. But we do *own* mines. Other than tourism, that's how we generate income to repair the pods and to purchase goods—like medical supplies—that we can't manufacture here at Elysia. The mines are worked by people from Earth or the other colonies."

"Guest workers or permanent?"

Angelina frowned, considering. "About half of each, I think. They all get to vacation in Oeste for free. And after twelve years, the permanent workers can now apply to move here. We can't take them all of course, but there's a community built specially for them. They only have to work in the gardens here, which is much easier than working in the mines. The first group arrived last year. And once there are enough of them, they'll be able to send a representative to the Council."

"That's … interesting. Do they live here or in Capullo del Sur?"

"Neither. As Abuelita says, many of them are *ruidosos.* Some of them *work* in shops in del Sur, but their apartments are in Oeste. Not as nice as here, but very much better than the mining camps. I visited a camp once with Tia." She gave a little shudder. "They will be happier in Oeste."

"I'm sure," Claire said, returning the girl's smile. Given her age, she thought it likely that Angelina believed this was a fair and equitable arrangement, so she didn't press the point. The last thing she wanted was to argue political ethics with a child. But it was easy to read between the lines. Despite what Angelina had said earlier, there were *two* tiers of people in Elysia. One group lived and worked in the pods from birth, or when they bought their citizenship upon immigration. The other group *might* manage to work their way into citizenship, but only after twelve years of heavy labor in the mines. And even then, they faced restrictions.

All Elysians were equal, but some were more equal than others.

SEVEN

CLAIRE CLOSED her eyes as the shuttle peeled off the track and accelerated toward their destination. This time, Angelina didn't need to announce their arrival, because there was a slight forward tilt that let Claire know they had docked. The apartment they entered was similar to the first one, with another mobility scooter waiting nearby.

"It's only a short walk from here," Angelina told her as they left the building. "Maybe ten minutes. You'll be able to see the red cross once we round the corner."

If Capullo del Sur was like an upscale suburban community, del Norte was its urban counterpart. There were trees and a small park, along with a number of apartment buildings, but everything seemed spare and functional. Everything was also kept to a single story or two stories at most, and when she looked at the few two-story buildings, she understood that this was a conscious design choice to minimize the slant and keep it from seeming like the structures were about to tip over. The path between buildings was also divided into two sections here, one for delivery vehicles and one for pedestrians. Angelina carried on with her tour, pointing out a building where they made clothing and the vat meat factory she'd mentioned earlier.

The walk had been a nice diversion, but the closer they got to the hospital, the harder it became for Claire to pay attention. Her mind kept drifting back to the fact that she was being summoned. She knew it was unreasonable to resent it. Kolya could hardly come to her at the moment. But it didn't change how she felt. The bigger issue was that she was furious at the man about the crash.

The three of them had very nearly died, and while he might not deserve all of the blame, he'd certainly earned the lion's share.

Elysia's hospital was one of the two-story buildings—a long, pale gray rectangle. A narrow strip of grass separated it from the street and two squat bushes at the entranceway were the only nod toward landscaping. Her first thought was that it seemed too big for the few thousand people who lived in the Elysian pods. But then she remembered that most of the domes on Mars had only the most basic medical services. Anyone working in the mining camps or in the smaller outpost domes scattered about the planet who needed surgery or advanced care would have to travel to Elysia or Daedalus City.

They took the elevator to the second floor. When they stepped out into the hallway, Claire spotted the same young man who had waited with her for the emergency shuttle to arrive the previous night. He was leaning against the wall and tipped a teasing salute to Angelina. She grinned and blushed. They had a brief exchange in Spanish, then he tapped his earpiece and began talking to someone else.

"He says we should go to the lobby or just wait here," Angelina said. "Tia Marisol will be out shortly."

Almost as soon as she spoke, a door opened further down the hallway.

"Did you give her the grand tour?" Marisol asked when she reached them.

"Not the *full* tour. Only the trail through the park in del Sur. I'll show her the shops on the way back. And no, we didn't go to Oeste or inside Jardín. We just circled around so that she could see the gardens."

Marisol responded with something in Spanish. Angelina gave her aunt a little nod and told Claire she'd be back in about an hour.

"Your niece is an excellent tour guide," Claire said as the girl rolled off on her scooter. "I learned a lot about your history."

"I'm pleased to hear it. Perhaps you will write a story about

Elysia for your science show and drive tourists our way as you did for Kolya?"

"Maybe," Claire said. "I'm no longer working with the *Atlantic Post*, but I'm sure I can find an outlet that would be interested in the story. Which room is Kolya in?"

"Room 307. He's been taken downstairs for a test but should be returning soon. Jaromir is awake, however. He's in 306 and he's expecting you." She nodded down the hallway. "You should make it quick, though. He needs rest."

When Claire reached room 306, she realized it was the same room that Marisol had been in when they arrived. The door was partially open, but she gave it a quiet tap before stepping inside.

"Surprised you're awake," she said.

Macek chuckled. "Surprised either of us is alive."

She nodded toward his leg, which was clad in a boot almost identical to the one she'd been wearing when she left Mars the last time. "How did that happen?"

"I waited awhile after our communication went out." His words had a slurred, lazy quality that told her that whatever he was on had left him drowsy and feeling very little pain. "Then I decided to test my thesis on that ceiling panel's inability to hold my weight."

"Looks like your thesis was correct. Had you already opened the hatch?"

"No. Like I said, I was testing my thesis first. I figured if I made it halfway up, I'd slide back down and open it. But it snapped in half when I was maybe four feet off the ground. I twisted around trying to avoid landing on the shoulder ... only to break my leg. Luckily, it is on side where I can still use a crutch. But getting lifted out of that shuttle..." He winced at the memory. "I was tempted to tell them to just leave me."

"If President Alvarado had her way, that's exactly what would have happened. She called you a *pendejo*. What did you do to piss the woman off so badly?"

He was quiet for a moment, and she was pretty sure he was

going to tell her it was none of her business. Then, he heaved a sigh. "I fell in love with her daughter. Pilar was not so opposed at first. Not approving exactly, but she accepted, you know? Then her son decides to go back to Earth, which means Marisol becomes next in line to lead Elysia. Pilar said she'd still agree to our marriage, but only if I quit my job with Kolya and lived here full time. No real job, just..."

"Like a royal consort?"

"Pretty much. And ... Marisol knew that was never going to happen. And I knew she could not leave Elysia. So, we broke it off. But her mother and I had words. Quite a lot of them. I may have called her a bossy old hag." He was quiet for a moment, and Claire thought he might have dozed off. Then his mouth quirked upward. "And some even worse things in Russian that she apparently looked up later."

"I should let you get some sleep. I'll tell you all about my adventures at Hyblaeus Camp when you're better."

He looked like he wanted to argue but then nodded. "Thank you for pleading my case."

"I don't think my pleading was what turned the tide. You should thank Marisol."

"Already did. When do you leave for Ehden?"

"Paul will be picking me up in a few hours."

Macek's eyes, which had been half closed, opened wide. "I thought he was staying in Daedalus with Stasia until ... until we could join them. There's likely to be some ... trouble."

"Wyatt stayed. Paul and Beck were already headed to Ehden when we crashed."

He gave a half chuckle. "King Asshole is not going to like that at all."

"Too bad. And I'm going to go now so that you can get some sleep."

"Good luck at Ehden."

"Thanks." She slipped out and crossed the hall to tap on the door to room 307.

The muffled noise from inside might have been *come in,* so she pushed it open to find Kolya propped up in a hospital bed with a brace on his neck. Or at least it was *shaped* like a neck brace. It seemed to be made of some sort of gel. A bandage covered most of the left side of his forehead.

"Don't you look happy," Kolya said glumly, moving his mouth as little as possible. "I'm surprised you didn't simply leave us out there to rot."

"Oh, come on. You know I couldn't do that. Macek got me out of the chamber at Icarus. I owed him a rescue."

Kolya laughed at her subtle emphasis on the word *him,* then winced at the movement. "Well, it doesn't matter. Whatever this is that you're planning, it's not going to happen. I may be stuck in this bed, but I *will* be conferenced in during the negotiations." He paused for a moment and then pinned her with a very purposeful stare as he repeated, *"I will."*

"I wasn't arguing with you."

"No, but your expression was screaming *fat chance, old man.*"

She ignored the first part of what he said because it was exactly what she'd been thinking. He might manage to get himself conferenced in for the actual negotiations with Shepherd, but he would not be there to keep her and Beck from finding the beacon.

"I don't think of you as old. Egomaniacal, out of touch, and a few other unflattering things, but you have a few more years before you're actually *old.*"

"You're too kind. Caruso tells me you met Wes Junior."

"Not exactly. I overheard him and Jason Boudreaux plotting to attack Nepenthes. Although Wes seemed to be trying to push him to do some other job first."

"Rather convenient, don't you think?" He adjusted slightly, and the gel substance seemed to ripple around his neck. "You just happened to be in the right place at the right time to hear Wes spell out their entire plan. How incredibly lucky."

She bit the inside of her lip, trying to keep her temper. Did he actually think she was *lying* about them planning to attack?

"I don't know, Kolya. I certainly didn't feel lucky when I was hiking across the freakin Martian tundra in the middle of the night trying to get help. Or when I nearly slipped into a chasm, or when I spent the better part of an hour terrified to breathe because a security drone was locked onto me. And Wes didn't exactly lay out their plan. I have no idea when they're going to attack or exactly how they expect to carry it out. Boudreaux is, based on everything I've heard, very much an opportunist. Westmoreland may have convinced him that this other job he's planning is a more lucrative target. What I do know is that they have a lot of weapons, including drones, and they're offering ten thousand credits to people willing to join them. As for me being in the right place at the right time, assuming Westmoreland hasn't flaunted your orders by opening up his other mines, Hyblaeus is probably the *only* place where they could have landed the *V1* without attracting too much attention. Wes's people were stripping the *Velox One* down for parts when I left, so you should be able to find conclusive proof of at least that part of my story if you send someone on a hunting expedition. Thanks largely to me, you survived with just a banged-up head, but I'm not the one who crashed the damn shuttle within walking distance of not just the *V1,* but possibly our only source of rescue. That was you. Maybe *you're* the lucky one."

Something passed over Kolya's face. To her surprise, it looked a bit like guilt. That was an emotion she wouldn't have thought the man capable of feeling.

He was quiet for a moment, then exhaled slowly. "I saw … something. Not long after we passed over Elysia. Looked like another ship on our starboard side. It was just a blip, though, so I wrote it off as an optical illusion. But then I thought I saw lights on the surface. Which was almost certainly Hyblaeus Camp. If I hadn't let myself get distracted by that I'd have kept control of the shuttle."

Neither of them spoke for a long moment. Claire suspected he was waiting for her to agree with him but her memory of exactly when he began losing control was a bit different, and she wasn't in the mood to absolve him or say it wasn't his fault.

Kolya eventually broke the silence, gesturing toward the chair near his bed. "Have you read the information that I gave you?"

She had to stop for a moment and think. "Oh! You mean your messages with Davy. No. I haven't really had a chance."

"Fine. Get up to speed before you arrive. As I said before, we'll have the negotiations at my cabin, where you'll be staying. Tell Garcia that he'd better not include the coordinates in any story he writes."

She nodded, opting not to correct him. If he didn't know that Wyatt wasn't joining her at Ehden, she saw no reason to fill in the blanks.

"Okay, then. Why don't we go over what you remember hearing at Hyblaeus?"

She gave a bitter laugh. This was becoming a recurrent theme in her life. First, sitting in a tiny office onboard the *Ares Prime*, with Macek grilling her repeatedly about the drone attack at the debate. Then, the multiple interrogations in New York after Dr. Leffler's murder, Agent West forcing her to repeat her story over and over after they discovered Devin Shepherd's body in New Haven, and now Kolya was trying to poke holes.

"Are you sure you don't want to call Macek in?" she said. "He could shine a light in my face while you interrogate me. Or there's a pitcher of water over there if you're interested in a little light waterboarding."

"Tempting. But I doubt Macek would be much help with just the one arm at the moment. He might not cooperate anyway. He never did have the stomach for torture, and he's gone even softer lately."

Kolya's sense of humor was so dry that Claire often had trouble figuring out when he was serious and when he was joking. It was probably the latter this time, but she had a flashback to when they were leaving Daedalus on the day that Westmoreland crashed. Kolya had arrived at the departure dome well ahead of her, saying he always liked to doublecheck a ship he was piloting, especially when he had passengers. He hadn't been nearly as diligent about safety checks when they were leaving Ares Station, although to be fair, they had been under pressure to leave quickly. And then there was Macek's comment about Kolya just before they crashed. *He's a better pilot than I am, but he knows far less about how to fix them. Breaking them, on the other hand…* Maybe she'd had it wrong all along and Kolya was the one who tampered with Westmoreland's plane.

Kolya seemed to pick up on at least part of her internal monologue, because he said, "Seriously, Claire. I'm simply trying to figure out how much was lost in translation, between what you told Garcia, who told Caruso, who finally told me."

"Okay." She sat, poured herself a glass of water, and began. "I was hiding in the back of the buggy that the two Hyblaeus workers—Ajay and Bowen—used to rescue me. Westmoreland, Boudreaux, and another man came in. I could only see them from about the knees down, but I'm pretty sure the third man was an *ipret-tai,* one of Durav's guards."

"How do you know that?"

"I *don't* know, which is why I said I'm only pretty sure. I'm basing it on something that Bowen said about the guy's freaky facial tats. I'm more certain about it being Westmoreland, because Boudreaux called him Wes. Oh, wait. I heard his first name, too. I'm guessing it's Steven. One of the guys who rescued me called him Little Stevie. He's apparently not fond of the nickname. Boudreaux was wearing cowboy boots, which is apparently his thing. I'm assuming you know that, since it's part of the description KTI Security has been circulating. He's also a fan of sarin gas, according to an article Wyatt wrote a few years back. Wes said he hadn't been able to get hold of the sarin but suggested that he could use the *Azospira oryzae,* instead. Said that it would do the trick just as well if they released it into the tunnels, and … that he'd have used it on the last attack at Nepenthes if he'd been handling it. Claimed it would have been poetic justice. But he wasn't the one who handled that one. Some guy named Berger was in charge. I didn't get a first name."

"I know who you're talking about. Used to work for Wes. I thought he went back to Earth."

"Apparently not."

"Okay. Let's assume I believe all of this. Why in the bloody hell would Durav send someone to attack Nepenthes? According to you, he's just waiting on this communications window to open so that he can contact the big bad aliens and have them destroy Earth. And Mars, too, from what you said earlier. Why go to all this effort now?"

Claire's mind began to spin, as she tried to think of a response that didn't involve the beacon. One option was to just tell him. He was in a hospital bed, with doctor's orders not to budge. But he still had plenty of employees at Nepenthes who could be assigned to keep her in line. The only other possibility she could think of was to say that Boudreaux might not be working for Durav anymore, that he might be working for one of Kolya's other rivals.

That didn't explain the *ipret-tai,* but it seemed like the best bet. She was opening her mouth to say it when a look of recognition came onto Kolya's face.

"It's because of Stasia, isn't it? He wanted to get revenge for her turning against him, but I took her off planet. We were scheduled to go to Nepenthes, so he must have assumed she'd be there, too. They'd probably have found out that wasn't true when they landed in Lyot. I'm sure even their pathetic rag of a news service will have picked up on the fact that Stasia is at Daedalus."

Claire nodded, relieved that he'd found something to fill in the blanks on his own, but also worried that he'd completely dismiss the threat to Nepenthes.

"How many weapons did they have?" he asked.

"I can't be sure. There were maybe twenty crates—I saw them after the men left, when I was heading out of the shed. And Wes told Boudreaux that it was only a small portion of what he had..." She shook her head, trying to remember exactly what he'd said, but it was a blank. "Of what he had for the other job. He said he had two more crates there of some rifle he was showing Boudreaux. An M4 … something. There was some disagreement between the two over how many men he'd need to take Nepenthes. Boudreaux seemed to want more, saying they needed to get in and out before you could send reinforcements. Wes said fifteen or twenty men would be plenty, because all of your reinforcements were going to be needed in Daedalus."

"What else did he say?"

"About Daedalus?"

"Yeah."

"Nothing," Claire said. "Judging from his tone, though, I wouldn't be surprised to learn he has people inside gleefully stirring the pot."

"Did he give you any indication where this other attack might be?"

Claire frowned, trying to remember if either of the men had mentioned a specific location. "No. The only other place he mentioned was a city in Lyot, where he has the rest of the weapons stashed. I remembered it because the first part sounds a bit like my name—Claritas."

Kolya stared at her for a moment, eyes widening. Then he began feeling around on the bed for something. He tried to turn his neck but couldn't get far due to the brace. "My phone. Do you see—"

"It's on the nightstand. Why?"

"Because Claritas isn't a *city* in Lyot. It's one of their external mining colonies. The one sitting practically on the border of Daedalus."

FROM AWAITING THE SENTINELS

BY TOBIAS SHEPHERD

Appendix: The Sentinel's Manifesto (Lesson Six)

AND ON THIS day of reckoning, what will become of those who have been caretakers, those who have used their time to mend and heal their broken planet, those who have treated their home with the proper reverence? Do not fear, my children. We have given unto you a flare to light the heavens. This gift is sealed by our own blood sacrifice. By this sign, we will know the faithful and we will lead you to a new home where the water is clear and the air is clean. The Sentinels will not abandon the faithful in their hour of greatest need.

Walk in the light of the Sentinels.

Res esdoden ojiri ensilar ufretas.

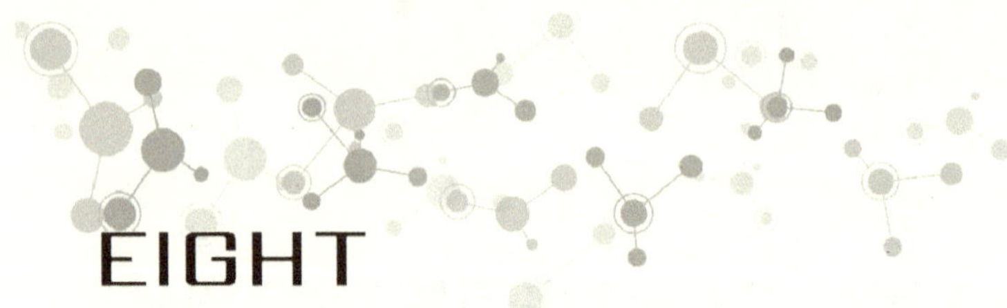

EIGHT

Thursday, October 5
Nepenthes Station

BECK BLINKED AWAKE, surprised at the amount of light flooding into the small plane. Even though Paul had managed to find an empty room for him and Wyatt to share at the Red Dahlia, he hadn't been able to sleep, in part because they were still waiting for news from Claire and in part because he knew he'd just have to wake up in a couple of hours. Wyatt, who seemed to have mastered the skill of catnapping even in tense situations, would snore for half an hour, wake up to check his phone, and then be back asleep ten seconds later.

He and Paul had left around five in the morning Daedalus time, taking a back route around the perimeter of the dome that avoided the chaos at the main gate into the resort, where protests were in full swing. Wyatt had vacillated back and forth but finally decided that he should remain at Daedalus. It was mostly because they'd agreed that someone should stay behind to ensure that KTI Security fulfilled their agreement to keep Stasia safe at the Red Dahlia. As Wyatt had noted, he was the expendable one. But Beck thought the information they'd gotten from Jordan Mercer and the sound of gunfire outside the gates had played a role, as well. Wyatt's journalistic spidey sense told him there was a story brewing that was right up his alley.

Beck had finally dozed off about an hour into the trip to Nepenthes, lulled to sleep by the slight motion of the craft and the flickering light from a movie that Paul was watching on one of the screens. Now both displays showed a small landing field and Paul was talking to someone about landing. For a station in the middle of lockdown, Nepenthes seemed unusually busy, especially given that it was just after midnight local time. Four other planes were currently on the field with maybe a dozen people in biosuits standing around them.

"What's going on?" he asked when Paul signed off the conversation. "It doesn't look like there's enough room for you to land."

"Yeah. They're going to open the smaller field on the other side of the hangar for us. The others just got back from a search and rescue mission." As if on cue, a bank of lights behind the hangars flashed on. Paul tapped something into the console as he spoke, and the plane veered slightly to the left.

"But the only ships that were out…" Beck pulled in a breath. "Claire. My god. Did they locate the shuttle?"

"No. But she's fine. They called off the search after they got word that Elysia had already sent a rescue team. Kolya and Macek are alive but injured. I don't know how badly. They told me that Claire…" Paul shook his head in disbelief. "Claire hiked out to get help. Hiked out to *where* I have absolutely no idea, but she's safe in Elysia. Their search and rescue team should be back with Kolya and Macek soon, so we're waiting on an update."

Nepenthes Station's rear landing field had three triangular icons. Their craft homed in on the one in the center, which was flashing orange, and began its descent.

"So, Claire is meeting us here, then?"

"No," Paul said. "We'll have to go get her in the morning. It's nearly fifteen hundred kilometers, well past the range of fully autopiloted shuttles. I need to check on Kolya and Macek anyway, although I am definitely not looking forward to those conversations given that we forged Kolya's credentials to requisition this plane."

"Of course, if you hadn't, we'd still be in Daedalus, and it would be even longer before Claire got here to begin the negotiations, right? Kolya needs you at the moment, which means he can't fire you. Not immediately, at any rate."

"Doesn't have to fire me. I'm quitting, remember? Although I guess I'll have to postpone that pleasure until we're all back at Daedalus, hopefully with this beacon of yours."

They left the plane and headed toward a small pad where several maglev shuttles were charging.

"I'm going to try to get a call in to Elysia before we go, so I can see if there's any word on the rescue," Paul said, "There are only a few spots in Ehden with decent coverage to the other colonies, and Kolya's cabin isn't one of them."

As they were placing their bags in the rear compartment, a tiny figure in a biosuit emerged from the hangar and began walking toward them. At first, Beck thought it was a child, but as the individual drew closer and he could see the face inside the visor, he realized it was an elderly woman.

He nudged Paul, who looked up and smiled. "Oh. Hey! Surprised you aren't already asleep. What happened to early to bed, early to rise?"

"I damn well *should* be in bed." The woman's voice had a faint hint of a Scottish accent. "Very nearly was, too. These fools dithered around for half an hour after Anton's shuttle was supposed to arrive, trying to decide whether to ask me to break lockdown protocol to search for him. I came down to enter the code and there was no way I was sleeping until we had some news. Once we finally heard back that they're both alive and on the way to Elysia, they told me you were due to arrive in ten minutes or so. I figured I'd wait and let you know I've already notified Shepherd of the delay and the reason for it. Which literally means I've been writing out notes by hand to have them delivered through the airlock since the fool doesn't have a bloody phone."

Beck was pretty sure that wasn't true. He and Claire both had exchanged messages with Shepherd. But telling this woman that Shepherd had apparently chosen to inconvenience her by not sharing his number seemed like a good way to derail the negotiations before they even began.

"Anyway," she continued, "I told Shepherd I couldn't guarantee it, but I thought you'd be back soon enough for us to start our talks around dinnertime tomorrow. Is that doable?"

"Should be," Paul said. "As long as I'm out of here by around eight and Kolya doesn't keep me for too long."

"If he gives you trouble, tell him I said you need to be back here by six." She turned to Beck. "Are you the reporter or the alien?"

He laughed, thinking he now had something to append after his name. "John Beckett, alien. But most people call me Beck. You must be Dr. Monroe."

"I am. And assuming Caruso here is willing and able to fetch our intrepid hostage negotiator on his own, I'll see you at the lab tomorrow."

Paul glanced at Beck, then shook his head. "Uh, that might be a problem. Technically, Beck is the property of Jonas Labs."

She barked out a laugh. "Do you think I'm planning to stick him full of needles? Our lab on Earth already sent me a full breakdown of all their DNA samples. I don't need to collect more of my own. I merely thought that given his work with Joe Echols he might be more interested in touring the lab than in flying halfway across the planet and back again. But if he'd rather spend the entire day with you in a—"

"No. Not at all," Beck said. "I'd love a tour. But ... aren't the domes still on lockdown?"

"Officially, yes. The only travel allowed was through the tunnels that connect the domes. But since two of those were destroyed in the attack, I sent a crew out last week to collect samples from the Nepenthes region. Call it a dress rehearsal for what we'll be doing everywhere else as soon as I get my field director back from that damn fool Anton has running Ehden. Nepenthes is clean. No signs of Azospira or anything potentially hazardous to human health. I haven't announced that though, so they're still going to make you go through decontamination."

Paul groaned.

"I'll have someone meet you here at eight tomorrow," she told Beck. Then she unfastened the outer pocket of her suit and handed Paul a written note. "That's directly from Shepherd. It will get you through the gate at Ehden. One of his Flock will escort you to the cabin and back to the gate tomorrow morning. I would have housed you at the lab and avoided all of this, but between the damage we took in the bombing and the suspects we're holding, we're short on beds." She pressed her palm against the door of one of the other shuttles to open it. "Don't be surprised if they're waving weapons about. They're a bit on the jumpy side since that asinine attempt at a rescue."

After Dr. Monroe left, Paul tried his call to Elysia again but couldn't get through to anyone. "Let's just go. There's nothing we can do from here anyway and I need sleep. I'll try again before I leave in the morning."

A little over ten minutes later, they arrived at the Ehden gate and transferred their bags to one of several KTI buggies parked on a charging pad outside the airlock gate. When they entered the tunnel, the buggy stopped automatically.

"We're going to be here a while," Paul cautioned. "Full sanitization protocol for stage six takes about five minutes."

It was closer to seven minutes before they were cleared. Once the lights went green, they pulled the buggy through and were greeted on the other side of the tunnel by two women and one man. All three looked to be in their twenties. They were armed with rifles, and visibly nervous. Beyond them, the road dipped rather sharply downhill, running through fields of what looked like corn, although it was hard to tell for certain in the dark. Further into the dome, he could make out a faint cluster of lights that must be the village.

Paul handed the girl closest to him the note from Shepherd. She glanced at it, then responded in a voice with a Midwestern accent. "You're cleared to go to your cabin, and back here in the morning. But stop by the dining hall on your way in and pick up the basket of food that Dr. Ademola prepared for you. He told us that the cabin may be without provisions."

"That was kind of you," Paul said.

"The Earth Watch Alliance doesn't allow anyone within our borders to be hungry. Go in peace and may the light of the Sentinels guide your journey."

Once they were out of earshot, Beck said, "Ademola. He's the botanist, right? The one from Claire's video about the bamboo?"

Paul nodded absently, as if his mind were somewhere else, barely hearing the question. Then he yanked his attention back. "Yeah, yeah. Idi's a good guy. He also knows Kolya keeps the cabin pretty well stocked, so I'm not sure what's up with that. I mean, it's all shelf-stable food, but…" He shook his head, glancing back toward the guards at the airlock tunnel. "My mind is stuck on what she just said. I mean, I knew they were the Earth Watch Alliance, even if pretty much everyone calls them the Flock. And in his memoir, Shepherd said that this Professor Everett guy chose that name, right? Which means Watch and Alliance have been right there in the freakin name all along."

"Yeah," Beck said. "It's not exactly subtle."

"So, you guys knew all along?"

"The Triad did. I mean, Shepherd was protected by Uden's right of *ufrete*, which is sort of like a last will and testament."

"Uden was Professor Everett."

Beck nodded. "And … the Flock's idea of the Sentinels seemed almost the reverse of what we were doing as the Watch—or so we all thought until a few months ago. The Triad kept an eye on Shepherd, but the group wasn't slowing down Earth's progress on the two objectives, so I guess even Durav didn't see them as much of a threat. I mean, no one did, which kind of makes sense. They were pacifists under Shepherd. They didn't start blowing things up until Drex took over."

"Yeah, well, personally? I'd be a lot more into their peace and light message if they weren't armed. And if I knew where they got the weapons."

"I was wondering about that. Guns don't really seem like something Shepherd's people would have brought with them."

"They weren't. We left two rifles, and Shepherd even seemed a bit nervous about that. This was right after the bombing at Millex, and there had been a few other incidents. He was all up in arms—pardon the pun—about bringing his people into another dangerous situation when they'd just left one on Earth. Insisted that anyone visiting Ehden would have to leave their weapons at Nepenthes Station."

"Well, at least we didn't end up with them giving us an armed escort like Dr. Monroe said they would."

Paul shrugged. "I'm guessing Shepherd trusts me a little more than he does the mad scientists keeping his people hostage. I spent several days with him when he first arrived in Ehden. Helped him get set up and kept him company until Kolya and Macek arrived to negotiate the specifics of bringing his followers to Ehden. The guy was obviously on edge after nearly getting killed on the *Ares Prime*, and I'm not saying we're best buds or anything like that, but after the first day, we got along fine. To be honest, I think if Kolya had let me talk Shepherd down after the bombing, this whole situation could have been avoided. He wouldn't listen, though. Never does. He always thinks he's the most personable person in the room, but the truth is he puts a lot of people off." With that, he launched into several anecdotes from the past few years, none of which cast Kolya in a favorable light.

"That certainly syncs with what I've heard from Claire," Beck said when Paul finally paused for breath. "And what I've gleaned from his media persona. Although I guess I should withhold judgment until I actually meet the man."

"Yeah, the only difference between his media persona and the real Kolya is that we try to make him look aloof, like he grows weary of public adulation. Truth is, he thrives on it. The animosity brewing in Daedalus is going to both confuse and infuriate him."

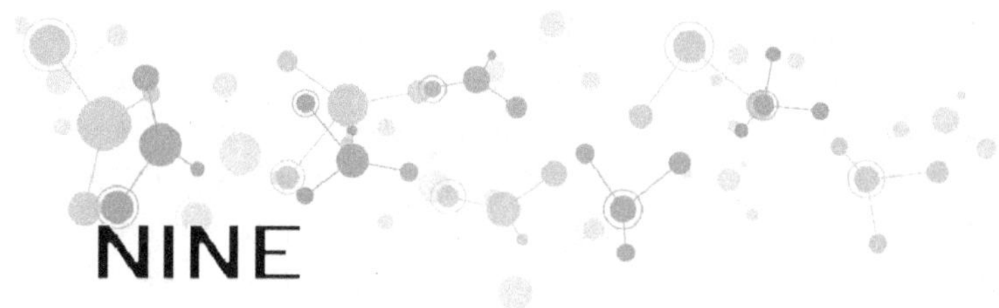

NINE

ALL OF THE windows in the tiny village of Ehden were dark, except for one. Light shone through the large front window of the café, the first of the five single-story buildings on the left. Three newer four-story housing units on the opposite side of the street dwarfed the other buildings, giving the town a lopsided appearance. Beck was about to ask why they hadn't opted to build out instead of up, given that there was plenty of land. Then, he remembered the chaos of all the rotating hotels at Daedalus and realized the traditional-looking exteriors were probably a façade that kept people from having to stare at buildings constantly in motion.

Paul parked the buggy on the charging pad outside the café. "You can wait here if you want. I'll just step inside and grab whatever Idi…" He trailed off as the door opened and a man holding a basket stepped outside.

"Caruso! It is so good to see you." Idi Ademola had the same lilting accent that Beck remembered from Claire's *Simple Science* video where he'd described the fast-growing bamboo. "Shepherd told me that Kolya and Macek were injured. Have you any news?"

"I'm afraid not," Paul said. "I'll try again in the morning. They're in good hands, though. The medical care at Elysia is as good as our hospital at Daedalus City. Better in some ways." He peered through the window into the main dining area, which was empty. "Where is everyone? I thought they were holding all of the KTI people here at the café."

Ademola nodded. "They did, for the first few days. But sleeping here was uncomfortable, and we are accustomed to being in quarters with full gravity. Not all of us intend to live here permanently, after all. There were empty rooms across the street, so Shepherd moved us there. It's a little disconcerting having an armed guard in the hallway, but they have treated us very kindly." He turned to Beck and nodded. "I am Idi Ademola, chief botanist for KTI here at Nepenthes."

"John Beckett, Dr. Ademola. Formerly of Jonas Labs. I'm here to assist Claire Echols with the negotiations."

"Oh. Good, good. And please, it is just Idi. The only one around here that anyone calls *doctor* is Davina Monroe." Idi handed Paul the basket. "These are just a few things that we put together for you since, as we told Shepherd, there may not be fresh food at Kolya's house. But truthfully, I mostly wanted a moment to talk with you before everything begins."

Beck glanced around the street. "Your captors let you come here alone?"

Idi smiled sadly. "Renata remains in our temporary quarters. They know I will do nothing that would put her at risk. Although ... I will say that they've gotten fairly relaxed with guarding us the longer we've been here. We play chess and Scrabble and charades with Flock members in the meeting house. We eat with them during mealtimes at the café. Some of us help prepare food and work in the fields. To be honest, it is an odd hostage situation. I do not think Davy would harm their people, but I doubt that she is treating them as well as we are treated. I almost wish we'd kept Amara here with us, because I do not feel we are in danger now and being away from our daughter is our main source of stress. But maybe this will be over soon?"

"I hope so," Paul said. "We should probably get going—"

"Hold up a minute," Beck said. He didn't know if or when he'd get a chance to talk with the other KTI hostages, and he had questions. "Dr. Ademola—sorry. *Idi.* Do you believe the Flock members KTI is holding were the ones who bombed the lab?"

He hesitated, then shook his head. "I do not. At first, I wasn't certain. But as I thought about it, I don't see how it is possible for them to have been involved. Our buggies passed a team working in the wheat fields, maybe two and a half kilometers from the village, around three-thirty."

"Why were you coming into Ehden that day?" Beck asked.

"For a softball game." Idi laughed. "I know. It sounds odd, right? But Shepherd instructed his people to be sociable with their new neighbors, and they were putting forth a solid effort. About a month after lockdown, they sent a message to the lab suggesting a weekly softball game, assuming we could get enough people to form a team. I had already been over here a few times to give them tips for dealing with the peculiarities of the soil inside these domes, and they were never unkind or hostile, so I took the lead. Renata joined, too, and I found six others. This was our seventh game, and team members often brought their partners and children to cheer us on. The people that Dr. Monroe captured as suspects were about a kilometer from the entrance to our maglev tunnel when we passed them. We waved, and they waved back."

"Did they have a buggy?" Paul asked, apparently sensing where Idi's argument was going.

"No. They were on foot. That is standard here unless you're harvesting. Our game began at four, and early in the sixth inning, we heard the explosion. Amara was recording our game, and the video shows that the noise occurred at five o'clock on the dot. The Flock members that KTI security apprehended running were definitely the people we saw out working the fields. If the only explosives planted had been at the entrance to that tunnel, they could have done it. But once we knew the extent of the damage? It isn't possible. They don't have access to the maglev tram, and the lab is nearly thirty kilometers from here. I've read in the Daedalus news that some explosives were placed in the tunnel between Doba and the lab, as well. Is it possible that someone from here in Ehden was involved?" He shrugged. "I cannot rule that out. But it could not have happened the way they seem to think. And I believe we were close to convincing Dr. Monroe of that before the failed rescue effort. Three Flock members were killed evicting the two security officers from Daedalus who sneaked in with the repair crew."

"Was the guard whose body they sent back to Davy one of the men who sneaked in?" Paul asked.

"No. Both of those men got away alive, minus their weapons. The guard whose body they returned was from the lab. I did not know him well, but I had seen him around. And the Flock did not kill him. He died of injuries from the explosion. Some Flock members found him half-dead in the fields the same day that Shepherd released the children and they reached an agreement about repairs to the domes. I think Dr. Monroe believed he was taken hostage with the rest of us. When they found the man, it looked like he tried to crawl to the road. Internal injuries. Broken limbs. He never regained consciousness and died overnight. They were debating whether to tell Dr. Monroe what happened or simply bury him."

Paul shook his head. "That doesn't make sense. I've seen the pictures. He was shot in the head."

Idi winced and made a little gesture of admission. "They were afraid Dr. Monroe would double-cross them again, like she did with the repair crew, and more Flock members would die. Shepherd's people were panicking and he needed to send a strong message that he would protect them."

"Have you tried telling her that?"

"No," Idi said. "Like I told you, Shepherd wanted her to believe his people were a threat, so that she wouldn't pull any more stunts."

"Um..." Paul hesitated for a long time. Beck and Idi just watched as a battle played out on his face. Finally, he said, "If you get a chance, tell Shepherd that wasn't Dr. Monroe. It was planned by KTI Security in Daedalus."

"Yes, yes. And maybe if you get the chance, you can tell Dr.

Monroe that Dawit was already dead. Several of us saw him and we will all tell her the same, but I'm not sure we'll be allowed at the negotiations. And…" He shrugged. "The woman has an entire lab full of scientists. Surely one of them is capable of performing an autopsy?"

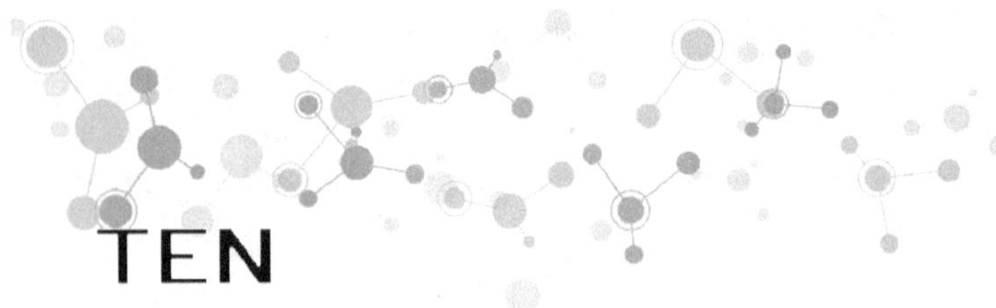

TEN

Thursday, October 5
Nepenthes

BECK AND PAUL arrived back at Nepenthes Station a scant eight hours after landing the night before. By the time they'd finished their conversation with Idi Ademola and made it to Kolya's cabin, it had been nearly two a.m. and they'd both collapsed immediately. He felt pretty good considering that he was running on less than five hours of sleep, but then he'd also napped a bit on the plane. To the best of his knowledge, Paul had not, and he definitely wasn't his usual chatty self on the ride from Ehden to Nepenthes. Of course, that could just as easily be trepidation about dealing with his soon-to-be-former employer as lack of sleep.

The worker that Dr. Monroe sent to fetch Beck was waiting inside a maglev shuttle when they arrived at the station. Beck told Paul goodbye and good luck, then switched to the other shuttle. His assigned escort had either been instructed not to converse with visitors or was extraordinarily taciturn. Even the most innocuous questions were met with some variant of *I really wouldn't know, sir* or *you'll have to ask Dr. Monroe, sir*. The only question that he'd answered definitively was how long the trip to the lab would take, and that had been a nonverbal response. He'd simply tapped the console of the shuttle to light up a screen with a small map of the region, their current speed, and an ETA of 9:04 a.m..

On the plus side, the lack of conversation gave Beck plenty of time to go through the messages from Claire and Wyatt that popped up on his phone when they arrived at the station. Aside from Claire being safe—which he'd already known secondhand—none of the news was good.

Wyatt took the easy route and forwarded the draft of an article he was sending his editor about the current situation in Daedalus City, which seemed to be getting steadily worse. Claire's message, which she'd written the previous night, was even more alarming, confirming that the man he'd seen at Ares Station was indeed Boudreaux. He was traveling with one of the *ipret-tai,* and she said they were planning an attack on Nepenthes. She'd also sent along some emails between Monroe and Kolya that read like a family squabble. All of it was strictly for his own information, since Claire said she didn't think the attack was imminent. She said she was sending the same information to Paul who would probably be in a better position to warn Shepherd and Dr. Monroe since he knew both of them better. Beck was fairly certain that Paul hadn't read Claire's message before he left, though. He wasn't sure who would be handling his tour of the lab. Hopefully, he could arrange at least a short private conversation with Dr. Monroe during his tour.

When they arrived at the edge of the dome, however, he found Monroe waiting outside the airlock tunnel. Two security guards stood next to her like bookends, each holding a large sack. All three wore gun belts over their biosuits. The guards placed the sacks in the outer storage compartment and then she waved them back toward the airlock.

"You're late." She looked at Beck for a moment, as if trying to decide something. Then she turned to his escort. "Go on with you, Gentry. Get some sleep."

"Are you sure?" the man asked. "I thought—"

"Of course, I'm bloody sure. If I wasn't sure, I wouldn't have said it. You've been on duty for twenty-seven hours, so I think my eighty-year-old reflexes are better than yours at the moment. I'm armed and I'm telling him upfront that I'd welcome the opportunity to autopsy an alien in the unlikely event that he decides to give me trouble."

"Nope. Definitely not planning to give you trouble." Beck kept his smile pleasant, even though he didn't like her casually referring to him as an *alien.* He hadn't assumed that was common knowledge, although come to think of it, she had told him the previous night that the lab had analyzed their DNA. Had his genetic code already been the subject of a KTI white paper or a lunch-and-learn session?

The autopsy quip also reminded him of Ademola's comment the night before. If he was to take Dr. Monroe at her word, there was indeed at least one person at the Nepenthes Lab capable of doing an autopsy, but she hadn't bothered. To be fair, a bullet in the head of the corpse had probably convinced her that it wasn't needed. The real question was whether she could be talked into doing it, assuming the body hadn't already been buried or cremated. Damage from a bullet wound to a living body would be markedly different from damage to a corpse. Idi Ademola would undoubtedly tell her the same thing that he'd said the night before. Beck wasn't sure Monroe would believe him given her quip to Kolya about Stockholm syndrome in the messages Claire had forwarded, but if she had concrete evidence that backed up his assertion and absolved Shepherd of murdering one of her people? That could go a long way toward resolving the standoff.

Monroe tapped the console. "Moghbeli. Maximum speed."

The screen lit up and one of the smaller, unlabeled domes on the map began to blink as the shuttle took off at a considerably faster pace than they'd traveled from Nepenthes Station. She settled back into her seat, folding her small, gloved hands in her lap.

"I decided we could tour the main lab later. We're expecting a bit of a windstorm between eleven and three. While that won't affect us *inside* the domes, it might make it somewhat tricky to travel between them. And I didn't think you'd want to miss seeing the fruits of KTI's labor in their *natural*"—she made air quotes around the word—"habitat, although you may already have seen some of the video from Anton's presentation to the Ares Consortium. The dome is officially called Moghbeli, but if you've heard of it at all, it's probably as the notorious Island of Doctor Monroe."

Her bright blue eyes watched him carefully as she said the nickname, probably trying to gauge which side of the debate he stood on, because middle ground didn't seem to be an option. Most of the public and many within the scientific community had labeled her experiments with hybridization and lab-created species an abomination, but Beck wasn't among them. That was mostly because he'd recognized the value of the work in understanding evolutionary processes and genetic variation. He didn't think her lab-grown creatures should be released into the wild, but Dr. Monroe had never argued for that.

The fact that her experiments were confined to habitats inside labs didn't stop groups like the Flock and the Gates of Destiny, both of which were in their infancy in the 2050s, from raising hell, however. More traditional religious groups had joined them, arguing that she couldn't be allowed to play god. In the end, legislation was passed in the newly *mostly* re-United States that placed strict limits on the field of synthetic biology. Some experts in the field shifted to more acceptable realms of study. Others continued their work in countries with fewer regulations. Davina Monroe did neither. She cut a deal with KTI—then under the leadership of Anton's uncle, Ryhor Kolya—and moved her lab to this area of Mars, which was the one place she would be granted the opportunity to continue her work unfettered.

"I've heard the nickname," he said. "And I'm looking forward to seeing your work. I never got a chance to see the videos Kolya showed at that dinner. Everything has been kind of hectic since then, and communications were limited on the *Velox One*."

"Right. You were one of the mad bombers assigned to Jonas Labs."

"Yes," he admitted. "Although I did do my best to limit the damage."

She gave a derisive little snort. "I'm surprised Kai Jonas didn't have her people shoot you on sight. But maybe she decided that owning you was a better punishment."

The ownership agreement was technically between the Watch and Jonas Labs, not Kai, and it had been done to give them some protection against potentially landing in the hands of the government. But Beck didn't see the point in correcting her.

"I've worked for Kai Jonas for more than a decade with barely any time off," he said. "She already considered me property of Jonas Labs. But … given that you're aware of my role in the bombings, I'm surprised you left your guard behind."

"We're understaffed and Gentry was tired. He was one of the people out searching for Anton's shuttle last night. Anyway…" She patted her gun. "My guard is right here."

He didn't have much to say in response to that, so they rode in silence for about a minute. As the shuttle began to decelerate, Dr. Monroe pointed toward a dome coming into view. "If you look near the lake over there, you can see one of our future dairy herds."

About a dozen shaggy, dual-humped creatures were congregated around the water.

"Camels, right?"

She nodded. "Bactrian, for the most part, since they can withstand major temperature fluctuations on Earth. We also added elements of *Camelus knoblochi* in the mix, to adjust for the even colder temperatures. We're around Pleistocene levels now outside the dome, so it's a good fit. Plus, I did some minor tweaking of the heat shock proteins. We hope to be able to move the herds outside the domes entirely within the next five years."

They left the shuttle on the charging pad. Dr. Monroe removed the two large sacks from behind the seat and carried them to the buggy parked near the airlock tunnel. "Snacks," she said as she tossed them into the back. Before the decontamination cycle finished, the herd left the lake and began gradually moving toward the road.

"They were the first batch gestated in the lab," Monroe said. "Genetically selected for mostly females given that space is still limited and the males get nasty with each other during breeding season. They're a little over three years old—Martian years, that is—so about six Earth years. We got our first two calves this season."

As they drew closer, Beck could see the two smaller camels, their heads rising just above the tall, dark green grass.

"Are the mothers adapting well?" he asked.

"For the most part, yes. We made some adjustments to the oxytocin receptors to compensate for their lack of socialization." She stopped the buggy. "Can you hop out and empty one of those sacks next to the road? Be quick about it, because they'll pick up speed as soon as they see the bag."

Beck did as she asked, then sprinted back to the buggy as the herd moved from a leisurely trot to an all-out run. They watched the camels eat for about a minute, then she started the buggy again.

For the next half hour, they drove around inside the dome, sometimes on the path, and sometimes veering off into the fields. Along the way, he got a running commentary on the wildlife currently populating Moghbeli. He was surprised to learn that it was a fairly small list.

"We only create animals that serve a purpose," she said when he asked why. "Technically, we don't *need* animals. We could do just fine on plants and vat meat. But Anton is right that people feel like the place is barren without other creatures. Creating animals with a specific function is our compromise. The lemur-dogs, for example. You'll see a domesticated version back at the lab, but the wild ones help break down the scraps from the bamboo harvest. The camels will eventually provide milk which is slightly less labor intensive than making it in the lab. We are also introducing a variety of earthworms to help turn the soil. The rabbits ... well, they may be the exception. They're here mostly because a few children put in a request for bunnies. And likewise, we'll soon have a version of the honeybee because the biggest child on Mars wants them."

"Kolya?"

She gave him a single nod. "For apple trees to make his krambambula. He swears that the versions made with self-pollinating apple varieties don't taste the same, but I'll be damned if I can tell the difference."

"What about predators?"

"None. I assume you are familiar with the *Jurassic Park* movies?"

Beck laughed. "Saw the first one in the theater in the early 1990s. And yeah, I guess it might be best to avoid going down that path. But aren't you going to be overrun with bunnies?"

"We will not. The bunny population here in Moghbeli does not, as the saying goes, breed like rabbits. Only a small number are actually fertile, just enough to maintain the current population."

He dumped the second bag of carrots at the other end of the dome. The younger herd was nowhere to be seen, until Dr. Monroe sounded the buggy's horn. Almost instantly a group of around twenty slightly smaller camels rose up en masse from the middle of a field near the edge of the dome and began thundering toward them.

"Teenagers," she said, shaking her head. "Lazy, but still food motivated. I know, I know, they're busy growing."

She reversed the buggy and they headed back toward the airlock, and he decided it was as good a time as any for that private conversation.

"Dr. Monroe, I thought I should let you know—"

"About the upcoming attack on Nepenthes?"

Her comment took him by surprise, but then he realized that Claire hadn't exactly been circumspect in her message. Evading KTI's censors was no longer necessary given that she was planning to tell Kolya everything she'd learned as soon as he was awake. Monroe was in charge here, so anything KTI picked up was probably sent to her security people.

"Okay," he said. "I guess that saves time. If you have the message Claire sent me last night, you know as much as I do."

"I might know as much about the who, what, when, and where. But I think you know a whole lot more about the why. I also suspect that the *why* behind the attack is directly connected to our ongoing hostage situation. Here's what's been puzzling me. Three weeks ago, I believe Shepherd and I were on the verge of hashing out this hostage *clusterbùrach*. He'd agreed to let Kolya mediate remotely. We were all set. The next thing I know, he's insisting that the only person he'll accept as a mediator is the girl Kolya was sniffing around on his last trip." She raised an eyebrow, apparently picking up from his body language that he didn't particularly care for her description of Claire. "No disrespect intended to the young woman, if she's a friend of yours. She obviously wasn't having any of Anton's nonsense, which means she's smart. He was better matched with the mother. She's a fine piece of work, isn't she?"

"She is, indeed," Beck said. "Claire's nothing like Kai, though, just to be clear."

"I'll take your word on that. Anyway, this was *before* Shepherd outright murdered one of the hostages, one of *my* people."

"Three of his people were killed, too, right?"

"That's beside the point. I had nothing to do with it. As I've told him. My point is that I can't help wondering whether we might have avoided both tragedies if these negotiations had been allowed to proceed without pulling in two people who, to the best of my knowledge, have even less experience in this sort of thing than Anton. The argument I heard was that Shepherd trusted Claire because she saved his life onboard KTI's fancy-pants cruise ship. But now it looks like you've brought a couple of hired assassins in your wake, presumably to get another crack at Shepherd. Only that means Nepenthes is in the crosshairs, too."

"Okay, first, I'm fairly certain the hired assassins didn't *follow* us. I'm not even sure that they know we're here. Claire overheard a conversation that..."

"I already know what she told you. If it's true, I'm aware it casts some doubts on the guilt of the individuals we're holding at the lab, *but*." She paused for emphasis. "That's assuming she's to be believed and assuming these men weren't aware of her presence. They could have been feeding her false information. I will note, however, that I'm not worried in the slightest about those fools pumping our *own* patented version of *Azo* into the lab. Do they really think we aren't aware of the danger? And that we wouldn't have filters and several different levels of safeguards?"

"What if they have someone on the inside, though? Couldn't they shut the filters down?"

She shrugged. "Not unless it's more than one or two people acting alone. Even then, not without setting off alarms. I'm more worried about Ehden and Nepenthes Station than the lab. If this is a real threat, they need to suit up and be on alert. And you still haven't told me *why* this is happening. Why they're after Shepherd and willing to kill a bunch of innocent people in the process."

"Can I ask you something first?"

Monroe narrowed her eyes, but she didn't say no.

"Okay," he continued. "You've referred to me twice as an alien."

"I have. Please don't tell me you're going to try and convince me I'm wrong?"

"Of course not. I'm just curious why you're willing to accept evidence that Kolya is not. He's made it clear that he thinks everything we've told him is an elaborate ruse, probably in league with—"

"Yes, yes. I know. Anton thinks this is something Shepherd cooked up. I've told him that this Sandjeel is not engineered, but he didn't want to hear it. He also didn't want to hear my view that the creature's DNA is very, very old, although a normal epigenetic clock is obviously not accurate in this case, given that we don't have a comparison for the species. I was able to give him a more accurate estimate in the case of cloned bodies like your own and that of the *ipret-tai,* although even you carry a few odd markers that aren't entirely human. I told him your bodies are between a hundred and thirty and a hundred and forty years old."

"And what did he say to that?"

"Mostly he ranted and raved about how our company physical could have missed it in Stasia's case, since we require a DNA sample. But we simply store it for future reference. It's not like we do a full genetic analysis unless there's a reason. And then he balked at my *expert* opinion that the genetic engineering that produced Stasia, you, and the others—and most certainly Sandjeel—could *not* have been accomplished in any lab using current technology. I'll talk him around to my view once he's here. We've done this dance before. It just means getting him into the lab and showing him concrete proof."

"Do you think he's hesitating because other scientists have given him a different opinion?"

"I doubt he's even bothered to ask. The unfortunate reality is that Anton believes everyone else's ego is like his own—a gargantuan beast that must be fed constantly. So, until I break it down and show him the proof, he'd prefer to believe I reached my conclusion because I'm unwilling to admit there might be some other synthetic biologists whose abilities exceed my own."

"Are there?"

"No." She pointed a finger at him. "But that is not ego, young man. It's simple fact. There are a few who come close, including two in my lab, both of whom confirmed my analysis of Sandjeel's DNA. Someone *will* surpass my work in the coming decade—or sooner, if I keel over tomorrow, which is always a possibility at my age. But those samples." She shook her head. "Nope. There are chemical building blocks in Sandjeel's DNA that I've never seen and could not replicate in my lab. I told Anton that I don't know why you're on Earth, but I know at a bare minimum that Sandjeel didn't *come* from Earth. And … based on changes I've noticed in the samples they've taken over the past few weeks, I don't think being on Earth agrees with him."

"We know. There are some nutrients he can't get from Earth foods. We had a small Ufretan replicator in the tunnels under the Triad's headquarters, but now that it's gone…" He shook his head. "Joe is working on it, but he doesn't have his full lab at this point, and he hasn't had any luck so far."

"I might be able to assist. But I'm not inclined to offer my services when you still haven't told me *why*."

They were back at the airlock now. Beck took advantage of the time required to shift from the buggy to the shuttle, trying to decide exactly how much he should tell her. The only reason he was here was because Claire acted on her intuition that he might be able to reach Shepherd, to convince the man that he was some version of these Sentinel deities he'd built up in his mind. But he didn't think that was going to work. He couldn't talk the language of faith and miracles. Yes, he was a member of the Watch, but at his core, he was a scientist.

Like Dr. Monroe.

That's when he realized Claire's instinct that he needed to be here was right. But not to convince Shepherd. To convince the only person in the world who might sway Anton Kolya. The data from the samples that contained the Eberin Das journal was in his phone, along with the translated sections.

And so, Beck climbed into the shuttle seat across from Davina Monroe and began telling her everything.

FROM THE ATLANTIC POST (DRAFT)

OCTOBER 4, 2084

Erika – This is rough, so use your red pen as needed. I trust your judgment. I've been awake for more than twenty-four hours. And yeah, I know this isn't the story I traveled all this way to get. But events have taken an unexpected turn and I'm thinking this may be even more interesting to our readers. Expect a follow-up on this tomorrow or possibly sooner if KTI's security forces can't hold them off.

ARMED STANDOFF AT KTI'S FLAGSHIP RESORT RED DAHLIA
by Wyatt Garcia

SEVERAL DOZEN Daedalian citizens stormed the Red Dahlia, the flagship Martian resort of Kolya Terraforming International (KTI) around two a.m. local time today, demanding that KTI Security turn Stasia Ljubic over to the local police. Ljubic, who is accused of orchestrating terror attacks that killed several dozen people in multiple colonies, is currently being held under house arrest at the resort, pending trial. The crowd was pushed back to the outer gates of the resort after about an hour, but it more than doubled in size as the day progressed and security forces are concerned that they may be planning a second attempt this evening. There are scattered reports of looting along the Strip and observers outside the gates have noted that a number of the protesters are armed, in open defiance of the colony-wide ban on guns.

This is not the first time that violence has erupted in Daedalus over the past few months. A combination of greed, poor planning, and last-minute labor concessions appear to have turned this normally peaceful colony into a failed social experiment, with a sharp increase in crime, a public lynching, and a rising tide of animosity toward colonial leadership.

The lockdown is expected to end within the next few days, and it cannot come soon enough for everyone interviewed for this article. This includes not only colonists and the miners who were assigned to the dome, but also tourists and researchers who seized on what they viewed as the deal of a lifetime and got more than they bargained for. Vacation packages for the entire lockdown were offered for less than the cost of a typical two-week stay, with hotels subsidized by KTI and the merchants' association, who banked on the revenue from the casinos, restaurants and other entertainments to cover the cost. Scientists who would normally have waited years for their application to be approved found themselves with free passage on a worker transport as long as they were willing to cover lodging, food, and incidentals. Nearly three hundred people jumped on these special deals.

Still, all might have gone smoothly except for the last-minute clash between the planet's major mine owners and the fledgling Martian Federation of Labor (MFL) that threatened to delay the beginning of stage six. Sources within KTI inform the *Post* that a meeting was held at the Red Dahlia a few weeks prior to lockdown in order to avoid a threatened multi-colony strike. The issue under contention was the mine owners' refusal to include the six-month lockdown period in the payment of worker bonuses. This provision would have effectively cut bonuses (which are a substantial portion of their pay) by twenty-five percent for guest workers, which they would not be able to make up given the strict two-year limit on contracts.

The negotiations were cut short due to an attack on the Millex facility in Cerberus, but an agreement was eventually reached between the mine owners and the MFL. One of the key concessions on the part of KTI was that Daedalus would house an additional five hundred miners for the duration of the six-month lockdown. A KTI construction team was pulled from an assignment in the Nepenthes region and tasked with building temporary housing to accommodate the miners, most of whom are assigned to the eastern region of Tharsis.

Those who follow Martian colonial politics closely may recall that Tharsis, along with Lyot, are the primary players in the colonial prison transfer program initiated when terraforming began. Since then, an estimated 60,000 incarcerated workers from seven countries have volunteered for mining work and for the early, labor-intensive stages of the terraforming project, including the laying of more than twenty thousand kilometers of superconducting wire along the planet's equator to create the artificial magnetosphere that helps shield the surface from radiation. In exchange, they received room, board, a small salary, and a substantial reduction in their sentences.

Tharsis and Lyot are still active participants in the prison transfer program, with incarcerated workers making up approximately half of the mining workforce. According to our sources, the agreement was that the miners would remain in the hastily constructed village, which includes a commissary and various entertainment options, while the tourists and researchers would occupy the hotels in Daedalus City. No one seems to have explained this to the miners, however. Every worker interviewed for this article expected a six-month vacation at Daedalus City, with easy access to the various clubs, shows, and casinos. When they discovered this wasn't the plan, and that there was no shuttle service between the camp and the Daedalus City strip, they "liberated" a shuttle from the security motor pool, hacked into the system to trigger the manual override, and took turns acting as the driver.

Clashes between residents of Daedalus City, visitors, and the miners have escalated over the past few months, causing many colonists to seriously question the colony's system of government, which is technically under the leadership of the elected fifteen-member Daedalian Council. But aside from a sales tax on tourists, the majority of funds for the colony come in the form of direct grants from Kolya International. This essentially gives Anton Kolya veto power over any law requiring funding. A former councilmember who spoke on condition of anonymity said that during his two years in office, there was never a single instance in which the council was able to push through a policy that Kolya opposed.

In a recent interview with the local paper, *The Red Planet*, Käthe Vogt, current chair of Daedalian Council, noted that support for the proposed constitution was already waning prior to the lockdown. Vogt, who will not be running in the elections slated for next month, said she does not think it will pass now, at least not in its current form. "People want more control over their lives. They're angry. A solid majority in Daedalus and Elysia would push it through—together we have just over seventy percent of the permanent colonists on Mars. But I'm not sure that majority exists at this time, at least not here in Daedalus."

One city official noted that anger at Stasia Ljubic was the only thing that unified the colony, including the current mix of visitors. This anger seems to stem as much from her role as the public face of Kolya International as from the role she is accused of playing in the bombings at Icarus Camp and elsewhere on the planet. Rumors were flying among the crowd last night. One man interviewed claimed that the woman being held at the Red Dahlia is not actually Ljubic, but rather an imposter that Kolya has hired to take her place in the trial. Another argued that it was indeed Ljubic who was taken to the resort but added that she's already been moved out of Daedalus and will never actually face trial.

City officials have instituted an eight p.m. curfew for the next two days, hoping to prevent additional violence.

ELEVEN

Wednesday, October 4
Ogunquit, Maine

THE CAR'S headlights cast an eerie, elongated shadow as Alice waded through thigh-high weeds toward the ancient gate. A crooked NO TRESPASSING sign dangled from one wire near the center, adding an extra touch of creepiness that she really didn't appreciate, given that they were miles from another living soul, and it was pitch dark.

She felt exposed and vulnerable—probably not a surprise after her alien zombie encounter the previous night—and wished she hadn't volunteered to type in the gate code. How old must the interface be if you couldn't connect via phone? But after the past hour, she'd jumped at any chance for even a minute of solitude, a minute when she didn't feel the need to keep up a bogus conversation in order to maintain their cover.

After yanking open the cracked plastic door to the lockbox, she tapped in the eight-digit code Wilson had given her before they left Boston. The code didn't take the first time because one of the keys jammed, so she tried again. This time, the light went green and she began pushing the gate open. Tall grass crunched beneath it, still bone dry from the heatwave. The storm must not have carried much rain this far north.

The afternoon had been a lesson in exactly how fast things could move when money was no object. As soon as they decided to act on the plan, Wilson had retreated into the house to make phone calls. Housen had dredged up two possible matches for the address that were within about an hour of New York City. One was in Long Branch, New Jersey and the other was in Massapequa, New York. Given the direction in which the Pulsar had been headed when the *ipret-tai* ditched it, Massapequa was by far the most likely. This was then confirmed by property records that showed the beachfront rental was managed by a company that Arbet recognized as handling a number of the Triad's financial investments. Wilson contacted someone he knew, and a little over two hours later, they were getting drone surveillance video back from the property.

After a long discussion about logistics, Alice had offered to go along as lookout. She wasn't certain she could pull the trigger herself unless she was in danger or protecting someone else, but she had experience with guns and was willing to keep watch. Durav had, after all, ordered her abduction. And based on what Arbet had said earlier, she was pretty sure the man would have killed her if not for Housen's quick thinking. The least she could do was watch his back for a few hours.

They'd left Everly Estates around ten p.m. for Ogunquit, Maine, with the combo tracker and listening device once again affixed to her glasses. A few minutes before they crossed the Maine state line, she disabled the blocker inside her bag, which should mean it had also started transmitting their conversation. So, for the past hour, she and Housen had carried on a fake conversation entirely for Durav's benefit. They'd chatted about the charter boat he'd reserved for the next morning, whether a current storm in Pennsylvania was likely to reach this far north by then, how far out they'd need to go to ensure that they were in deep enough waters that Durav wouldn't be able to track the beacon, and whether they'd be likely to see whales off the coast this time of year.

Although it would be more accurate to say that *she* had carried on the conversation, because Housen was distracted. He kept running his thumb over the oval object she'd seen Arbet give him just after they arrived in Boston. It was apparently a video device of some sort, because his eyes moved like he was watching something. She couldn't see anything, so he must have special lenses. And she couldn't ask what the damn thing was because they had to assume that Durav or one of his people was listening. Or at least they hoped someone was listening. Otherwise, everything they were doing was pointless.

The plan was to enter Beck's cabin just long enough to drop off the tracker, along with a burner phone on which she and Housen had recorded about an hour of fake conversation followed by sleep noises from the four or five hours they grabbed before leaving Camp Ufrete. They'd leave the sound on before they left to make it seem as though they were crashing at the cabin before heading out bright and early on the rented boat to dump the beacon.

In reality, as soon as they dropped off her glasses and the burner phone, they would be driving to the hyperloop terminal in Kittery, catching the next train south, and sending the car back to Joe. It would take a little less than an hour on the loop to reach New Rochelle, where a car would be waiting at the station. From there, it was maybe a forty-minute drive to Massapequa, by which time they'd hopefully have confirmation that at least some of Durav's men had taken the bait and were heading to Maine. And by the time his men reached the cabin, more than a dozen Jonas Labs security officers would be in place inside and around the property, ready to give them a warm welcome.

"You could have skipped closing the gate," Housen said when she got back into the car. "We're just going to have to open it again in about five m—"

She cut him off with an alarmed look, pointing to the frame of her glasses. "Five more *hours*. Yes."

He made an apologetic face, and Alice waved it off, but she couldn't help thinking how ironic it was that the guy who had been living a double life for at least ten times as long as she had was the one to slip up.

"And I know we're in the middle of nowhere," she said. "I'll still feel better with the gate locked." That was true. The dilapidated gate was a poor substitute for the battalion of locks and bolts on her apartment door, but it still felt better than nothing.

A white car with rental plates was parked in front of the cabin. It was the car Beck had left behind, the one he'd used to transport Reese from Jonas Labs after the bombing, and the one they'd be taking to the hyperloop tonight, just in case they'd been observed leaving Everly Estates. The car had been thoroughly cleaned, but Joe said he'd decided to purchase it rather than risk any questions about the interior damage.

Beck's cabin was a small gray box, with a porch barely wide enough for the wooden chair and tiny table on the left. Housen pulled a key out of his pocket and flipped on the light when they stepped inside. The place carried a faint disinfectant smell. A basic kitchen sat on the left, separated from the sparsely furnished living area by a bar and a couple of stools. The worn and sun-faded wooden floors in the living room had two shiny footprints left behind by a sofa and an oval rug that had apparently been trashed after occupying those spaces for many years.

Housen opened one of the two doors behind where the couch had sat. It was a bathroom. "Okay if I go first?"

"Sure. I'll see if I can find sheets for the beds. Although I'm tired enough that I'd settle for just a pillow."

There was no overhead and she couldn't find a working lamp, but the light from the living room revealed an empty wooden bed frame. The mattress must have been trashed, too. She took off her glasses and placed them on the nightstand. Her plan had been to peel off the tracker, but Wilson had pointed out that her fingers brushing against it might make an odd noise. That wouldn't have been an issue when the gate guard did it because sound transmission was blocked, but they couldn't afford to take any risks now. The glasses were entirely cosmetic, part of the physical makeover she'd undergone to change from Cecilia Cooper to Alice Dobroski, but she'd worn them for so long that her face felt naked and exposed without them. She left the burner phone on the dresser near the door, and pressed *play*.

"Do you think there's any food here?" Housen asked in the recording. "Not sure I can sleep yet."

Her own voice answered. "Guess we can hunt around. God only knows how old it would be, though. Wish we'd thought to bring something with us."

As she backed out of the room, her armscreen vibrated with an incoming message. She glanced down and saw that it was from the same unknown number that had contacted her earlier in the day. With everything going on, she'd completely forgotten about it. This time, however, the subject wasn't blank. It was just two words, and they sucked every bit of air from her lungs.

Hello Cecilia.

She braced herself against the kitchen bar before opening the message. The first thing that jumped out at her were the two photographs. On the left was a picture taken just before her junior year of college, back when she had shoulder-length hair that she diligently straightened each morning and kept dyed the honey blonde shade it had been when she was a small child. The girl staring back from the photo was unnaturally thin, basically a stick figure with breasts. Her mom had once joked that women in their family would even have boobs as skeletons and nineteen-year-old Cecilia Cooper had clearly been putting that theory to the test.

On the right was an engagement picture, taken about eighteen months later. She wore one of the demure dresses that were the basic uniform of women in the Gates of Destiny. Mitch stood close behind her, his hands on her waist.

The message itself was unsigned, and it went straight to the point.

If you want your secrets to stay secret, bring me the device.

Below the message was a string of data. Addresses where she'd lived since leaving Colorado. Jobs she'd held. Her mom's current address, complete with a street view image, followed by her new name, new phone number, and where both her mom and her stepdad worked. The high school her mom's stepchildren were attending. Links to several police reports, the oldest being the bullshit theft charge in Colorado when she left Mitch and the most recent being the interview in New Haven after she and Claire found Devin Shepherd's body. Old social media accounts, too, including the memorial account her mom had set up for Cecilia Cooper after her car crashed and Alice Dobroski emerged from the ashes.

"What's wrong?"

Alice jumped, looking up from her armscreen to find Housen directly behind her. She hadn't even heard him come out of the bathroom.

She closed the screen, then pressed her finger to her lips and jerked her head toward the recorder on the nightstand. He nodded and followed her outside, closing the door softly behind them.

"What's wrong?" he repeated as he pulled up the entry code for the rental car.

"Nothing," she said. "I just—"

"It's obviously not *nothing*. You looked like you were about to faint."

"I wasn't going to faint! Jesus Christ, I was reading a private text. Is that *okay* with you?"

"Sure, sure. Whatever." He raised one hand as if warding off a blow and opened the car door with the other.

The car reeked of the same disinfectant she'd smelled in the cabin. She got in, trying not to think about how messed up the upholstery must have been to require that many chemicals.

"Actually, it's *not* okay," Housen said before she could even shut the door. "I got a clear enough look to see that the message included a picture of you from your previous life. I know, because I saw several of them when I was researching you at that club last night. Since I didn't send that message, I'm guessing Durav had someone do a little digging, too. I'm about to kill the man and you're my shadow, which means that message is directly relevant to this whole scheme. And to be perfectly honest, if you were planning to keep that from me, I've got serious questions as to whether I can trust you to have my back."

Alice leaned her head against the seat. "I'm well aware that this affects the plan. It also affects my entire *life*. My safety. The safety of my mom and her family. And I would have told you if you'd given me a minute to process instead of sneaking up on me. You nearly blew our cover, too, for the second time in the past five minutes."

"Sorry."

"You should be. The real question is what do we do now?"

"I guess the good news is that it sounds like Durav is taking the bait."

"No. We don't know that yet. Because that's the *second* message I've gotten. Another one came in just before I joined you guys on the patio this morning. I didn't recognize the number and there was no subject, so I decided it could wait." She tapped the screen to open the first message. Aside from the missing subject line, it was identical to the one that had just come in.

"Do you mind if I read it?"

She kind of did. But it probably wasn't anything he hadn't dredged up in his own search, so she flipped the screen in his direction.

"Okay," he said, after scanning it quickly. "Will he be able to tell that you opened it?"

"Not unless he has some alien tech that gets around my privacy settings."

Housen shook his head. "Nothing I know of. I say we go ahead with the current plan. I mean, would it be all that surprising if you didn't check your messages before going to bed, given how little sleep we've had?"

It would be very surprising to absolutely anyone who knew her personally, but since Durav didn't fall into that category she gave Housen a little shrug to concede the point.

He tapped the console. "Kittery Station." Then he turned back to her. "You're thinking the primary threat is to your mom and she's in ... Philadelphia, right?"

"Pittsburgh."

"Okay. I don't think you need to worry about her if Durav sends any of his men here. He doesn't have that many people to spare. And if all goes well, he won't be alive to threaten anyone when the sun comes up."

"Sure." He was probably right about any immediate threat to her mom, who was nearly as security conscious as Alice herself after all that they'd been through. What he was missing was that it wouldn't take any manpower at all for Durav to send the information that he had to Mitch. Just one tap of his finger. He might even have done it already.

They were at the gate, so she got out and entered the code again. When she got back inside, Housen was on the car's phone.

"That would be great. We're probably being overly cautious here, but—"

Joe's voice cut him off. "No, no. Better safe than sorry. I'll get Wilson on it."

"What was that about?" she asked when he ended the call.

"I asked if Jonas Security could send someone to Pittsburgh. Or at least contract with someone local to keep an eye on your mom's place overnight."

"That's ... kind of you. And Joe, too."

"I'm not entirely heartless. Even if everyone thinks I'm about to engage in *cold-blooded murder*." He delivered the last two words with a melodramatic twist, adding a flicker of a grin at the end. "Also, if I'm being completely honest, it's a little self-serving. I would actually prefer to come out of this alive—for *both* of us to come out of it alive—and that's a lot more likely if you're not distracted with worry about your mom. And, I don't know, maybe there's even a small silver lining to all of this."

"Really?" she said. "And what might that be?"

"If something goes wrong with Plan A, maybe we can turn Durav's demand into a Plan B."

Alice nodded but didn't have much enthusiasm to offer. Housen was trying, but he didn't seem to realize that temporary surveillance on her mom's house, as comforting as it was, couldn't erase the fact that Alice Dobroski was no more. Her graduate degree, her position at Columbia, everything that she'd worked for over the past decade had been for nothing. She would obviously continue to do everything she could to help. What choice did she have when the alternative was the complete annihilation of the planet? But it didn't change the fact that she was going to lose big time, even if they managed to win.

TWELVE

Thursday, October 5
Massapequa, New York

ALICE SLID an extra-large cup under the dispenser, pushed the button, and then turned to browse the snack foods on the other side of the aisle. By the time the coffee brewed, she'd made selections from each of the three major after-midnight food groups—crunchy, chewy, and chocolate—and grabbed Housen's bottle of water. She added a bit of ice to cool the coffee down, then snapped the lid on the cup and headed for the register. Wilson had said she should pay in cash, just in case there were complications that got the police involved. She supposed that made sense, but it unfortunately required ringing the bell for an employee not once but twice. The woman had apparently been snoozing in the back and was not happy that her nap had been disturbed. Which meant Alice's face was on the store's security camera for probably five times as long as it would have been otherwise. She should have just pressed her thumb to the pad.

They'd picked up the car at the New Rochelle hyperloop terminal about an hour earlier and were now maybe five minutes away from the house on Riviera Drive. A small duffle in the storage area of the car held communications gear, Housen's pistol, which he'd retrieved from its burial spot before they left for Maine, and a second handgun that Wilson claimed was fairly close to the Glock 73-X that was back in Alice's apartment in New York. Wilson had also added two stun grenades, which might be useless, since Housen didn't think they would work on Durav or the *ipret-tai*. A heavy-duty drone jammer was also in the bag, but Housen said the only way that would be helpful was if Durav was using an off-the-shelf system, and he was fairly certain that he would have brought the drones that once patrolled the Triad's headquarters. The only thing missing from the bag had been provisions, and since they were both running on fumes, they'd decided to pull into an all-night convenience store before their scheduled two a.m. final check-in with Wilson.

When she got back to the car, Housen was again watching something on the device that Arbet had given him. He quickly stashed it in his pocket, and she tossed him the snack bag. He rummaged around until he found the chips and then nodded toward her coffee. "You sure about that? Won't it make you jumpy? That's generally a bad idea in this situation."

Alice was tempted to ask him exactly how many stakeouts he had under his belt. She suspected that the answer was zero, and all of his sage advice was based on old buddy-cop movies. It was also annoying that he seemed to function better than she did on very little sleep, with only his cup of tea at breakfast.

"Would you prefer me asleep?" she asked. "Because that's the other option."

"Fine. Chug away."

She did. It occurred to her as she was drinking, however, that the one thing she wouldn't have on stakeout was easy access to a bathroom, so she left half of the coffee in the cup and grabbed one of the chocolate bars instead.

"So … what's with the egg-shaped thing?" she asked. "Is it like a Ufretan tablet? I can tell you're watching something from the way your eyes move."

He shrugged. "Sort of. It's called a *rezlat*. It's how we got messages from friends and family back in the Ufretan system. We could only use them at Conclave, so that was the main thing we all looked forward to when we arrived. We'd watch what they sent and then record messages to send back during the communications window. Or at least, that's what we thought we were doing. They were actually heavily censored. Friends and family got fake messages based on the same fake memories that they planned to implant in us when they revived our bodies. The responses we got back were fake, too. I'm guessing that Arbet told all of you about Sarah, given the abrupt change of mood when I returned to the patio earlier?"

"Yes. She said you were married."

"Correct. After Durav killed Sarah, he sent someone in to trash the house we shared. I had to get a full new identity along with facial alteration, because he set up evidence to suggest that I was the one who killed her. He wiped my iPhone, too. This was in 2010, before you had cloud backups and so forth. But what he didn't know was that I'd sent some vacation videos back home to my mother. Videos of me with Sarah. Grainy as hell—the videos on those old phones were crap. But I was glad to have them, even if I only got to see them at Conclave. Arbet knew it was the only thing I have left of her."

"And she saved it from the fire?"

"Yeah. Mine and as many of the others as she could. Most of the Watch had already turned theirs in when Durav killed them, which is good, because even if we stop him, Arbet will need to keep sending fake reports every three years or so when the comms window opens. Otherwise, they're going to know something is up and this won't buy Earth much time at all."

Wilson appeared on the car screen a few minutes later. His face was haggard and the hint of a Southern accent that she'd detected when they spoke at Arbet's place now bordered on a full-fledged drawl, so she was pretty sure that this was way past his bedtime.

"Okay," he said. "As I noted earlier, I need to keep as much official distance between Jonas Labs and this little adventure as possible. Fortunately, I was able to pull in one of Claire's friends who I met when he brought Jemma's cat up here a few weeks back. Kes has handled tech and surveillance for Wyatt for a couple years, including setting up the cameras at your Conclave a few months back, and was happy to take the loop up from DC to set all of this up. The bad news is that they've got decent security on the place, and that holds for pretty much the entire neighborhood. No big surprise, I guess, given the price tag of these houses. Kes wasn't able to get much of anything from the front of the property aside from this..."

Wilson's face was replaced by a video that moved slowly across the front of a large sand-colored brick contemporary, with a portico and a paved courtyard. It was flanked on both sides by a tall hedge of arborvitae. "The drone couldn't get low enough or at the right angle for any sort of interior imaging," he said, "but I'll send you the floorplan from the last time the house was sold. They also only got two things of interest from the front. One is this house on the other side of the street."

The image shifted to show a smaller place with an industrial dumpster on the front drive and a similar line of hedge trees.

"This is 158 Riviera," Wilson said. "Currently unoccupied and undergoing renovations, as you can see. That's true for a number of the houses in the neighborhood. Some of the older waterfront properties that aren't on elevated land flooded when Hurricane Yvette zipped past. Same for those that are canal-front, and between the two, that's maybe fifty percent of the houses. The power is off in this one, which means no motion-activated floodlights or security cameras, so that driveway will be the lookout spot. That big hedge and the dumpster provide some cover, but you should still have a mostly unobscured view of the target house through the car's front cameras if you back in and inch out just a bit beyond the trees."

The screen flicked back to the same aerial view of 167 Riviera, but it was now nighttime, with the courtyard illuminated by floodlights from the house and parallel rows of recessed lights where the pavement met the lawn. As they watched, the garage door opened and a sedan emerged.

"A second thing we picked up from this position was this bit of activity just after midnight." The drone followed the car. Wilson increased the speed on the video so that the car appeared to whip through the neighborhood and onto a main road. It eventually pulled into a park and stopped at a helipad at the far end, where an AeroLyft was waiting. Three men emerged from the car and entered the aircraft.

"The lighting isn't great here, but we're fairly certain those men are Vaughn Delroy and his baby brother Casem, both formerly with the Lone Star militia group. The third man is Ben Severne, formerly with an offshoot group of the Boise Bois that operated out of North Dakota. They're all known associates of Jason Boudreaux, and two of them have records that are going to make Agent West very happy if we're able to hand them over. The chopper they just entered is privately owned, and no flight details are available. But the flight time from there to Maine is about two hours and fifteen minutes, so within the next half hour my team should let me know whether or not we caught our three little piggies up at Beck's place. Regardless of where those men are headed, however, we at least know that they are not at your target house."

"Which is very good news," Housen said.

"It is indeed. Quick question—do you know how to row a boat?"

Housen frowned. "Uh ... yeah, although I'll admit it's been a while. Why?"

"Because we think that's gonna be your best bet for getting into the house." Wilson switched to the next video. It began over the water and slowly zoomed in on the back of the property, which consisted entirely of a multilevel deck that stretched from the house to the waterfront. A series of steps led down to a private pier, now partially underwater. Off to the left of the house was a smaller building, which looked like a guest house or maybe an extra garage. "The body of water you see here is Massapequa Cove. Kes rowed out earlier and popped one of those little sticker cams on top of a buoy that marks off a sandbar in the middle. It's not high enough up to get any footage from inside the house given that the property is elevated, but we hit the jackpot a little after six."

The video on the screen showed four men on the deck, eating barbecued ribs at a long table under a white pergola that cast striped shadows across their faces. They moved around enough, however, that their faces were easily identifiable in the composite images Wilson extracted.

"Those three on the right side of the screen are the militia members I mentioned earlier, the ones whose AeroLyft I assume is somewhere around the Maine border about now. And the man on the left is Durav, as Housen undoubtedly knows."

Durav was tall and barrel chested, with pale skin and dark hair. He wore one of the tiny, obscenely tight swimsuits that her mother always called a *banana hammock*.

"No wonder he's in a rush to get home to his actual skin," Alice said. "That's the most body hair I've seen outside of a zoo."

"As a member of the Triad, he had his pick," Housen said. "And he's from Ufretas Prime. Pretty sure the fur coat was a selling point for him."

Alice wasn't sure why Durav's country—or maybe it was his planet?—played a role in his choice of bodies. But it didn't seem relevant to their current discussion, so she just gave him a vague nod and focused on the screen. Wilson had skipped ahead a bit, and the four men were now lounging in and around the pool. They'd been joined by two young women, one blonde and one brunette, in barely-there bikinis.

Housen let out a slow breath. "You didn't see them leave? The girls, I mean."

Alice would normally have protested his phrasing, but on closer inspection, she decided that *girls* was probably the correct word. Neither of them appeared to be of legal age.

"Nope. But they might be happy to see you." Wilson zoomed in even closer on the girls. The brunette was mostly in the shadows, but the blonde's cheek was swollen and there was a bruise on her upper arm.

Housen's jaw tightened. "That tracks. Bruises are Durav's favorite calling card. But two innocents being in the house is going to make this a whole lot harder."

"I know. Just … try to keep them from getting shot. We'll handle the girls after. Either get them back home or into a shelter."

"Claire's roommate volunteers with a women's shelter in Baltimore. She can probably help with that."

"Okay. There's also another guy in the house … I'm going to guess *ipret-tai*." Wilson fast-forwarded through about an hour of the six of them in the pool until the man entered the frame. She recognized him instantly as Do'djat. He was carrying a tray with three beers, a highball glass, and an oddly shaped red bottle.

Housen huffed. "The contents of the drinks tray tracks, too."

Alice gave him a questioning look.

"The red bottle contains *evir*. Ufretan drink, similar to vodka, but there's a salty undertone, a bit like seaweed or anchovies. Durav clearly packed up the Triad's supply before torching HQ, and he's hoarding it as usual, sticking his underlings with beer."

Wilson grimaced and Alice was in full agreement. Based on Housen's description, she thought the *underlings* were probably more than happy to take the beer and leave the fishy vodka to their boss.

"One more bit of bad news," Wilson said. "They *do* have security drones. Only two, as best we can tell. Kes says they look like the ones from the footage Wyatt recorded outside your Conclave. That means you're gonna need to time it carefully and move fast. The zapper in that kit is top of the line and of … questionable legality. Kes says it's anybody's guess whether it will take the drones down, but it will temporarily disrupt the motion sensor lights on the deck and the security alarm on the entrances. As for the drones, they seem to be running a fairly regular route. During the time we've been doing surveillance there have been forty-three occasions when both drones were patrolling the front of the property, roughly once every eight minutes. Alice will let you know when that happens. You'll then have a window of about two and a half minutes, which should be enough time to run down the pier, up those stairs, across the deck and ... assuming that other gadget works, get inside the patio door."

"Got it," Housen said. But for the first time, Alice detected a twinge of hesitation in his voice.

Wilson must have picked up on it, too. "Like I said, you need to be quick, but Kes says the device has been tested on similar houses, including one in that same neighborhood earlier today." He chuckled softly. "Kes claims to be a white hat, and I sure hope that's true. Anyway, have the car drop you at the entrance to what used to be Alhambra Park. It's mostly swampland now, and the road is closed off to vehicles. But Kes says there's a narrow path that's reasonably dry. It's maybe a quarter of a mile down to the landing where the kayak is waiting."

They spent the next few minutes talking through the logistics and getting instructions on how to sync up their comms equipment.

"Any chance this Kes is still around and interested in making this a two-person operation?" Housen asked as they were about to wrap up the call.

Alice shot him a dirty look. It was *already* a two-person operation. Apparently, sexism wasn't merely global, but also universal. Although, to be fair, she'd only agreed to be lookout, not act as a backup shooter.

Wilson sighed and shook his head. "Asked and answered. They told me they do cameras, not guns. I'll drop you a few pins with the park entrance, the spot where Kes left the kayak, and another with your target location so you don't end up breaking into the wrong house. The landing is a little over half a mile to the north. Depending on how fast you row, you should be able to get from there to the dock in fifteen minutes or so. Alice, the car will have to take a slightly more circuitous route through the neighborhoods, so I'm guessing you'll only arrive five minutes or so ahead of Housen."

Then Wilson said, "I'll be here monitoring. There will be a

chopper waiting at that same helipad with a clean-up crew. That might be crossing a line with Dr. Jonas, but like Joe said, we can't risk leaving altered DNA that will raise questions. And to be honest, after seeing the bruises on that girl's face, I was half a mind to take off this uniform and head down to join you even if I can't in good conscience send JL staff." He gave a wry chuckle. "But I'm pretty sure a man three months shy of sixty who spends most of his time at a desk these days would only slow you down."

THIRTEEN

BEEP. BEEP. BEEP.

Alice jumped at the sound, even though she'd been expecting it. Maybe Housen had been right about the mega-mug of coffee.

Three beeps meant he was in position under the dock. She tapped her earpiece once to indicate that she'd gotten his message, then went back to staring at the front lawn of 167 Riviera where one black saucer with a tiny blue light was currently making its rounds, flitting in and out of the floodlights. As soon as she spotted both drones in the front, she was supposed to tap the earpiece twice, letting Housen know that it was go time. She'd already logged two instances of double drones. The first happened about three minutes after she backed the car into the space between the dumpster and the hedge, and the second at 3:06. It was now 3:11. If Wilson's estimate was right, Housen had around three minutes to catch his breath from rowing across the cove.

Their earpieces had an audio connection, but they'd decided to avoid using it as much as possible. Wilson said Kes assured him that the channel was secure, but after they ended the call, Housen told her that they might not be dealing with Earth tech. He had no idea what equipment Durav might have scavenged from Triad headquarters before the fire. Once he was in place, he was supposed to turn on his microphone so that she'd be able to track his progress. Aside from that, they were on silent mode.

Technically, if she heard gunfire and didn't get a response from Housen, she was supposed to leave. She hadn't agreed to do anything other than watch. But things had changed. On the patio when they were planning everything out, she'd told them she wasn't sure she could kill someone she hadn't even met, and it was true at the time. The threat had been more abstract than immediate at that point, and she hadn't known for certain how she'd react in the moment. It might also have been because she didn't want Wilson and Joe to give her that same wary look they'd given Housen before they called it murder.

Any hesitation that she felt, however, had vanished when she read Durav's message. The threat was direct and personal now, both to her and to people she loved. She had no doubt that she could pull the trigger. If Housen failed, she'd wait until the drones crossed paths near the garage and circled around to the back. Then she'd take off across the street and do her best to finish the job.

She took several deep breaths, then pulled the handgun out of the bag and placed it on the seat within easy reach. If things went wrong, she would have to move quickly. Most of these properties were vacation rentals, and the area was practically a ghost town due to the flooding, but it was still possible that someone might call the cops. Or there could be police drones patrolling the area.

About twenty seconds after the clock flipped to 3:15, Alice spotted the second drone. She tapped the earpiece twice. Housen's confirmation beep sounded. Then she heard a faint splash, a series of movements that were probably Housen climbing onto the wet dock, followed by feet slapping across the wooden slats. The sound changed when he hit the cement walkway, where he paused. This was when he was supposed to test out the blocker. If all went well, both drones would drop to the ground.

But the drones continued their dance, with the second one making a quick loop toward the small, landscaped island in the center of the courtyard drive. She tapped the earpiece twice to let Housen know there were still two drones heading his way in a little over a minute. He cursed softly, then took off running across the deck.

When he stopped, the only thing she heard for about twenty seconds was breathing and the occasional rustling noise. Something was wrong. He should have the door open by now.

She tapped the earpiece once to let him know that drone number one had just rounded the corner, heading toward the pool house or whatever that outbuilding was that they'd seen in the images. They now had just over thirty seconds before it would be close enough to spot Housen.

Thirty seconds passed. She tapped four times, their agreed-upon signal for time's up. Two more seconds, and then she heard a faint thud and the tinkling of breaking glass, followed by the door sliding open. No alarm, though, unless it was the silent variety, so Kes's gadget had clearly done at least part of the job.

She realized then that the second drone was no longer in the front yard. It must have picked up the sound of the break in and circled around to the deck early to join the other one. They didn't have a specific signal for that, so she improvised, tapping twice. Hopefully, he would interpret it as two drones are *again* heading your way. He was in the house, though, so maybe it wouldn't matter.

"Shh. Shh."

At first, Alice thought Housen was shushing her for sending the extra warning. But then she heard a clattering sound, like someone dropping a plate onto a carpet.

"No disparéis!" The girl's words were followed by a faint whimper.

"Shh. No dispararé. Estás a salvo," Housen whispered. *"Entiendes?"*

I won't shoot. You are safe. Understand?

Another whimper.

"Está bien. Dónde está Durav?"

The girl didn't answer for a moment, then the words came pouring out in an urgent flood of Spanish. She told him that Durav was in the large bedroom upstairs with a girl named Ximena. Three doors down. Then she begged him to be careful, and not to hurt the other girl. There was something in the mix about a gun. She was trying to be quiet but also crying and it was barely intelligible.

Housen shushed her again, saying he would be careful, and then he asked the girl her name.

"Sara."

Alice heard Housen's sharp intake of breath, almost as if he'd been punched. It was a common enough name, but damn, what were the odds?

Housen shushed her again and told her that he'd find Ximena, but she needed to go. He said that she should run to the house across the street.

"No, no," the girl hissed. *"Los tatuados tienen cámaras que vigilan la puerta."*

The men with tattoos have cameras that watch the door.

Something beeped inside the car, and it took a moment for her to realize it wasn't from the earpiece, but from her phone. A text from Wilson popped onto the screen.

Three little pigs in cabin.

Between Housen's voice in her ear and reading the message, the tap against her window barely registered. When she saw Do'djat crouched outside, his gun aimed directly at her head, she jumped so hard that she knocked the earpiece loose.

Where the hell had he come from? There were only inches between the dumpster and the house, so he couldn't have come around the back of the car. He must have squeezed through the hedge. It was still baffling, though, because she hadn't seen anyone leave the house or cross the street.

Her own gun was within easy reach, but Do'djat could see it, too. Time for Plan B.

"Please don't shoot! I'm here to see Durav. He messaged me earlier. I can show you the email."

"Stop. Do not touch the weapon."

She held up both hands. "I was going to show you the message Durav sent me. He has information about me that I want to keep secret, so I came here to tell him I know where they're hiding the beacon. The *brelat*. It's just ... it's the middle of the night and I didn't want to wake anyone up. That's why I decided to park over here and wait until morning."

Alice held her breath, hoping he wouldn't ask how she'd gotten the address, since that definitely wasn't in the message she was about to show him. But he asked a different question instead.

"Then why do you have a gun?"

"Because I'm a woman traveling alone at night! A woman you abducted two nights back. Why do *you* have a gun?"

The last part was pure sarcasm and probably not the best idea under the circumstances, but Do'djat's brow creased as if he was trying to figure out how to answer. It reminded her of his face in the car when he was on the phone with Durav. It wasn't the exact same expression, but they were the only times she'd seen his face display any emotion at all.

"I have a gun because sometimes I am required to kill people." He opened the car door and grabbed her arm. "Get out."

The command was unnecessary because he yanked her arm so hard that she had no choice but to follow it. He then pushed her against the car and began a thorough, almost clinical pat down. When he was satisfied that she didn't have any hidden weapons, he latched onto her upper arm again. "Let's go."

Do'djat jerked her forward again, moving so quickly that she stumbled, knocking the strap of her sandal loose. As she leaned down to pull the shoe back on, the *ipret-tai's* grip tightened briefly, jerking her backward, and then went completely slack. He slumped to the ground, smacking the back of his head against the driveway. His eyes stared up at the sky, blank as always. But she didn't think he was seeing anything now, given the trickle of blood coming from the tiny dark circle near his tattoos.

Given the way he'd moved, she was fairly certain that the shot had come from across the street. She grabbed the gun next to his hand and began moving backward toward the car, quickly scanning for any movement on the balconies or along the tall hedge that separated Durav's place from the house on the left. Nothing, aside from the two drones, one in the center of the house and the other near the far-right corner. It couldn't have been a drone hit, because they were equipped with lasers, and this was a bullet wound. And even if she'd somehow switched the mic on by accident, she doubted that Housen could have made it to the front of the house to take the shot. This was confirmed when she grabbed the earpiece from the crevice between the seat and the console and could still hear him trying to calm the girl down.

She was about to tell him what had happened when the garage door opened. The light flashed on briefly and then flickered out. A second later, a figure dressed entirely in black—pants, jacket, even a balaclava—darted out from behind the fountain. They were crouched over, but she could tell that the runner was tall, and most likely male.

And where were the drones? She'd seen both of them in the front of the house only a few seconds ago. The fact that they weren't firing at the man, weren't even visible, probably meant that he had disabled them. Which almost certainly meant it was the other *ipret-tai*. But why would he have shot Do'djat? Unless … had he been aiming at her and simply missed when she lost her balance?

Or maybe Kes had decided to help after all?

She held her finger against the earpiece. "Do'djat is dead. But the second *ipret-tai* may be here. I just saw a very tall man entering the house through the garage."

A single tap from Housen. Message received. Then he whispered again to Sara, repeating that he would protect her and Ximena, but she needed to hide.

This finally seemed to calm her down a bit. "*Gracias, gracias.*"

The girl's last *thank you* was followed by the subdued *thwump* of a suppressed gunshot.

FOURTEEN

ALICE TOOK OFF IMMEDIATELY, gun in hand. She scanned for the drones as she ran, praying that they didn't come zipping around the corner. As she stepped into the empty street she heard a second round of gunfire through the earpiece. The pitch was slightly different, though, so she thought it was from a different weapon.

Then he spoke. Just a single word, *wait*. She thought at first that he was talking to the girl, but then realized he'd spoken in Ufretan. His voice was faint, but he was alive.

"Housen?" she said, holding down the button on the earpiece. "Hold on. I'm coming."

A single beep came back in response. Message received.

She spotted the first drone as she entered the driveway. Its top half was jutting out of the bushes near the portico at a forty-five-degree angle. The other drone lay flat on the strip of lawn near the left corner of the house. She didn't have time to puzzle out how this bit of good luck had happened, but she was relieved that she now only had to worry about the second *ipret-tai* and Durav.

Pistol drawn, she ran into the darkened garage, surprised to find that the *ipret-tai* had left the door to the mudroom open as well. Beyond that, she saw a faint glow of light. From what she remembered of the floorplan that Wilson had shown them, it should be the dining room.

It was actually the kitchen. Housen was slouched next to the refrigerator holding one hand to the hollow between his shoulder and his chest. Blood seeped through his fingers and down his bare skin. The blonde girl, Sara, who was naked aside from the dark green shirt Housen must have given her, cowered behind the bar, her back against the dishwasher.

What confused Alice most was the *second* body, lying face up on the floor. It was the second *ipret-tai,* the one who'd tracked her to the club in New York, and he was very obviously dead. A bullet had torn away part of his neck. But he was wearing *khaki* pants. Which meant he couldn't be the person she'd seen enter the house.

Alice snatched a dish towel from a nearby rack and pressed it to Housen's wound.

He grabbed her wrist. "Upstairs. Help … me."

"No. You're bleeding like crazy. You'll slow me down. Who shot *him*?" She nodded toward the dead ipret-tai. "You or the one in black?"

"In black. Durav must … have a third ipret-tai. Might have thought … that one was … me."

It was the same thing she'd thought when he shot Do'djat. It had seemed implausible the first time, but twice? She didn't have time to talk it out, though. If Housen was right, the man was probably already warning Durav.

"Stay here." She switched to Spanish and told Sara to keep pressure on Housen's wound. Then she bolted through the dining room toward the foyer, where a curved staircase led up to the second floor. Moonlight coming in through the glass wall that spanned the back of the house reflected from every surface of the room, which was entirely white from the ceiling to the marble floors. There was no point in stealth when she was dressed mostly in black, so she opted for speed.

Halfway up the stairs, she heard another gunshot, followed by a high-pitched scream. The girl had told Housen earlier that Durav was in a room three doors down, but there were actually *two* hallways, one going left and one going right. All of the doors in both directions appeared to be closed from this far back, so that provided no clue, but she was almost certain the shot had come from the left. As she passed the first door in that hallway, a light flipped on in the third room, and she could now see that the door was partially open. She moved forward, very nearly firing off a shot on accident when she heard a mechanical whirring behind her. When she turned to look, however, nothing was there. Probably just the air conditioning kicking on.

When she reached the room, she pressed her back to the wall and shot her foot out to kick the door. As it flew open, Housen's voice came through her earpiece, barely audible. "Coming out ... of elevator. Don't shoot me."

She tapped once. Message received.

Stepping into the room, she saw Durav, sprawled across the center of the bed. A circle of red blossomed on the white sheet under his body. He was still alive, staring openmouthed at the man who had shot him in the side and who was still pointing the gun at him. The dark-haired girl she'd seen in the video, also nude, was curled in the corner next to the bed hugging a pillow to cover herself.

Durav's hands clutched at the wound on his side. He barked out a weak laugh and began to speak in Ufretan, asking the gunman why he wore a mask. "Don't want me to know it is you, Housen?"

"Not Housen." The man grabbed the top of his balaclava and pulled it backward. The first thing she saw was the tattoo over his eye. But there was no Ufretan number above it and as he pulled the lower half of the mask down to his neck, she realized it was Denny.

A look of complete bafflement crossed Durav's face. Then, he laughed again as Housen stumbled into the room. The towel that the girl must have tied around the wound was already sliding from his shoulder, but his gun was out and pointed at Durav.

Durav's eyes went to Alice, then back to Housen, and he shifted to English as he struggled to prop himself up on one elbow. "I see you've taken up with another *assera-sai*. Did you learn nothing in school?"

The word *assera-sai* was Ufretan, but Alice knew it well from one of the Aveezi Forest stories in Shepherd's files. Professor Everett—or whatever his Ufretan name was—had translated it as *starsprite*.

"This one will die soon, and just as easily as the last. And then they will *all* die. Even if Arbet continues filing her fake reports, the Alliance is not so easily fooled. So go ahead and shoot me. What do I care? They will revive my body on Ufretas Prime soon enough. And your body will be executed as a traitor to our ancient lineage. Only a fool would give up eternity as an Ufretan when the most your betrayal buys your pathetic earthworms is a few years."

"Earthworms?" Alice said. "I've read the Eberin Das journal. Our DNA comes from the ancient Ufretans, same as yours. Your ancestors seeded this world, and seeded Mars before it. We have as much claim to that *ancient lineage* as you."

Alice saw Durav reaching under his pillow even before the girl yelled "*Pistola!*"

Housen beat her to the shot, though. His bullet hit Durav just above the left temple and the man's body went slack before his hand closed around the gun.

Denny let out a long breath and holstered his pistol.

Ximena stared at them, dark eyes wide, biting the edge of the pillow as if it were the only thing keeping her from screaming. Alice grabbed a blanket from the chair next to the bed and wrapped it around the girl. She told her that Sara was okay and waiting downstairs in the kitchen. Then she said they should get dressed so they could leave as quickly as possible. The girl nodded and flew from the room, nearly tripping over the hem of the blanket.

"I will page the car," Denny said. "Then I will move Do'djat inside."

She pulled up the message from Wilson and responded.

Got the big bad wolf. Alert medic that H is injured. Both girls fine.

The *ipret-tai* was still tapping something into his phone when she finished. She watched him for a moment, still confused about the timeline. He had to have been just standing there for a good forty seconds after shooting Durav in the abdomen. Had he wanted to watch Durav suffer, to bleed out slowly? That didn't fit with what she understood about their training or their psychological makeup.

Housen was heading for the door now, clutching the towel to his wound. Denny stepped forward to support him and they all moved into the hallway.

"I'm glad you were here," Housen said to Denny. "But … Arbet should not … have ordered you to come."

"Arbet did not order me."

"Fine," Housen said, exasperated. "She shouldn't have … *asked* … you to come. This wasn't your battle."

Denny's face held the same blank expression as they headed down the hallway toward the elevator, but there was a hint of steel undergirding his usual monotone delivery when he responded. "You are wrong, Housen. I asked her to *let* me come. I was given the same security training. I knew their weaknesses. And I have handled the drones. They changed the password, but I know the algorithm they use to create new ones, so it did not take long to figure it out."

Housen leaned against the wall of the elevator, eyes half closed. "But if she said no, you would have … obeyed."

"That is true. But she would not have denied me this. I know you had reasons for wanting Durav dead. I remember when he killed your *amali-tai*. But he also hurt Arbet and Dora. He killed my *ufrenai* David and many, many other *ipret-tai* and Watchers. If the people he sent to Mars obtained the *brelat*, he would send the signal to kill everyone else. So, I also had reasons to want him dead. *Vraidar paitel.*"

Vraidar paitel. Alice's translation for *vraidar* was *pure evil.* Eberin Das had used the word many times, mostly hoping that he'd find evidence that his people weren't *vraidar*, that there was some element of good. And *pait* was die. The last two letters, *el,* turned it into an imperative, so … *evil must die.*

They reached the ground floor. When Housen made no move toward the door, Denny bent down and scooped him up like a child. He was clearly taking care to jostle him as little as possible, but the movement started another freshet of blood from the wound.

"Then why didn't … you kill him?" Housen asked. "You can't have been … out of ammo."

It was the same thing that Alice had wondered a few minutes earlier.

Denny didn't answer immediately. He seemed to be waging some sort of internal battle. "Durav was *vraidar,* but he was a member of the Triad. I injured him, but my training…"

He trailed off at the end, ducking his chin slightly as if he regretted that he hadn't been able to finish the job. But the reason rang false to Alice. She'd seen his eyes as he stared at Durav, seen his finger twitching on that trigger. He was lying, and she was pretty sure she knew why.

Whether he'd arrived at it on his own or had been instructed by Arbet, Denny had waited, hoping Housen would be able to make it upstairs to avenge his *amali-tai* and finally get closure after seventy-five years.

FROM AWAITING THE SENTINELS

BY TOBIAS SHEPHERD

Appendix: The Sentinel's Manifesto (Lesson Nine)

THOSE WHO WALK in the path of the Sentinels have no need for the wheels and cogs that gnash against the Earth like demon's teeth. Machines have long since ceased to serve humanity and have now become the idols that we worship. But these false gods demand far too much in sacrifice. In our efforts to feed and appease these demons, we are now slaves to the very machines that they claimed would set us free. Only by kneeling down and sinking your hands into the soil can you become worthy of the Sentinels' salvation.

Walk in the light of the Sentinels.

Res esdoden ojiri ensilar ufretas.

FIFTEEN

Thursday, October 5
Near Nepenthes Station

Claire was sitting on something that looked a bit like Angelina's scooter. Only it was purple, like her first bicycle, and her father was standing next to her. He was showing her the biodome and telling her she could ride on the path around the edge, but she had to ride very, very fast or she would tumble straight down. All of the familiar landmarks were there—the playground, the rainbow eucalyptus, the falls, and the lake—only they were inverted, defying gravity as they clung to the sides and even the top of the inside-out dome. When she looked back at her father to ask how the water kept from pouring to the bottom, she found him in the hospital bed, with tubes and wires, barely conscious as he'd been so often during those last days before he died. And then the scene morphed into Kolya in the hospital bed, only this time, her mother was there instead of in the lab and…

CLAIRE JOLTED AWAKE, thrashing against the seat harness. She shook her head to clear it and looked around the plane. It was a smaller version of the one that Paul had flown from Ehden to Icarus on her previous trip, only Ayman had been with them that time.

"Where are we?" she asked.

"About ten minutes from Nepenthes Station. Looked like you were going to jump out of your harness just now. Were you reliving Kolya crashing the shuttle?"

"No. It was a different dream … pleasant enough until the

monsters showed up." She yawned and glanced at the time on the inside of her helmet visor. It was nearly six thirty. They were supposed to have been at Ehden half an hour ago, and it would still be another thirty minutes or more after they landed before they arrived at the village. "Sorry for falling asleep."

"No problem. I've just been listening to my marching orders from Kolya."

"Oh. Are we in comms range of Nepenthes?"

"No. He dictated these before I arrived in Elysia."

"Did he say anything about your ... insubordination?"

"Nope. Nothing beyond the patented Anton Kolya Squint of Disappointment that he gave me in person before sending me off to arrange a medical transport to Daedalus. I'm sure he's planning to wait and fire me as soon as it's practical, and he probably thinks the threat of it gives him leverage over me in the interim. The main thing he said in the recording was not to give you and Shepherd any time alone. My orders are to record the proceedings and report back on every move you and Beck make. I am so looking forward to giving that man the middle finger when this is over."

Kolya's determination to be conferenced in for the negotiations with Shepherd had evaporated instantly in the face of a possible—although, he'd stressed repeatedly, not *likely*—armed assault on Daedalus. Which made sense, but it still highlighted how very petty his insistence on taking part had been in the first place. A medical transport from KTI's fleet had been requested immediately in order to transport Kolya and Macek to Daedalus City. The doctors at Elysia protested, noting that neither of them was fit to travel. But given that Kolya was obviously an awful patient and their president wanted Macek out of the colony ASAP, Claire thought the protest had mostly been for show.

"What are you planning to do after..." Claire laughed shakily. "I was going to ask about your future job plans, but I'm guessing that depends heavily on whether we manage to delay the Alliance attack."

"Yeah." A somber look crossed his face. "Ayman and I had talked about having a couple of kids at one point, before I took this job, and I always thought of that as my fallback if I quit. That's obviously off the table now. Even if you hold off the Alliance, we still have a sword dangling over our heads, and I'm not bringing kids into that kind of uncertainty. Too bad, though. I liked the idea of relaxing. Taking it easy for a few years, just being a stay-at-home dad."

"You really haven't been around kids that much, have you? Wait until they hit the tantrum stage."

"Claire, I've been taking care of a fifty-two-year-old infant for the past several years. I think I could handle the terrible twos."

Once they were in range of Nepenthes Station's communications array, Claire checked for updates from Wyatt. There was nothing new, however. He'd sent a brief note earlier, along with the draft article he was submitting to his editor. She understood why he'd stayed behind, and it was almost certainly safer than most of the conflicts he reported on, but she was still worried. Between that and her nerves about this negotiation, her stomach was in knots.

Kolya had told her that they would hold the meeting on the back porch of the dining hall where he and Macek had negotiated the Flock coming to Ehden. Davy would be conferenced in from her office at the Nepenthes Lab. The tunnel between the lab and Ehden had been cleared a few days earlier, and while they needed to get a structural crew to ensure it was sound before running the express shuttle, it was sturdy enough for one of the KTI buggies. If they reached an agreement, they'd meet at the tunnel entrance to exchange hostages an hour later. The key point of contention was that Davy insisted that the person who shot her security guard turn himself or herself in for prosecution under Daedalian law. Shepherd said that none of his people would do that, and Claire wasn't at all sure how she was going to navigate around that impasse.

A little less than an hour later, Paul pulled up in front of the dining hall in Ehden. She ran her fingers through her hair and grabbed her helmet and the bag with the few essentials she'd picked up at Elysia.

Being back here gave her a warped sense of déjà vu. The building itself looked exactly the same, but the village and land around it had changed considerably since she was here with Kolya. For starters, there had been three Flock members guarding the airlock tunnel when they came through, all armed, and all dressed in puffsuits, which confirmed Paul's earlier assurance that they'd been informed of the security threat. Some people apparently hadn't gotten the memo yet, however, or they were short on biosuits, because they'd passed two small groups coming in from one of the new greenhouses who wore the standard Flock uniforms of logo t-shirts over jeans or skirts.

Inside the village, the housing unit that had been under construction was now complete. It loomed over the other buildings, making the road between them feel more like an alley than a street. There were also more people around now. At least twenty were gathered on and around the porch of a building a bit farther down the street that she thought Paul had identified as a community center. She couldn't see their faces clearly, but she thought they looked skeptical. And who could blame them? Claire Echols, unemployed science reporter, former host of *Simple Science,* and now … hostage negotiator. It was a sick joke.

"Come on," Paul said when he turned back to find her still standing next to the buggy. "You're not going to the gallows."

"Sure feels like it." Her phone vibrated in her pocket as she followed him through the door, but it would have to wait. "Where's Beck?"

"Probably out back with Shepherd. I hope this doesn't take long because I am absolutely starving." He breathed in deeply. "I also hope they have leftovers. That smells good."

He was right. The dining hall smelled much better than it had the last time they were in Ehden, when the predominant odor had been stale grease. This time, she picked up a whiff of spice. Curry, maybe?

Paul pushed the back door open. "Sorry we're late. Kolya was…" He trailed off, staring at the three people seated around a bamboo picnic table with what looked like beer in front of them.

Shepherd and Beck rose to greet them. Davina Monroe remained seated.

"Wait," Paul said, looking at Davy. "I thought I was supposed to conference you in from the lab?"

"No need for cameras or gadgets or even negotiations," Shepherd said. "We reached an agreement this afternoon. Dr. Monroe graciously brought my people with her when she arrived around six, and hers will be returning with her when she leaves."

"I don't understand," Claire said, taking a seat on the bench next to Beck. "I mean, I'm *very* happy to hear it, but…"

"Mostly a big misunderstanding," Beck said. "Once we cleared up the fact that Shepherd's people weren't involved in the bombing, that Dr. Monroe knew nothing about the rescue attempt, and we proved that there was no actual murder, things just sort of came together." He squeezed her arm under the table as he spoke. She had a vivid memory of Wyatt doing the exact same thing in the very meeting where she'd gotten pulled into all of this. The meaning was as clear now as it had been then—*just go along with it*. And Beck would get no argument from her.

"That's exactly right," Shepherd said, giving her a tiny nod and slightly narrowing his eyes, telegraphing as clearly as Beck had that something was going on.

This felt much too good to be true.

Paul came back with two more beers and handed one to Claire. It was light and floral, and very clearly a homebrew judging from the plain white label that simply read *Bamboo Brew (Batch 3)*. Shepherd made a toast to good neighbors, which was echoed a bit less convincingly by Davy, who quickly finished off her beer and stood up.

"We should really be getting back," she said. "I know my

people are looking forward to getting home and seeing their children."

Shepherd stood up as well. "I'll go with you so that I can say my farewells."

"Very good to see you again, Ms. Echols." Davy leaned forward to squeeze her hand. Looking Claire directly in the eyes, she gave the same knowing look that Shepherd had just given her.

Claire glanced at Paul, wondering if he was as baffled as she was. But if he'd picked up on any of the subtext whirling around them, he clearly didn't care. He was already on his phone, almost certainly trying to call or text Kolya to let him know the mission was a success.

What the hell was going on?

SIXTEEN

CLAIRE LEANED her head against the back of the bench, took a long sip of her beer, and let the tension flow out of her. After a quick glance through the window to be sure that Davy and Shepherd were out of earshot, she turned to Beck. He was now grinning.

"You want to tell me what that was all about? They were both practically winking at me, like they were letting me know they were in on some big secret."

"Yeah. Shepherd did the same thing with me, and to be honest, I'm not at all sure what *he's* up to. Dr. Monroe, however? I … told her everything, Claire. Yes, I know I should have checked with the rest of you, but after talking to her for a while, I just went on instinct. She doesn't question that Sandjeel is an alien, and she is adamant that it couldn't have been done with current Earth technology. Her views were based on the genetic evidence she had in hand, and she didn't need to be convinced, unlike Kolya and … some others." He shot a furtive glance in Paul's direction, then continued. "That's when it occurred to me that I had other scientific proof that might help convince her. I showed her the Eberin Das manuscript, along with the translation. I showed her the videos we took while we were analyzing the *Deinococcus aganippe* sample in Joe's lab. Then I told her why the Watch is really here, what the Alliance is planning, and why Durav's people could be headed this way. It took a bit of time, but I was able to convince her." He shook his head. "Actually, I take that back. Convincing her didn't take much time at all. But it was followed by several hours of her complaining to her lab staff, wondering why none of them had picked up on the anomaly in the bacteria. Which wasn't entirely fair, since that falls a bit outside their job descriptions."

"Okay ... but how did that resolve the hostage situation?"

"Oh. Sorry. I also told her something Idi Ademola shared with me the night before. The Flock didn't actually kill the security guard but just wanted it to look that way so that KTI wouldn't try any more rescue attempts. They *did* fire the bullet," he added in response to her confused expression. "But the man was already dead. They think it was due to injuries from the explosion. And she was able to confirm that, so..." He shrugged and grinned again. "You haven't checked your messages, have you?"

"No. Several came in when we entered the dining hall, but we were running late, so..."

"You were cc'd on the one I got from Joe. Durav is dead."

For several seconds, Claire couldn't speak. When she finally found her voice, it came out as a whisper. "Oh my god. You mean, we actually..."

"Yes. It's over. Housen, Alice Dobroski, and Denny apparently tracked him down."

"That makes absolutely no sense, but I'll take it." Claire grinned back at him and looked around for Paul, who had apparently gone back inside. She tugged her phone out of her biosuit so that she could read the message for herself and forward it to Wyatt.

Shepherd stepped onto the porch just after she hit send.

"Just wanted to let you know that there is food in the kitchen, if any of you are hungry. The volunteers who cooked dinner tonight made a delicious African stew with the first of our sweet potato and peanut harvests. Caruso has already found it. But first, could I have a private word with you, Claire?"

His eyes had that same insider twinkle she'd noticed earlier. After a quick glance at Beck, she agreed and followed Shepherd down the steps toward a bench overlooking the lake. When they were seated, he leaned toward her and said, "First, I'm delighted that you and the others decided to join us at Ehden. I think you're going to like it here, although it is of course only temporary."

"Yes, of course. Thank you for having us." She returned his smile, trying to keep her confusion from showing.

"I'll admit that I am curious as to why Housen isn't with you, though. He was very obviously pushing for me to insist on you being the hostage negotiator, which seemed a bit odd. I didn't even know you knew him. But then I realized that he must be signaling that he'd changed his mind about joining me here. We grew quite close when he was with the Flock, although I'm afraid he has some very odd ideas about the intentions of the Sentinels. And maybe even some…" He made a rueful face. "Delusionary episodes, I guess? I don't know if you're aware, but for a while, he was claiming to *be* one of them, using information that I suspect he found in the notes for my memoir. And I know that can't be true. If the Sentinels were still on Earth, they would have reached out to me. Anyway, I assumed Housen was counting on your connections with Kolya to secure passage to Mars. Is he okay? I've been trying to reach him using the contact information he gave me, but I've had no luck."

"Housen is fine. We were worried, too, but we just heard back from him. He's in Boston, now, and..." The last part wasn't at all relevant, but she needed a couple of seconds to try and remember everything Wyatt had said about Housen. He'd said that Housen had told Shepherd everything about being a member of the Watch but hadn't been able to convince him. And there was also something about Shepherd hoping to eventually get the entire Flock to Ehden… "I think KTI may be censoring some communications," she added, "because we had trouble contacting him, as well. And yes, he planned to come with me initially, but he's still trying to work out transportation for some other members of the Flock."

Claire smiled again, hoping she hadn't said anything wrong. Shepherd had always reminded her a bit of a rabbit, perpetually on the verge of being startled into retreat. There were so many holes in their story, but with Durav out of the picture, did it even matter? It wasn't as if she needed to convince him of anything now. Shepherd could keep the beacon on his bedside table, use it as a paperweight, or whatever. She did feel kind of bad lying to him about Housen bringing more of his members, but there were armed guards belonging to the Flock between her and the plane out of here and her main goal was not to upset the zealot who gave them their marching orders.

The zealot in question clasped his hands together and bowed his head briefly in a gesture of gratitude. "That is wonderful! I just … I do hope they hurry. Because I don't know if the Sentinels will wait. It will *probably* be at least three or four months from the time they received my message, based on what Professor Everett told me. But technically, they *could* arrive at any minute."

Received my message?

The odd, tearful quality of Shepherd's smile made her almost as uneasy as what he'd said. She didn't entirely trust her voice, so she just repeated his last two words back. "Any minute?"

"Yes." He nodded vigorously. "It took a lot of soul searching, but I know now that my people won't be safe here after all. We've made peace with Kolya's scientists, but we received word of another safety threat just this morning. Now I know that I made the right decision when I used the beacon. We've done our best for the Earth. It's time for the Sentinels to take us home."

She struggled to keep her face neutral as she processed what he'd told her. Shepherd might *believe* that he'd sent the signal, but it took the biosignature of two members of the Triad to use the *brelat*. On the other hand, they already knew it could be forged. That's why Durav had stabbed Sandjeel before setting the tunnels on fire. Uden had been a member of the Triad before his death, so he'd only have needed a sample from one of the others.

But even if it was technically possible, why would Uden have given Shepherd a way to contact the Alliance and bring destruction down on the planet? Wasn't that why he'd killed himself—because he didn't want to be part of something so monstrous?

Shepherd reached into his pocket and pulled out an oval

device that was almost identical to the one she'd seen in the Triad's chambers, the one that had been planted as a fake. But this one was a pale shade of blue and there were two little dips, one at each end. And the indentation in the fake version hadn't glowed, while both of these pulsed with blue light.

"I was afraid I'd failed because nothing happened at first. Well, except for the lights," he said, tapping next to the one on the right. "Those showed up as soon as I applied the samples. The professor provided enough in the two vials that I could try again, if I needed to, but I decided to wait. I listened day and night. And then about two days later, I got a response. I couldn't understand much of what they were saying. Professor Everett warned me in his letter that might be the case. But I understood enough. I heard them say the word *ufrete*. And I repeated the line exactly as he taught me. *Res esdoden ojiri ensilar ufretas. Res esdoden ojiri ensilar ufretas.*"

Claire's brow creased as she tried to remember where she'd heard the words before. Or maybe she'd read them? She didn't think it was in the Eberin Das journal, though. There had been some words that weren't translated, but usually not entire phrases.

"What does that mean? Is it Ufretan?"

"I can't translate it precisely, aside from *ufretas*, which as you probably know is similar to family or clan, I guess. Professor Everett said it was a variant of the language that only the Sentinels speak. He said it would indicate that we are loyal and ensure that they would not abandon us. I made it part of my mantra during prayers and lessons, so that I wouldn't forget how to say it."

The memoir. That was where she'd seen it. It was how he closed out each of the lessons or sermons or whatever they were in the appendix.

"And when was this?" Claire asked, her voice breaking slightly. "When you sent the signal, I mean."

"About two weeks ago. They've messaged every few days

since then. Every fifty-six hours and seven minutes. The same message, and I think the signal is getting clearer." Shepherd beamed at her. "I just repeat back what the professor told me to say each time. And that's how I know they're coming to take us to our new home." He frowned, clearly picking up on her changed mood. "Don't worry! It's true that you were not part of my Flock. But you are welcome to join us, as are your friends. I would prefer that you didn't bring Kolya or your mother, because I think the Sentinels will refuse them. But I will tell them that you *earned* a place here. If you hadn't been on the *Ares Prime* to save me, I wouldn't be alive today. Without you, there would have been no one to send the signal."

SEVENTEEN

AS SHE WALKED BACK to the porch with Shepherd, Claire was intensely conscious of Beck's eyes on her. She couldn't look at him, though. If she did, she'd crack. She'd devolve into her teenage self, crying on his shoulder, and she could not afford that right now. Not in front of Shepherd. The man believed that he'd rescued his followers from an apocalypse. How would he react if she told him the truth—that he'd actually called that apocalypse down on the entire Earth, and probably Mars, too? She didn't think he'd believe her, but either way, she doubted that it would go well. And right now, she just wanted to leave. To get back to Earth, so that she could spend every possible minute with the people she loved.

So, she'd kept the smile frozen in place as she told Shepherd she needed to get to Daedalus immediately so that she could bring Wyatt back and they could await the Sentinels together. She promised him as well that they'd try once again to contact Housen, to see if there was any additional news on transporting the rest of the Flock. Now she just needed to hold it together for a few minutes longer.

"I'll see about getting some food packed up for you," Shepherd said and disappeared into the dining hall.

"What's wrong?" Beck asked.

She held her hand up and sat down across from Paul, who was typing out a message as he ate from what looked like a bowl of the stew they'd smelled when they walked in.

"How soon can our plane depart?"

"The plane? It can go now, but the pilot is…" He looked up,

caught her too-bright smile, and fell silent. "Immediately. We can go right this minute."

"Good." She lowered her voice. "I'll explain everything once we're out of here. I've told Shepherd that we'll be back within a day or two at the most, so just smile and thank the man for his hospitality."

"Okay." He retracted his armscreen and shoved a few more bites of stew into his mouth, then picked up the bowl to carry it inside.

Beck handed her the helmet and bag she'd left next to her chair. "What happened? Are you okay?"

"Please don't," she said sharply. "Not until we're in the buggy."

"Okay. But you are seriously freaking me out."

They followed her lead, taking the package of hastily assembled sandwiches that Shepherd offered and waving goodbye to him and the assortment of Flock members who had gathered outside the dining hall. Claire squeezed into the smaller back seat of the buggy, just as she had a little over twenty-four hours earlier at Hyblaeus. She almost wished she was back there. She'd been terrified, but at least she'd had hope. Shepherd had just extinguished that.

"Hurry home, child," he called as they backed out. "And tell Housen to hurry, as well. Time is short."

As soon as the buggy was on the main road, Beck said, "Did you pick the beacon out of his pocket or something? Is that why you were in such a rush to get out?"

"No. He still has it."

"That's okay, though, right?" Paul said. "I mean, Beck said that Durav is dead, so…"

"It doesn't matter. Shepherd activated the beacon about two weeks ago. Shortly after the failed rescue attempt, I think. He's exchanged messages with the Alliance multiple times since then. He said he couldn't understand them because he hasn't heard Ufretan spoken since he was a kid, but he repeated the message that Uden gave him each time." Her voice began to quaver, exactly as she'd feared it would. "And we're all welcome to join the Flock here to wait for their arrival, because according to him, if I hadn't been so damned eagle-eyed on the *Ares Prime*, he'd have died and there would have been no one to send the signal."

Beck shook his head. "Claire, wait. This doesn't make sense. How could Shepherd activate the beacon?"

"The same way Durav would have. The only difference was that he needed *two* DNA samples from Triad members for the scanners, instead of just one. Uden left him with everything he needed."

Beck was still shaking his head, but she could read his face well enough to tell that he knew that part, at least, was possible. "What was this message that Uden gave him?"

"Hold on. It's in his memoir." After a quick search, she pulled the document up on her phone and navigated to the appendix. "Here it is. *Res esdoden ojiri ensilar ufretas*."

He took the phone from her and handed it back immediately. "This isn't Ufretan."

"I know that. It's just a phonetic rendering. What does it mean?"

"No, no. You're missing the point. Aside from *ufretas*, this is all gibberish. I remember seeing it when I thumbed through the memoir and wondering what language he'd cribbed from to make the other words."

Claire's shoulders relaxed the tiniest fraction, then tensed right back up. "But does it even matter what he told them? If the Alliance gets gibberish back from the person with the beacon, they're going to assume the mission has gone wrong. Also, the two indentations were lit up, with a pulsing blue light. He said that happened after he used the samples. Do they always look like that?"

"No," he admitted. "And you're right that it's concerning. Unfortunately, I don't know the full process for using the *brelat*. I'll message Arbet. All I'm saying is that we shouldn't assume the worst. Shepherd is a nutcase. You *know* that. Sure, there's some factual basis for his insanity, but he's built a cult and an entire mythology around it with him as the Glorious Leader. I think there's a decent chance that we'll learn those voices were just another of his delusions."

"He's right about Shepherd," Paul said. "I've spent more time around him than either of you. He's lucid and practical most of the time, but his eyes get this glazed-over look when he talks about the Sentinels."

"Okay," Claire said. "You both raise good points. I guess we should wait and see what Arbet says."

Beck reached back and squeezed her shoulder. "I'll message her from Nepenthes Station. Hopefully we'll hear back by the time we get to Daedalus."

Claire nodded and then just stared out at the rows of corn and the greenhouses the Flock had erected over the past five months. In the distance, a tiny blip of light shot up into the sky from Nepenthes Station. She focused on taking deep breaths to steady her nerves, which had been on a rollercoaster over the past hour, from worrying over the negotiations to absolute joy at the news that all of this was over, and then complete devastation minutes later. The journey had left her drained.

She wasn't at all convinced that she'd overreacted, though. Paul clearly still had some doubts as to whether any of this was real, so it was probably easier for him to dismiss the risk, but she didn't think Beck was convinced either. She could tell he was worried. He kept looking back to check on her. It was a relief when they approached the airlock tunnel and she was able to put on her helmet. If a stray tear happened to slip loose, it would be much easier to hide behind the visor.

Claire's phone buzzed twice as they approached the station, with messages from Wyatt and Joe. Her response to Rowan's earlier message was also in her drafts. She ignored them all. Anything she typed right now that didn't mention what Shepherd had told her would feel like a lie. And even if she'd been certain that Shepherd was telling the truth, it wasn't the sort of news she wanted to give anyone via text. The only person she was even slightly tempted to message was Alice. How had she wound up as part of some sort of hit squad going after Durav with the missing Watcher and Arbet's *ipret-tai*?

Nepenthes Station had been almost empty when she and Paul arrived a few hours earlier. Now, it was a hive of activity. She'd seen two more aircraft take off during the shuttle ride from the Ehden gate and the air control system had informed Paul that there were still four more in line ahead of them when they reached the station.

"Davy's field director is back in the lab," Paul explained. "These teams have been on standby, waiting to head out to various measurement stations around the planet. Once they send the all-clear, the lockdown will be over, and things can get back to normal around here. Finally."

Claire exchanged a look with Beck, who was already reaching for his phone to message Arbet. Sure, they'd agreed to hold off on freaking out until they heard back from her, but Paul had apparently decided to take the path of complete denial.

EIGHTEEN

Friday, October 6
Daedalus Station

BETWEEN THE THREE-HOUR flight and the time zone change, it was midmorning when Daedalus came into view. Claire had kept her helmet speakers turned off and feigned sleep for most of the trip, worried that Beck or Paul would keep giving her more reasons that Shepherd's story couldn't be true if given the chance. She couldn't get it out of her head, but that didn't mean she wanted to talk about it. And maybe they felt the same. The only one who had spoken at all about the situation since they left Nepenthes was Beck, and that had simply been to note that the time difference in Boston meant Arbet was almost certainly asleep ... so it would probably be at least five or six hours before they'd get a response.

On her first visit, Daedalus Station had been busy, but most of the action had been confined to the gates near the main dome. The station was several kilometers long and nearly the same across, counting the various smaller domes along the edge, and at least half of the space had been empty. Today, it was packed, not just with planes and shuttles, but with the buggies and trams that normally transported passengers along the Strip. It looked as if every vehicle in Daedalus City was outside the dome now.

A second, smaller cluster of vehicles was gathered along the right edge of the dome, about two thirds of the way around the outer perimeter. She turned her comms system back on to ask Paul if he knew what was going on over there but realized he'd just joined a call with someone. She was close enough to hear his side of the conversation and managed to piece together that Kolya and Macek had arrived a few hours earlier. They were currently at the Red Dahlia. Beck had apparently been eavesdropping, too, because when the call ended, he asked why they weren't at the hospital instead.

Paul tapped something into his armscreen before responding. The plane decelerated, and once it began taxiing into a lane near the front of the landing area, he said, "The Dahlia's security situation is better at the moment. We keep a medic on staff, and there's not much doctors would be doing at the hospital other than keeping them in bed. Which isn't going to happen anyway. Well, at least not for Kolya. Three members of the Daedalian Council are demanding that he turn Stasia over to the city police. He's heading down to the Executive Pavilion in about fifteen minutes for a private meeting with the council, the chief of police, and a delegation of local business owners, hoping to calm things down a bit. I'm supposed to meet him there. I don't know if Macek is going or not. And then we have a—well, he called it a public press conference, but that's gilding the lily a bit when it's just Jordan Mercer's paper and Wyatt as the press. It will be at the amphitheater in the resort gardens at one and it will be open to all permanent citizens, so I'm guessing there will be a crowd, even with the relatively short notice. I suggested, given his injuries, that we simply record a video statement and play it on all of the monitors, but that idea was rejected without discussion."

"Do you think Kolya is planning to turn Stasia over to them?" Beck asked.

"He says he won't. She stays at the resort until after the trial, which will probably be next week. But, if she's found guilty, and I assume she will be, there's not much he can do after that. I think he can make a compelling case to keep her at the Red Dahlia with the rioting going on downtown and the lynching of that miner last week. The city police will *definitely* be on his side, given that KTI is having to keep the guards who would normally be inside

Daedalus outside the dome to protect the station. Those guards would be their backup in case of an emergency."

"Seems like the number out here is overkill, though," Claire said, looking around the station, where there were at least fifty vehicles and two or three times as many people. "Why not keep more security inside the dome?"

"Because the city isn't what Westmoreland wants," Paul said. "I know you think he has people inside stirring up trouble, and that's very likely true, but if so, the goal is for security to be so distracted that they'll miss an attack out here." He nodded toward one of the smaller domes at the edge of the station where maybe a third of the vehicles and people were milling about. "Dome Five houses the maglev tunnel to the hyperlift at Arsia Mons. That's what he wants. And if they manage to take control of it, no one's getting off this planet without his permission."

Dome Five was maybe half a kilometer beyond the dome that housed the Icarus chamber. An underground tunnel of nearly two hundred kilometers ran from there to the Arsia Mons hyperlift, which launched shuttles and small aircraft into orbit so that they could catch the laser propulsion boost at Ares Station for the trip back to Earth. Claire had made that trip up the mountain the last time she left Mars, but the medical team had sedated her heavily before departure, and she had no memory of it at all.

"Westmoreland isn't happy with the current monopoly on the hyperlift?" Beck asked. "That's what all of this is about?"

"Oh, he doesn't have any problem with it *being* a monopoly. He just doesn't want Kolya *having* that monopoly. And based on what I know about the guy, Westmoreland's terms for using the system wouldn't be as generous. I could easily see him charging a king's ransom to any shuttle or ship trying to get back to Ares Station, which could give us a much larger hostage situation than the one we had at Ehden. But that's not going to happen. Macek has a team headed that way to intercept them."

"So … he *is* headed to Claritas?" Claire tried to keep the told-you-so out of her voice but failed. It wasn't that she *wanted* Westmoreland's people to attack Daedalus. But Kolya's implication that she was probably wrong, that she'd misheard, or might even be making it all up still chafed.

"Yes. You were right. Feel free to rub it in when you see His Majesty again. Satellite imagery over Lyot showed two worker transports heading out toward Claritas about four hours ago. Another one left from Hyblaeus around the same time. All in clear violation of the lockdown, I might add, since Davy's field director hasn't greenlit either region yet. She's prioritizing Tharsis, so that we can get their miners out of here, and Daedalus, so that we can relieve the pressure on Ares Station. Lyot is near the bottom of the list. Their worker transports move pretty slow compared to our security craft. And we're about six thousand kilometers closer to Claritas, so the KTI team will beat them there."

"Then, why is Claritas under Lyot's purview?" Beck asked. "I mean, if it's closer to the border with Daedalus, wouldn't it make more sense for that to be a KTI property?"

"Nothing about the way land was divided up on Mars makes sense. Claritas is Lyot's for the same reason Nepenthes belongs to KTI even though it's eight thousand klicks from Daedalus. The corporations that own the various colonies picked out the areas that had mineral wealth, especially those where it was easier to mine—cliff faces like Claritas Rupes or trenches like Cerberus Fossae. They basically sat down with a map like the European powers did with Africa and Asia and carved out spheres of influence." Paul unstrapped his seat restraint and grabbed his bag from the net. "Fortunately, here on Mars, there are no indigenous people attached to the land, but the colonies still squabble over who got the better deal. Anyway, our guys are setting up drones along the border. If Westmoreland's little militia tries to cross, they'll be stopped."

"And there's no sign of Westmoreland or Boudreaux?" Beck asked as he handed Claire her bag. "I doubt they'd be traveling on one of the worker transports."

"There's no sign of either of them *here*, if that's what you meant. But we think they're already at Claritas. A small Engelbrodt left Lyot a few hours before the worker transports. It may be the same plane they had at Hyblaeus. Although, you'd think he'd avoid that brand since that's what his dad was flying when he crashed."

Unless he doesn't believe it was a mechanical failure, Claire thought, again remembering Macek's comment in the shuttle about Kolya's skill at breaking things.

"Westmoreland would *have* to go to Claritas first in order to distribute weapons," she said. "The crates have biolocks, and from what he told Boudreaux, he's the only one who can open them."

"I should pass that along to Macek," Paul said. "Just in case our guys get any bright ideas about storming their arsenal and helping themselves."

They followed him outside and over to a waiting buggy. Instead of heading for the closest airlock gate, however, he told it to circle around toward one of the smaller domes.

"This isn't the scenic route," he said once the guards let them through the gate. "But you've both had the VIP tour, already. This way has the advantage of being quick and we won't run into any protests."

The route in question was a dimly lit tunnel that dipped down sharply for the first hundred meters or so and then forked off into three spokes. As their buggy shot off along the middle path, Paul filled them in on their accommodations, saying that Beck would be in his guest room. "Claire, you're with Wyatt, one floor down. I'll send the key and the room number to your phone."

She thanked him, then pulled off her helmet and stretched her neck. It wasn't heavy, but it limited her range of movement. And it was hot. Same for the suit. The shorts and tee she wore under it were plastered to her body. It felt like she'd been trapped in a sauna for most of the past few days, and she was looking forward to a long, cool shower.

Realizing that she couldn't put it off any longer, she took her phone out and messaged Wyatt that they had landed, saying she'd meet him in their room when they reached the resort. His response was immediate and she held her breath, waiting for his inevitable question about the beacon. But all he said was that he'd meet her there in ten minutes.

The buggy emerged into a cavernous room filled with maintenance robots and other equipment. Paul said, "Welcome to the Red Dahlia's sub-subbasement. That lovely roar you hear is the filtration system for the lake above, and..."

Someone moved out of the shadows and pivoted toward them, gun raised. "Stop and get out of the buggy! Now!"

"Jeffries!" A second man was now running across the basement toward them. "Hold off! He's KTI. Jesus Christ, man."

"Okay, okay," the first guy said, slinking back toward the shadows. "Sorry."

"Yeah. Sorry about that, Mr. Caruso." The other guy was slightly out of breath. "Jeffries isn't regular security and we didn't expect anyone to be coming in this way. He usually works in the casino, but we had to send a bunch of people out to the hyperlift and a few more to the outer perimeter to help the city cops deal with the traffic incident."

"Traffic incident?" Paul asked, glancing down at his armscreen again.

"Yeah. Don't know if you heard, but a group of Tharsans stole a tram last week. They don't normally go beyond the city limits, but they hacked and triggered the manual override and have been using it since then to bring people in from the temporary units so they can party on the Strip. The city forces ignored the theft, hoping to avoid another bout of riots, but the Tharsans must've failed to designate a driver last night. The drunk operating it lost control and crashed into the side of the dome a little before dawn. No one killed, but there are injuries and it's just a godawful mess. Again, though, sorry about Jeffries. After the past twenty-four hours, we're all a little jumpy."

"No problem. Just caught me by surprise," Paul said. "Not used to there being guards down here at all."

"No sir, but like I said, after last night ... it's turning into an all-hands-on-deck situation. And drones can't take up the slack because Chief Macek has most of them deployed to deal with…" The guard glanced at Claire and Beck and apparently decided discretion might be in order. "With an issue along the colonial border."

They left the buggy on a charging pad, stripped out of their biosuits, and entered the elevator. It went straight up for the first three levels, where Paul got out to join Kolya's meeting, then the cube did the weird hiccupping little sidestep she remembered from the previous trip as it ascended to the upper levels to bring the resort up to an acceptable facsimile of Earth's gravity. Her room was on the ninth floor, two floors below Kolya's penthouse.

"Are you going to the press conference?" Beck asked as they approached her floor.

"Maybe? I need to get a shower and talk to Wyatt and … I guess I'll see how I feel after."

When the elevator door opened, he grabbed her arm. "Listen, um … Wyatt knows, okay? I cc'd him on my message to Arbet. I'll understand if you're mad, but I knew how much it hurt *me* to have to tell Arbet that there's even a chance this was all in vain, especially after they were all elated that Durav wouldn't be around to push the button. You'd already had to break the news to me and to Paul. I thought the least I could do was spare you having to do it again."

"It's okay. I'm not mad." She wasn't, not really, and she managed to muster a smile as the elevator door closed. His motives had been good, even if she did think he'd overstepped.

When she opened the door to her room, Wyatt was there. He just pulled her into his arms and held her as she let out the tears she'd been holding in for the past four hours. No explanations required, no words at all.

It was exactly what she needed. As Beck had clearly known.

NINETEEN

WHEN CLAIRE STEPPED BACK into the elevator at around a quarter of one, she barely recognized her reflection in the mirrored tiles. She'd pressed an ice-cold washcloth to her face for a full ten minutes after Wyatt left, but her eyes were still puffy from crying. Any makeup she might normally have used to disguise that fact was now floating in the frozen void outside Ares Station. The demure, calf-length shirtwaist dress she'd purchased at a little boutique in Capullo del Sur gave off strong 1950s sitcom-mom vibes. But with Paul due to arrive at any minute to transport her to Ehden, she'd had no time to hunt for anything more suited to her tastes. And judging from the other women she'd seen walking around Elysia, she had serious doubts as to whether the stores even carried anything she'd normally wear.

Maybe it was for the best. This way, there was a decent chance that no one would recognize her. Wyatt had suggested that she just stay in the room and he'd give her the play by play later, but she'd told him to save seats for her and Beck. She really didn't want to be alone with her thoughts right now. Left to its own devices, her brain just kept replaying Shepherd's reminder that if she hadn't been on the *Ares Prime*, he wouldn't have been alive to signal the Alliance.

Beck was waiting near the front desk, holding a pair of oversized sunglasses. "Found these at the gift shop. Thought they might come in handy."

"Thank you. *Again*. Because yeah, you were right about telling Wyatt." She slipped the glasses on, and even though she was pretty sure he'd have said something if there was news, she asked the question anyway. "Any response from Arbet?"

"No. But it's not even eight o'clock there and if left to her own schedule, she's not an early riser. I think we've got a couple of hours, and that's assuming Kolya's censors aren't up to their usual tricks. Do you know where this amphitheater is?"

"It's near the edge of the resort. I passed it when I went into town last time in search of souvenirs. It's one of the few resort facilities that's open to townspeople as well as guests, which is probably why Kolya is speaking there. I don't think you'd need directions anyway. Just follow the crowd." She nodded toward the door, where a small group of guests were heading outside. Beyond them, several dozen more followed a path through the gardens toward the line of trees that separated the resort from Daedalus City.

The venue was officially named the Daedalus Amphitheater, but that was typical Kolya hype. It was actually a small bandshell —red, of course. Six chairs were currently on the stage, positioned in two groups of three, with a wide transparent screen hovering several feet above. Low curved benches faced the stage, arranged to mimic the flower-petal balconies of the Red Dahlia. She knew this only because she'd seen the place empty. Today, the benches were packed, and the attendees seemed a bit on the surly side. People were also seated on the hill, with others still coming in through the back entrance, where two guards were checking identification and performing a weapons scan.

Wyatt sat in the front row near the center, with a wide empty space between himself and a smartly dressed woman. He slid over to make room. The woman had just introduced herself as Jordan Mercer, editor of *The Red Planet*, when a black van with tinted windows pulled around the side of the bandstand, followed by one of the buggies used by the city police. A uniformed officer and a middle-aged woman with wispy red hair got out of the buggy and took the two chairs on the far right of the stage.

Kolya was the first to get out of the van. He still wore a neck brace, but this one was in a more subtle flesh tone and partially camouflaged by the high-necked sweater under his suitcoat. To her surprise, Macek was with him, wobbling slightly on a single crutch propped under his uninjured arm.

Claire thought that seemed like an exceptionally bad idea, especially given the four steps leading up to the stage. Paul looked like he agreed, although she soon realized his wary expression could easily have been because he knew who was getting out of the van next.

Stasia was accompanied by two armed guards. She'd gotten a full makeover since Claire last saw her at Tranquility Base. Her hair was once again her trademark blonde and in her crisp white pantsuit, she looked much more like Kolya's former right hand and ever-present KTI spokeswoman. The key difference was her bearing. Stasia had none of her former confidence and authority, although that would have been hard to muster in handcuffs and a neck monitor, let alone with the two guards and a low chorus of boos coming from the audience.

Beck leaned across and whispered to Wyatt. "Did you know about this? What the hell is he up to?"

Wyatt shook his head. "My best guess is he's trying to squelch the rumors about her being sneaked out of Daedalus. Or the competing theory that the woman being held at the Red Dahlia was not actually *her*."

"I guess that explains why he wouldn't listen to Paul's suggestion about simply recording a message," Claire said.

Jordan sniffed loudly. "I do *not* trust that man. He probably changed his mind about turning her over. Wouldn't even put it past him to have been planning something like this all along."

For Stasia's sake, Claire hoped that wasn't true. But she couldn't discount the possibility. If Kolya had decided that keeping her at the resort was a battle he couldn't easily win, it would be very much in character for him to make a grand show of it so that he could act like turning her over had been his idea all along.

Macek awkwardly lowered himself into the chair next to Stasia. The guards took up position several steps behind them. Paul stood off to the right, holding a clicker of some sort. Except for Stasia, who was staring at her shoes, all eyes were on Kolya as he made his way to the center of the stage. Wyatt tapped his body cam to begin recording.

Kolya cleared his throat and looked around at the audience, much as he'd done when he took the stage at the debate onboard the *Ares Prime*. "I'd like to thank all of you for joining me here today. I'm going to keep this brief on advice from my doctor—as you may have heard, our shuttle crashed on the way to Nepenthes and Chief Macek and I are both a bit worse for wear. But we have several serious matters to address, and I felt it only right to do so face to face. First and foremost, I have an announcement to make that I believe will meet with your approval."

"Not unless you're turning over Ljubic." The voice came from somewhere in the back and was cheered on by others.

Kolya ignored the interruption. "The field team in charge of final clearance for stage six of the terraforming project has sent their report to the Ares Consortium, and they have declared the lockdown *officially ended* in Daedalus." He paused, possibly holding for applause. Some people clapped, but it was an embarrassingly small number and just slow enough that it felt sarcastic. He pushed on. "We have just received word that Tharsis has been given the green light as well, which means that our guests will be departing over the next few hours."

The screen behind him now displayed animated fireworks and the words *LOCKDOWN ENDS!!* Claire thought the display was overly effusive given the general mood of the audience, but at least they applauded this time, and she sensed a slight decrease in the tension of the crowd behind her.

"We expect the other colonies to be cleared in the next twenty-four hours, and while some of the more remote areas will take a bit longer to certify, we should be able to declare stage six completely over within a week. I understand that the past few months have been awkward, especially given the events that occurred just prior to lockdown. My goal is to have us back to normal operations by late October. Both the *Ares Prime* and the *Diamante* are fully booked for holiday travel."

This drew murmurs of approval. Kolya's smile broadened, and he seemed more at ease now that the crowd was moving, albeit grudgingly, in his direction.

"Second, Daedalus cannot be a prosperous colony if it is not also a *safe* colony. Those who violate our laws must face justice. That was one reason that I was not here with you during lockdown. Knowing that Ms. Ljubic had escaped to Earth, I followed her, oversaw her apprehension, and transported her back to the colony to stand trial."

That was a lie. Claire explicitly remembered Kolya telling her that he was going back to Earth for business reasons.

"The trial is tentatively scheduled for next week," he continued, "as leaders from several other colonies have expressed an interest in attending. Earlier today, I met with our own council and the leader of the Daedalus police, and we discussed the best way forward. I'll let Colonel Weaver take it from here."

Kolya stepped back and a man in uniform, who was apparently Colonel Weaver, took his place centerstage. "As Mr. Kolya noted," he began in a terse monotone, "we met this morning at the Red Dahlia. At that time, I informed the council and Kolya that I cannot guarantee Ms. Ljubic will be safely delivered for trial in the current environment. Kolya has acted in good faith by bringing her here today, in order to dispel some of the rumors that are circulating. Given the comments that my officers have heard on the streets—including, I am sure, from some of you who are here today—I believe the best course of action is for Ljubic to remain in the custody of KTI Security through the end of her trial. Depending on the outcome of that trial, we may need to figure out how to deal with a long-term inmate, as the maximum time we've housed anyone to date is six months."

Weaver returned to his seat to the sound of jeers. As Kolya stepped forward again, a woman in the audience shouted, "Send her to Tharsis! That'll solve the problem."

This drew the loudest cries of support so far. Kolya waited for the noise to die down and was about to speak again when a young man in the front row stood up.

"Better yet," he said, "put it to a vote. Ask the citizens of Daedalus how *we* feel about the death penalty. That's not even addressed in this new constitution you expect us to vote on. Just because you're personally opposed to capital punishment doesn't mean that your will should be the law of the land. I actually oppose it, too, but it should be the people's decision." He turned slightly to face the audience. "Vote no on the corporatist constitution. Demand a constitutional convention so that we actually have some say in the laws that govern us. Oh, and while you're at it, vote Brent Hadler for Daedalian Council," he added, with a grin.

"I appreciate your input, Mr. Hadler," Kolya said in a voice that suggested he did not appreciate his input in the slightest. "But I would argue that the past six months is a clear indicator of why the proposed constitution should be adopted as quickly as possible, especially the security provisions. Six months of minor discomfort and this place descended into chaos, with a lynching in the streets." He held up his hand as audience members started to protest. "This is not, however, the time for campaign speeches or division. We can debate the death penalty later, along with any other issues, and even what our friend Mr. Hadler referred to as the *corporatist constitution*." His voice dripped with sarcasm. "At the moment, however, we have an existential threat on our border."

The screen flickered and the announcement about the lockdown was replaced by a video of two worker transports arriving at a small domed encampment at the base of a towering cliff.

"This was taken about twenty minutes ago at Claritas. For those of you who are unfamiliar with Martian geography, Claritas is a Lyotian mining outpost, about two hundred kilometers from our colonial border, and about twelve hundred from Daedalus City. Those worker transports are carrying Lyotian mercenaries. Our intelligence indicates that their objective is to seize the Arsia Mons hyperlift."

No one was jeering now. Kolya had their full attention.

"They believe they have the element of surprise, but we have dispatched KTI Security forces to the border, along with a sizeable contingent of drones. To be honest, though, I'm not at all sure we'll be able to stop them, because we've just learned that seven additional transports are en route."

Seven additional transports? That didn't match at all with what Paul had said earlier. Had they received new information? Or was Kolya simply playing this up to redirect the crowd's anger?

Claire looked at Paul to gauge his reaction, but his face was shadowed by the rim of the bandshell. Macek, however, was right there on the stage, and Claire had seen that look on his face more than once in the past few days. It was the same expression he'd worn when Kolya was rambling on about Wyatt being the most probable suspect for stealing the *Velox One* … and again when Kolya had insisted on winging the landing rather than listening to guidance from the shuttle's computer.

"Most of you are owners or employees of businesses here in Daedalus. I don't need to tell you what will happen to this colony if Lyot takes over the hyperlift." Kolya said and then proceeded to tell them anyway. "They will levy a tax on every incoming and outgoing passenger shuttle."

Claire kept her eyes on Macek's face, watching for his reaction, but she could see Kolya pacing the front of the stage from the corner of her eye.

"It may be a small tax at first," he said, "but any of you who have done business with Westmoreland know that the son, just like the father, is a pirate with no code of ethics. If we pay their ransom once, they will demand a higher price. It will increase, and increase, until—"

Three shots rang out, one after the other. *Bang. Bang. Bang.*

TWENTY

SHE TURNED her head just in time to see Kolya drop to one knee. The woman directly behind her screamed and then Kolya pitched forward, landing less than a meter from the front row.

Wyatt pushed Claire to the ground on the other side of the body. Everyone was screaming now, scrambling to their feet, and tripping over the low benches in their efforts to flee. Her cheek was pressed against the foundation of the bandshell, and she could feel the vibrations of people running above as Macek shouted orders. A fourth and fifth gunshot sounded almost in unison, then something thudded heavily on the stage.

She was now inches away from Kolya. He lay face down in the grass. She felt like she should do something. Check for a pulse, maybe. But there was so much blood, so much that it was seeping into the fabric of her dress. And she'd seen him just before he fell. He was almost certainly dead before he hit the ground.

A horrible, awful voice at the back of her head screamed that it was good, that he deserved it. He hadn't pushed the button himself, but if he'd listened to Drex, if he'd listened to *Claire* when she tried to tell him about the Alliance, the sequence of events might have unfolded differently. They might have avoided everything that happened at Nepenthes. They might have reached Shepherd in time, might have delayed the Alliance for decades. There might have been time for Jemma and millions of other children to grow up. And maybe time to find a way to fight.

Wyatt reached across her to grab Beck's arm. "Stay down and get her out of here as soon as you can."

She looked up to see that Jordan was already gone and realized what Wyatt meant. "No. Are you crazy?"

His answer was a quick kiss. Then he tapped his backup cam and took off, stepping over the blood and Kolya's body. Running in a crouch, against the crowd, toward the story.

"Come on, Claire," Beck's arms were wrapped around her waist. "He knows what he's doing. He'll be fine."

She caught a brief glimpse of the stage as Beck half-dragged, half-carried her away. One of the guards who'd been standing behind Stasia was down, the right side of her face a mask of red. Macek's crutch was propped against the bottom edge of the screen, where the video of the two personnel transports continued to play in a loop.

"Claire!"

Paul was behind them, motioning toward the van. She searched the crowd for Wyatt but couldn't find him. Cursing under her breath, she piled into the van with Beck. Stasia and the remaining guard were already inside, both covered in blood and wearing almost identical expressions of shock.

Macek hobbled toward the van, as several of his guards tried to hold the crowd back. "McMann!"

The guard next to Stasia jumped, jolted out of his state of shock.

"Go get my crutch." Macek moved aside for the guard to get out and then he climbed into the van.

Paul slammed the door behind him, just as several people broke through the line of guards and shoved the back of the vehicle, setting off the automatic alarm.

A man pressed his face to the window. "Give us Ljubic!"

"Some of these people are *not* from Daedalus," Paul said.

"No kidding. Someone let a group of the miners in through the other gate." Macek looked at Claire and then at Stasia as the van began rocking again. Then, he leaned forward and tapped the console. The alarm increased in pitch and then people began screaming.

"What did you do?" Beck asked.

Macek arched an eyebrow. "It's non-lethal. Do you want them to push the van over?"

Non-lethal didn't exactly answer Beck's question, but none of them pressed the point. And whatever Macek had done, it did seem to be keeping the crowd away from the van.

Macek glanced out the window again and then turned to Paul. "You need to get them *out* of Daedalus. Take the *V2*, or whatever ship you can get. Let me know if you run into trouble."

"What about Stasia?" Paul asked. "I can't take her back to Earth. She'd be arrested the second we landed."

"I don't know. Maybe just..." Another gunshot sounded off in the distance. "Maybe just take her to Ares Station for now. Anywhere other than here."

"What does it matter?" Stasia said, with a hysterical little laugh. "None of us will be here in a few months anyway."

Beck leaned forward to squeeze her hand, and Claire realized he must have told her about Shepherd using the beacon. Which meant she was also working through some major guilt. It was hard enough knowing you'd killed for a cause that *saved* billions of lives, but to have killed for a cause that failed?

Macek gave Stasia a baffled look. "What the hell you talking about? I'm not going to let them lynch you."

He, of course, still had no clue that all of their days were most likely numbered in double digits. Once they knew for certain, he would be one of the few people that Claire told. He'd made it very clear that he would want to know the truth in that situation. And maybe he'd find a way to spend what time he had left with Marisol.

"I ... may have an idea where Stasia can go," Claire said.

Macek frowned. "No. Do not tell me where. Just go."

"Fine. But is it true that Westmoreland is sending seven additional transports to Claritas? And have you heard anything more about that transport from Hyblaeus?" What she really wanted to ask was whether Westmoreland was sending people to Ehden, but that would be giving it away completely. Even this was skating on very thin ice, but it would give him plausible deniability.

"No. I haven't heard anything about Hyblaeus or about these additional transports." He glanced at Paul, who shook his head.

"Although ... Kolya *was* talking to someone just before we left the penthouse. And it's not like I was in the loop at the moment." Paul's voice was very tight, like he was barely holding it in.

It seemed to be contagious. Macek squeezed his eyes shut for a moment, then took a ragged breath and reached for the door handle.

"I'll have my people clear a path for the van. I need to get back out there and see if he..."

"He's gone, man. I was looking straight at him when the gun went off." Paul looked at Claire, maybe wanting her to say something, to confirm Kolya's death.

But Macek's eyes told her that he already knew the truth. "If Kolya is dead, that's all the more reason I have to get back out there." He stepped out of the van, wincing slightly when he stumbled and some of his weight landed on his bad leg. "There are thousands of people under this dome, and thousands of employees elsewhere and like it or not, I have inherited the role of King Asshole." He gave Claire a nod. "If I see Garcia, I will tell him to get to the Red Dahlia immediately. If he ignores me, I will provide him with an official escort."

McMann handed him the crutch and started to get back into the van.

"No," Macek said. "I need you out here."

"But..." The guard nodded toward Stasia. "What about her?"

"She's wearing cuffs and a containment collar. I think they can handle her. And where the hell would she go anyway with all these people out for her blood?" Macek slammed the door behind them.

"That's a very good question." Paul instructed the van to take them to the executive pavilion and then turned to Claire. "I do hope your idea wasn't for us to go back to Ehden. Because in case you've forgotten, the only hyperlift is *here* and there's at least an outside chance that we won't have control of it much longer. We need to get to Ares Station while we still can."

It was a good point. She hadn't exactly forgotten either of those complications, but maybe they needed to be weighed more heavily in her analysis. "All I'm saying is that I think I can talk Shepherd into taking her."

Stasia shook her head. "Are you crazy? First, I'd rather be on Ares Station than with a genocidal monster. Second, I'm the one who targeted the nanodrone that nearly killed him."

"I don't think Shepherd is genocidal. Not really. He didn't fully understand the consequences of using the beacon. He just thought he was getting his people off what he considers to be a dying planet. And does he know that you were directly involved in the drone attack? I didn't even know until just before we left Earth. Either way, I'm the one Shepherd credits with saving him, so maybe if I plead your case…"

She rolled her eyes. "Leaving all that aside, I doubt Davina Monroe would want me next door after we targeted her lab."

"I told Dr. Monroe everything," Beck said. "I'm not saying she's happy that the Flock hired someone to damage her lab and kill multiple people in the process. But she understands what was at stake."

Claire ran one hand through her hair. "Davy. That's one more person we still have to tell about the beacon. And … about Kolya."

Stasia winced. "She's going to take Anton's death very hard. He irritated her to no end, but … they were very close. Once, after the divorce when he'd had too much krambambula and was feeling sorry for himself, he said Davy was the only person who'd really loved him since his mother died. Which left me with many questions about his family."

Claire thought he should have added Macek, as well, but how like Kolya to casually dismiss his most loyal friend. And what about her mother? Claire was pretty sure that Kai had loved him, too, at one point, although her love was *always* conditional, so perhaps it didn't count. Still, she probably needed to tell Joe so that he could give her a heads up.

She pulled her phone out, but Beck quickly grabbed her hand.

"Why don't you hold off on that? At least until we hear back from Arbet?"

She looked up from the phone, confused. "Oh. I wasn't messaging Davy. I don't even have her contact information. I was going to tell Wyatt where to meet us. In case Macek doesn't see him. And … I thought Joe should probably let my mom know about Kolya."

He relaxed. "Good. Because I still think there's a decent chance that Shepherd hallucinated the whole thing. As I said when we left and as I told Stasia earlier, the message he claims Uden gave him is *not* in Ufretan and it definitely doesn't mean *walk in the light of the Sentinels*. If you show Stasia that copy of his memoir, she can back me up on that."

Claire finished the message to Wyatt, then said, "I believe you, okay? I'm sure you know your own language. I'm just not convinced that the words have to be real in order for the rest of what he told me to be true. Shepherd could have been chanting fake Ufretan for years and still have sent a signal to the Alliance, right? But sure. I've got it right here if Stasia wants to look at it."

She scrolled through, pulled up one of the lessons in the appendix, and gave it to Stasia, whose hands were now free. The cuffs were on the seat next to her, along with the collar.

"When did that happen?" she asked.

"Right after Macek got out of the van. He must have turned them off." Stasia glanced at the words on the phone, then shook her head and gave it back. "*Definitely* not Ufretan."

The van was in front of the executive pavilion. Paul told them to stay put until he got back.

Claire switched to her messages and was relieved to see a thumbs up from Wyatt. Which didn't confirm that he was heading back to the resort, and meant he'd be getting a follow-up text in a few minutes, but at least it was proof he was still alive. She quickly tapped out a message to Joe, saying that Kolya was dead and she'd follow up with more details. Before hitting send she remembered that this was Joe she was dealing with and he might not pick up on the next step unless she added explicit instructions for him to tell Kai before she heard it elsewhere. But since he didn't know about the affair, she made a joke of it, saying that it might be bad for the company if she learned the news in public and someone caught video of her doing a happy dance.

When she looked up, Stasia was staring at her. "Can I see that passage again?"

"Sure." She opened the memoir again, and noticed Stasia's hand shaking as she took the phone. "What's wrong?"

"Maybe nothing. Just let me think. *Res esdoden ojiri ensilar ufretas.*" Stasia closed her eyes, then repeated the words with a slightly different intonation. "*Res esdo**dan** oj**iri** en**see**lar … ufretas.*" Her eyes flew open. "*Ojiri. Ojiri ensilar!* That's it."

Beck shook his head. "I am not following you at all, Stace."

"God, you really weren't kidding about flunking that class, were you?" She laughed. "It's *Hodjeri,* Beck. If this is what Shepherd's been saying, he's telling them we're seeking the Hodjeri Union's protection from Ufretas."

TWENTY-ONE

CLAIRE TOSSED WYATT'S bag and her own into the rear of the buggy and began getting back into her biosuit. She was relieved that the guards who had been on duty when they arrived were now gone, probably called to the amphitheater or the front gates. Beck was the only one there, and he informed her that Paul was helping set up something for Macek, but he and Stasia would be down soon.

Paul had given them ten minutes to pack up whatever they had in their rooms and meet him at the buggy. She'd messaged the location to Wyatt, along with their estimated time of departure and a teaser that they might have some good news for a change. She hadn't given any details, though. If he wanted more, he could get his ass to the Red Dahlia. His response? Another thumbs up.

Five minutes later, Paul and Stasia still hadn't arrived. She sent another message to Wyatt, telling him that they were still on Level B3. Still waiting. He sent a heart emoji instead of a thumbs-up this time and she wasn't at all sure how to interpret that. It could be *love you, thanks for waiting, on my way.* It could also be *love you, not coming, hope you understand why I can't leave yet.*

And she did understand. Didn't agree, and didn't like it one bit, but she understood.

Beck had been pacing pretty much nonstop since they got to the basement, and the clack of his boots slapping against the hard floor was beginning to grate on her nerves. She supposed it could be a delayed reaction to the shooting. But she was also wondering about his earlier optimistic insistence that Shepherd had imagined voices coming from the beacon. Maybe Beck had been in denial as much as Paul, because it was only now, when they had a tiny ray of hope, that his nerves seemed to have kicked in.

To be fair, his pacing was bothering her mostly because she was also on edge. They were now in three different holding patterns. Actually, *four* if you counted waiting on Paul, Stasia, and Wyatt. The other three were mostly due to the time zone differences. They'd been waiting for hours to hear back from Arbet, both in regard to his first set of questions *and* the follow-up Beck had sent asking if there was any way Uden might have tweaked the beacon to a different frequency or otherwise enabled it to contact the Hodjeri. Finally, they were waiting on a response to the message Claire had sent to Shepherd, which she was a little surprised hadn't come by now. It was already seven in the morning in Ehden. Weren't farming communities supposed to wake at the crack of dawn?

Claire hadn't tried to explain things to Shepherd. She'd simply told him it was urgent and asked him to get back with her as soon as he was awake. That was mostly because they'd been debating how much to tell him. Stasia still preferred steering clear of Ehden and Shepherd. Her idea was to go back to the original plan—send someone in to simply *take* the beacon. Beck leaned toward that as well. Paul thought they should tell Shepherd everything, lay all of their cards on the table, although he added that he'd be convinced by whatever plan was likely to get them off Mars the fastest.

Personally, Claire wasn't keen on Stasia's plan, in part because she suspected she'd be the one tasked with taking the beacon. And while she generally believed honesty was the best policy, she also thought Paul was placing far too much trust in Shepherd behaving as a rational actor. While he could present a rational front, she'd seen the fanatical joy in his eyes as he told her that the Sentinels were on their way. Shepherd had built this Professor Everett and the Sentinels up in his mind until they were veritable deities, to the point that he hadn't been able to accept Housen's claim to be one of them, even though he clearly liked him. Unless they went in with pyrotechnics or worked a few flashy miracles, she didn't think Shepherd would accept that any of the other members of the Watch were Sentinels, either.

She also suspected that Shepherd would reject any reality that didn't include his gods arriving to whisk him and his Flock away to their reward with cries of *well done, my good and faithful servants*. And she'd heard plenty of stories about what happened when cult leaders were forced to face reality. It generally didn't end well for them or their followers.

Even if it turned out that Shepherd's message hadn't reached the Ufretans, Earth was still on their list for imminent destruction when they inevitably grew tired of Arbet's false progress reports. Simply put, if they had the chance to ask a favor of the Alliance's sworn enemy, rescuing the Flock was not going to be at the top of their wish list.

A sound like a chair scraping across the floor shook Claire from her thoughts. She gave Beck a confused look and then realized the noise was coming from the speaker system when Macek's voice filled the room.

"This is Jaromir Macek, chief of operations for Kolya International. For any of you who have not yet heard the news, Anton Kolya and two other people were killed in a public forum this afternoon in Daedalus City. I am now speaking to you as the chief executive of the corporation. One of the individuals directly responsible for this heinous act is among the deceased and we have the other in custody. The primary gunman has been identified as Jason Boudreaux, a member of a now-defunct terrorist organization called the Lone Star Militia. We believe that he received assistance from others to enter the dome last night and to enter the amphitheater itself this afternoon. Anyone in attendance today, or who may have information about the tram that crashed into the dome last night, please contact either the city police or a KTI Security officer and give them your statement. We will be offering a substantial reward for information that allows us to apprehend anyone who assisted the assassin."

"Unfortunately," Macek continued, "this is not the only immediate crisis facing Daedalus City. Shortly before his death, Kolya stated that Lyotian mercenaries were preparing to storm the dome. That was a ... slight overstatement, based on more recent intelligence. What we know for certain is that approximately one hundred armed militia are on their way to the border from Claritas, where we believe Lyot has a sizeable cache of weapons. Their goal is to take control of the hyperlift and Daedalus Station. KTI officers have been deployed to intercept them. I will provide additional information as we receive it but let me say that I have every reason to believe our forces will be successful. Should they fail in holding the attackers off, however, we will need volunteers to help defend the station, the hyperlift, and potentially the dome itself. I know you will do what is necessary to protect your homes, your businesses, and your future in this colony *that I firmly believe should be governed by the will of its citizens*. Macek out."

"Whoa," Beck said. "That last bit seems like a slight departure from Kolya's view."

"It does. Although Kolya would have denied it wholeheartedly, all the while pushing policies that kept control in his own hands. I just wonder how well Macek's view will sit with KTI's investors or even the Ares Consortium."

"In the short term, maybe it will at least buy him enough good will for the locals to overlook the disappearance of the planet's public enemy number one." Beck glanced at the elevator, and Claire followed his gaze, ready to start listing the reasons she'd been rehearsing to encourage Paul to wait at least a few more minutes.

But it was Wyatt who stepped out.

"You made it!"

He gave her a sideways grin. "Macek didn't exactly offer me a choice in the matter. He was headed back here to make his announcement and said I could either get in the buggy or get my ass kicked. And I'm not inclined to fight a human tank, even when he's operating with only one good arm and one good leg. I got the footage I needed, anyway, and I think I'll have some good still photos, too."

"Is a Pulitzer really worth getting your head blown off?" Beck asked.

Wyatt made a so-so gesture, then faked pain when Claire dug her elbow into his side. "I'm joking, I'm joking. But I don't regret sticking around. I got a short interview with the woman who saw Boudreaux shoot Kolya and then saw the *ipret-tai* take *Boudreaux* down when he shifted the gun to the left."

"You're kidding," Claire said.

"Nope. She thought Boudreaux was aiming at Macek, but that's only because she didn't have the context to make sense out of what the *ipret-tai* was saying…"

He pulled up the video and turned the screen toward them. A middle-aged woman began speaking in a faint South Asian accent. She wore a floral-patterned kurta and a look of shock. "I was running late because I only decided at the last minute to close up the shop so I could hear what he had to say. I entered the gate directly behind the two men. Either the guards at the gate are in on it, or maybe the men already had the guns out because they are wearing body armor, and you'd think they would have stopped them, right?"

"Sure," Wyatt said. "What happened next?"

"Almost immediately, maybe two steps inside the gate, that first man? He fired at the stage. Three shots, at Mr. Kolya. I crouched down behind a bench, too scared to run back to the gate because he was so close and because the other man, the one with the face tattoo, he had a gun, too, you know? He was waving it at the police, and he fired once like he was trying to give the first man cover. Then, the first man fired again, I think at a police officer, and he whips the gun toward the stage as he's backing toward the gate. I think he was pointing at the man in the arm sling that time. The big one. I do not know his name. That is when the one with the tattoo aimed his gun at the first gunman and shot him right here." She pointed to her temple.

"Perfect shot. The gunman dropped dead. Just like that. Then the police grabbed the face tattoo man and cuffed him. I think he may be … off balance, you know, because he is saying over and over as he stares at the body that a hipra…or *something* like that … could not allow an Earther to kill a washer. So … he must be crazy, right?"

"Yeah, that's kind of odd," Wyatt said. "Did he say anything else?"

The woman shook her head. "Not really. As soon as he saw the police he stopped babbling. They cuffed him and he told them to contact his attorney. Someone in New York, so I'm not sure how that will work."

"So … it sounds like Boudreaux was aiming at Stasia, but the bullet hit the guard standing behind her." Claire turned to Beck. "Is what the *ipret-tai* said true?"

"That they're supposed to protect the Watchers? Yes. If he thought Boudreaux was aiming at Stasia, he'd have to stop him. Had Durav or another Triad member ordered a member of the Watch killed, I suspect the *ipret-tai* would have carried it out without a second thought. But if Durav ordered an *Earther* to kill one of us?" He shook his head. "I think he'd have to prevent that. And that would go double if there wasn't an explicit order and Boudreaux was just doing it on his own, thinking that Durav would approve given his anger at Stasia. The bigger question, though, is why Durav would have ordered him to shoot Kolya."

"He didn't. That was the private matter Westmoreland mentioned. He blamed Kolya for his father's crash." Claire didn't add that he might have had good reason. That was only a gut feeling, not anything she could prove. "I just don't see how Boudreaux got here so quickly from Claritas."

"Maybe he got off the plane early," Wyatt said. "One of Jordan's sources told her that security found two parachutes about four klicks from the dome. My guess is that Westmoreland dropped Boudreaux and the *ipret-tai* via parachute last night and then continued to Claritas. It was probably his man on the inside who arranged for the tram crash last night that breached the dome. So … you said there was good news?"

"*Possible* good news. The quote in Shepherd's memoir…" Claire trailed off as her phone began ringing. For a moment, she didn't even recognize the sound. When was the last time she'd gotten a voice call? Certainly not since leaving Boston.

She gave Beck a panicked look when she saw the screen. "It's *Shepherd*."

This was not what they'd expected. The plan, to the extent that they had one, had been to play it by ear, and discuss as a group how to respond to his *text messages*. They hadn't even considered the possibility that he'd call.

Putting the phone on speaker mode, she said, "Dr. Shepherd. I'm surprised to hear from you so soon."

"Well, you did say it was urgent."

"I did. Yes. I … just … thought … um. You said the Sentinels have been calling every few days, right? On a regular schedule?"

"Yes. Every fifty-six hours and seven minutes. Approximately."

"When do you expect them to call again?"

"Today. At eleven minutes after noon, Ehden time, so … a little less than five hours from now. Why? Will you be back by then?"

"No. It's just that…" Her mind was spinning and she was very close to just spilling everything, but she remembered that almost ethereal glow on his face as he told her the Sentinels were on their way.

No. It was time for some pure fiction.

"It's just that there's something I didn't tell you when I was at Ehden," she said. "I didn't want to get your hopes up. I've been in contact for a while now with someone who once worked as an assistant to the Sentinels. She understands spoken Ufretan, or at least, the dialect she says they used among themselves. I'm very worried that they might be giving you specific instructions or asking questions that you need to answer. Would you be willing to let her listen to the message?"

Beck waved his arms wildly and began typing something on his phone.

There was a very long silence on Shepherd's end, which she was grateful for, since it gave Beck more time to finish whatever he was writing. Finally, he said, "This is someone you trust? And she's here on Mars?"

"Not on Mars. But I'm headed to Ares Station. There's some … chaos here in Daedalus that I'll explain later. And KTI has something on the station—an experimental new voice-only technology linking to Earth. It's almost instantaneous."

Wyatt gave her a look that clearly telegraphed his view that she'd gone too far. And maybe she had, but Shepherd was a major technophobe. He wouldn't have any idea how big of a lie she'd just told. Probably…

"And as for trusting her, yes I do." She looked down at what Beck had written, which was actually something he'd mentioned in the video he sent to her before the bombings. "And you corresponded with this woman briefly several weeks ago. She messaged you asking about someone named Professor Uden, and you told her he was deceased."

"Yes. That was very strange. An anonymous message, using Professor Everett's real name. I assumed it was Housen again."

Paul and Stasia stepped out of the elevator. Wyatt held up a hand to shush them.

"No, it wasn't Housen. But she realized after she sent the message that it might have alarmed or upset you, especially given your recent security concerns. She decided it might be best to approach you through a third party. I was going to tell you after the hostage situation was resolved, but … then you gave me the good news about the Sentinels' message. It was only later that it occurred to me that she might be able to help us."

She held her breath, waiting for his answer. It was a completely ridiculous story, with massive holes, even with Beck's bit of information that might tie it to Shepherd's reality. He was going to realize she was lying, which meant they'd not only need to go with Stasia's option of stealing the beacon, but would probably have to pull in Davy and Macek and have KTI Security take the thing by force.

"Well," Shepherd said. "If you trust her, I don't suppose there's any harm in it. And I'll admit I have been worried that maybe I'm not saying the words exactly right or that there's something else the Sentinels need from me. They sound a little … frustrated, maybe? … when I repeat the same thing back."

"That's wonderful, Dr. Shepherd! I'll set everything up and call you back at a little after noon your time." Claire ended the call and sank down onto the floorboard of the buggy.

"That was *Shepherd?*" Paul asked. "What exactly did you just agree to?"

"Yeah, it was Shepherd," Claire said, "And I think I've just set up a conference call for this afternoon between Stasia and the Hodjeri."

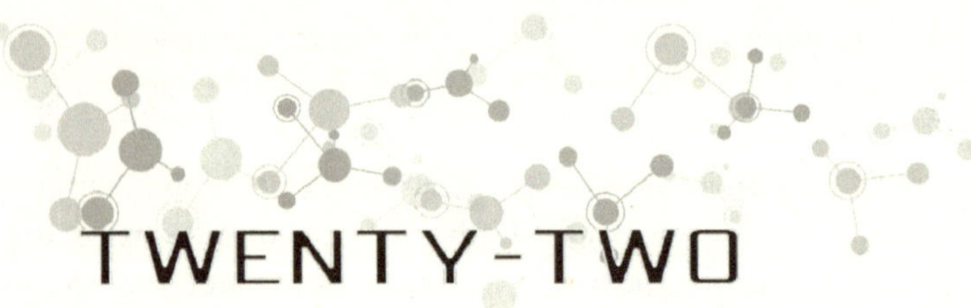

TWENTY-TWO

Friday, October 6
Ares Station

THEY REACHED the conference room at Ares Station with about ten minutes to spare. Once everyone was gathered around the table, Claire unlocked her phone and handed it to Paul, who began working with a KTI tech employee to sync it up with a recorder, a speaker, and something to enhance the audio quality.

The room was cold, and she was stuck in the same shirt and shorts she'd worn when they left Ares Station two days earlier, since the dress she'd bought at Capullo del Sur was streaked with Kolya's blood. The first thing she was going to do after this phone call ended was go down to the station's promenade and purchase clothes for the trip home that were warm and didn't reek. Then she was going to toss her current outfit straight into the trash.

She'd actually hoped to do that before the call, but they were running late. Daedalus Station had been a madhouse of outgoing planes, mostly heading to Tharsis with the miners who'd been temporarily housed at Daedalus and a bunch of new arrivals who'd been stuck at Ares Station. Bringing new people down to the surface seemed risky given the possibility of an attack by Lyot, so either KTI had already stopped Westmoreland's militia, or Macek was even more worried about potential violence due to the overcrowding at Ares.

They'd had a brief problem with one of the security guards who refused to let Stasia board the *Velox II* until he had clearance directly from the top. That was understandable, but it had taken twenty minutes for them to track Macek down for his explicit okay.

The delay had been good, in one sense. While they waited, Beck had gotten replies to both of his messages to Arbet. She'd told him that while she'd never seen the beacon used, she was responsible for transmitting the outgoing messages from the Watchers' *rezlats*, the personal devices they used to keep in touch with family and friends back home. She said that the DNA scanner on those devices did indeed light up in the same fashion that Claire had seen on the beacon. As for tweaking the beacon to contact the Hodjeri, she didn't think it was possible ... but she also didn't think it was necessary. The Hodjeri were undoubtedly intercepting Alliance communications. If they were in range of the beacon, they *could* have picked up the signal.

Arbet also confirmed something that Beck said he'd wondered about but hadn't thought to ask directly—she was the attorney who met with Shepherd the year before he graduated high school to inform him of the legal trust that Professor Everett had established to help him form the Earth Watch Alliance. She gave Beck a basic overview of the meeting and said that she'd used the name Barbara Windham, adding that Stasia should feel free to impersonate her if it helped in dealing with Shepherd.

By the time Macek cleared their departure, there had been a line of outgoing shuttles waiting at the hyperlift tunnel in Dome Five. Paul had to pull rank to get the *Velox II* to the front, and even then, it had taken nearly an hour before the ship zipped up the side of Arsia Mons and the hyperlift spat it out for the ascent into orbit. Claire was glad she'd been conscious this time. It was, as Kolya had once said, one hell of a ride.

She squeezed her eyes shut at the memory, fighting back tears.

Wyatt took her hand under the table. "You okay?"

"Yeah. Just tired. And cold. And ... maybe having a bit of a delayed reaction to the shooting." She sighed, shaking her head. "By the end, I couldn't even say I liked the man. He was stubborn, and selfish, and his interminable ego very nearly got all of us killed."

She decided to wait and share her other thoughts with him later, when there weren't as many people around. Because she couldn't help thinking that as awful as the shooting was, it was in some ways a prophetic ending. How many times had Kolya compared Mars to the Wild West? He'd said the planet operated, for the most part, under a code of frontier justice. He'd even told her that if the people responsible for the explosion at Cerberus were found, he thought their fate should be decided by that code. If her suspicions about his involvement with Westmoreland's crash were true, that code had decided his own fate as well. But it was complicated, because Kolya also said that he wanted Daedalus, and eventually, all of Mars, to become a more civilized place, with a real legal code that didn't operate on lynchings and private vengeance.

"Whatever his faults," she said, "no one deserves to die like that. And that poor guard. An inch or two in the other direction and she'd still be alive."

"An inch or two in the other direction," Stasia said, "and *I'd* likely be dead."

Claire winced. "Sorry. I didn't mean it like that."

"I know. Don't worry about it. It's all starting to catch up with me, too. We just need to get through this call. I only wish it hadn't been so long since I heard or spoke Hodjeri. It's entirely possible that I won't understand a word they say." She shot a look at Beck. "Although as our reigning pessimist noted earlier, it's *also* entirely possible that they've been speaking Ufretan back to him and Shepherd just can't understand it."

Claire suspected she owned a share of Beck's pessimist crown, even though she wouldn't jinx things by speaking her worries out loud. Her biggest fear was that they'd call Shepherd and no message would play at all. Which meant they'd *never know.* Had Shepherd simply imagined it? Had the Hodjeri grown tired of trying to communicate with a man who kept repeating the same few words over and over? Or had it really been the Alliance all along, as Beck feared, and the naidar drones were already on their way?

Paul handed back her phone. "All set. We'll dial out from your number in about ninety seconds. That will give Stasia a bit of time with Shepherd to sell herself as Barbara Windham before the message from the beacon begins."

If the message begins. She mentally shoved the thought aside, took several deep breaths, and waited for the call to begin.

Shepherd seemed a bit on edge when he answered, and she was worried that he might have changed his mind. But his nervousness seemed to settle as soon as she turned the call over to Stasia. Her impersonation of Arbet was uncanny, although it probably didn't need to be, given that the meeting with Shepherd had been three decades ago. He seemed to remember her clearly, however—perhaps not surprising, given that he'd been an eighteen-year-old boy and a stunning woman had arrived on his doorstep to offer him a scholarship to Yale, a house near the campus, and the funds to start an organization that would be his life's work.

It occurred to her then that Arbet might have been the one person who could have convinced Shepherd that *she* was one of his Sentinels, especially given that she probably hadn't changed physically since their original encounter. If nothing else, though, maybe she could help soften the blow, since the one thing they'd decided for certain was that no matter what message they actually received from the beacon, the translation Stasia gave Shepherd would have to include the news that the Sentinels wouldn't be arriving in the near future and they had no idea how he'd take it.

For now, though, Shepherd was so caught up in his conversation with the woman he believed to be Barbara Windham that Claire had to remind him that it was almost time for the transmission and he needed to keep the beacon close to his phone. There was about thirty seconds of silence, then a deep voice began speaking in another language.

Claire looked back and forth between Beck and Stasia, trying to determine from their faces whether the news was good or bad. And then Stasia began speaking excitedly, stumbling a bit over her words. It seemed like she was asking the man to repeat himself on a few occasions, but there was absolutely no mistaking her expression. Whatever the person was saying, they were saying it in Hodjeri. The conversation went on for about five minutes, with Stasia jotting down a string of numbers near the end.

To his credit, Shepherd didn't interrupt at all while Stasia was talking, but as soon as the call was over, his questions tumbled out in a frenzy. "What did they say? And what did you say back?"

The frustrating thing for Claire and everyone else in the room with her was that Stasia had to feed Shepherd some version of the fake translation they'd agreed on earlier before she could end the call and tell them what they'd actually said.

"Okay," she began. "I'm not sure if you'll consider this good news or bad news. First, the Sentinels are currently very far from here, dealing with a crisis in another sector of the galaxy. They must still be receiving information from Earth, though, because they're very much aware of your efforts and they are impressed with the improvements in air and water quality that you've helped achieve over the past decades. Largely as a result of your work, they believe there is still hope for the planet."

"How could that be bad news?" Shepherd said. "It's very *good* news, indeed. They are showing mercy!"

"Yes, but it may be a very long time before they reach Mars."

"We will wait," he said. "We are faithful."

"I also told them of your recent work in Ehden. Claire says you've already made real improvements in just a few months. They hope that you'll keep up the good work. They've also asked me to stay in touch with you and keep them informed about progress on Earth and on Mars. You'll receive another call in about a month and I told them I'd be happy to translate again. You can write out any questions you have for them, as well."

"That's ... *wonderful*. I have so many things to ask them."

"Maybe just a *few* questions at first," Stasia cautioned. "My translation skills are still a little rusty."

"Certainly. I wouldn't want to impose too heavily on their time, either, when they have so many worlds to watch over."

Claire cut in. "Dr. Shepherd? I'm getting word that our time is up for the voice relay. And I don't want to abuse the privilege since we'll apparently need to ask them to use it again next month."

"Yes," Stasia said. "I will message you with the time he gave me for our next conversation, Dr. Shepherd. May you walk in the light of the Sentinels!"

"And you. Both of you!" Shepherd almost sounded as if he were in tears, which Claire had half expected—although she hadn't assumed they would be tears of joy.

As soon as the recording light went off, Stasia collapsed back into her chair and took a deep breath before speaking.

"The Alliance is on the verge of falling. Fourteen additional planets have defected to the Hodjeri in the last cycle, including Parda."

Claire wanted to give a happy whoop, but she realized that while the news might be good for Earth, it was probably mixed for Beck and Stasia. Even if their home planets were no longer in the Alliance, they remained in danger if the war was still raging around them.

"I take it Parda is your planet?" Paul asked in response to Beck's audible exhale.

"Yeah," Beck said. "And this also means the Alliance is down to about one-third the number of member worlds it had when we left Ufretas Prime."

Stasia shook her head. "I think it's lower than that. Somar—that's his name, I think he was the ship's captain. He didn't say it explicitly, but I got the sense that other worlds that were actively fighting against them are now under Hodjeri control, too. The one thing he did tell me was that every Ufretan ship is being used in battle, and the area where they'd normally travel to intercept our signals—or to send out naidar drones, for that matter—is now fully under the control of the Hodjeri. Even if Durav had gotten his hands on that beacon, the Hodjeri would have been the only ones in range to pick up the signal."

"And you requested protected status for Earth?" Beck asked. "Or whatever their equivalent is?"

"Requested and granted on a provisional basis. Mars, too. I don't have the authority to make the request, but I made it. That's what he's supposed to get back with me about in…" She glanced at the number she'd jotted down. "I'll need to do the math, but about thirty-four days."

"What exactly does protected status mean?" Wyatt asked.

Beck smiled. "On a practical level, it means that one thing she told Shepherd is true. Earth has been granted a reprieve. If it works the same way that it did under the Alliance, it's like putting a temporary protective zone around the planet."

One of those words bothered Claire. "How *temporary*? And is there any way to make it permanent?"

"Hard to say for sure," Beck said. "But it's important to remember that the Hodjeri were once members of the Alliance. They've already achieved biological immortality, so their concept of temporary would probably be measured in Earth centuries. And yes, there's a path to make it permanent—by joining the Union. But that's way, way down the pike. Before we can even think about that we need to get Earth ready for official first contact."

EPILOGUE

FROM THE JOURNAL OF EBERIN DAS

Translation by Alice Dobroski
[undated]

MANY MONTHS AGO, I mused in this journal about a little girl who found herself ejected from the game she was playing with her peers. I was merely an observer, and a poorly informed observer at that, with no understanding of why she was removed from the game. The girl seemed to know the rules, however, at least well enough to know that she had broken one of them. She accepted her expulsion with grace.

I think about that day often, especially on nights like this one when I've had far too much to drink. Too much at this point to search through this missive and find my exact words, and definitely too much to recall my words verbatim. But the gist was that people have a right to know the rules. Without that knowledge, it's not a fair game at all, but merely the strong forcing their will upon those who lack the power to resist.

There is no honor in using strength as a weapon against the weak. Its best and highest use is, now and forever, as a shield.

But what chafes the most is that I believe my people once understood that principle. It is at the heart of the stories we learned as children. It is in the lyrics of the songs we sing, and in the ideals that we claim to cherish. At what point did we lose sight of those ideals? Or were they always fiction, just useful tools to keep us pliant and obedient, to keep us from learning the true nature of our leaders?

I know now that I cannot change the tide. But my final wish is that their cruelty becomes their downfall. May they one day face an opponent who understands that true power can only come from bringing these dark little worlds into the light so that they, too, may fight the darkness.

Until then, my heart breaks for the worlds that the Alliance has destroyed and will continue to destroy in its single-minded pursuit of power long after I am gone. It breaks, too, for the people of the Alliance, because I truly believe we *could* be the union that our songs and legends proclaim us to be if we tempered our strength with wisdom and mercy.

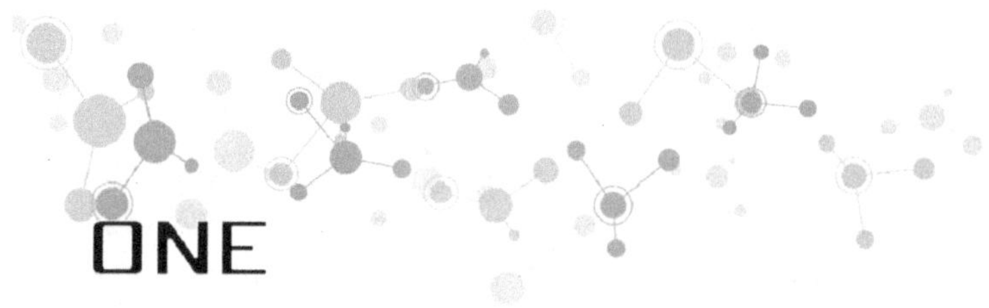

ONE

Sunday, April 8
Lynn, Massachusetts

ALICE HANDED her invitation and ID to the guard at the security gate with an apologetic smile. "I know the opening reception isn't until six, but I'm supposed to meet Joe Echols and some others here for a private event at four-thirty. Although, I guess I'm a little early even for that."

"Yes," the woman said. "Dr. Echols hasn't arrived yet. But you can have a seat in the lobby or browse some of the exhibits while you wait. The biodome is open, too."

"Thank you."

Alice retrieved her bag from the scanner and stepped into the multistory atrium of Jonas Labs. It was an impressive room, filled with direct sunlight from glass panels above and the more diffuse light from the wall that it shared with the biodome. She had no idea how much of the building was new construction, since she'd never visited the campus prior to the bombings. Based on Claire's comments and her own personal interactions with Kai Jonas, however, she was willing to bet that some version of the floor-to-ceiling wallscreen had existed in the original. The main section now displayed a closed-captioned interview with a much larger than life version of Kai, as a carefully curated montage of Rejuvesce distribution centers cycled through on the smaller screens.

While it was true that the chaos had quieted down considerably in the past few months, these images were like watching an alternate reality. No rioters. None of the protest signs and sit-ins she'd seen in coverage of the early weeks of the New York City rollout at the Javitz Center. Nothing but happy campers waiting patiently in line for their longevity boost.

"And this is *truly* just the beginning," Kai was saying. "It's still a bit too early for an *official* announcement, but our Phase II tests have been extremely positive. We're back to full production levels, even after the hiccup last fall."

Someone behind her snorted. "*Hiccup,* she says."

Alice recognized the voice instantly. But when she turned around, she thought for a second that she'd made a mistake. She hadn't seen Housen since they both left Camp Ufrete in mid-October. His long, somewhat shaggy hair now barely brushed his collar. He'd added a neatly trimmed beard and traded his jeans for a suit. If not for the square jaw and slightly off-kilter nose, she wasn't sure that she'd have recognized him.

"I'm impressed. You clean up quite nicely." She lowered her voice. "I didn't think you were coming. Claire said…"

He tilted his head toward the biodome. "Maybe we should take a walk?"

She followed him into the dome. They walked along the tree-lined path for a couple of minutes in silence. Her privacy app would have shielded their conversation, but it was probably best to find a spot where there were fewer cameras, too. Once they were about a quarter of the way in, he motioned toward some benches under the canopy of a banyan tree in the middle of a clearing. The tree was missing branches on one side and she wondered if it had taken damage when the dome collapsed.

They took a bench facing the path so that they could watch for the others. Alice launched the privacy app on her armscreen and then Housen continued.

"You're right. I wasn't planning to come. But Arbet pleaded my case to Wilson, saying it would be wrong to exclude me. I do have to clear out before the grand opening crowd arrives and the rest of his security team shows up. Although, I don't know why we need to be so secretive. I mean, Kai Jonas apparently thinks the bombing was only a *hiccup*."

They both knew Wilson was advising Housen to keep a low profile for another reason. He had told them he was *fairly* certain the clean-up crew had cleared up any evidence at the house in Massapequa. After the bodies were removed, he sent in a team to do "mold remediation"—something that half the houses in the neighborhood needed after the flooding. They'd debated torching the house because that was the only way they could be certain that no trace of modified DNA remained behind from Durav's blood, that of the dead *ipret-tai,* and even Housen. Wilson had thought there was an excellent chance that the three militia members they turned over to Agent West would cough up whatever name Durav had given them during questioning along with the address where they'd last seen him. But they'd kept surveillance on the place and there was no evidence that police had searched it. And once the militia members learned that Boudreaux was dead, they opted to pile everything on him. So had the *ipret-tai* who shot him at Daedalus.

"So," he said, "how are you doing now that things have … quieted down?"

Quieted down? Alice wondered if using a euphemism of his own was intended as a touch of irony, given that he'd just called Kai Jonas out for doing the same thing. But if so, his expression gave no clue.

"They're going okay. I was worried that I'd have a mess to clean up at my apartment, but Durav's people never got inside. And … I'm actually leaving Columbia after this semester. Yeah, yeah, I know. I was all stressed out about keeping my job. But new opportunities are opening up, and the truth is, I'd rather be exploring brand new living languages than teaching about old dead ones. Plus, I think there's going to be a lot of publicity once we publish the journal."

"Oh, right," he said drily. "The journal you never even bothered to tell me about. The one I learned about when we were both pointing guns at Durav."

"It wasn't by choice. I was under an NDA."

"Fair enough," he said. "When does it come out?"

"Probably not for another six months. Maybe even more. We need to move slowly, but this makes sense as the best first step for Project First Contact or whatever they end up calling it. Releasing the journal will get people accustomed to the idea that aliens exist, or at least that they existed long ago. We can use the example of ancient Mars to build up a little fear that Earth could potentially be in the same danger. And then, hopefully, we work through the Ares Consortium to *gradually* suggest the prospect of an alliance with the Hodjeri."

He grinned. "So, that will keep you busy for what … a year? How about after?"

She rolled her eyes. "Yeah, right. I'm thinking it will keep me busy for a decade, at a bare minimum, given all of the files Stasia is receiving. But if I do find spare time, Stasia thinks I should translate Iberian's journal into Hodjeri. Given the anti-Ufretan theme, she says it might find a market."

"So, you're working with her on the translation projects?"

"Yes. She's been forwarding me the language lessons she's getting from the Hodjeri. Macek is keeping her pretty busy. At least it keeps her mind off being stuck on the station. Hopefully, that will be resolved soon, and she'll at least be free to travel on Mars."

"You should make the trip sometime, too. I'm … actually heading there myself next week. Arbet thinks I should clear out for a few months until she can arrange a new identity for me and Shepherd has been hounding me about bringing additional members of his Flock to Ehden. I wasn't inclined to do it, to be honest. Shepherd *seems* to be okay with the idea that his Sentinels aren't fast-tracking his rescue, but putting more colonists into the dome with him feels like a bad idea. Then I found out that a group was planning to go anyway, so I decided to tag along. I'll rest easier if I see for myself that this hasn't made him unstable. Okay, he's always been a bit unstable, so let's make that *dangerously* unstable."

Alice decided this was probably as good of an opportunity as she was going to get to broach the subject of the other reason he might need to keep a low profile, the one that none of the others knew about. If he claimed that he'd had nothing to do with it, she wouldn't press the matter. She could always say she was thanking him for killing Durav. But she knew that Housen was the reason she breathed easier at night. She still turned every lock, but she didn't feel compelled to check them again at bedtime.

Had Durav sent Mitchell Morris her contact information? Or had she just gotten more careless with everything going on and left some thread dangling? She didn't know. But either way, on December 14th, about six weeks after she returned to her apartment, she'd noticed a nanodrone following her through Morningside Park. The drone stayed outside of the one-meter zone, just tagging along behind her.

A giant bumblebee hanging around in a New York City park. In mid-December. *Right.*

When she was certain no one was watching, she'd opened her app and zapped the nasty thing. It should have died instantly, but instead it spiraled to the ground, and a tinny recording of a familiar voice she'd hoped never to hear again said, *Dogs shall devour the flesh of Jezebel, by the walls of Jezreel. Her corpse will be like dung in his fields, and none shall mourn her.*

She zapped it again. This time, the light flickered out and Mitch's voice went silent.

As she had after her last unpleasant encounter in the park, Alice went straight to DLS and ordered her usual drink. It was only half-past noon, and a bit early for a drink, but she told Juno she'd just taught her last class of the semester (true) and was celebrating. Juno had said congratulations and then went back to unloading a delivery that had just arrived. She'd taken a seat at the end of the bar and began checking her messages and socials.

She had checked everything frequently after she got back from Boston, but between her translation projects and grading final exams, she'd slacked off a bit in the past week or so. The memorial page for Cecilia Cooper had received two new messages since her last login. A week earlier, Mitch had posted a candle along with the message, *Hard to believe you're gone. Still feel like you're out there somewhere.* Two days after that, another candle, with *RIP, Ceci. I'll see you soon.*

Taken individually they might be seen as innocuous, but combined with the preachy little bugbot? She hadn't even bothered to pack but headed straight from DLS to Grand Central. Her only question had been whether to go to her mom's place in Pittsburgh or back to Boston. In the end, she'd just booked a hotel room near the terminal at New Rochelle for two nights so that she could finish grading. As soon as she had everything posted online, she'd make up her mind.

On the day she'd planned to check out, however, she was awakened early by a song. That was confusing, because she didn't remember setting an alarm. Also, it wasn't her usual wake up music, but a dark little tune that had been briefly popular when she was in college called "I'll Dance on Your Grave Every Day."

And sure enough, when she opened her mail, she found an obituary in the *Colorado Post-Gazette.* Mitchell Morris, middle son of the lead pastor of the Denver Gates of Destiny, had been killed the previous afternoon while on a hunting trip near Newcastle, Wyoming.

The hunting trip checked out. Mitch had been going on a week-long trip each year with three sons of Gates of Destiny elders, guys he'd grown up with, since they were teens. One of those friends had posted pictures of them arriving at the hunting camp on Wednesday and another of a rather puny-looking deer that one of them bagged on Thursday. And then on Friday, someone bagged Mitch.

Which meant that he'd been on vacation stalking deer at the

same time someone that he hired was stalking her through the park with a bugbot. Had he been following along on his phone?

Alice posted her final grades and decided to go to her mom's house. Christmas was only a week away, after all. For the next week, in between holiday baking and a trip to the light show at the Botanical Gardens, she followed updates on the story in the news and on the social media accounts for the Gates of Destiny. On Christmas Eve, two days after she read that Mitch had been interred at Fairmount Cemetery, she shared the news with her mom, telling her it was just something she'd happened to stumble upon.

It was a very merry Christmas.

Nothing that she'd read said that foul play was suspected. The authorities seemed to think it was a stray shot from another hunter. It happened sometimes.

And she might have been able to convince herself that it was true if not for an odd comment among the hundreds of anonymous messages on his memorial page. The comment had seven likes, last time she checked, even though none of those reacting to it could possibly have had the slightest idea what it meant.

Just two words. The same two words that Denny had said about Durav.

Vraidar paitel.

Not *evil dies,* but *evil* ***must*** *die.* If not for those last two letters, she could have believed that Housen had simply left a snarky bit of commentary on Mitch's memorial page. She still might have wondered, but that tell-tale imperative suffix pretty much removed all doubt in her mind.

She glanced off to the left and saw Beck and Arbet coming up the main path. If she was going to say something, it had to be now.

"Speaking of dangerously unstable men, I'm glad there's one less in the world." She placed her hand on his and squeezed it tightly. "*Thank you.*"

Housen looked up and held her gaze for several seconds.

"You're welcome. After I saw his messages on Cecilia's memorial page, I did some digging and found out he'd hired a private surveillance company in New York a few weeks back. Add both of those together and his messages were a pretty obvious threat."

"Yeah. I had a nanodrone escort through Morningside Park, complete with Bible verses about evil women. I was trying to figure out where to go and what to do next when I got the obituary alert. Again, *thank you*. I'm glad. Given the opportunity, I'd have done it myself. But you shouldn't have taken on that risk."

"Worth it. Like I said before, I *know* his type. They don't stop on their own. And … you had my back with Durav. If I hadn't been able to make it up to that bedroom, you'd have taken the shot."

It was true. Although she still didn't think she'd have needed to, despite the prevailing theory that the *ipret-tai* on Mars had shot Jason Boudreaux because his "programming" required him to protect a member of the Watch. That might have been true in the Mars case, but she'd seen Denny's eyes as he stared down the barrel at Durav.

If Housen hadn't shown up, Denny would have pulled that trigger again in a heartbeat.

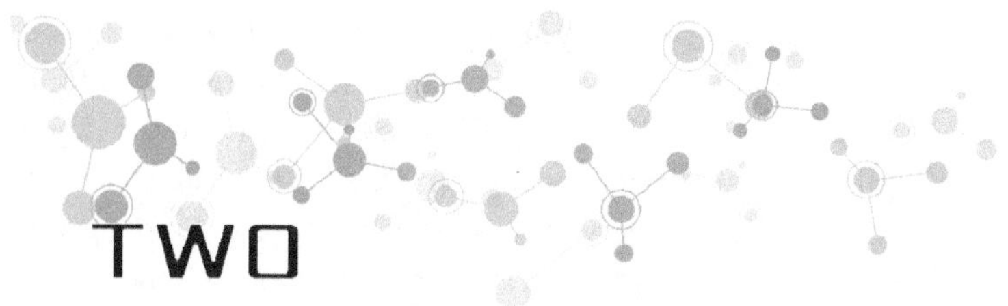

TWO

BECK PAUSED on the steps between the parking garage and the biodome to take a deep breath. He couldn't remember if he'd done that the very first time he entered, but it had been his pattern every visit since. Stop, breathe in, and savor that faint trace of crisp mintiness in the air.

It was his first time inside the biodome since the bombing. He'd been up to the new Olympus to help Joe set up the lab, but he'd avoided the dome. It was partly penance for not being able to stop the destruction, but also a very selfish fear that he had lost the one thing on Earth that had always felt like a tie to his family in Parda. Holding on to that tie felt even more important now, given that he had no idea when or if he'd be able to contact the family and friends he'd left behind. The trees near his grandmother's house didn't have quite the same sinus-clearing pungency as standard eucalyptus trees he'd seen elsewhere, but the scent was very similar to that of the brightly colored rainbow eucalyptus grove near the small lake at the center of the dome.

It was still there, under the stronger scents of plumeria and gardenia. He hadn't been sure that it would be when he heard that several of the trees had been lost. They had all been at risk, given their tropical origins, but the grounds crew had apparently managed to keep them sufficiently sheltered from the cold during what had thankfully been a fairly mild winter.

And it was finally quiet again, unlike the times he'd visited in the months before the bombing when the sounds of the protest reached you even inside the dome. That was one reason that Kai had decided to hold this meeting on Sunday. Gates of Destiny still sent a contingent on the other six days, but they'd always considered Sunday a day of rest from hounding the employees at Jonas Labs. And while the Earth Watch Alliance had kept a seven-day-a-week vigil, their bus rarely showed up these days. Many of them had decided to rejoin society. It was probably hard to hold a group together when their spiritual leader was millions of miles away. But Beck suspected it was mostly due to Shepherd's video announcement several months earlier. He'd told his loyal followers that the Sentinels were pleased with the Flock's progress on Earth and would not, therefore, be arriving to whisk them away anytime soon. Without the imminent arrival of the mothership to hold them together, the earthbound Flock had withered away to only a few thousand members.

"Are you okay?" Arbet stopped on the bottom step and looked back to see what was keeping him. She carried the smaller of the two urns, the one with Reese's ashes.

Her cheeks were still slightly pink from their recent vacation. It was still far too cold in Maine this time of year, so they'd spent two weeks on a beach in Fiji, one of the places neither of them had visited on their sabbaticals from the Watch. They slathered themselves with sunscreen, wore hats and rash guards, and both still managed to pick up a mild burn. It was worth it, though, to lie in the sand and stare up at the sky without the worry that it would soon be clouded by a swarm of naidar drones.

Still, it had been a bittersweet vacation, and one he probably wouldn't have taken had Arbet not insisted. He'd returned from Mars to find Joe fully immersed in his new project—saving Sandjeel. Beck had joined in, spending his days and the better part of his nights in the makeshift lab they'd created at Everly Estates, AKA Camp Ufrete, trying to formulate the right mix of nutrients to keep the Triad leader alive and healthy. Nothing seemed to work, though, and in early January, Dora had awakened him and Arbet with the news that Sandjeel had died in his sleep. What the *ipret-tai* hadn't realized—and what Arbet had asked everyone never to tell her—was that Sandjeel had adjusted the dials on his air tank at some point during the night. The only person he had told beforehand was Joe.

Arbet had bought the tickets to Fiji a few weeks later. She pointed out that he'd promised her a beach that afternoon in the Triad's chambers. It was the only chance they'd have to get away together for a while, since she was leaving soon for the trials in Daedalus, where she was scheduled to represent both Stasia and Nine, the *ipret-tai* who'd killed Boudreaux. To his surprise, Joe hadn't objected to their trip and had even interceded with his mother to get permission for her "property" to travel. They'd had no issues with the government so far, and the ownership agreement remained private, but that didn't stop Kai from mentioning it on occasion.

Beck smiled at Arbet and shifted the larger urn to his other arm. "Just catching my breath. We're supposed to meet down there." He pointed toward the center of the eight-acre dome, where glimpses of water were visible through the trees. "I think we may be the first ones here."

They headed downhill, but as they rounded a curve in the path he discovered they weren't the only early arrivals. Alice Dobroski sat on a bench beneath the banyan tree. And even though he'd known the man with her for much longer, he almost didn't recognize him.

"Still not sure that was a good idea," he said.

"It's a risk," Arbet admitted. "But I think it's a small one. Wilson hasn't heard from Agent West since February. And Housen deserves a chance to say goodbye, too."

For Beck, Arbet, and Housen, as well as Dora and Denny, this was a farewell not merely to Sandjeel and Reese, but to all of their fellow Watchers and *ipret-tai* who were poisoned or shot by Durav at the end of Conclave. There had been no time to mourn them in the wake of their escape. Beck didn't even know which members he would consider worth mourning, since Arbet steadfastly refused to tell him who had rebelled after he passed along the information that revealed the truth about their mission. All he knew was that enough of them had stood up that Sandjeel changed his vote. Her view in keeping the names secret was that some of the others might have come around to that position eventually, too, and either way, Durav had made certain that they *all* paid the price.

They'd also had a long debate over whether the memorial was appropriate, since their original bodies might be revived. Ufretas Prime was still fighting, but the Hodjeri claimed that they had firm control of the sector that was close enough to Earth for the Alliance to communicate with the Triad. Without that communication, would the Academy wake the bodies that were currently in stasis or simply leave them there? In the case of the Watchers from planets that had rebelled, Beck suspected they would pull the plug. And as he'd noted, were they even the same people without the memories they'd gathered over more than a century on Earth? He didn't think so. Housen had been equally adamant on that point, and Arbet had gradually come around.

Arbet squinted at Alice and Housen. "Looking at the two of them, I'm wondering now if the memorial was Housen's only reason for wanting to attend. Maybe we should just head straight to the lake?"

It did look as if he and Alice were in the middle of a rather intense discussion, so Beck took her advice and followed the fork to the left instead. "Let's just be sure he gets out of here before any of the guards who might recognize him show up to cover Kai's grand reopening."

Kai's reception was one of those events that snowballed, as anyone who knew her could probably have predicted. At first, it was supposed to be a small affair preceding an in-person meeting of the board of directors, just to reassure them that the lab was back up and running. It soon morphed into a reception with the board, major stockholders, and a few members of the local press. But now that Kai and Joe had reached a compromise on the formal announcement of his "stretch goals", she had turned it into a full-fledged company gala.

Even though Beck was still listed as a key employee and would normally have been forced to share in the agony, he'd be leaving after the memorial. Kai had messaged him earlier in the week suggesting that it would be best if he kept a low profile, given the questions surrounding his actions on the day of the attack. That was fine with him.

The compromise between Joe and Kai had been delayed for several months, pending further communication with the Hodjeri. Continuing work on either of the two milestones was risky if there was any chance of the Alliance turning the tide. They also needed guidance on the Hodjeri position about Earth's possible long-term expansion to exoplanets. Neither the fact that the Hodjeri were fighting against the Ufretans nor the fact that they believed planets in their own system should have greater autonomy guaranteed that they would be more amenable to allowing that same prospect for Earth.

Once they'd established a communications channel between Stasia and the Hodjeri that didn't involve Shepherd holding the beacon and Stasia pretending to be Arbet, they asked for clarification. What restrictions would Earth be required to meet if they wanted to leave the door open to a future application as a member of the Hodjeri Union?

It had taken more than a month before they had an answer, and Stasia had been forced to ask for a number of further clarifications. The gist was that there were no hard and fast rules, but the Union strongly discouraged Earth from pursuing the scattershot method of seeding planets that Kolya had been planning, aiming at multiple "barren" worlds and hoped for the best. That was, as they pointed out, very similar to what the Ufretans had done prior to and during the First Alliance, and the lack of control made it an irresponsible method of expansion. They asked for the top two planets from the list that Davina Monroe had suggested to Kolya, and eventually said they had no problem with either of those worlds being terraformed remotely.

So Kolya would get his wish, to some extent. Maybe they'd

even pack some of his ashes in with their advanced evolution biobots. Growing beyond those two planets wasn't expressly forbidden, but failure to consult with members of the Hodjeri Union in advance before adding to that list would be considered a negative if Earth ever reached the point of applying for membership.

With that understanding in hand, Joe had agreed in early February that Kai could announce a new series of trials for Rejuvesce at the quarterly meeting. The statement that Jonas Labs would officially release tomorrow would note that preliminary data suggested the strong possibility that earlier administration of the drug could add several decades of life beyond the original twenty-five-year projection. Kai had already been hinting at this much with her public comments about Phase II, and she clearly wanted a more dramatic statement, so Beck still suspected that she would be whispering sweet nothings like *biological immortality* into investors' ears behind the scenes.

Their plan was to extend the program first to those who were above the current age cutoff of seventy. Rejuvesce was still less effective for that age group and would probably add only a few years of life, but it was an equity issue that needed to be addressed. After that, they would gradually lower the age at which the drug was administered. They would also be pulling in younger recruits for the *in silico* scans, so that they weren't relying solely on the data from Virtual Claire.

All of this meant he'd be returning to the lab full time starting on Monday. Things weren't fully back to normal between him and Joe. Maybe they'd never be. But they were close enough, and the changes weren't entirely bad. Joe asked for his opinion a lot more often … and Beck no longer felt compelled to hold back.

A happy squeal came from off in the distance. He turned to see Jemma dragging Wyatt toward the double-helix slide in the playground, with Claire and Joe bringing up the rear.

"I'm glad they decided to bring her," he said. "The downside of Sandjeel waiting until they left was that Jemma didn't get to say goodbye. Maybe the ceremony will help her find closure. And … I think having a kid around will be good for everyone else."

A cloud crossed Arbet's face, and he was pretty sure she was thinking of her own daughter. But the cloud cleared quickly, replaced by the smile he was beginning to cherish as much as the one that he'd first fallen in love with across the padjit board.

"That's true," she said. "It's hard to be *too* somber when there's a child running around. And when remembering those whose lives have passed, it never hurts to have a visual reminder of the future."

THREE

CLAIRE SAT NEXT to Joe on the steps leading down to the biodome, watching as Jemma climbed up the ladder for another trip down the slide. "Kai is going to murder you if you get that suit dirty."

He cast a wry glance at her dress. "I could say the same."

"Yes, but *I'm* not going to be photographed."

"I wouldn't count on that. This is your first time attending one of these, and that will not escape the attention of the press. I doubt they'll miss a chance to snap a few shots of Kai with the prodigal daughter."

Claire groaned, realizing that he was probably right. "Want to run away after the memorial service?"

"Yes. But I need to be there to keep an eye on her and you need that introduction. So suck it up."

He was right, although she was now questioning the life choices over the past few months that had her schmoozing at corporate events. But if Project First Contact was going to get off the ground, they needed people in positions of influence on the Ares Consortium. Macek was planning to nominate her for a seat on the executive committee at the next conference. But she needed someone to second the nomination. Macek's political capital was close to maxed out at the moment trying to maintain control of Kolya International. He had inherited half of Kolya's shares, with Davy inheriting the other. Combined with their previous shares and Paul's much smaller stake, it *almost* gave them a majority, but Macek was having to do a delicate dance to keep at least a few shareholders in his corner.

Stasia could potentially put them over the top. Her voting rights were frozen, pending trial, although she and Arbet were both hopeful that the testimony of Nine, Durav's *ipret-tai,* would clear her or result in her paying restitution. Claire had no doubt that it would be coached testimony, and she wasn't sure how it would balance against witnesses who heard Nine's original story at the scene. But he had followed protocol very literally. The *ipret-tai* were trained to refuse to say anything until their lawyer arrived, and he had not said a single word to anyone since.

Regardless of what happened at trial, Stasia wouldn't be serving Kolya International in a public capacity in the near future, but she was very involved behind the scenes. Paul opted to delay his resignation if KTI hired Ayman as government liaison to help draft a new constitution after Kolya's proposed solution failed in the December election.

They also had to deal with Lyot, after Westmoreland was arrested at the Daedalus border. Lyot was under the temporary joint control of Daedalus and Elysia. Claire was sure there was an interesting story there, and she hoped to pull Macek aside and get the full scoop the next time they were on the same planet.

With all of that going on, Macek had told her that it would be best if she looked outside KTI for someone to second her nomination. The head of Columbia's Science Council was on both the Ares Committee and the board of directors for Jonas Labs, so here she was, sucking it up.

"What you don't realize is that you're getting off easy," Joe said. "Mom was going to suggest you repay the favor by doing a piece on *Simple Science* to help recruit younger people for the Phase III scans. She claimed it couldn't possibly be a problem, since you don't have to worry about objectivity and editors now that you're doing the show on your own."

"Except it's pretty much the exact opposite. *Simple Science* is completely under my name now. I have to be *more* diligent if I want to maintain credibility."

The deal she'd worked out with *The Atlantic Post* gave her

the right to create new segments, which they could add to the *Post's* archive after three months. She was now able to produce them on her own schedule, leaving her free to travel with Wyatt when his assignment allowed. She also needed time to help Alice with publicity for the Eberin Das journal. And, assuming she mastered the fine art of schmoozing, she would eventually need to focus most of her attention on groups like the Ares Consortium and the UN, in order to gradually coax people toward the point where first contact with the Hodjeri was feasible.

"I know, I know," Joe said. "I'm the one who I talked her out of it. Which means *you owe me*, Claire Bear."

"I suppose I do. Come down for our housewarming next week and I'll order dumplings from a place that I swear is even better than the one in New York."

"Hmm. I could probably manage that. Has Jemma's furball chilled out about the paint smell yet?"

"Pretty much. We've kept the windows open as much as possible for the past week and it's starting to clear a bit. She still twitches her tail every time she's in the room with me or Ro, but the fact that Wyatt moved in seems to have appeased her somewhat."

"And the whole communal living thing is working out?"

She laughed. "You make it sound like we're the Flock. It's four people and a cat sharing a house. With a pool, so our little mermaid is quite happy."

For several weeks after her return from Mars, Claire had waited, expecting Ro to tell her that they needed to come up with new living arrangements. Not just a new house—that much was obvious with the old one now completely gone—but *separate* arrangements. Ro had managed to pick back up with her residency program after the leave of absence. Her supervisor never even mentioned the prescriptions she'd written in Maine. But Ro only had five months left in her program. She could make ends meet on her own for that long, and her salary would be much higher after residency. Plus, Jemma was now in kindergarten, so the childcare issue was more manageable.

To her surprise, Ro and Wyatt had approached her together with a stack of blueprints they'd printed out from files Joe had given them. They were the plans for a house that her father had wanted to build before he died. Like all of Martin Echols's designs, it was modern and quirky, and in Claire's estimation, pretty much perfect. With some minor tweaks, it suited their mutual needs, and it fit nicely on her current lot. She'd hired a builder, paid them enough to expedite the project, and they'd finally been able to move in the previous week.

"Kind of surprised Ro didn't come with you," Joe said. "I hope she knows that nobody here blames her. She did her damnedest to keep both Reese and Sandjeel alive."

"No, it's not that. She's lost patients before. She actually told me to tell *you* to cut yourself some slack. It's just that she's still walking on eggshells, worrying that she'll do something wrong and her supervisor will suddenly start asking a lot of uncomfortable questions about those prescriptions she wrote in Maine. So, when they need someone to work weekends or take an extra shift, she volunteers."

Joe stared down at his feet for a minute. "Um, tell her to relax, okay? I took care of it. In exchange for there being absolutely no questions about that incident and no flak about the leave of absence, Johns Hopkins got a new endowment. I needed a tax write-off anyway."

"Okay," Claire said. "Not sure how she's going to take that…"

"Why do you think I didn't tell her myself?"

"Here's my proposal. I'm going to say thank you very much on her behalf … and *not* tell her. Because I'm pretty sure it won't make her do anything different. She'll still take weekend shifts so that they don't think she's trying to coast. And it's just going to make her feel weird. Maybe we can keep this as our little secret."

"You mean like you keeping the information about Mom and Kolya from me?"

She winced. "When did you find out?"

"When I told her Kolya was dead. I was telling her what you said. You know, about how it might look bad if she learned the news in public. And she ... erupted. Was absolutely livid that you'd told me. She yelled that she and Dad had an understanding, and said she told you that, but no, you couldn't leave well enough alone. When I told her you actually hadn't told me anything, she burst into tears and stormed out of the room. I didn't see her for nearly a week. So now I'll ask you the same question. When did *you* find out?"

"On my first trip to Mars. It's a long, somewhat embarrassing story and I'll tell you over a drink sometime. I knew you had to work with her every day, and..." She sighed. "I'm sorry, Joe."

"No, I'm actually relieved. I mean, I'm not happy you didn't tell me, but I thought maybe you'd found out when Dad died and had been carrying it around for over a decade. That maybe it was part of the problem between the two of you."

"Nope. Just icing on the cake." She thought for a minute, then said, "But maybe you're right."

He gave her a questioning look. "You're going to have to narrow it down, since I'm *always* right."

She elbowed him. "I meant about keeping secrets. I'll tell Ro. Or you can tell her. But maybe we wait until her residency is over and she's working somewhere else? She'll still feel weird, but at least that way, she'll know she put forth her very best effort the entire time and she won't have to go in and wonder who knows what every day."

"Deal. Now, let's go pry Wyatt and Jemma off the swings so we can pay our last respects to the Watch."

"Are you going to be okay?" she asked as they walked toward the playground.

"Yeah. I was in a blue funk for a while. Kind of felt like I failed him."

"How surprising that you'd take the entire weight of a group effort on your shoulders. I mean, no offense, but it was really more in Davina Monroe's field, and she didn't have any luck, either."

"Yeah, only it wasn't personal for her. She never even met him. And it's complicated for Beck, because he blames Sandjeel for more than a century of lies and for being part of the system that condemned Earth. Which is fair. I realized I was mostly being selfish, thinking of how much I could still learn from him. We had some incredible conversations over the padjit board. But he wasn't here by choice and even if we'd found the right cocktail to make him better ... Earth could never be home for him. In general, but *especially* if we're going to extend lives indefinitely, people need the right to decide when they've had enough and are ready to check out." He crouched down as Jemma ran toward them. "Want a piggyback ride?"

"You're way too big to be a piggy," she said in a serious tone. "I want a *giant* back ride."

Claire slipped her hand into Wyatt's, and they followed behind to the wide ledge where she'd sat alone for so many hours. It felt very different today. Some of the stones in the waterfall had been replaced, and the water didn't cascade in exactly the same way from the twin waterfalls that began on the fifth-floor terraces. A few of the trees also hadn't survived the winter without the dome and smaller versions had now been planted in the barren spaces.

The strangest thing, though, was having so many other people here. They were only ten in total, but the area was small and they had to cluster together.

Arbet gave each of them a tiny packet of ashes. The urns were merely symbolic. Beck had joked that if they scattered all of Sandjeel's ashes, it would probably clog the filters. She sat down on the ledge and helped Jemma open her packet. The girl sprinkled them along the water's edge and said the words that she'd practiced on the ride to Boston.

"Goodbye, Sandjeel. You were my friend and I miss you."

They each followed suit, with a personal remembrance or line of poetry. Her favorite was the quote by Carl Sagan that Wyatt had chosen—*The cosmos is within us. We are made of star-stuff.*

When everyone finished, the remaining members of the Watch sang a song, which Beck said was the traditional Ufretan song of remembrance. And between the choruses, Arbet read the names of every member of the Watch, including the *ipret-tai* and the three Watchers at the service.

The only member omitted from the list was Durav.

Instead, they added a final member from an earlier Watch. They didn't have any of his remains. His final resting place had been millions of kilometers away, and his final rites were millions of years overdue.

But Claire liked to imagine that some tiny fragment, maybe just a single atom of his being, resided here with the others on this planet that his warning had, at least for now, saved from destruction.

It wasn't impossible. Eberin Das was also made of star-stuff. And the cosmos is within us all.

AUTHOR'S NOTE

Thanks so much for reading *On Alien Skies*. This series was a bit of a departure from my usual style and subjects, so I truly appreciate the readers (old and new) who have stuck with me as I explored new frontiers.

A quick Griffin update: An earlier volume was dedicated to him in the middle of a health crisis. He's still going strong, still keeping my feet warm when I write, and more energetic than ever, especially when there's the possibility of a sweet potato chew as a treat.

An extra big thanks, as always, goes out to my family and friends, and especially those with whom I share a house. These poor unfortunate souls have to deal with me as I work through the inevitable stage of writing where I'm convinced that the book is a steaming pile of garbage that will never be (and never *should* be) finished. Counting co-authored works, this is my twenty-eighth novel and it happens *every single time*.

Some of the people listed below were involved in the current project. Others helped along the way. I owe them all a debt of gratitude: Peter Walniuk, Steve Buck, Karen Stansbury, Teri Suzuki, Oleg Lysyj, Chris Fried, Theresa Kay, Caleb Ansel, Ian Walniuk, Mary Freeman, Lilly Sparks, Meg A. Watt, Aletia Meyers, Alexa Huggins, Alexis Young, Allie B. Holycross, Amelia Elisa Diaz, Angela Careful, Angela Fossett, Ann Davis, Antigone Trowbridge, Becca Levite, Bianca Najjar, Billy Thomas, Brandi Reyna, Chantelle Michelle Kieser, Chaz Martin, Chelsea Hawk, Cheyenne Chambers, Chris Fried, Chris Schraff Morton, Christina Kmetz, Claudia Gonzaga-Jauregui, Cody Jones, Dan Wilson,

Dawn Lovelly, Devi Reynolds, Dori Gray, Emiliy Marino, Erin Flynn, Fred Douglis, Hailey Mulconrey Theile, Heather Jones, Hope Bates, Jen Gonzales, Jen Wesner, Jennifer Kile, Jenny Griffin, Jenny Lawrence, Jenny MacRunnel, Jessica Wolfsohn, John Scafidi, Karen Benson, Katie Lynn Stripling, Kristin Ashenfelter, Kristin Rydstedt, Kyla Michelle Lacey Waits, Laura-Dawn Francesca MacGregor-Portlock, Lindsay Nichole Leckner, Margarida Azevedo Veloz, Mark Chappell, Meg Griffin, Meredith Winters Patten, Mikka McClain, Nguyen Quynh Trang, Nooce Miller, Pham Hai Yen, Roseann Calabritto, Sarada Spivey, Sarah Ann Diaz, Sarah Kate Fisher, Shari Hearn, Shell Bryce, Sigrun Murr, Stefanie Diegel, Stephanie Kmetz, Stephanie Johns-Bragg, Summer Nettleman, Susan Helliesen, Tina Kennedy, Tracy Denison Johnson, Trisha Davis Perry, Valerie Arlene Alcaraz, and the person (or, almost certainly, *persons*) I've forgotten.

THE DELPHI EFFECT

BOOK ONE OF THE DELPHI TRILOGY

It's never wise to talk to strangers...and that goes double when they're dead. Unfortunately, seventeen-year-old Anna Morgan has no choice. Resting on a park bench, touching the turnstile at the Metro station—she never knows where she'll encounter a ghost. These mental hitchhikers are the reason Anna has been tossed from one foster home and psychiatric institution to the next for most of her life.

When a chance touch leads her to pick up the insistent spirit of a girl who was brutally murdered, Anna is pulled headlong into a deadly conspiracy that extends to the highest levels of government. Facing the forces behind her new hitcher's death will challenge the barriers, both good and bad, that Anna has erected over the years and shed light on her power's origins. And when the covert organization seeking to recruit her crosses the line by kidnapping her friend, it will discover just how far Anna is willing to go to bring it down.

MORE FROM RYSA WALKER

IMPROBABLE

Improbable

Slipstream

Split Infinities

The Icarus Code

The Cold Light of Stars

First Watch of Night

Dark Little Worlds

On Alien Skies

The CHRONOS Files

Timebound

Time's Edge

Time's Divide

CHRONOS Origins

Now, Then, and Everywhen

Red, White, and the Blues

Bell, Book, and Key

The Delphi Trilogy

The Delphi Effect

The Delphi Resistance

The Delphi Revolution

Enter Haddonwood (with Caleb Amsel)

As the Crow Flies

When the Cat's Away

Where Wolves Fear to Prey

Novellas

Time's Echo (A CHRONOS Novella)

Time's Mirror (A CHRONOS Novella)

Simon Says (A CHRONOS Novella)

The Abandoned (A Delphi Novella)

Graphic Novels

Time Trial (The CHRONOS Files)

Short Stories

"The Gambit" in *The Time Travel Chronicles*

"Whack Job" in *Alt. History 102*

"2092" in *Dark Beyond the Stars*

"Splinter" in *CLONES: The Anthology*

"The Circle That Whines" in *Tails of Dystopia*

"Full Circle" in *OCEANS: The Anthology*

Time's Vault: A CHRONOS Anthology

AS C. RYSA WALKER

Thistlewood Star Mysteries

Baskerville for the Bear (novella)

A Murder in Helvetica Bold

Palatino for the Painter

A Seance in Franklin Gothic

Courier to the Stars

Comic Sans for the Ex

Coastal Playhouse Mysteries

The Phantom of the Opal (novella)

Curtains for Romeo

Arsenic and Olé

Offed Off-Broadway

Exes! Stage Right

ABOUT THE AUTHOR

RYSA WALKER is the award-winning author of many books, including the best-selling CHRONOS Files. *Timebound,* the first book in that series, was a Grand Prize winner in the Amazon Breakthrough Novel Awards. *The Delphi Effect* was an Amazon Editors' Pick and a finalist in the ITW Thriller Awards. Rysa's books have sold nearly a million copies worldwide and have been translated into fourteen languages.

In addition to speculative fiction, Rysa writes mysteries as C. Rysa Walker. She currently resides in North Carolina.

Check out rysa.com for the latest news or to order signed copies.

www.ingramcontent.com/pod-product-compliance
Lightning Source LLC
LaVergne TN
LVHW041053080826
845145LV00007B/1556

* 9 7 8 1 7 3 5 8 6 6 9 9 4 *